PRAISE FOR J. M. HOCHSTETLER

"*Daughter of Liberty* is a magnificent book, well written, researched, and developed. It is the best historical novel I've read since I can't remember. Besides the smooth-flowing style and pacing that simply carries one from one page to the next, the characters are people who rise from the page. Even the secondary characters have personal issues, conflicts, human desires, and fears and resentments. The author weaves real people and events seamlessly into the story. The real events of 1775 Boston are integral to the plot and the actions of the characters. That takes a great deal of detailed research. Since I know this time period well, ulous in her details and rese of the characters' everyday someone who researched novel I love to read and find too few to read. That it is Christian fiction makes it all that much better."

—LAURIE ALICE EAKES, AUTHOR OF *Heart's Safe Passage*

"J. M. Hochstetler tells the story of *Daughter of Liberty* in a style I love. She takes fictional ch in history to describe ever that history in school shou tory is taught with the dry and names—something gu historical moments are al heroism, sacrifice and pas drama while still delivering series of novels by Hochs more."

"This is an exceptional book. I read the last 150 pages in one sitting. Heart racing, tears falling, I suffered the anguish and indecision that Elizabeth and Jonathan experienced. Hochstetler has created a magnificent, well-crafted story that will endure with the classics. . . .To read *Daughter of Liberty* is to live in 1775 and to experience the spirit that made our country great. Read this book for pleasure, but don't be surprised when you receive an awesome history lesson that brings you an appreciation of the United States of America in a deep, new way."

—LOUISE M. GOUGE, AUTHOR OF *At the Captain's Command*

Chapter One

THE CRACK OF THE PISTOL'S REPORT came from directly behind the courier. Sizzling past so close to his ear he could feel the heat of it, the musket ball whined off into the windy night.

Instinctively he crouched, bringing his head close to his mount's straining neck. *"Go! Go!"*

The mare responded with a burst of speed, stretching the distance between her and the pursuing British patrol. Flying strands of mane whipped tears to the courier's eyes as he fumbled beneath his cloak for the handle of the pistol shoved into the waistband of his breeches. His hand shaking, he tore the weapon free and cocked it with his thumb.

"Hold! Pull up and surrender, you blasted rebel!"

The shouted command reached him faintly above rushing wind and pounding hoofbeats. Mouth dry, stomach knotted with fear and exhilaration, he searched the shadowy landscape for an escape route.

In the darkness off to his right, beyond a high stone wall, wooded hills loomed up. Inside the line of trees the woodland dropped to a winding creek, then rose again into the hills, the courier knew. Reining his mare hard right, his breath coming in sharp pants, he glanced over his shoulder at the same moment the wind shredded the clouds high overhead.

For an instant splintered shafts of moonlight rippled across hill and hollow, gleaming on icy remnants of a late snow that still clung in sheltered areas. Touching the irregular stone walls that wound through the rolling farmland, the light glimmered across the blood-red uniforms of the soldiers stampeding after him through the murky Massachusetts countryside.

The quick glimpse revealed three soldiers in the patrol. The one who had fired had dropped back, and the officer now held the lead. He hung stubbornly close, trying to aim his pistol while he swung wide in the attempt to cut off his quarry.

The dim bulk of the stone wall raced toward the courier. A tangled growth of brambles topped the wall on the far side, reaching thorny fingers well above the stones. With reckless determination, he urged his mount on, raising in the stirrups at the exact instant the mare gathered her haunches under her and took flight.

She skimmed over the seemingly impossible height as effortlessly as a gull and lit softly on the other side. Hardly breaking stride, she fled toward the line of trees. A crashing sound reached the courier, and he hazarded another anxious glance back.

The officer had angled his mount off to a partial break in the wall some yards down. One of the two soldiers was riding hard toward the wall's far end.

The other had tried the wall at the same point as the courier but had miscalculated the jump. Before his mare swept around a bend that for the moment cut him off from the patrol's sight, the courier caught a brief glimpse of dislodged stone slabs spilled across the ground and the thrashing legs of the fallen horse.

He urged his mount between the trees. A dozen strides into the woods he pulled up hard and guided his mare into a narrow space behind a head-high outcropping of rock screened by slender saplings and dense undergrowth. Shoulders hunched, head bent so the wide brim of his hat shaded his face, he sat motionless, calculating that his black cloak and the midnight black of his mare would render them all but invisible in the shadows.

The mare stood silent, head down, lathered sides heaving. Gripping the reins with one hand so tightly the leather cut into his palms, the courier aimed his pistol with the other, holding it steady with difficulty. His heart beat so hard that for a moment he was overwhelmed by the irrational fear that his pursuer must hear it.

He could make out the sharp crackle of fallen branches and rustle of dry leaves underfoot as the officer fought his way through the dense growth, cursing in frustration. The muted creak of leather and jingle of metal drew steadily closer.

As he watched fearfully, the dim shape of a horseman materialized between the ghostly trunks of the trees. The thud of hoofbeats slowed, then for long, heart-stopping moments paused within eight feet of the courier's hiding place.

He became aware of the stinging tickle of perspiration that wound past the corner of his eye onto his cheek. Holding his breath, he aimed his pistol at the rider's breast at point-blank range, his hand grown suddenly steady, finger tightening over the trigger.

The mare's ears pricked, but she made no sound. When the tension reached the point at which the courier feared his nerves would snap, the sound of other hoofbeats approached from the left.

"Captain! Scott's horse fell on him," a hoarse voice called out. "He's in a bad way."

Muttering an oath, the rider reined his horse around to face the oncoming rider. "I'll be right there."

The courier could hear the second rider move off, but still the officer did not spur his mount forward. Instead, he brought him in a circle until he again faced the courier's hiding place.

"I know you're there somewhere, you rebel devil!" he rasped. "Come on, you cursed Oriole, show yourself! I know it's you!"

Motionless, eyes fixed on the officer's indistinct form, the courier willed him to ride on. The pulse of his blood sounded like thunder in his ears.

The officer waited for several moments more, head tilted as though he listened for a betraying sound. Finally he taunted, "One day you'll make a misstep, and then we'll have you. And you'll hang at last."

Giving a harsh laugh, he moved past the courier's hiding place, fighting through the low-hanging branches. Within seconds he vanished into the night as completely as though the earth had swallowed him up.

Trembling uncontrollably, the courier lowered his weapon. For some minutes longer he waited, every sense strained to the breaking point. But no sound reached him except for the moan of the wind through the bare limbs of the trees and the creak of interlaced branches high overhead.

Taking a shaky breath, he took the pistol off cock and shoved it back into the waistband of his breeches. "Thanks be to God!" he muttered. "That was entirely too close."

The mare tossed her head, and he patted her lathered neck. When he was certain the patrol had to be well out of sight and sound, he spurred her out of their hiding place, urged her down the slope and across the shallow creek. Silent as a specter, they moved up the flank of the hill on the other side and slipped over the summit.

Thus unnoticed, the courier known to General Thomas Gage and the British garrison in Boston only by the name "Oriole" for the whistled notes of his characteristic signal melted into the impenetrable cloak of the forest beyond.

"IT WAS A QUARTER OF MIDNIGHT that Friday, April 14, 1775, when the courier reached the nondescript tavern on the outskirts of Lincoln. The building faced the dusty road that pointed through the hamlet toward the village of Concord some six miles northwest.

In spite of the late hour, the flicker of candle- and lamplight illuminated the lower windows of the tavern and the one-story addition at its rear. Half a dozen horses still switched their tails patiently at the hitching rail along the building's near side.

The courier took the precaution of scouting the area before approaching the tavern. The road was deserted in both directions, the windows of the houses in the vicinity blank and black. High above, the wind seethed through the overhanging treetops, but he could discern no other sound beyond the snort of his mare and the measured beat of her hooves. Reassured, he dismounted and found a place for his mare at the hitching rail.

Slim and straight in stature, the courier had regular features markedly more handsome than those of the average farm boy. Although his pale complexion had been reddened by the fast ride in the icy wind, his sole concession to the April chill was a frayed black cloak, beneath which he wore the loose tan smock and brown breeches common to the region's farmers. The straight brown hair visible under the drooping brim of his dusty, sweat-stained hat was pulled back and tied with a black ribbon.

As he unbuckled the leather pouch behind the saddle, the door of the tavern's rear addition creaked open. A lanky figure slouched in the doorway, outlined black against the light behind him.

"Will, tell Pa he can quit worrying," said a terse voice.

"Hey, Levi," the courier greeted his cousin wearily. Slinging the pouch over his arm, he strode to the door beneath the peeling paint of a worn wooden sign that proclaimed the establishment to be simply "Stern's."

The tow-haired youth who held the door open with one spare, sinewy arm was about the courier's age. He moved out of the way and beckoned the courier into the passage between the kitchen of the main building and the enclosed lean-to at its rear.

Once inside, the courier pulled off his hat and wiped the clammy sweat off his brow with the back of his hand. Levi scrutinized him, his pale blue eyes growing keen.

"You're more'n an hour late. Any problems gettin' through?"

"You could say that, Cuz."

To his left, through the wide doorway of the tavern's kitchen, the courier could see into the taproom. The long, narrow room was crowded, the atmosphere thick with the yeasty aroma of ale and the blue tobacco smoke that gathered in a dense haze against the blackened beams supporting the low ceiling. The grim-faced patrons who bent their heads together over their pints were all members of the local militia.

Farmers, merchants, and tradesmen, they sported clothing that indicated varying degrees of prosperity. Most were clad, as was the courier, in simple homespun, a necessity for the vast majority of colonists because of the despised taxes Britain had imposed on imported goods. Even the more prosperous members of the group were soberly suited in a reflection of their Puritan stock as well as the temper of the times.

"Was Uncle Josh expecting trouble tonight?"

"Naw." Levi shrugged. "Will dismissed the company a couple hours ago, but most of 'em decided to hang around a while. I guess we're all thinkin' trouble's bound to come right soon."

The courier gave a rueful nod. "I got a taste of it tonight."

Before Levi could question him, a tall man stepped out from behind the door to their right. About thirty years of age, he was lean and tanned as a hunter, though spotless white linen, a waistcoat of dove-grey silk, breeches of fine black wool, and the silver buckles of his shoes marked him as a member of some profession.

The courier grinned at his oldest cousin in grudging admiration. A lawyer who was gaining some reputation in the area, William Stern was also captain of the Lincoln militia and chairman of the local Committee of Correspondence, which was responsible for distributing information about the activities of the British to other committees throughout the thirteen colonies.

He was, as well, a delegate to the illegal Provincial Congress currently convened in Concord under the direction of thirty-four-year-old

Dr. Joseph Warren. Samuel Adams's right-hand man, Warren was considered to be the most personable incendiary in the colonies, reluctantly admired by his enemies even though they despised his politics.

"You'd better get in here," Will said with a relieved grin. "Pa's been fretting. He's about worried himself sick."

With Levi at his heels, the courier squeezed past him into a low-ceilinged room hardly larger than a closet. The constricted space was pungent with the scent of mingled tobacco smoke, whale oil, and the musty leather bindings of the books that crowded shelves occupying every available inch from floor to ceiling along the bare plaster walls. To one side of the single window stood a large, scarred desk piled with an untidy clutter of books and papers that threatened to crowd a battered whale oil lamp off its edge.

Behind the desk, in the lamp's flickering light, Joshua Stern, proprietor of the establishment and colonel of the Lincoln militia, threw down his quill pen with a sigh and looked up, his square, genial face softening into a smile. Transferring his blackened clay pipe to an ash-filled saucer with one large paw, he reached for the courier's pouch with the other. When he had tossed it on top of the papers in front of him, he stretched back in his chair and, yawning, ran his fingers through the unruly mop of curly grey hair that wreathed his head.

"I was about to send a party out to hunt you down." He turned to direct a pointed glance in the direction of the ancient oak clock that ticked on unperturbed from the wall to his right.

The courier dropped into the chair Will shoved forward, weighing how much he could safely confess. He threw his cousins a look of appeal, knowing all too well that in spite of every attempt at evasion his uncle would eventually pry every incriminating detail out of him.

Will slouched into a dilapidated wing chair, while Levi leaned against the closed door. Both watched him with a mixture of amusement and concern.

"You didn't run into any trouble, did you?" Stern fixed the courier in a gaze that had become piercing.

"There was a patrol this side of Brooklyne," the courier admitted, resigned to his fate. "I'd swear they were on the lookout for me, too. They just rode up out of nowhere and came after me."

Stern scrutinized him narrowly. "It appears you got away unscathed."

The courier grimaced. "It took some creative riding to shake them off."

"They get close enough to get a good look at you?" Will demanded, his tone sharp.

"I don't think so. Luckily they were poor shots, and—" He stopped, thoroughly disgusted.

Levi's jaw dropped. "You mean they fired at you?"

"I guess they meant business this time." At memory of his narrow escape, the courier suddenly felt weak.

"I had a feeling you needed my prayers tonight," Stern said, his voice sober. "I've said it before, though no one's listening. You're testing God's patience too far. One of these days he's going to remove his hand of protection."

Ignoring him, Will leaned forward in his chair. "This is serious. Gage ordered his troops not to shoot except in self-defense. So either they took matters into their own hands or the general has changed his policy."

Stern packed a pinch of fresh tobacco into his pipe. Clenching the stem between his teeth, he took the stub of a candle from his desk, lighted it at the lamp, then applied its flame to the pipe's bowl and drew on it until the tobacco glowed cherry red.

"Someone's putting them on to you," he said, releasing a cloud of fragrant smoke. He blew out the candle and set it aside. "Gage is going to keep his hounds hot on your tail until they bring you to bay."

"He's not going to catch me—" The courier bit his lip the instant the impulsive words slipped out, but too late to take them back.

Stern's eyes narrowed. "So you're too clever for the king's men, are you? How long do you think you can keep tweaking Gage's nose before he comes down on you with an iron fist? But having some experience with your complete inability to exercise reasonable caution, I suspect it hasn't sunk into your thick skull that you're playing with fire. Do I have to remind you that Gage has spies planted even in Revere's circle of mechanics? All it would take is a hint dropped in the wrong ears—"

"There's no one in Boston, except for Mr. Longworthy, Mr. Revere, and of course, Dr. Warren, who has any suspicion I'm not as zealous a Tory as my father. I'd trust any one of those gentlemen with my life."

"They aren't the ones I'm worried about! There's a reward on your head. Sooner or later you'll make a misstep, or someone will put two and two together. If Gage manages to capture you, the most your father's influence will gain you is a quick exit in front of a firing squad instead of slow strangulation at the end of a rope."

"I'm not afraid of the Regulars," retorted the courier with some heat.

"That's the trouble! If you understood the consequences that could result from your actions, you'd stop behaving as if this were nothing more than an amusing game!"

Levi and Will exchanged glances. The courier flushed and opened his mouth to protest, but Stern cut him off, emphasizing each word with a jab of his pipe.

"I fought Tess about your involvement from the beginning, and I'd have won the argument if she hadn't persuaded Warren to intervene. If any harm comes to you, I'll never forgive myself."

"You couldn't have stopped me," the courier protested. "From the time I was a child, you and Will and Papa have debated whether the rights God gave us as free beings take precedence over our allegiance to an earthly king who is a tyrant. I listened to all your arguments and came to my own conclusions.

"I love and respect my father more than any man, but on this issue,

I cannot agree with him. The last thing I want is to hurt him, but I have to follow my own conscience, as you did. Yes, Aunt Tess encouraged me to take an active part in working for the Sons of Liberty. But I alone made the decision to act, and I think I've proven of some value to the patriot cause."

"You're the most daring and resourceful courier we have, and you have the perfect cover. With your close ties to so many of the officers on Gage's staff, there's no end to what you can learn just by keeping your mouth shut and your ears open." Will grinned. "And so far, at least, even Uncle Samuel doesn't suspect you—or that his own sister is storing enough powder in her barn to blow up a good part of Boston."

Levi gave the courier a wink. "Don't pay Pa any mind. His bark is considerably worse than his bite."

The courier laughed, but Stern puffed thick smoke from his pipe, exasperated by their apparent unconcern. "You may consider this a fine joke, but you'd better heed my warning or you'll likely find your head in a noose in short order."

"I'm not the only one taking risks, Uncle Josh. All of us are. It's too late for us to turn back, even if we wanted to. As for me, I refuse to live as any man's slave—even George the Third's!"

"Well said, Cousin," Will murmured as Levi nodded approval.

"All very well and good, but I get the impression that more often than not you're following your own desire for excitement rather than seeking God's guidance and purpose. In my experience, that's a sure recipe for disaster." Stern fixed the courier in a warm look.

The courier flushed and raised his chin. "I pray for guidance every day."

"And do you ever listen for the answer?"

Will and Levi guffawed. Throwing them a reproving look, the courier changed the subject.

"Gage has ordered all the men-of-war in Boston harbor to keep their longboats on standby. That has to mean there's a move afoot and soon."

Sobering, Will frowned and shifted in his chair. "Gage doesn't dare wait much longer. The more he delays, the stronger our position becomes. If he expects to arrest Sam Adams and John Hancock, he's going to have to move within the next few days, before they leave Concord for Philadelphia and the next session of the Continental Congress."

Still frowning, Stern unbuckled the straps of the courier's pouch and shuffled through the papers it contained. Those from the Boston Committee of Correspondence he handed to Will. As he scanned the report from the Committee of Safety, charged by the Provincial Congress with overseeing the military defense of the colony, he stiffened.

"Gage received a dispatch from Parliament yesterday. They're sending substantial reinforcements as well as several high-powered generals: Clinton, Howe, and Burgoyne. Looks like the Ministry is determined to stir Gage to action."

"Another confidential dispatch arrived today. I haven't gotten wind of its contents yet, but I should be able to learn something at the general's ball tomorrow—or rather tonight," the courier corrected himself when the clock chimed the quarter hour past midnight. "If he's set a definite date, I may be able to discover it as well."

Sitting forward on his chair, he went on, "By the way, I chanced on another bit of information you may find interesting. The other night we had Lord Percy and Major Pitcairn to dinner, and they mentioned they're expecting the arrival either today or tomorrow of a captain of the Seventeenth Light Dragoons who's being posted here from Virginia."

"I hadn't heard any dragoons were stationed in the colonies," Stern responded.

"None have been, so far at least. The captain has been on leave from his troop."

Stern raised his eyebrows. "What was he doing in Virginia?"

"He was reared there. According to Lord Percy, when the captain was very young he was adopted by a wealthy old bachelor uncle from Virginia, who needed an heir. Since the captain's older brother was set to inherit their father's estate in England, it was a mutually beneficial arrangement. At any rate, the captain returned to England a few years ago, where he became fast friends with Major Pitcairn and Lord Percy and took a commission in the dragoons. When his uncle died last fall, he came back to Virginia to settle the estate."

"So what's his business in Boston?" Will asked, puzzled.

The courier glanced over at him. "I gathered Percy and Pitcairn persuaded the general to have him attached to his command. The Seventeenth is included in the reinforcements Parliament is posting here, so the captain would have ended up in Boston anyway. But it's interesting that Gage intends to place him on his staff as an advisor of sorts."

Will was plainly mystified. "Why all the fuss over a mere captain?"

"It turns out this 'mere captain' is not only rich, but also happens to be blessed with influential friends at court and in Parliament who might be induced to do Gage a good turn. As you know, the general hasn't exactly been in favor in either place of late. And Pitcairn says the captain knows this region like the back of his hand and is exceptionally knowledgeable about the political and military situation here."

"But you said he grew up in Virginia," Levi pointed out.

The courier's gaze remained on Will. "He did, but he also spent considerable time in Boston overseeing his uncle's business interests. In fact, Captain Carleton graduated from Harvard."

Startled, Will shot upright in his chair. "Carleton? Not Jonathan Stuart Carleton?"

The courier smiled with satisfaction. "I thought you might know him."

"The younger son of Lord Oliver Carleton, George II's closest advisor? I should say!" Will exclaimed. "He was a year ahead of me at

Harvard. I had him home to dinner a couple of times, Pa—tall, blond fellow, very agreeable sort."

Stern broke into a smile. "Oh, yes. I used to wish you'd bring him around more often."

"He was a brilliant student, though I rarely saw him crack a book."

"From Percy's description, I'd hardly have taken him for a scholar, Will," the courier chided. "I got the impression he's a bit of a dandy and very much the lady's man."

Will laughed and propped his long legs up on the edge of the desk. "That would be Jon, all right. We all heard rumors about Sir Harrison Carleton's vast fortune, and from my acquaintance with him, I'd say Sir Harry could have bought and sold even John Hancock without batting an eyelash. And Jon had the most attractive penchant for spreading the wealth around. The parties he threw were memorable, to say the least."

"Lord Percy did mention that his reputation is notorious even among the officers," the courier said with some severity. "It appears your old friend has found it necessary to cultivate an exceptional proficiency at the duel."

"I shouldn't be surprised. He was a crack shot and an elegant swordsman when I knew him."

"Really, Will, I wouldn't think him at all the sort you'd find congenial."

Will's grin widened. "On the contrary, I liked him more than I can say. When he wasn't charming himself out of some absurd scrape or other, he was fast-talking one of the rest of us out of trouble. He provided me an alibi on more than one occasion."

Grumpily the courier said, "Well, I suspect I'm not going to like him one whit."

Will's expression was skeptical. "Don't make any judgments until you meet him. Personally, I've always hoped we'd meet again one day."

"You may very well as adversaries on a battlefield. Still, considering that the captain spent his childhood in the colonies, who knows where his real sympathies lie."

"In Jon's case, I wouldn't rule out either alternative," Will said. "None of us ever came close to figuring out what made him tick. He was exceptionally close-mouthed about himself, though on the surface he could seem as transparent as glass."

"Well, as luck would have it, our tenants sailed for England a couple of weeks ago, so of course Papa offered to billet Captain Carleton in our town house, along with a lieutenant who's traveling with him. And if I know my father, he'll find occasion to entertain both of them at Stony Hill on a regular basis."

Will leaned forward in anticipation. "Which opens up all sorts of possibilities for you."

"The contact may turn out to be . . . useful."

"See how much you can learn," Stern approved. "The next few days are going to be critical, and we need every scrap of intelligence you can pry loose."

He broke off, then said, "One more thing. Warren has made contact with someone on a high level in Boston who has offered to provide us with the most sensitive military intelligence. They're meeting tonight to work out a way to pass the information safely."

"What do you mean high level, Pa? An officer on Gage's staff?"

"That's something none of us need to know, Levi," Stern reproved. "He's putting himself in considerable danger by passing intelligence on to us, so it's best if we mind our own business."

Levi flushed and clamped his mouth shut. Stern did not appear to notice. Rising, he began to pace up and down the cramped room with an agitation he couldn't conceal. For several moments, all of them silently marked the steady ticking of the clock.

At last Stern turned to the courier. "As much as I'm reluctant to involve you any further, we need someone to rendezvous with this contact—Patriot, Warren called him—then relay the intelligence back here to me. It'll mean meeting him in or pretty close to Boston."

"You know I'll do it—"

"Now hear me out. This intelligence will be so compromising that if you're caught with it, they'll likely string you up on the spot."

"Since there's already a price on my head, what difference does it make?"

As though he were trying to convince himself, Stern admitted, "I thought of that too. It's a virtual certainty they'd hang you anyway. But you've proven that you're resourceful in a tight spot."

On impulse the courier got to his feet and embraced the older man. "Please don't worry. Look how much effect your prayers have had already."

Stern patted him on the back, then released him. "Heed what I said about putting God to the test. Still, if Gage moves tomorrow, this will be a moot point."

Will rose and stepped to the desk. After placing a thick sheaf of papers into the courier's pouch, he fastened it and handed it to his cousin.

"There are the reports from our Committees of Safety and Correspondence for Longworthy. You'd better get along before you're missed at home. It'll be dawn by the time you get back."

"Sunday is Easter," Stern reminded them as they went out through the tavern's rear door. "Let's hope everything remains quiet for a couple more days. Warren is leaving Concord for Boston this evening so he won't have to travel on the Sabbath. He'll leave your instructions in the usual place Monday morning."

"Pa said you're bringing out the last of the gunpowder today," Will noted.

The courier brightened. "We've gotten hold of some muskets and a fair supply of cartridges too—though since the fines have been raised, the soldiers aren't nearly as eager to sell them as they used to be."

"Gage has a sight of gall to put a price on our heads for taking back the munitions he stole from us!" Levi broke in. "The citizens of this colony bought and paid for every last ounce of that gunpowder, and he just walks in and takes it without a by-your-leave. We even pay his soldiers premium prices to take their worn-out muskets off their hands!"

Will pushed the door open. "That argument won't hold up in a royal court. The king can claim everything you own, and you don't even have the right to demand payment."

"On your way now," Stern growled, waving the courier off. "And be especially careful just in case another patrol is out there waiting for you."

He and Levi went back inside while Will walked the courier to his horse. The tavern's customers had all gone home, and the mare stood alone at the hitching rail, head drooping.

"How's Rebekah doing?"

Will smiled. "Moving slow, but the baby's due any day now."

"And little Will and Anne?"

"Full of mischief and growing like weeds."

The courier finished buckling the pouch behind his saddle, then turned to give his cousin a probing glance. "I notice you've taken down your shingle."

Will shoved his hands into his pockets. "With the royal courts shut down, we're handling as many legal cases as possible through the local committees. My days are taken up with the sessions of the Provincial Congress, committee meetings, drilling the militia, and trying to scare up enough guns and ammunition to go around, none of which brings in cold coin. I believe in what we're doing with all my heart, but it's sure hard to support a family on rhetoric."

The uncharacteristic bitterness in his voice wasn't lost on the courier, and he touched his cousin's arm in sympathy. "Rebekah knows how important your involvement is to the cause right now. She doesn't begrudge the sacrifices."

"I know. If anything, she feels more strongly about it than I do. But I'm hardly indispensable."

"All of us are indispensable if we're serious about opposing tyranny."

Will frowned and looked away. His voice muffled, he said, "I know you're right. It's just that I can't help wondering who'd take care of my family if I couldn't."

An unaccustomed tightness closed over the courier's heart. "Everyone keeps saying Gage won't dare press the issue to the point of war."

Will's answering look was hard. "Do you still believe that after tonight?"

The courier mounted without answering, but as he reined the mare round, Will caught the halter. "No more of your daredevil exploits, all right? Stick to spying. That should be dangerous enough even for you."

"I can take care of myself."

"Pride goeth before a fall," Will warned. "And be doubly careful where Jon is concerned. I witnessed several incidents that led me to believe he'd be a dangerous adversary. He has a keen eye for the little details others miss—and an extraordinary ability to figure out what they mean."

"Thanks for the warning."

Although Will returned the courier's smile, his eyes remained serious. "While you're at it, guard your heart well, little Oriole. If I know my old friend, he'll try to steal it."

The courier threw back his head, laughing as the wind ruffled his long cloak around him. "Don't worry about me on that score, Cuz. My heart is proof against all attempts."

Chapter Two

IT WAS BARELY FIRST LIGHT when the courier skirted the village of Roxbury along its western and southern boundaries. At a little distance, through the light mist, he could make out the indistinct shapes of the nearer houses and cottages. Above the rooftops loomed the ghostly spire of First Church.

He kept well off the road, cutting through the hazy fields silent as a wraith until he reached the brow of the heights just beyond the last houses. There, where the land dipped sharply to the bay, he crossed the road and pulled his mare to a halt in the deep shadows beneath a row of green-black pines. For some moments he sat motionless.

To the east, toward the sea, the first rosy streamers of dawn faintly streaked the thin skein of clouds high above the verdant hills brooding over the mouth of the harbor. A short distance off Dorchester Point the melting light caressed the walls of Castle William, the fortress atop Castle Island whose hundred guns guarded the sea roads leading into the bay.

Pale fog rose from the grey-black surface of the water. Hovering above it circled the gulls roused by the strengthening light from their nests on the rocky islands along the coast. Their piercing cries reached the courier from a distance as they skimmed in toward land.

Lifting his face to the cool salt breeze, he gazed down the length of Orange Street, which pointed like a spectral arrow along the narrow neck of land that connected the mainland to the shadowed peninsula at its end. On all sides of that jutting prow of land slapped the slow, dark waves of the bay, lightly tipped with pearl. Amid its silent hills, where orchards and gardens were just beginning to show the faintest tentative blush of green, the rooftops and church spires of Boston slumbered in deceptive serenity.

The only visible movement was the rhythmic sway of the bristling masts of the men-of-war rolling sluggishly on the outgoing tide at their anchorages just beyond the wharves. His Majesty's navy. An implicit threat sent to enforce the will of king and Parliament on England's rebellious colonies.

Under normal conditions the port would have been coming alive at that hour with the traffic of a wide variety of vessels. An assortment of fishing sloops, an occasional skiff, longboats from busy merchant frigates, schooners, the ferries to Charlestown and Winisimmit all would have presented a constantly changing panorama of color and motion to the observer.

But Parliament's imposition of the Boston Port Bill the previous year had changed all that. In retaliation for what the local wits had inevitably immortalized as the Boston Tea Party, the British government had closed the harbor to all vessels except the ships of the British navy and a limited number of carefully regulated fishing vessels that supplied the town.

To add insult to injury, Parliament had also removed Massachusetts's seat of government from Boston to Salem and had made the town of Marblehead its port of entry until the colonists paid for the ruined tea. This the indignant colonists refused to do, even when a military governor, General Thomas Gage, had arrived the previous May with an impressive armed force to occupy the rebellious town and enforce compliance. Instead, Committees of Correspondence had been organized throughout the thirteen colonies to keep each informed of events in the others. And colonies as far removed as Virginia and South Carolina had begun to ship supplies overland to the embattled town.

Resistance had a price, however. Inevitably, businesses that owed their existence to the sea trade had been forced to close their doors. Activity in and around the ropewalks, sailmakers' establishments, import offices, shipyards, and customs houses had dwindled and at last died away.

The loss in jobs and income had taken a heavy toll on almost every household in Boston. The result had been to harden public opinion against the king, which made General Gage's thankless task all the more difficult, especially as the rebels had taken full advantage of every opportunity to make life miserable for him and his troops.

Although the citizens of the colonies were required by law to provide lodgings for Britain's soldiers, every house had suddenly been full. Few quarters could be found, and the majority of the troops had ended up living in tents for months on end. Nor had barracks been built until winter due to the outright refusal of most of the local contractors to work for the hated "lobsters." This included those whose politics were less scrupulous but who feared the violent reprisals by the Sons of Liberty that had become epidemic. Only a staunch few found the courage to provide the goods, services, and supplies needed to maintain Gage's army.

Hence the present stalemate. Daily, sullen dockworkers idled in the taverns and lounged on street corners looking for trouble, which the bored, defiant soldiers cooped up in the town were eager enough to provide. And all the while Paul Revere's circle of artisans kept close watch on the troops, reporting any unusual movement to Warren, the acknowledged leader of the patriots in Massachusetts since Samuel Adams's election to the Continental Congress meeting in Philadelphia.

Dismounting, the courier studied the foreboding bulk of the recently completed fortifications directly outside the double brick arches of the town gates. With a calculating eye, he took in the menacing batteries that frowned down on Boston's sole landward access. From where he stood he could make out an occasional flash of red and glint of steel where sentries kept watch along the tops of the walls.

Gradually the brightening light brought the landscape into clearer focus, and his gaze returned to the peninsula. Just visible between the two steep promontories of Beacon Hill and Copp's Hill on Boston's landward side rose the highest of the three hills that dominated the Charlestown peninsula straight north across the bay. Known only by the name of the farmer who pastured his cattle there, it was called Bunker's Hill.

A nameless foreboding caused the courier's hand to tighten unconsciously, until the mare tossed her head at the pressure of the bit. Becoming aware of the cutting sharpness of the wind, the courier shivered and drew his cloak more closely about his shoulders.

A cock's hoarse crow and the soft lowing of a cow drew his attention to the sheltered hollow that lay below him. Along its western and northern sides the land fell away to marshes and tidal mud flats where the Charles River and several minor tributaries drained into the Back Bay.

Because the site overlooked the small rivulet called Stony Brook, it had been dubbed Stony Hill. Its protected location welcomed the first signs of spring earlier than the surrounding countryside. Already the imposing brick mansion of English Georgian design that dominated the hollow was partially hidden behind a delicate tracery of yellow-green bursting into life along the branches of the trees that dotted its park-like lawn.

Noting that a thin ribbon of smoke curled from the kitchen's tall chimney, the courier led the mare at a swift walk down the rocky slope at the rear of the estate. At his approach, the chickens pecking in the dirt outside the tidy barn scattered. He slowed his stride as he neared the low, whitewashed stable at the far end of the paddock fence.

The figure of a man materialized out of the shadows of the building's rear door. Catching sight of the courier, he loped toward him and took the mare's reins in his broad hand.

"You're up early, Isaiah."

A free black man of medium height and muscular build, whose wiry hair was liberally salted with grey though his dusky face remained as unlined a youth's, Isaiah fixed the courier in a stern glare. "And you comin' home mighty late. A couple soldiers bring one in hurt bad, and they say Oriole done it."

"It was an accident. They came after me, and I had to make a run for it. What happened?" he added anxiously.

Isaiah snorted. "What you think? I convince Dr. Sam I can help and he don't need to call you down. So we work on the soldier for near three hours, then they all go take him back to Boston not half an hour ago. But if Dr. Sam decide he need your help or if he lay eyes on that empty stall, you can bet he start askin' some questions we sure not goin' to want to answer."

"The soldier's all right?"

"He goin' to live, but look like he be crippled."

The courier followed him into the stable. "I'm awfully sorry it happened. I never meant to hurt anyone, but my only other choice was to give myself up—or get shot."

Isaiah gave a curt nod as he turned the mare into her roomy box stall. "Sarah got the fire goin' for breakfast by now," he said, referring to his wife, the family's cook. "Miz Anne be up a'fore long, so you better git to the house."

"We need to smuggle the last of those munitions out of Boston today. Have the phaeton ready to go right after lunch," the courier ordered over his shoulder on his way out of the stable.

Making sure no one was in sight, he strode toward the house. Clipped box hedges bordering the gravel path on either side shielded him from view as he passed through the kitchen and herb gardens in the direction of the wide stone terrace that ran the length of the mansion's rear.

The windows were still shuttered, but as soon as he came within sight of them, he left the path to cut across the lawn and around the kitchen to the front of the house. Tall oaks, elms, chestnuts, and pines along with graceful maples and gnarled dogwoods shaded the circular carriageway and lawn and threw muted shadows across the weathered rose of the mansion's bricks, the curved, cream-colored lintels of the windows, and the massive pediment over the central doorway.

He came to a halt beneath the ancient apple tree that grew outside the dining room, its branches reaching to the level of the third-story dormers. Fighting the fatigue that was beginning to make every movement an effort, he caught hold of one of the lower branches and swung himself lightly up. With practiced ease he climbed to the level of the second story.

As he paused, the pouch-like nest of an oriole hanging from a nearby branch caught his eye. Each spring for several years he had watched a nesting pair raise their brood in its secure confines, and he had begun to take great interest in their welfare.

Damaged during the winter storms, the nest showed signs of recent repairs. A quick look inside confirmed that the residents had returned from their winter's absence and begun to prepare for a new family.

On impulse the courier softly whistled the high warble of the oriole's call. After a moment, from a maple on the far side of the lawn, came the answer. Smiling, he reached for the window nearest his perch.

It had been left open just far enough for him to find a fingerhold under the frame. Giving a quick tug, he slid it all the way up. Then clinging to the bough above his head, he swung feet and legs in through the window. With a sideways twist of his body, he released the branch and landed as lightly as a cat on the Turkey carpet that covered the plank floor inside.

The room he entered in this stealthy manner was his own, its furnishings simple but elegant. The counterpane of the high poster bed and the crocheted canopy seeming to float above it glowed a ghostly white in the faint light. A sturdy wooden trunk with a domed lid stood

at the foot of the bed, and along the walls were ranged a finely proportioned writing desk, chair, and highboy, and a washstand on which stood
a blue-flowered china basin and pitcher.

Sitting down on the floor, the courier pried off his boots, then tiptoed across the room to the washstand, where he wiped dew and bits of
grass and leaves from the leather with a rag. Carrying the boots back to
the trunk, he opened the lid and lifted out the blankets stacked inside. A
hidden catch released the trunk's false floor to reveal a capacious secret
compartment below, into which he laid the footwear.

Gloves, cloak, and hat followed, along with the wig of brown hair.
For the moment he left in place the silken cloth wound around his head.

Rolling up the sleeves of his shapeless farmer's smock, he returned
to the washstand, where he poured water from the pitcher into the basin
and scrubbed dust and sweat from his face, neck, and arms. The banked
embers of the previous night's fire glimmering on the grate beneath a
thick covering of grey ash did nothing to warm the room, and he shivered in the early morning chill as he flung the water from the window.
Taking care to make no noise, he closed both window and shutters and
carried the basin to the washstand.

This done, he slipped off his smock, and then unwound the length
of silk from his head. Pulling out the hairpins that held a mass of dark
curls in place, the young woman thus revealed shook her head to release
the waist-length cascade in a gleaming flood over her bare shoulders.

With a sigh of relief, she removed the wide linen wrappings that flattened instead of emphasizing the full curves of her bosom. Wasting no
further time, she peeled off breeches and hose. When the last article
had been added to the secret compartment, she secured the false floor
and replaced the blankets. After retrieving a small key from behind a
loose baseboard along the wall beneath the window, she locked the
trunk and returned the key to its hiding place.

On the mantel the clock chimed the third quarter after four. Her
shift was where she had left it, rolled up and stuffed under the pillow on

her bed. As she began to pull it on over her head, she heard a tentative knock at the door.

For a breathless moment, she neither moved nor answered. But just as her pulse had begun to steady, the knock was repeated more insistently.

She settled the shift over her shoulders with a deft shake before answering in a sleepy drawl, "Mama . . . is that you?"

"Beth! It's me—Abby," came the anxious, whispered reply.

The young woman let out her breath. Pulling the bedclothes into disarray, she hurried to unlock the door.

In the darkened hall outside a child of about ten years of age jiggled from one bare foot to the other. She wore only her thin linen shift, and shivering in the chill, she hugged herself in an effort to stay warm.

Her sister drew her inside and closed the door behind them. "Faith, but you gave me a fright, you naughty goose!" she accused in a vehement whisper, bending over the child. "Whatever are you doing up at this hour?"

Abby reached up to wind her arms around her sister's neck, her voice plaintive. "I couldn't help it. I had a bad dream."

Contrite, the older girl picked her up and carried her to the bed. "Tell me what happened," she said as she tucked her under the covers. "You know, if you tell your dream it stops being scary."

Abby snuggled under the warm covers, shivering. "It was real dark, and this big red monster was chasing you. You were screaming and running away, but it kept getting closer. I called you, but you didn't hear me, then I heard something bump, and I woke up."

A pang of guilt stabbed through the young woman, and she slipped in under the covers to hug her sister fiercely. "You know Sarah always says God takes care of us, and see—I'm here, and both of us are safe."

The child kissed her cheek. "I know. I'm glad God gave me a big sister. I always feel safer when I'm with you. I just wish there weren't so many bad things happening right now."

A quiet tap at the door interrupted them, and an anxious voice called, "Elizabeth, is Abby with you? She's not in her bed, and I can't find her."

"She had a bad dream, Mama, and I took her to bed with me."

"Well, go back to sleep, then." Their mother's voice sounded relieved. "I'm sorry I disturbed you."

When her muted footsteps had faded down the hall, Elizabeth smiled down at Abby, and brushed her fine, blond hair off her forehead. "I'm glad He gave me a little sister, too. I know things have been scary, but I'll always be here to take care of you. Promise."

She laid her head on the pillow beside the child's, the small form gathered against her. Sighing with contentment, Abby closed her eyes, a smile touching her lips.

Gradually the room brightened with the sun's rising, but neither of them saw it. Their arms wrapped around each other, cheeks touching, they slept.

It was late when Elizabeth Howard awoke. Deciding not to call her maid, Jemma, to assist her, she took longer than usual to dress and arrange her hair. It was almost eleven before she descended the broad central stairway of Stony Hill, one hand skimming the polished wood of its ornate, carved banister.

Beneath a delicate gauze cap, she wore her hair piled into a gleaming crown on top of her head, a style that complemented the delicacy of her features. Her emerald brocade robe à l'anglaise, with its elbow-length belle sleeves trimmed in a froth of lace and a petticoat that fell open down the front to reveal silken under-petticoats striped in apricot and cream, emphasized her slim figure, pale complexion, and dark eyes.

At the bottom step, she paused and cocked her head to listen. The house was silent. No sound of voices or movement reached her ears.

Lost in thought, she went to lay her cloak and feathered hat on the settee opposite the stairway, then dropped her reticule and gloves on the small table beside it. For a moment she studied her reflection in the tall mirror hanging above the table. After adjusting the fichu of pale lace that softened the revealing cut of her gown's décolletage, she leaned closer to the mirror to fluff the soft curls clustered against her temple and cheek.

The only trace of last night's courier that remained to betray her this morning was her hands. Small and square, they were boyishly strong as a result of a great deal of hard riding, the palms calloused from the reins, fingernails cut short because she was forever breaking them. She frowned down at them, thanking heaven that custom required ladies to wear gloves for all social engagements.

Turning away from the empty parlor, she crossed the foyer and went into the dining room, where a fire crackling on the hearth took the chill off the air. This room also lay empty, dappled by the flicker of sunshine and shadow through the long windows. As in her bedroom, luxurious, hand-woven Turkey carpets overlaid the wide, unpolished plank floors in each of the rooms, but downstairs the walls were either paneled in rich wood to the ceiling or wainscoted, with imported fabrics covering the upper portion.

Throughout the house the colors were restful to the eye, each detail designed to impart a sense of graciousness and harmony. For a moment she paused to drink in the peace that surrounded her and the sensation that the house stood as a solitary, but invulnerable, bastion against the turmoil that raged all around it.

With an unconscious sigh she passed through the double doors at the back of the room that opened into the adjoining drawing room. Crossing to the rear door, she stepped down into the enclosed porch that joined the main portion of the house to the separate building housing the kitchen. The plain, whitewashed room she entered was fragrant with the rich aroma of baking bread.

On the bricks in front of the massive fireplace, codfish balls sizzled in the cast iron Dutch oven. Beans, the usual Saturday fare, simmered in

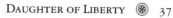

a black kettle hanging over the flames. Overhead, long strings of dried fruit and vegetables and bunches of herbs festooned the ceiling's blackened beams, adding their pungent scent to the air. Elizabeth took a deep breath, her stomach reminding her insistently that she hadn't eaten since dinner the night before.

At the plank table her black maid, Jemma, sat on a tall stool, her back to Elizabeth as she dreamily stirred the contents of the large crockery bowl she balanced on her lap. She was watching her mother, a statuesque, coffee-colored woman whose red-turbaned head bent over the fire.

Neither of them noticed Elizabeth. Biting her lip to stop a giggle, she tiptoed toward the child, arms outstretched, careful to keep her high-heeled slippers from clattering on the brick floor.

Without warning, she pounced. Jemma jumped and gave an ear-splitting shriek as batter slopped down her apron and onto the floor. The bowl was narrowly saved from disaster, and the two of them dissolved into helpless giggles.

"Miz 'Lizabeth, if you keep on misbehavin' like that, I'm goin' to have to take this here wooden spoon to you like I did when you was a child." The cook brandished the instrument of discipline.

"Oh, Sarah, can't anyone have a little fun?" Elizabeth teased.

Shaking her head in tight-lipped disapproval, Sarah wiped her floury hands on her apron. Grabbing a couple of thick pads of cloth, she removed a large tin from the reflector oven that faced the flames. She set the tin on the table to cool while she turned another loaf she had set out earlier onto the cutting board. With deft, sure strokes, she began to slice the still steaming brown bread.

Over fourteen-year-old Jemma's vehement protests, her mother sent her out of the room on an errand before fixing Elizabeth in her stern gaze. "Isaiah tell me what happen with them soldiers and how late you git home this mornin'. You mark my words, young lady, if you keep on pressin' your luck, one o' these days, you goin' have to pay the piper."

"Keep your voice down!" Elizabeth pleaded in a loud whisper. Glancing toward the door in alarm, she asked, "Where are Mama and Abby?"

"Out back in the garden 'long with Pete and Sammy. They gettin' the herb beds ready for plantin'."

"Papa's not home yet?"

"I 'spect he makin' his rounds, him bein' in town anyways," Sarah allowed.

Relenting, she placed a thick slice of the brown bread in front of Elizabeth along with a small pitcher of milk and a bowl of porridge she had obviously been keeping warm for her. When Elizabeth wrinkled her nose, she admonished, "An' that all you gettin' from me till lunch. If you wasn't traipsin' all over the country ever' night doin' Lord knows what, you might show up on time for breakfast."

"What I was doing is just a little bit more important than punctuality for meals!"

Sarah shook her finger in Elizabeth's face. "When your ma and pa find out what you been up to, you goin' to break their hearts."

Elizabeth knew Sarah's dire predictions masked genuine affection and worry, and she laughed the warning off. "Since you and Isaiah are as deeply involved with the patriots as I am, you'd better keep praying I don't get caught, or it'll mean all our necks."

Her teasing had the desired effect. While Elizabeth devoured her breakfast, Sarah had to struggle to maintain her stern look. But she inserted one last warning.

"I know one thing for sure—the good Lord gonna send somebody to take you down a peg or two. You jus' wait and see."

Giving a merry laugh, Elizabeth escaped out the door and went back into the house, her head tilted at an assured angle. She crossed the parlor to a door that opened into the wing on the opposite side of the house from the kitchen.

The long, narrow anteroom she entered was furnished with a single bench, which stood against the wall across from the window, and a peg-board for cloaks. The door to her left led outside, the one opposite her into the dispensary.

Entering this generously proportioned room, where a row of glass-doored cabinets held bottles of various tinctures and boxes of medicinal herbs, she went on into the surgery beyond it. Her father's surgeon's case was gone, she noted, and the cloth-covered tray of surgical instruments that rested on a smaller table beside the large one used for surgeries had been disturbed, the scattered instruments left bloody. On the floor below, a large basin held blood-saturated cloths.

From the peg behind the door she pulled down her apron, tied it around her waist, carefully covering the front of her voluminous petticoats, and then pinned the bib to her bodice. After carrying the basin to the kitchen so Sarah could soak the cloths, she had Jemma carry a bucket of hot water to the dispensary.

When the young woman had gone, Elizabeth began to wash the assortment of lancets, scalpels, forceps, needles, and scissors. While drying the instruments with a clean cloth, then arranging them in proper order on the tray, she let her thoughts drift to the changes the past year had brought to her life.

The arrival of the British troops the previous spring had brought many of the officers to Dr. Samuel Howard's surgery, as much due to the social ties the genial doctor shrewdly cultivated with General Gage and his staff as to her father's acknowledged skill. It was these useful—and increasingly treacherous—contacts that had drawn Elizabeth into the vortex of the escalating conflict between England and her fractious colonies. And at the moment, in addition to Gage's plans for the next few days, they were the source of her most troubling concern.

With the sudden influx of so many young, unmarried officers shortly after her father had broken off her betrothal to David Hutchins, the son of a prominent Boston Whig, the ranks of her suitors had swelled to amazing proportions. Within a very short time the ardent offers for her hand had become the subject of tight-lipped envy on the part of her girlfriends. To the mounting distress of her mother, however, Elizabeth's response to each proposal had been the same sweetly courteous, but unmovable, refusal.

For his part, her father regarded her dalliances with indulgent good humor, which strengthened Elizabeth's resolve to guard her independence, especially after the painful experience with Hutchins. Dr. Howard made no secret of his pride in her skill as his assistant. A natural teacher, he had taught her as he had his students, before his political loyalties had led them to desert him.

It was the one conflict between him and Elizabeth's mother, who objected that a chaste young woman should never be exposed to the indelicate matters common to a doctor's profession. But he took such great pleasure in Elizabeth's assistance, her comprehension of his medical texts, and their long discussions of new procedures and theories that in this matter he refused to be moved.

Although she suspected that in some measure her interest in medicine soothed his regret at siring no sons, she was drawn to the art of healing by more than the desire to gain her father's approval. She could not help being conscious that the calm, steady confidence of her manner reassured and won over patients who initially resisted the presence of a young woman. She had also noted from the beginning that her touch on the injured or ill had a markedly soothing, even healing, effect. That this gift was of God and not due to any effort of her own impressed itself on her consciousness each time she ministered to someone in need, and she was humbled by it.

The sound of a door opening and closing and the thump of footsteps roused Elizabeth from her thoughts. Hurrying into the dispensary, she met her father coming in, his face reflecting the strain of the long night.

"I was wondering how late you were going to be," she grumbled as she helped him off with his cloak.

"I thought I'd better take care of my calls this morning if we're to make it to the general's ball tonight."

Dr. Samuel Howard was little more than an inch taller than his daughter, with a head disproportionately large for his slight frame and fringed with black curls touched with grey at the temples. From him Elizabeth had inherited her vivid coloring, the large, expressive brown eyes that were her finest feature, and her delicate hands and feet.

And much of her sense of adventure as well, she suspected. Trained in medicine under the most prestigious surgeon in his native London, Samuel Howard had been resigned to an uneventful career. But when his strong-willed elder sister, Tess, who had emigrated to Massachusetts years earlier, had summoned him to Boston, he had found her offer to cover his expenses until he could establish a practice impossible to resist.

On settling in Boston, through Tess's influence he had acquired as one of his first patients the lawyer Jeremiah Stern, head of one of the oldest families in Massachusetts Bay Colony. Within a few short months Samuel had met and married the Sterns' demure, Paris-educated daughter, Anne, acquired an elegant town house, and established a thriving medical practice.

This peaceful life had been shattered by the escalating conflict between England and her colonies, turmoil in which Anne's eldest brother, Joshua Stern, had from the beginning taken an active part. Already a disappointment to his family for choosing the quiet life of a country innkeeper, an occupation he regarded as more honest than involvement in the British-controlled establishment, he had further disgraced them by taking up the rebel cause with passion and unexpected talent.

In this Elizabeth's father had opposed him with every fiber of his being, and their disagreement had opened a rift that had by now widened into an unbridgeable chasm. Elizabeth's mother kept her opinions private and chose to remain loyal to her husband. Neither she nor Samuel exhibited any suspicion that Samuel's sister, Tess, might also be deeply involved in the patriot cause—much less that she had drawn Elizabeth into their treasonous activities as well.

Now, before going to hang up her father's cloak, she dropped an affectionate peck on her father's cheek. Somehow, someday, she told herself, she would win him over to the patriots' point of view.

"Isaiah told me about the soldier they brought in last night."

"That cursed Oriole again! He's slipperier than the devil himself. My fondest wish is to see him hang."

Careful to keep her back to him, Elizabeth led the way into the surgery. "I'm sorry I slept through it. The soldier's injuries weren't too serious, I hope."

With a sigh Dr. Howard pulled up a chair and sat down. "A shattered leg, a couple of broken ribs, a punctured lung. He'll survive, but I doubt he'll walk without a cane. His career in the military is finished."

She threw him a searching look. "Were they at least able to get a close look at that awful spy?"

"I'm afraid not. All they could tell was that he was slight in build, possibly just a youth, and that he was riding either a black or dark bay horse. Not much to go on. But according to Lord Percy it's the first time anyone's actually seen him in the flesh."

Elizabeth came instantly alert. "Now I hope you didn't drag poor Lord Percy out of bed in the middle of the night. We ladies are going to be thoroughly provoked with you if he's too tired to dance at the ball."

"Don't lay that charge to my account," Dr. Howard protested. "He was waiting for the patrol's return when we got to the barracks."

Elizabeth carried a basket of cloth strips to the table. "When I was in town yesterday a ship from England had just docked, and I overheard talk that an important dispatch was rushed off to Province House."

Dr. Howard nodded. "Another letter from Dartmouth."

At mention of Lord Dartmouth, the British secretary of state for the colonies, Elizabeth pretended to concentrate on folding bandages.

"Percy said he has finally issued direct orders for Gage to seize the rebels' munitions without further delay and to arrest anyone who has committed acts of treason and rebellion. We're going to see some action at last, my dear."

Elizabeth stared at him, stunned. She had expected this, but the reality of it struck her like a blow in the pit of the stomach.

"Oh, Papa, if Gage tries that, it's going to mean war."

Dr. Howard snorted. "Percy says the army has but to make a show and these cowards will lie down meek as lambs. I must say I wholeheartedly agree with his assessment."

Elizabeth bit her lip to keep from blurting out the first words that came to her tongue. She had heard some of the patriot leaders express the very same sentiments about the courage of the Regulars, and she couldn't help wondering what would happen if both sides were wrong.

"What about men like Uncle Josh, and Will, and Levi?" she said after a moment, choosing her words carefully. "You know the strength of their convictions. I'm very much afraid they won't run away if Gage tries a raid."

Dr. Howard's face hardened. "No one forced them to make the choices they have, and they'll have to pay the consequences. Or rather, their unfortunate families will."

"You know I agree with you, Papa, but they feel the actions taken by the Ministry in the past ten years have placed an intolerable burden on the colonies, made it impossible to earn a living or to—"

"What has happened is a direct result of the rebels' breaking the laws—"

"I'm only repeating what they say as an example of how strongly they feel, not because I agree with them."

"The Scriptures tell us to submit ourselves for the Lord's sake to the government God has instituted, to the king and to his governors."

"I know." Elizabeth tried to force down the rebellious answer that sprang to her lips and failed as she too often did. "But the patriots say that the king has become a tyrant and therefore has forfeited the right to rule. They give the example of the kings God removed from the thrones of Israel and Judah because of their wickedness, and of how God destroyed Pharaoh for his refusal to heed Moses' warnings and free God's people."

The expression on her father's face told her she had gone too far— as usual. His face reddening, he said with a frown, "That's quite enough, daughter. I won't have this treasonous talk repeated in my own house."

Elizabeth ran to put her hands on his shoulders, her expression contrite. "Oh, Papa, don't be impatient with me for repeating the silly talk I hear on the streets. It's just that I don't want either our friends on General Gage's staff or anyone in our family to get hurt."

His face softened as she knew it would. Although he struggled to maintain his sense of outrage, it was a losing battle, as always, when it concerned this favorite daughter of his.

"Well, I can't blame you for having a tender heart. I pray none of us will have occasion to grieve over the stubbornness of a radical few."

Elizabeth forced a smile. Removing her apron and dropping it over the surgery table, she tucked her arm through his.

"If I know Mama, she'll be wondering where you are."

"Then we'd better go find her and lay her concerns at ease," he answered, his good humor restored.

ANNE HOWARD WAS THE SOURCE of Abby's fair coloring, but both her daughters reflected her delicately modeled features and slender, graceful form. As soon as she saw them approaching, she left Isaiah and Sarah's two teenage sons at their work in the garden and came to meet them, Abby skipping at her heels.

Putting his arm around her shoulders, Dr. Howard drew her to him, smiling down at her with the warmth in his eyes Elizabeth had often marked. When Abby tugged on his coat, he bent down to swing her up, squealing, into his arms.

Watching her parents, Elizabeth thought how even after twenty-two years of marriage each submitted in love to the other, as Paul had admonished the Ephesians. Even her spinster aunt, Tess, had admitted to Elizabeth more than once that she envied the closeness they cherished. And Elizabeth was determined that unless she found a relationship as genuinely loving and filled with mutual respect as theirs, she would remain a spinster no matter what earthly advantages a particular match might offer.

Especially would she refuse to marry anyone who did not share her allegiance to the patriot cause. And since her father had made it clear he would never consent to her marrying a rebel, she remained determined to never marry at all. Indeed, it was the safest course if she was to avoid a repetition of the misery she had been subjected to by one she had loved and trusted.

The memories of her unhappy betrothal were still too raw, and she hastily pushed them back into their carefully guarded prison. She had no desire to explore that well-trodden territory again.

"I trust the young man they brought in last night is much improved," Mrs. Howard was saying with concern.

Dr. Howard set Abby down. "He's resting comfortably, Dearest— no thanks to that villain, Oriole."

"Then I'll continue praying for him. But you look tired, Samuel. Abby, please go tell Sarah to serve lunch right away so your father will have time for a long nap before we have to leave for Province House this evening."

As Abby raced off toward the kitchen, Mrs. Howard turned to Elizabeth. "You were quite late abed this morning. Are you feeling all right, dear? You look pale."

"Yes. Yes, I'm fine," Elizabeth answered hastily. "I sat up reading until past midnight, that's all."

Her reply didn't erase her mother's worried frown. "You've been spending far too much time alone in your room. I hope you're not still brooding over David. He hasn't bothered you again, has he?"

Elizabeth swung away so her parents wouldn't see the spasm of pain that crossed her face. When Hutchins had openly joined the Sons of Liberty, her father had ended their betrothal and forbidden her to see him again.

In private, she had been forced to admit that if she continued their relationship, Hutchins' involvement with the radical patriot organization must compromise her own clandestine role. But the break had gone far deeper than that. For after the announcement of their engagement, Hutchins had become increasingly demanding, jealous, controlling, and manipulative, though in the presence of others he maintained the masterfully charming front that had won her heart.

In truth, she'd been relieved when her father broke their engagement, but that didn't assuage her grief at losing the sweet ideal of love she had cherished. While over time the raw ache in her heart had dulled, the memory still hurt.

She became aware that her father studied her, frowning. "What's this?" he snapped. "If Hutchins has had the effrontery to—"

"I haven't seen him for weeks, Papa, not since that last incident. And, Mama, please don't concern yourself. I don't think of David at all anymore."

In spite of the steadiness of her voice, misery twisted inside her breast. Why did her mother have to bring up that painful episode again? Elizabeth wanted nothing more than to put the memory of that involvement behind her forever.

If only Hutchins would stay out of her life.

Forcing a cheerfulness she did not feel, she led the way into the house. In a short time lunch was served, and while they ate Elizabeth made sure their conversation stayed on superficial matters.

As they rose to leave the table, she said carelessly, "Isaiah is taking my phaeton into Boston to have Mr. Longworthy look at the wheel that's been giving trouble. I thought I'd ride along and stop at the town house to make sure Mrs. Dalton has made suitable arrangements for Captain Carleton's arrival."

Mrs. Howard nodded her approval. "Both Mrs. Dalton and the new cook come with high recommendations, but I'll feel easier if you oversee them. Be sure to remind Mrs. Dalton she's to take care of any changes the captain may want."

Her father scowled. "I wish you wouldn't do business with Longworthy."

"I'm not responsible for his politics, Papa. He's the best carriage-maker in town, and Isaiah won't deal with anyone else. You know how stubborn he is."

Mollified, Dr. Howard allowed, "Well, Isaiah knows horses and carriages better than I do. Go ahead then, but just be sure you're back in time to leave with us for the ball. I'll have no more of your tardiness, young lady. There's no use in taking two carriages into town when you can ride with us," he blustered, as he often did when he had been circumvented.

"I'll try," Elizabeth promised with proper meekness, "but I want to stop by Felicity Whyte's to check on little Jimmy. I'm taking cinchona in case his fever hasn't broken. Oh, and I promised to bring Aunt Tess those gloves she wants to borrow for church tomorrow, so if I'm not back in time, you'd better go on without me."

Not waiting to hear his exasperated response, she escaped into the foyer. She took her time putting on her cloak and tilting her forest-green hat with its drooping, apricot-colored plume at a fetching angle atop her curls, delaying so she could kiss her parents good-bye on their way upstairs. When she was finally alone, she made sure that Abby had run outside to play and that no one was about before she slipped into the library.

She took the precaution of locking both the hall and the parlor doors, then went to sit at the escritoire. For a long moment, however, she remained motionless, staring down at her hands. At length she got up and began to pace up and down, her fingers pressed against her temples, Sarah's warning about breaking her parents' hearts echoing in her ears.

It was not the first time a nagging sense of guilt over the routine deceptions she practiced had forced itself into her consciousness with paralyzing intensity. Most of the time she could dismiss any unwelcome reflections through the assurance that her double role was vital to the defense of the colonists' right to govern themselves. But in that moment she could not entirely justify her actions in her own eyes. The thought of her father's devastation if he were to learn of her passionate sympathy with the patriots, and worse, the extent of her active involvement, rose up to accuse her.

From the moment she had undertaken the role of courier, smuggler, and spy for the patriots, she had lived with secret terror at the thought of what the consequences of her actions might be. At the same time she felt an equal exhilaration in the risk-taking that carried her forward without her being able to understand why.

Remembering the glib assurances she so often gave of God's protection, she had to admit that the words sprang to her lips even while she was running after her own desires. *Am I being presumptuous?* she questioned, the knot tightening in her stomach. *Do I really have faith in God—or is my faith in myself?*

Not introspective by nature, she found self-doubt and the attempt to analyze her motives uncomfortable and confusing, and at last banished her doubts one more time. She would think about it later. At the moment, the need for action was too pressing.

Returning to the escritoire, she sat down, found paper, and hurriedly outlined the contents of Dartmouth's latest letter to Gage. Finished, she folded the page and sealed it with wax. On the outside she wrote "Philanthrop," one of the pen names used by Dr. Warren on letters printed in the *Boston Gazette*. Under this, she added the inscription: *Urgent.*

She placed the letter into her reticule, then drew on her gloves and left the house by the front door. Her phaeton waited at the foot of the steps as she had directed. Attired in formal black livery, Isaiah stood beside the door, ready to hand her up.

Today the black leather folding top of the elegant carriage was raised over its gleaming, moss-green body to give protection against the cold wind and threat of rain. Every detail had been exquisitely executed, from the padded, velvet-covered seats to the narrow scarlet stripe that edged its body, the shafts, and the rim of each wheel. There was no hint in its graceful lines to suggest that it had been designed for a single purpose.

Only the most rigorous inspection would reveal the hidden compartments under the false floor, beneath the cushions of the seat, and behind the seat back. Designed by Isaiah following Elizabeth's directions and executed by the master hand of the patriot carriagemaker Robert Longworthy, during the past ten months the carriage had become an indispensable medium of supply for the arsenals of the local militias.

Stepping up into it, Elizabeth threw a furtive glance toward the second-story windows. Reassured, she pressed a hidden spring beneath the seat cushion that released a lock, allowing the top of the seat to be easily lifted. After she had transferred the letter from her reticule to the capacious interior of the box, adding it to the pouch already inside, she secured the seat and sat down on it, carefully arraying her petticoats around her.

At her sign, Isaiah shook the reins over the back of the gleaming dark bay gelding, and the phaeton rolled forward. They skimmed along the curving drive that wound through the tree-dotted lawn to the road, and within moments passed through the brick columns and wrought-iron gates at the estate's entrance.

Turning onto Orange Street, the carriage began the descent to the brooding fortifications that guarded the gates of Boston.

Chapter Three

ELIZABETH RETURNED THE SICK CHILD to his mother's arms. "You should see improvement within a few hours, Felicity, but be sure to continue the same dosage until the fever is gone."

Her face drawn with anxiety, the young woman settled her son in his small bed, then led the way into the adjoining room. "Everybody says not to have nothin' to do with ye 'cause ye're a Tory, Miss Howard, and 'cause yer father is in tight with Gage. But I got no money for a doctor, and Miz Harton said ye'd come. Now ye've been so kind and I've no way to pay ye."

Elizabeth bit her tongue to keep from blurting out her thoughts. Forcing a smile she said, "I don't expect payment. Whether you're Tory or Whig doesn't matter when someone's sick. I'm just glad I came today. The fever has gotten worse since I saw him yesterday morning, but he should be out of danger shortly."

Without seeming to, Elizabeth noted the young woman's swollen abdomen, her thin arms, and the discolored, puffy area on her cheekbone, then directed a discreet glance around the cramped room. It was spotless, though the furnishings were poor and worn, as was the clothing of the woman and her little boy. There was no fire in the fireplace nor wood to build one, and the thin ray of sunshine admitted by the single window did little to warm the rooms.

"When is your baby due?"

Felicity blushed and gave her a shy smile. "I'm not right sure—a month, I'm thinkin'."

Elizabeth had her sit down, then knelt beside her and gently pressed her fingers against several points around her abdomen, feeling for the size and position of the baby. "That seems about right. It hasn't turned or dropped yet. Do you have a midwife?"

"My mother helped me birth Jimmy. She's been real poorly, but I ain't got nobody else."

Elizabeth reached up to touch the swollen mark on her cheek. "How did that happen? Did your husband strike you?"

She said it so kindly the woman nodded in mute acknowledgment, tears welling into her eyes. "He didn't mean no harm, Miss Howard. It's just that he's been out o' work 'cause o' them redcoats . . ."

"And he's been drinking," Elizabeth concluded.

Felicity looked away, but not before Elizabeth saw the haunted look in her eyes that told her it was worse than she would admit. Remembering the brutish lout of a longshoreman she had seen leaving the house at her first visit, Elizabeth realized it would be useless to try to give Felicity any advice. Her husband would not take kindly to his wife's standing up to him, and Felicity had nowhere else to go, no means to support herself and two children.

Anger and frustration formed a tight lump in Elizabeth's throat as she stared at the young mother's bowed head. Anger at the British who had closed the port and thrown countless men out of work. Frustration at the grinding poverty that, over time, stole the last ray of hope from the human breast.

Of course, Elizabeth's more fortunate social status provided no protection from the type of degradation Felicity suffered. Once married, Elizabeth reflected, a woman was at the mercy of her husband in almost every way. For almost two years Elizabeth's relationship with Hutchins had spiraled ever deeper into verbal abuse, though thankfully it had never gone beyond that. Criticism had escalated into irrational accusations, followed by apologies and pleas for forgiveness. Confused and believing herself somehow at fault, too ashamed to confide her plight to her parents, she had felt trapped and without recourse. If her father had not intervened and she and Hutchins had married . . .

She shuddered at the thought. Getting to her feet, she took several coins from her reticule and pressed them into the young woman's hand, ignoring her protests. "This is for food and wood for the fire. Keep it from your husband, and don't tell anyone where it came from. If Jimmy isn't much better by tomorrow or if you need help for whatever reason, please send for me. And be sure to let me know as soon as your pains start. I know an excellent midwife, and I've helped to deliver several babies as well."

Felicity followed her to the door, her anxious expression replaced by the faint glimmer of hope. "I can't thank ye enough. God bless ye, Miss Howard. It's sure he sent ye to us."

Elizabeth gave her an impulsive hug. "If I don't hear from you tomorrow, I'll check in on you in a couple of days."

Church bells were just beginning to peal two o'clock when she made her way down the stairs of the dilapidated building. Her nose wrinkling, she held her petticoats out of the muck as she picked her way around the fetid puddles of household sewage flung from the overhanging upper stories of the decaying houses that shouldered each other on either side of the lane. Still preoccupied with Felicity's difficult circumstances, she followed the narrow, crooked alley to where it terminated at Dock Square.

Across from her stood Faneuil Hall, its ground-level market stalls relatively quiet today. As she stared at it, she could not help thinking of other occasions when surly crowds had gathered for the tumultuous town meetings ruled by Samuel Adams and Joseph Warren in the spacious hall that occupied the building's second floor. It had been at these meetings that the murmurs of resistance to royal authority had been skillfully fanned into active rebellion.

Atop the hall's graceful cupola, a gilded weathervane in the shape of a giant grasshopper turned its green glass eyes toward the sea. The brisk wind that blew out of the east cut through her fluttering cloak, bearing on it the tang of salt and smoke mingled with the redolence of hemp rigging and sun-warmed canvas, the more pungent odors of tar, decayed seaweed, and rotting piles. She drew in a deep breath of the scent, familiar from her earliest childhood. Surely it ebbed and receded on the tide of her blood, for it always brought with it an exhilarating sense of unbounded freedom.

Her expression pensive, she passed through the square and turned south onto Cornhill Street. There, another flash of gold brought her to a halt to stare up at the gilded figures of a lion and a unicorn that stood on opposite edges of the Towne House roof across the street.

Until recently, all legislative and judicial business of the colony had been conducted in that building. In its council chamber in 1761 brilliant, eccentric James Otis had presented forceful arguments against the writs of assistance that empowered customs officials to search for smuggled goods without showing cause. Thus Otis had fired the opening salvo in the colonies' battle against the increasingly oppressive powers of crown and Parliament. One of General Gage's first acts on arriving in Boston had been to suspend these legislative and judicial sessions in enforcement of Parliament's Coercive Laws, which the enraged colonists had promptly christened the Intolerable Acts.

Against her will, Elizabeth's eyes were drawn down King Street in the direction of the docks. A few doors down from where she stood, she could see the building that until last year had been occupied by the Customs House, the visible and hated symbol of British taxation. It was now also shuttered, since the citizens of Boston no longer needed its services.

Indelibly etched in her memory was the night little more than five years earlier when an enraged mob had taunted and tormented a small detachment of British soldiers posted near the building until, in fear of their lives, they had fired into the close-packed crowd. With a shudder she glanced down at the cobblestones beneath her feet, seeing again the horrifying image of the stones splattered crimson with the blood of those slain or wounded in the encounter, hearing the crowd's screams of agony, fear, and rage.

It had happened just weeks before her fifteenth birthday. Rioting crowds had prowled the streets with torches and clubs, crying, *"Town born, turn out!"* And ignoring her mother's terrified insistence that her children stay locked in their upstairs bedrooms with their windows tightly shuttered, she had managed to slip from the house to follow her father down to the docks. His anger at finding her among the jostling crowds that surrounded the victims of the shooting had made little impression amid the chaos of that appalling scene.

As clearly, she remembered the upheaval that had resulted and the fury directed toward her father and the other Tories in the town. The reaction had been so severe that Samuel Howard had felt it necessary to remove his family from their home in Boston to the relative security of Stony Hill on the mainland just outside Roxbury.

With an effort she shook off the disturbing memories and forced herself to continue down Cornhill to School Street, where she turned west in the direction of the Common and the Back Bay. As she walked, a lively din filled her ears. Overhead, gulls screeched, wheeling sharp-eyed in search of refuse flung from the decks of the ships anchored in the harbor. The clatter of wagons and an occasional fashionable carriage, the clop of hoofbeats, the hubbub of voices filled the streets all around her. Above the rest rang the shrill cry of fishermen hawking their wares.

The traffic that filled the maze of constricted, winding lanes was a trickle compared to the tide that had clogged it a year ago. Now, more often than not, the customers who frequented the taverns, coffee houses, and shops wore the hated red coats.

To Elizabeth, whose earliest memories included the clamor of the

shipyards, the loading and unloading of merchantmen at the overflowing docks, the bustle of ropewalks and sail lofts that had been the com-
munity's mainstay in happier days, the town seemed deserted by
comparison. And she wasn't alone in resenting the change.

Sullen, dispirited laborers lounged idle on every street corner. It did-
n't improve the general mood that squads of scarlet-coated soldiers mingled with the soberly clad inhabitants of the town. The soldiers'
contemptuous glances were met with bitter looks as they shoved their
way through the crowds in arrogant quick-step, refusing to turn aside
even for the old or the lame.

"Why, it's Miss Howard!"

Several other voices joined the first, all raised in excited recognition.
"Wait up, Miss Howard—over here!"

Elizabeth bit her lip hard to suppress an impatient exclamation as
footfalls hurried in her direction. The very last thing she wanted right
now was an encounter with the high-spirited officers who were already
crossing the street to intercept her.

By the time she turned to face them, however, her expression regis-
tered delight. "Lieutenant Sutherland, what a surprise!" she exclaimed,
extending her hand to the first officer who pressed to her side. "I was
certain Colonel Smith would insist on drilling all day in anticipation of a
march out into the country."

Laughing, one of his companions, Lieutenant Jesse Adair, put his
finger to his lips. "Hush, or you're going to sound the alarm!"

"By now there isn't a suckling babe in this cursed town who isn't in
possession of every last detail of our plans," growled Lieutenant John
Barker, his expression sour.

Lieutenants Henry De Berniere and William Sutherland exchanged
meaningful glances. "I swear, Miss Howard, it's impossible to keep a
secret around here for more than five minutes," De Berniere agreed.

Thanks in good part to the four of you, Elizabeth thought with amusement. She gave the officers a dizzying smile calculated to make each

believe himself the sole object of her favor. It plainly had the desired effect.

"Then why aren't you on duty protecting your secrets from these horrid rebel spies?" she teased.

Barker blurted, "Today's general orders relieved all the grenadiers and light infantry of duty until further notice."

Elizabeth didn't need any explanation to understand the significance of this information. The grenadiers were the army's largest, strongest soldiers; the light infantry, its fastest moving troops. If Gage planned a rapid, stealthy move, these were the logical troops to carry it out.

She didn't allow any hint of her conclusions to show in her expression as she laughed up at them. "Lucky you! The infantry must be positively mad with envy. And what have the grenadiers and light infantry done to deserve such good fortune?"

"We were just debating if it's good fortune or not," De Berniere said with a grimace. "According to the orders, we're to learn grenadiers' exercises and new evolutions, whatever that's supposed to mean."

Barker pursed his lips, his eyes narrowing. "My guess is it's a blind for some special duty Gage has in mind for us."

"A little adventure to Concord, perhaps?" Elizabeth guessed.

"Just between us, you may be right," Sutherland admitted with a grin. "Personally, I'm agreeable to an excursion, and the sooner, the better. We've been cooped up in this town far too long; and besides, it's high time we took these rebels down a peg or two."

"I can't think of anyone more qualified for the job," Elizabeth responded gaily, "but I do hope the general doesn't intend to send you off until after the ball tonight. I'm going to be heartbroken if I don't have the opportunity for at least one dance with each of you."

As they crowded around her, pressing their assurances that no force on earth could prevent them from attending the ball, she had to admit their attentions gave her a gratifying sense of power. At the same time, as attractive and amusing as each of them was, none of them tempted her to move beyond a casual flirtation.

Her indifference was due to more than that they were officers of the king whose authority she considered to be forfeit. She had placed a guard over her heart that she was determined would not be broken by any but the most extraordinary man, if such a one existed.

Before they would let her go, she was obliged to promise a dance to each of them. Relieved at her escape, she hurried toward the town house, where Isaiah was to pick her up as soon as his errand was finished.

Crossing Tramountain to head down Beacon Street, she threw an apprehensive glance toward the North End, where the tall steeple of Christ Church dominated the peninsula. There was good reason why she never openly accompanied Isaiah to venerable Richard Longworthy's carriage works. His establishment was located among the North End businesses and shops that included the foundry of his good friend, Paul Revere.

In fact, the carriagemaker served as the link between Oriole and the daring band of youths who stood ready to join in his escapades on the shortest notice. But because Longworthy was rightly suspected of involvement with the subversive circle of mechanics surrounding the well-known silversmith, Elizabeth took pains to avoid any contact with him except when she was in disguise.

After a short distance she rounded the corner of the almshouse, where Beacon angled westward to skirt the northern edge of the Common. Along the grassy meadow to her left stretched the Mall, a long, double file of trees where the eligible ladies of Boston had in happier days spent pleasant summer afternoons walking in company with their beaux. Now each morning and afternoon the air was most generally filled with the harsh shock of volleys, the rattle of drums, and the shrill pipe of fifes during drills and parades. Today, however, the wide field lay deserted.

Behind the houses ahead of her and to her right, the grassy peaks of

Tremont jutted skyward. The central and highest portion of the steep hill was named for the tall pole on its summit where hung an iron cage containing a barrel filled with tar that in times of danger was set afire as a warning beacon.

Elizabeth didn't slow her brisk pace until she reached the stately fence enclosing the lawn of John Hancock's imposing brick mansion. Her frown deepened as she stared at the sword cuts that scarred it, wounds inflicted over the past months by some of the British officers as a sign of their contempt for the patriot leader. Behind it, the house was shuttered, its owner miles away at Concord attending the last session of the Second Provincial Congress before traveling to Philadelphia.

At the far corner of Beacon Street, where it intersected and terminated at Charles Street, and beyond which a narrow strip of ragged salt marsh fell away to the sluggish water of the Back Bay, she came to her parents' town house. An elegant brick mansion that rivaled Hancock's for grace of design, it was set off from its neighbors by a wide expanse of emerald lawn and high hedges. The widely spaced, mature trees that shaded the property gave the appearance of a park. Following the brick path to the front door, Elizabeth took the key from her reticule and went in without knocking.

"Mrs. Dalton?"

There was no answer. Removing her hat and cloak, she dropped them with her reticule onto a chair in the parlor, then went down the hall, her footsteps muted by the thick runner. The sunny rooms were silent, but they had been cleaned and aired. A quick inspection reassured her that everything was in perfect order.

There was no one in either library or dining room. The kitchen at the rear of the house was also deserted, although several pots bubbled over the fire, filling the room with a delicious aroma.

The back door stood ajar. From it, she could see the plump, middle-aged cook her father had engaged standing at the property's rear hedge, deep in animated conversation with the neighbor's scullery maid.

At the side of the carriage house, the housekeeper, Mrs. Dalton, busied herself hanging out linens to air on a laundry line. Elizabeth smiled at sight of the slight, brown-haired woman whose sharp eyes and swift movements reminded her of a cheerful little wren.

Unknown to her, she and Elizabeth had more than one tie. Mrs. Dalton's brother-in-law captained the fishing boat by which, on occasion, Elizabeth slipped in and out of Boston in disguise on one of her clandestine forays.

Returning to the front of the house, she caught up the stack of neatly folded linens that lay on the hall table and carried them upstairs. When she had arranged them on the shelves of the linen press at the far end of the hallway, on impulse she went through the door on her right. Five years ago, this small bedroom at the rear of the house had been her own.

Inside, the door to the adjoining dressing room stood open, as did the door at the dressing room's far end. Through them she could see into the spacious bedroom at the head of the stairs that had belonged to her parents, which at Elizabeth's direction, had been prepared for Captain Carleton.

Happy memories flooded over her, drawing her through the dressing room into the front bedroom. Many times as a child she had run to climb into the safe haven of her parents' bed during a storm or on waking from a frightening dream.

Idly she smoothed the bed's counterpane and fluffed the pillows, then turned to survey her surroundings with satisfaction. Lost in thought, she wandered to the window. Drawing back the brocade curtains, for some moments she stared through the panes' wavy, grayish haze and across the still waters of the Back Bay toward the trees that marked the outline of Lechmere's Point on the mainland.

How safe and secure the world had seemed when her family lived in that house. But today that serene life felt unreachably remote. Happiness and security had been irrevocably torn from her family by the whirlwind of events that had forced them to flee this home for another.

And now this childhood refuge would belong, however temporarily, to an officer of an army of occupation.

In her preoccupation she paid no attention to the distant bang of a door somewhere below, assuming that either the cook or the housekeeper had come inside. But the sudden thump of boots across the floor in the downstairs passageway pulled her around in alarm.

A muffled burst of laughter was answered by a disturbingly masculine voice, husky and good humored. She threw an anxious glance at the door, but before she could move toward it, she heard the tap of boots and jingle of spurs as someone ran lightly up the stairs.

"Andrews!" the voice commanded. "Tell Stowe to bring my kit upstairs. First bedroom, Mrs. Dalton said. And find out who belongs to that cloak and hat in the parlor. I *am* intrigued."

Dismayed, she belatedly ran for the door, her slippers making no sound on the woven carpet. Grasping the handle, she jerked the door open and stepped across the threshold in the same motion—and collided headlong with the one who was in the process of entering.

She gasped, heard his muttered oath of astonishment.

"What the deuce—?"

She had a fleeting impression of a brilliant scarlet coat with the white facings of the Seventeenth Light Dragoons, the flash of a silver epaulet at one broad shoulder, the glitter of a sabre swinging from a wide, white shoulder belt. Then she looked up, cheeks burning, to find herself in the arms of a British officer.

Chapter Four

"WHY, WHAT HAVE WE HERE?" Amazed amusement tinged a British accent softened by the lingering trace of a lazy Virginia drawl.

Hastily Elizabeth took inventory from beneath a veil of lowered lashes. What that glance told her was far from reassuring: Her captor wasn't handsome so much as arresting in appearance, tanned from the outdoors, with sun-streaked blond hair and smoky blue-grey eyes.

In spite of their unexpected and most improper encounter, he didn't appear to be in the least taken aback. Nor did he make any move to release her, but held her appreciatively, laughing down at her as he took her in with a bold glance.

"How delightful. Do you come with this place too?"

"I most certainly do not, sir!"

"How disappointing." His tone reflected genuine regret.

She bit back a hot reply. This wasn't at all the decorous meeting she had envisioned. Instead, she found herself in a distinctly awkward, not to mention compromising, position.

His hands lingered with entirely too much familiarity at her waist, and the arms that held her captive were disconcertingly hard beneath the woolen fabric of his uniform coat. Unless he chose to release her, she realized with dismay, she would have considerable difficulty in breaking free.

Furious, she lifted her chin to meet his amused gaze with a coldly reproving one, determined to gain the upper hand. "If you'll be so kind as to let me go, Captain Carleton, I'll show you where to put your things." She kept her tone frigid.

"Ah, then you were expecting me."

"Not until . . . until this evening or . . . tomorrow—if you please, sir!"

Again she attempted to extricate herself from his arms, but it was at once apparent that if she intended to regain her freedom, she was going to have to resort to an undignified struggle.

"We got in late last night," he explained with a smile, adding pleasantly, "Major Pitcairn was kind enough to put us up."

"The major forewarned me of your arrival."

"Did he? And what else did he tell you, *enfant?* Only agreeable things, I hope."

She was uncomfortably aware that they stood just inside the bedroom that was to be his, as compromising a situation as one could wish for. It was obvious he took wicked enjoyment in her plight—and in the sensation of her nestled against him.

As though he read her thoughts, his glance lingered for a deliberate instant on her lips. She had played that same game more than once, however, and rage took over.

"Whether it was agreeable or not, his description seems to have been accurate. Release me at once, captain, or I shall scream."

"Scream away, then," he answered, seeming to anticipate the prospect with glee. "After all, you were in my bedroom, and you did throw yourself so accommodatingly into my arms."

"*Oh!*"

It took heroic effort to master the impulse to attack him with her fingernails. "Faith, but you certainly flatter yourself if you can think for one tiny instant I would ever throw myself at *you*, sir."

His response was a hearty and unapologetic laugh. For an instant, his grip slackened. Planting both hands against his chest, she gave a hard push and at the same instant stepped away from him. Unbalanced, he was forced to let her go.

Far from seeming disconcerted at her escape, he grinned and made a deep bow. "You have me at a disadvantage, fair vision. Do you have a name?"

She glared at him. "I am Elizabeth Howard, sir."

"Oh, that explains why you were lurking in my bedroom." Before she could gasp out a scathing reply, he added amiably, "I presume I do have the honor of addressing the daughter of my benefactor, Dr. Samuel Howard."

"Our citizens are obliged to provide quarters for His Majesty's soldiers whether they consider it an honor or not."

"I am familiar with the quartering laws," he conceded, his tone dry.

Having put him in his place, she was inclined to be more gracious, though as a precaution she put a safe distance between them. "And of course my parents are pleased to comply with them."

"Of course. And you?"

She frowned, wondering if he was always so annoyingly direct. "What pleases my parents pleases me."

He acknowledged the reproof with the slight lift of an eyebrow, a tug of laughter at the corners of his mouth that made it difficult for her to maintain a pose of outraged dignity. Throwing a swift glance at his surroundings, he said, "I didn't expect to be billeted in such gracious style, nor to find such hospitality in Boston. Your parents are too kind. I hope I'll have the opportunity to thank them personally."

"I'm sure they'll be delighted to have you wait upon them tonight at His Excellency's ball."

"Ah, yes, we've been informed we're to attend. You will be there, I devoutly hope."

When she inclined her head, he swept her with an approving glance. "It seems my stay in your fair town is going to prove more pleasant than

I anticipated."

Not waiting for her reply, he took two swift strides into the hall and bent over the banister to call downstairs in high good humor. "Charles! I swear we've lighted upon one of the clouds of heaven! Come see what a treasure I've chanced upon." He directed a lazy smile at Elizabeth as she stepped to the banister beside him. "She's no less than a very angel—though a somewhat ill-tempered one, I must say."

The officer who strolled through the open door of the library to peer up at them, a half-filled glass of brandy in his hand, was perhaps twenty-five years of age. Not as tall as his superior, he was more slenderly built, with a fresh, ruddy complexion and light brown hair.

"I might have known, Jon. We've hardly got our land legs back, and you've unerringly found your way to the sweetest rose this side of the Atlantic."

"Watch your tongue. She has a bad enough opinion of me already without your adding to it." Assuming a schoolmaster's severity of tone and look, he indicated the lieutenant's glass. "And put that down, you dissipated cub—it's a little early to be drinking. Where are your manners? Come here at once and be properly introduced to Miss Elizabeth Howard."

With no more urging, Andrews set down his drink and came bounding up the stairs to sweep Elizabeth an elaborate bow. As Carleton introduced Lieutenant Charles Andrews, the officer beamed down at her with unconcealed approval.

"I was right. This one really is as perfect as a rose."

"Beware her thorns," Carleton warned sourly. "I've already had occasion to feel their prick."

"Begging your pardon, Jon, but she'll need more than thorns to keep you in line. If you ever need a bodyguard, Miss Howard, I'd be delighted to volunteer."

Elizabeth gave a merry laugh. "I appreciate the offer, Lieutenant Andrews, but Major Pitcairn put me on guard. Forewarned, forearmed."

Carleton sighed. "The price of fame. I see my dubious reputation has preceded me."

"You'd better be prepared to suffer the consequences if you find it so amusing to be thought a rake."

His expression conveyed pained innocence. "My dear Miss Howard, I object. I can't believe my reputation has suffered that badly in transit. Why, I'm the most unassuming and virtuous man I know."

Andrews guffawed. Throwing him a murderous glance, Carleton possessed himself of Elizabeth's hand, tucking it in the crook of his arm with a proprietary air.

"Now, *enfant,* you did volunteer to show us our accommodations, and I can't conceive a more charming guide."

Smiling in spite of herself, Elizabeth showed them from room to room, indicating which they were to occupy, then led the way downstairs. As they reached the bottom step, the front door burst open and over the threshold staggered two private soldiers in the uniform of the Light Dragoons, each weighed down by an assortment of military gear.

She had to suppress a laugh at the contrast the two made. The younger was perhaps in his late twenties, about Elizabeth's height and slender, his bearing militarily erect. The older one was middle-aged, with a thick neck, brawny arms, and bandy legs that gave him the appearance of a bulldog. Elizabeth's first impression was that he was a pirate or some other desperate character. The livid scar that ran from his left eye to his jaw puckered the left side of his face into a perpetual, evil wink. In spite of this handicap, however, his expression managed to convey a reassuring amiability.

Carleton waved a lazy hand in the soldiers' direction, indicating first the elder. "Miss Howard, my servant, Mr. Stowe, and his accomplice in crime, Lieutenant Andrews's servant, Mr. Briggs."

As they dropped their burdens to touch their hands to their Roman-style helmets, Elizabeth noted that the two officer's matching brass helmets lay on the hall table. The headgear was striking, with a brilliant scarlet horsehair crest that flowed to the shoulders in back. But it was the white skull and crossbones on the black-painted frontal plate and the motto "Or Glory" that attracted her greatest interest.

She returned her attention to Stowe in amused wonder at Carleton's choice of a servant. "Foin place you got 'ere, Miss 'Oward," he was saying happily. "Not a'tall wot we was a'feared we'd foind."

"Why, thank you, Stowe. And what did you expect to find?"

"Considerin' wot we 'eard about Boston, we was suspectin' as 'ow we'd likely be gettin' a warm reception from some o' these 'ere rebels in war paint."

"Oh, you needn't worry. We reserve the war paint strictly for tea parties."

She said it with such gravity that Carleton had to choke down a laugh, which he gracefully transformed into a diplomatic cough. His eyes alive with mirth, Andrews directed the two men upstairs with their burdens before following Elizabeth and Carleton into the drawing room.

The lieutenant reclaimed his glass from the hall table, then crossed to the cabinet at the side of the fireplace where a tray held glasses and a decanter of brandy. Tossing down the remnant in his glass, he refilled it and added a generous measure to one of the others, which he offered to Carleton.

The older officer shook his head, and Elizabeth noted the sharp look that passed between them. Carleton frowned, his mouth tightening, but Andrews studiously pretended not to see it.

With an impatient movement, Carleton pulled his shoulder belt off over his head and dropped it with the sabre onto one of the wing chairs before wandering to the window to gaze out across the bay. Elizabeth settled herself on the sofa. Almost against her will she found herself studying him with a mixture of curiosity and puzzlement.

Although his features gave the impression of a singular, though subtle, irregularity, his nose was fine and straight, his brow and jaw firmly modeled. He wore his hair neither clubbed, queued, nor powdered, but simply brushed neatly back and tied with a narrow black ribbon.

Knee-length black riding boots encased his long legs below supple, buff-colored buckskin breeches that hugged the muscular thighs of a born horseman. His scarlet coat gave stark contrast to white facings with silver buttons and the closely fitted white waistcoat that emphasized the leanness of his waist.

There was a lazy elegance about him that she found disturbingly attractive. Yet beneath the surface she sensed a tightly curbed tension that the lithe, almost catlike grace of his movements couldn't quite conceal. Did he also struggle with the same restlessness against which she so often fought a losing battle?

As though sensing she watched him, he turned without warning to meet her gaze. She made a point of directing her attention to Andrews with a smile that was meant to take his breath away and clearly accomplished its purpose.

Without difficulty she elicited the information that he and Carleton had arrived in Virginia the last week of December after a stormy ocean crossing. Until Gage's summons reached them, they had planned to sail for England by the end of the month.

"It appears you'll be stranded here a while longer," Elizabeth sympathized. "I hope you aren't finding your stay unpleasant."

Andrews drained his glass and set it back on the tray. "Quite the contrary. The more I see of this country, the less I miss England. If I owned an estate like Jon's Thornlea, it'd take an army to pry me away from it."

Elizabeth considered the younger officer with renewed interest, weighing the possibilities his unguarded words suggested. Deciding to explore the same possibilities in regard to his superior, she glanced over at Carleton.

"Thornlea must be quite an extraordinary place if Lieutenant Andrews covets it so dearly he'd fight an army for it," she teased.

Carleton had returned to a moody contemplation of the Back Bay, and Andrews answered for him. "Oh, it's just a modest plot of land—twenty thousand acres or so running up into the Blue Ridge. Most of it is heavily forested, but enough is cleared to pasture about three hundred head of cattle and a hundred horses. I swear, the main house rivals the great manors of England, and the countryside around it is second to none for beauty."

Amused by the lieutenant's enthusiasm, Elizabeth asked, "Do you own many such small parcels of land, captain?"

"I'm hardly made of money. As it is, I'm probably going to be forced to sell the place before it bankrupts me."

"Rumor would have it you're far from bankruptcy."

He waved her words away. "I assure you, a man of my limited means—"

"Ye gods, Jon!" Andrews objected. "You'll have this charming creature believing you're destitute as a church mouse, when in addition to Thornlea you own a fleet of merchantmen and a thriving import business, not to mention—"

"My expenses are prohibitive and my profits minimal."

Andrews shook his head. "If that's true, why do you live so extravagantly? I've never known you to buy anything less than the very best, to refuse a loan to anyone in need, or to accept repayment of it. You pour favors on your friends as though money were water—"

"My dear fellow, you know very well I live an excessively frugal life."

Folding his arms across his chest, Andrews regarded him with amused affection. "The trouble with you is that your Scots parsimony is in direct conflict with your French liberality. In the war between the two, the Scot reigns supreme in matters of business, while the Provençal invariably wins out in matters of the heart."

Carleton made an exasperated gesture, muttering under his breath something about "madman." Andrews laughed. The picture of disgruntlement, Carleton turned his back to them and returned his brooding gaze to the bay.

It was obvious that the turn of the conversation didn't please him. More than one predatory female had shown a thinly veiled interest in his financial affairs, Elizabeth guessed.

Smiling at the realization that he must suspect her of similar concern, she said in perfectly accented French, "I know your father was Scottish, so I assume your mother must have been French. My mother was born in Boston, but she spent much of her childhood in Paris."

Pleased, he bowed in acknowledgment, good humor restored. In equally flawless French he explained that his mother had been a native of Nice and that, in fact, the Carletons were originally Normans who had arrived in England with William the Conqueror. They had acquired extensive landholdings in Scotland, intermarrying with the inhabitants until the blood that flowed in their veins was more Scot than Norman.

"I've heard Scotland is as wild as it is beautiful. I'd love to see it."

"Perhaps someday I'll have the good fortune to show it to you, *enfant.*"

"I'm hardly an infant, captain," she pointed out with annoyance, returning to English. "Or are you so old?"

"I'm a decrepit thirty-one. How old are you? Seventeen? Eighteen?"

"Twenty."

"Why, you're positively ancient. Why aren't you married with three children by now?"

"I haven't met the man who could tempt me to give up my freedom. To tell the truth, I can't say it'll break my heart if I never do."

He studied her for a moment, eyebrow raised, a smile tugging at his lips. "According to Major Pitcairn and Lord Percy you've cultivated quite a reputation for breaking hearts."

"So you did know who I was all along, didn't you?" When he grinned in confirmation, she demanded, "And what did they say about me, pray tell?"

"That you've conquered the heart of every officer in Boston, and that you've entertained more proposals of marriage than the rest of the feminine population combined, all of which you've callously spurned."

Stung, she pointed out, "You're not married either, though you're centuries older than I am. What's your excuse? Is your reputation as a lady-killer so satisfying to your masculine pride that you can't bear to see it deflated?"

Andrews howled in delight. "I'd say you've met your match, Jon."

Far from appearing insulted, Carleton gave a rueful laugh. "Believe me, I'm doing the feminine gender a favor by remaining a bachelor. I've become so set in my ways I doubt there's a woman in the world who could stand to live with me for a day."

"There are certainly enough who are willing to hazard the attempt," Andrews interjected.

Carleton paid him little attention. His gaze was fixed on Elizabeth, and she couldn't help thinking how warm a blue his eyes were and how expressive, though she couldn't read the emotion in them. He was no longer laughing, and suddenly she found it impossible to meet his piercing gaze.

"I suspect both of us are entirely unsuited to the sober estate of marriage."

He acknowledged her comment with the merest flicker of a smile, then straightened and came to reach out his hand for hers. "Will you show us the grounds? It would be a shame to stay indoors today. The wind is as soft as a lover's sigh."

Smiling at the description, she gave him her hand and rose. "Faith, it seemed quite cold to me. But you shall have your tour, and then I must be going."

He helped her on with her cloak, and after she had put on her hat and collected the rest of her things, she led the way into the garden. As they started down the path toward the stable, Andrews stretched and yawned.

"It's a relief to get a breath of fresh air after spending the morning cooped up with Percy, being brought up to date on your local politics."

"I vow, Boston is obsessed with rumors these days," Elizabeth ventured. "Everyone seems to think General Gage will act within the next week. It's common knowledge he's planning to secure the militia stores at either Concord or Worcester."

"From what we've been told so far—"

"Let's hope a confrontation can be avoided," Carleton cut the lieutenant off. "The situation is tense enough without adding provocation to it."

Andrews flushed at the implied rebuke. After securing Elizabeth's promise of a dance at the ball that night, he bowed himself off and returned inside.

Carleton accompanied her around the side of the house. They walked slowly toward the end of the carriageway, where Isaiah was by now waiting with the phaeton. Throwing Carleton a sidelong glance, she decided to probe a different area to see what information might surface.

"I understand you attended Harvard. I have a cousin who graduated a year behind you. His name is William Stern."

He swung to face her. "Will is your cousin? Tell me how he's doing! He was a good friend, and I've thought of him often. I suppose he's married and a family man by now. Did he become a lawyer as he meant to?"

Surprised and pleased by the rapid fire of questions, she answered in some detail.

"I'm not surprised to hear he's involved with the Sons of Liberty," he said when she finished. "Will was passionate about his beliefs even then. He was one of the most vocal in our endless debates on the authority of Parliament over the colonies."

"And what position did you take?"

Carleton chuckled. "I've always tended to play advocate for the devil."

She was silent for a moment, then on impulse said, "We were very close to Will's family until the famous 'tea party' a couple of years ago. Uncle Joshua, Will, and Levi made no secret of the fact that they took part in the raid, and that was the final straw for my father. He forbade us to have anything to do with them. I understand how he feels, but I still miss them terribly."

The words were no sooner off her tongue than she regretted them, but Carleton's reaction surprised her. Taking her hand, he squeezed it sympathetically.

"So many families are being torn apart. Unfortunately, I'm afraid it's bound to become considerably worse before this matter is finally resolved."

There was so much concern in his voice that she looked away, pain stabbing through the defenses she had built up with such care.

"I can imagine how painful it must be for you," he murmured, "and I, for one, wouldn't blame you in the least if you felt more than a little sympathy with their cause."

It was a subtle question, and she froze, a warning sounding loud in her mind.

During the past hour a turmoil she had never experienced before had taken possession of her heart, making it impossible for her to determine whether she liked Carleton or despised him. But it suddenly occurred to her he might be testing her even as she was testing him.

She tried to remember everything Will had said about him, but it was impossible to think clearly with him standing so close beside her, his strong fingers exerting gentle pressure on hers, his eyes warm with concern. Forcing her emotions back under control, she gave him a tremulous smile.

"You have more reason to be torn in your loyalties than I. In spite of your ties to England, you were reared here, you have close friends, not to mention valuable property and business interests, that are all affected by Parliament's policies toward the colonies. I would think you'd share many of the same concerns as the patriots."

For a moment he studied her with a faint smile that told her nothing. When he spoke, his tone was matter-of-fact.

"Before much longer all of us are going to have to decide on which side our loyalties truly lie. I've made my decision. Have you?"

His eyes were guarded, and she could read nothing in his expression. She had to remind herself that his uniform gave inarguable testimony as to where his allegiance lay.

"Of course, sir. I will always love my uncle and my cousins, but I grieve that their beliefs are so misguided."

Carleton gave her hand a quick squeeze then released it. "I wish there were some way I could see Will again—though I don't suppose it would make any difference."

"If things continue the way they are, I'm afraid you're likely to meet on opposite sides in battle."

They had reached her carriage. Stopping beside it, Carleton rested his hand on the seat and turned to face her.

"If you haven't promised away all your dances, enchanting child, perhaps I might persuade you to save the last for me."

"Not if you insist on being so patronizing."

Elizabeth's heart had begun to pound again, but for a different reason. Concealed inside the seat box, beneath the cushion on which Carleton leaned, now lay mute evidence sufficient to convict her a hundred times over of smuggling. And he had only to move his fingers a quarter of an inch to touch the hidden spring.

Breathless with apprehension and excitement, the color deepening in her cheeks, she met his amused gaze with a challenging one. The laughter faded from his eyes, and again a look came into them she could not decipher. Before either of them could speak, however, they heard the swift patter of hoofbeats moving at a gallop up the street.

They both turned as a sleek, black stallion swept around the phaeton and slid to a halt, scattering the stones of the carriageway. Restrained with difficulty by his rider, the horse pranced nervously, tossing his head up and down as he fought the reins, eyes rolling, ears laid back. The gelding shied in the phaeton's traces, and only Isaiah's firm hand on the reins kept the animal from bolting.

The rider was slender and darkly handsome, clad in coat and breeches cut in the latest style, the severe black of his garb unrelieved except by the ruffles of delicate white lace that foamed at neck and wrist. At the moment his face was pale and strained, and he took in the two of them with a burning glance that caused Elizabeth to draw involuntarily away from Carleton.

"David!"

"The latest of your many conquests, I presume." Sneering, he indicated Carleton.

Carleton surveyed him calmly before turning back to Elizabeth. "Are all your acquaintances as charming as this one?"

"Captain Carleton, this is Mr. David Hutchins," Elizabeth faltered. "David . . . Captain Jonathan Carleton of the Seventeenth Light Dragoons."

Hutchins gave Carleton the merest flicker of a hard, contemptuous glance. "Oh yes, I heard your father was intending to billet a couple of these strutting bloody backs. That certainly makes it convenient for your ambitions, doesn't it?"

His movements deliberate, Carleton straightened to his full height. To her consternation, Elizabeth saw that his eyes had gone as wintry as an icy December sea.

On the driver's seat of the phaeton, Isaiah had also tensed. The powerful muscles of his back hardened to a menacing tautness as he fixed a smoldering gaze on Hutchins.

Realizing she would have to act before the situation got completely out of control, Elizabeth drew herself up with quiet dignity. "I hardly think it necessary for us to air our private disagreements in public, David."

Hutchins hesitated for a moment, then dismounted and stepped to

her side, pointedly ignoring Carleton as though to convey that the officer's greater height and strength did not intimidate him. "Please forgive
me. I must talk to you alone. If you're leaving, may I ride a little way
with you?"

Anxious to end the confrontation as quickly as possible, Elizabeth
stiffly inclined her head. While Hutchins went to tie his mount's reins to
the back of the phaeton, she extended her hand to Carleton with a
forced smile.

"Until tonight, captain."

He bent to kiss her hand. "I'm looking forward to it."

Before he could move to help her into the phaeton, Hutchins shouldered his way between them and handed her up, climbing in after her.
He signaled to Isaiah, who clucked to the gelding and guided the
phaeton back down the carriageway, his body stiff with mute protest.

Elizabeth caught one last glimpse of Carleton staring thoughtfully
after them, then they turned onto the street and he was quickly lost to
view.

Chapter Five

"WHAT COULD POSSIBLY HAVE BEEN THE PURPOSE of that little display?" Her cheeks burning, Elizabeth clenched her hands in her lap.

"If you think I'll just stand by forever as though I cared nothing while you carry on flirtations with those detestable—"

"It isn't any of your business what I do."

Hutchins gritted his teeth, clearly checking a bitter outburst. With an effort at calmness, he countered, "It was once, or have you so quickly forgotten?"

"Our relationship is over. Can't you understand that?"

"Please, Elizabeth, lower your voice." He threw a warning glance at Isaiah's rigid back.

"Faith! It was you who asked for this interview, not I. I've no wish to discuss the matter further, as I've told you countless times. We have nothing to say to one another now or ever."

He stared at her, his eyes blank. "I can't believe you've changed so much after all we've meant to each other—I won't believe it!"

"You're the one who has changed, David. You're not the man I fell in love with. That man was tender and kind and admirable. What happened to him? You've become someone I don't know, someone I don't even like."

"Either you've been deceived by your father or you're nothing but a heartless trollop. I've never stopped loving you, even though you don't deserve my love!"

She fought down a sob. As so often before, they were once again locked in the same circular argument, with no apparent way out.

Keeping her voice level and cold, she said, "Leave me alone. If you try to interfere again—"

"I *have* left you alone for months in the hope you'd finally come to your senses."

"I came to my senses when I broke off our relationship."

Despite her anger, the sight of his stricken face cut through her heart like cold steel. Even after all those months he still held an inexplicable power over her. She had to turn her face away to keep him from seeing her instant remorse, but there was no disguising the tremor in her voice.

"Even if I felt differently, Papa would never allow us to see each other, much less marry. It's useless to talk about it."

For a tense moment he stared at her without speaking. "That's the real reason, isn't it?" he said at length. "Your father, not this pretense you've assumed. I know you too well to believe you're quite the ardent Tory you'd have everyone think."

"You don't know me at all! You never have. Stay away from me, David, or I'll take whatever steps become necessary to keep you from bothering me again."

The color left his face. They were screened from view by the phaeton's raised top, and before she could stop him, he caught her in his arms and strained her to his breast.

"I can't leave you alone—I won't!" he murmured hoarsely, his lips moving against the tendrils of hair that curled against her temple. "One way or the other, I shall have you!"

Shocked, she fought to break free as Hutchins bent over her, his face taut, his gaze burning. She caught her breath sharply at the pain of his grip, a choking wave of terror draining the strength out of her.

"I shall have you, Elizabeth," he repeated, his voice husky with desire, "or by God, no one will!"

He kissed her, his mouth brutally demanding against hers, and for an instant she felt as though she were drowning in the aching, tangled emotions of the past months. Then, uttering a muffled cry, she wrenched out of his arms, pressed one icy, trembling hand to her flaming cheek.

"Isaiah, stop the carriage!"

Isaiah pulled the gelding to an abrupt halt. Although he was careful to keep his back to them, his rigid posture made it clear to Elizabeth that he was struggling as hard to control his emotions as she was.

"Get out this instant!" Each word was spoken with icy precision. She indicated the knots of soldiers lounging at ease on the Common less than a hundred yards away. "And don't think about trying that again. If I call for help, every one of those soldiers will come to my aid."

Hutchins' face contorted with desire and fury. He reached out to touch her, but she shrank away, her jaw set with determination. He jerked his hand back.

White with anger, he stepped out of the carriage, tore his stallion's reins free, and mounted. He rode forward to stare down at Elizabeth, eyes narrowed.

"It's all a game to you, isn't it?" he said in a low, choked voice. "You break a man's heart as carelessly as a child crushes a toy it's grown tired of. But I won't be cast aside like all your other lovers. I promise you, I'll make you pay for playing me for a fool."

Keeping her eyes straight ahead, her back defiantly erect, she motioned to Isaiah. With a jerk the phaeton rolled forward.

As soon as they were out of Hutchins' sight, Isaiah drew the carriage to a stop at the side of the street and turned to give her a hard, probing glance. "You all right?"

She nodded. Seeing that she was shaking, Isaiah threw a grim look back in the direction from which they had come.

"If he touch you again, I kill him with these bare hands."

The deadly evenness of his tone terrified her. Swiftly she placed a restraining hand on the bulging muscles of his shoulder.

"And you'll be hanged for it. No, I depend on you far too much to lose you over such a trifle. Don't worry about me. If I ever need your protection, I'll call for you. Otherwise, do nothing."

His expression did not change, and he made no reply. Turning around, he gathered the reins in his massive fist and clucked to the gelding.

Huddled miserably in a corner of the phaeton, Elizabeth clenched and unclenched her hands to stop them from trembling. Drawing in a shaking breath, she angrily brushed away the tears that trickled down her cheeks.

"WE'RE IN A BIT OF A HURRY, Sergeant Miles. I'm expected at home and we're already late."

The soldier replaced his battered cocked hat atop his greasy, powdered hair and grinned up at her in apology. Standing beside the phaeton, he rested one weather-roughened hand on the wheel.

Since smuggling had grown to epic proportions, in considerable part due to Elizabeth's exertions, everyone was now forced to stop and submit to a search before leaving the town. Ahead of her carriage, reaching to the gates that spanned the narrowest part of the Neck, stretched a line of wagons and other conveyances waiting for their turn to be searched.

She allowed a frown to cloud her brow. "If it weren't for His Excellency's ball tonight, you know I wouldn't object to the delay in the least."

"I'm right sorry, Miss Howard, but I got my orders."

"But, Sergeant, you know very well I have *laissez passer* signed by General Gage himself. I've never been stopped before."

The sergeant was almost abject in his deference. " 'Course, we all know that, but orders come through for us to search every rider, carriage, and wagon. Rumor is there's a load of munitions bein' smuggled out today."

Shocked at the evidence that Gage's spy had been at work again, Elizabeth kept any hint of dismay from showing in her expression. Mentally she reviewed the names of everyone who knew she intended to smuggle out the last of the secreted munitions that day.

The list was a short one, every person on it unquestionably loyal to the Sons of Liberty. But, of course, there was always the possibility one of them had mentioned her plan in an unguarded moment to someone outside the circle believed to be trustworthy.

At the head of the line, the soldiers swarming over a farm wagon jumped down and raised the bars that blocked its way, motioning the driver through the gates. The carriages ahead of the phaeton moved forward.

While she was weighing the alternatives, she noticed a familiar figure striding toward her. Relieved, she smiled and waved to Captain Browne, holding out her hand in appeal as the officer hurried to her side.

The distress in her voice was real as she explained the situation. Obviously flattered by the plea he read in her eyes, he took the hand she offered and squeezed it.

"I do apologize for the inconvenience. It's an affront to you and your parents, to be sure."

Sighing, she dropped her eyes. "I hate to be late for the ball tonight, especially as I was so looking forward to dancing with you, captain. But you'll doubtless have a dozen ladies on either arm long before I arrive."

The captain swallowed hard. "Now, Miss Howard, you don't have to worry about that. You know I'd never turn down the chance to dance with you."

She knew he wouldn't, but time was evaporating and with it every hope of escape. Judging from the way he gazed at her, he was so preoccupied with a fantasy of the delights the evening might hold in store that he was oblivious to the ensign, who had already waved another carriage on. Two vehicles stood between hers and discovery.

Elizabeth's glance flew to Isaiah. To her horror, she saw that one powerful hand held the reins taut while the other clenched the whip as he measured the distance between the ensign and the gate, weighing the strength of the bars and the determination of the grenadiers in their tall bearskin hats who blocked their path.

Elizabeth pouted. "How do you expect me to believe you, Captain Browne? Why, I've seen how Miss Harrison smiles at you, and you've no more resistance to her charms than a babe to candy. Don't bother to deny it."

Her eyes fixed on him in appeal, she gave her shoulders an elaborate shrug that caused the plume on her hat to bob. Her hands closed over her reticule so tightly that its carved ivory clasp bit through her gloves into her palms.

The officer hesitated. Elizabeth's gaze flicked to the road ahead as the next carriage rolled through the gates, and the ensign impatiently motioned the one directly ahead of hers forward. Returning her attention to Captain Browne, she gave him a dazzling smile.

"Faith! Perhaps I won't bother going tonight after all."

Browne's answering smile assured her he was completely smitten. He squared his shoulders.

"Well, I can't allow that. Surely the general didn't mean to detain anyone from your family." Turning, he motioned the ensign to stand back. "You there! Open the gates! This carriage has clearance."

Nothing beyond the shaky intake of her breath betrayed a relief so intense she almost collapsed against the cushioned seat. She held out her hand, and he bowed over it.

"Thank you, captain. I'll save a dance for you this evening."

The phaeton rolled through the gates and out between the walls of the fortification that guarded them, the bay gelding trotting with plumed tail along the sandy road that crossed the Neck toward Roxbury heights. Within a short distance, they came abreast of the old gallows that stood at the side of the road.

Staring at it, Elizabeth shuddered. Isaiah pulled a handkerchief from his pocket and mopped the sweat from his brow.

"That hangman's noose come a little too close for me that time."

Elizabeth laughed, suddenly exuberant. "But we won the game, Isaiah! And in the end that's all that matters!"

THE RAMBLING CLAPBOARD MANSION belonging to Teresa Howard stood well back from the road that wound out of Roxbury and on to Cambridge, where it branched right toward Charlestown peninsula and left toward Lexington and Concord. Built late in the previous century on the bank of Stony Brook, which meandered down the steep bluff toward Boston's Back Bay, the house was screened from Pierpoint Mill on the opposite bank by dense, overgrown box hedges and a stand of towering pines and oaks.

Beyond the hedged garden behind the house stood a tidy brick carriage house and a stable, both built by the present owner. Farther back, down a rutted lane, a huge, ancient barn sagged at the edge of the bluff where the land dropped to Brindley's Meadow and the salt marshes below. From these heights the trees and rooftops of Stony Hill were just visible, and beyond, the hilly peninsula of Boston.

Without stopping at the house, Isaiah guided the gelding past the stone wall that marked the boundary of the gardens and down the rutted lane. The path curved around a wild, neglected growth of stunted fruit trees, brambles, and tangled blackberry vines that pressed right up to the barn's unpainted, mossy boards, effectively concealing it from view of the house and the road.

The moment they pulled up at the barn's yawning door, Elizabeth gathered her petticoats in one hand and jumped to the ground. As she did so, a lanky figure lounged out of the shadows and came to meet them.

"Levi! Gracious, but you gave me a start. What on earth are you doing here?"

Her cousin ran his tanned fingers through his pale hair. "Pa wanted me to make sure you came through all right."

"Almost didn't this time." Isaiah wound the reins around the handle of the brake. "Try it again, and we gonna swing like ol' Mark over by Charlestown Common."

At the reference to the mummified remains of the Negro who had hung in chains from Charlestown's gibbet for twenty years for the murder of his master, Levi paled. "I was just about to come lookin' for you. What happened?"

Elizabeth returned a merry laugh. "Isaiah's exaggerating. We were never in any real danger." She tiptoed to glance over his shoulder. "Did Will come too?"

Levi shook his head. "I reckon he's home puttin' diapers on that new son of his."

Elizabeth greeted the news with a flood of delighted questions, but Levi's recital of the details was interrupted by the swish of the long grass at someone's approach. Two figures rounded the side of the barn: the first, Perry, the stoop-shouldered old caretaker of the estate; the other a woman of middle age striking in appearance in spite of her garb of men's breeches, rough linen shirt, and boots. Her hands were encased in dirty work gloves, and she carried a hoe.

Elizabeth ran to embrace her gleefully. "Here we are, Aunt Tess, just as I promised!"

The older woman returned her embrace with affection. "I see Oriole has flown safely one more time."

An older version of her brother, Tess Howard was fully as tall as he, though age had added majesty to her figure and streaked her black hair with iron grey. Like Samuel, classically handsome features stamped a head somewhat too large for her body. Even though she was fifteen years his senior, she stood as ramrod erect as she had when she had sailed alone to America, a spinster of twenty-eight.

While she had been courted by many men of good family, including several of noble descent, she had fallen in love with none of them and had chosen to remain unmarried. Independent in spirit and means, she had settled in Roxbury, invested her inheritance with characteristic shrewdness, and prospered.

"I'm glad you're all right. I was beginning to think they'd caught you at last," she said with a wry smile.

"The way they be searchin' the others, for a minute there, I think our next sight goin' to be the business end of a noose."

Tess threw a questioning look at Isaiah, but Elizabeth swayed from heel to toe, arms spread wide. "Oh, that's the challenge of it!"

"Doubtless you found last night exceptionally challenging too," Tess reproved.

Elizabeth threw Levi an accusing look. "You've been telling tales!"

He grinned. "She pried it out of me."

"We'd better unload the incriminating evidence and send you home before you get into any further mischief," Tess intervened. "I won't rest easy until I know you're out of trouble—at least for a little while."

Elizabeth stifled a giggle. "Don't forget the Gages' ball tonight."

Her aunt rolled her eyes. "When I proposed your working for Warren, I didn't mean for you to throw all caution to the wind. Your arrest isn't going to help the cause of liberty one whit."

Elizabeth decided against confiding her unexpected meetings with Carleton and Hutchins. "If General Gage's troops were to inspect the contents of your barn—"

"That's not likely to happen."

"My point exactly," Elizabeth responded sweetly.

"I'm not galloping through the countryside at all hours with smuggled munitions and intelligence. Joshua is right. Please try to be careful for a change, though I know it goes against your nature. I'd like you to stay around long enough to inherit this property after I'm gone."

"Why, you're going to live forever!" Elizabeth protested

Laughing in spite of herself, Tess teased, "Whether I do or not, you mind my words, young lady." Sobering, she added, "From what Levi told me, it sounds as though Gage may make a move this coming week. We'll arrange to have you stay with me for a few days to help with my spring cleaning, as usual. That will give you freedom to go and come as necessary—and in the meantime, I'll have plenty to keep you occupied."

Elizabeth grimaced. "I can see me now in a mad dash for Concord with a kerchief wound round my head and a dust cloth in my hand!"

Tess chuckled. "At least, if you're dressed as a servant girl, no one's likely to shoot at you." She gave Elizabeth an affectionate hug and kiss before heading up the lane toward the house.

Within a short time the three men had disassembled the false compartments of the phaeton. Released by the hidden spring, the seat cushion lifted to reveal several small casks of gunpowder, which were quickly stowed inside the barn. Then the seat back was lifted away, and from its interior they removed a sizable stack of cartouche boxes filled with a precious supply of cartridges.

Working swiftly, the men stacked these on the ground to one side, then unlatched and lifted out the phaeton's false floor. A row of gleaming Long Land Pattern muskets alternating with their separated bayonets fit snugly into this narrow hiding place.

At sight of them, old Perry exposed his tobacco-stained teeth in a grin. Giving a soft, admiring whistle, he tenderly patted the smooth stock of one of the muskets.

"Whooeee! I sure cain't wait to pepper a few o' them redcoat hides with one o' these here beauties."

While they hurried to transfer the munitions into the barn, Levi said to Elizabeth, "It sure feels good knowin' we have our ammunition back and can defend ourselves if need be. But I'd give my right arm to know how you and the boys managed to smuggle all this out of the gunhouse right under Gage's nose."

Elizabeth's eyes twinkled with laughter. "This time we took a more direct approach than when we reclaimed our cannon. Instead of cutting through the wall, we walked right in—in broad daylight."

Levi set an armload of cartouche boxes on the remains of a moldering haycock and swiped the sweat from his brow with his arm. "How in tarnation—?"

"It helped that we were dressed in British uniform at the time . . . and carried orders personally signed by Colonel Smith."

Levi guffawed. "Don't tell me. I suppose you just walked right up to him pretty as you please, batted your big brown eyes, and asked him to lend you some spare uniforms, and while he was at it, would he sign orders allowin' you to cart off all the munitions you felt the Sons of Liberty could use."

Elizabeth pursed her lips. "Something like that."

Shaking his head, Levi picked up the stack of cartouche boxes and carried them into the barn, Elizabeth trailing at his heels.

In the center of the barn floor's broad expanse, the layer of musty hay that overlaid the wide planks had been swept back and a large trap door thrown open. Elizabeth followed Levi down the stone steps that led into the gloom below.

Just large enough for a man of average height to stand erect, the space was rumored to have been used by the original owner to conceal contraband smuggled into the colonies to avoid paying the taxes levied by England. Floored and walled with the stones yielded by the neighboring fields, it was cool inside, draped with tattered, dusty cobwebs, but dry.

And crammed to the massive beams that supported the floor just over their heads with kegs of gunpowder, cartouche boxes, and an ill-matched assortment of firearms that included four fieldpieces. The new acquisitions were soon added to the store.

When the trap door had again been let down and swept over with its concealing layer of hay, Elizabeth stood motionless for a moment, looking around her. Mote-dappled shafts of golden sunshine danced to the floor from the high window beneath the roof's swaybacked peak. Overhead, a fringe of hay hung over the edge of the buckling mows.

The great beams that formed these and the rafters had been roughly hewn from logs cut a century earlier. In places they still showed peeling bark between the lacerations of the ax.

As she had many times before, she mused at the barn's unearthly peacefulness. The stillness within its walls reminded her of an empty cathedral.

But a silent, deadly menace crouched there as well, she thought with an unconscious shudder. Beneath the moldering hay, beneath the rotting planks, lay death.

Shrugging off the sensation of foreboding, she reminded herself that she had to hurry if she was going to make it to the ball. And at the thought of the possibilities the night would afford, her spirits soared in anticipation.

Chapter Six

IT WAS PAST SEVEN AND FULL DARK by the time Isaiah guided the bay gelding through the elegant gate fronting the formal gardens of Province House and urged him up the curved drive. Built in 1679 by Peter Sergeant, the mansion had for many years served as the official residence of the royally appointed governors of Massachusetts Bay Colony. During the previous year it had become home and headquarters to its first military governor.

Elizabeth had come alone to the ball after all. Since Mrs. Howard was one of the ball's chaperons, her parents had been unable to wait any longer for their tardy daughter and had left Stony Hill more than an hour earlier, while Elizabeth hurried to bathe and dress.

Before the phaeton came to a halt in front of the brilliantly lighted brick mansion, a liveried footman was already waiting to hand her down, his shoulders hunched against the cold rain. Stepping out, she shivered, her eyes following the classic lines of the mansion upward, past the wrought iron balcony over the massive double doors to the octagonal cupola three stories above her head. There an enormous, gilded bronze weathervane in the shape of an Indian drew its bow and arrow into the piercing spring wind.

Its green glass eyes glittered faintly as though warning that it would not easily give up the secrets it guarded. But as she climbed the red stone steps, Elizabeth resolved that nothing would distract her from her object that night.

Inside the spacious foyer, the light of massed candles and shimmer of color and motion temporarily blinded her. Beneath the murmur of voices and bursts of laughter, she could hear the lively strains of a minuet coming from the third-floor ballroom.

Directly opposite the front door, a magnificent staircase wound through the center of the house, its carved balustrade of quaint twisted and intertwined pillars wound with festive lengths of orange and blue ribbon. A continuous procession paraded up and down: ladies gowned in every conceivable fabric and hue with petticoats extended to unwieldy widths over panniers, vying for attention from the officers in their brilliant scarlet uniform coats. Not to be outdone, the non-military men boasted rich satins and velvets, embroidered or brocaded waistcoats fringed with silk, and elegant smallclothes buckled in gold or silver at the knee.

Among all the men dress swords were the order of the day. So, for the most part, were powdered hair or wigs for both men and women. Many of the ladies had added to their own powdered hair towering creations embellished with a host of fantastic ornaments ranging from baskets of fruit to ships and tiny British flags.

Of the younger women, Elizabeth was one of the few who shunned this affected style. One of the last to arrive, she pushed back the hood of her cloak, revealing the narrow cream ribbons and small clusters of fresh violets that held back her glossy, upswept curls, then hurried after the butler to the receiving line where her hosts were greeting their guests.

Despite her opposition to everything his presence in Boston symbolized, Elizabeth had to concede a grudging respect for the British general. In spite of his high office, His Excellency Lieutenant General Thomas Gage, commander-in-chief of His Majesty's armies in North America, was in appearance and manner as mild, imperturbable, and undistinguished as his solid military career had been.

Caught between England's king and Parliament on one hand and the contentious colonies on the other, Gage had never failed to keep a tight rein on his temper, to patiently reason with both sides, to attempt to govern with what he thought proper firmness a colony that stubbornly refused to accept his authority. Now, belatedly, it was beginning to sink in that all his best efforts, his good intentions, and his good will came too late.

Only an eye as keen as Elizabeth's could have read his uneasy thoughts, however. As she curtsied, he bowed with a smile of genuine affection.

"We'd all but given you up, my dear. I can't tell you how many broken hearts there would be if you hadn't come."

"As usual, you flatter me, Your Excellency. Everyone would have survived my absence, I'm sure."

Margaret Gage held out both hands to take Elizabeth's and bent forward to kiss her cheek. "Then you shouldn't be. I've lost count of how many of your suffering conquests have asked after you. Your parents have been so beleaguered they're on the point of hiding in the cloakroom."

Laughing, Elizabeth regarded the older woman with frank admiration. In face and figure she seemed almost untouched by age. Her strength of will had also remained intact, even though it was no secret that some of the general's subordinates distrusted the influence his American-born wife exercised over him. A few went so far as to privately question her loyalty.

In fact, in private conversations during the past months, Mrs. Gage had confided to Elizabeth the anguish she suffered over her divided loyalties. Tonight, despite her elegantly fashionable Turkish gown and the proud tilt of her head, there was a haunted look in her eyes.

Noting that the general's attention was occupied with another late arrival, Elizabeth drew her aside. "You don't look as though you're enjoying your party very much. Is everything all right?"

Mrs. Gage gave an eloquent shrug. "To tell the truth, all this gaiety rings terribly hollow. I was so looking forward to this evening, but now I feel as though we're standing on the edge of a precipice and that after tonight everything will be changed."

"His Excellency hasn't decided to move against the rebels?" With difficulty Elizabeth maintained an air of indifference she was far from feeling.

"Lord Dartmouth won't allow him to delay any longer. Oh, Elizabeth, it's as if a dark cloud hangs over our heads. I'd give everything I hold dear to keep my husband from bringing harm to my countrymen."

When Elizabeth gave her an impulsive hug, she forced a smile. "There now—enough of my silly fears! This may be the last chance we have to dance and be gay. Run take off your wrap and join the others before we have a mutiny on our hands!"

Assured that her friend knew nothing definite, Elizabeth obeyed. Upstairs, the bedrooms overflowed, every inch of space adrift with young women preening and gossiping in front of the mirrors in a fever of excitement before they climbed the stairs to the ballroom. Taking little part in the excited conversation, Elizabeth removed her cloak, then smoothed her hair and shook out her petticoats.

The classic lines of her champagne-colored Spitalfield silk gown, brocaded with flowers and vines in a range of rich hues, heightened the effect of her natural beauty. The lace-trimmed belle sleeves were detailed, as was the bodice, with knotted silk fringe, while the petticoat, gracefully draped over panniers, fell open in front to reveal a shimmering under petticoat of violet silk that echoed the deep shade of the tight-fitting stomacher.

Finally satisfied with her reflection in the floor-length mirror, she squeezed back through the crush and out into the passageway. At once she was engulfed by a cluster of her friends, who swept her with them to the third floor on a wave of rapture over the newly arrived captain of the Light Dragoons. Halfway between amusement and scorn, Elizabeth gathered that Carleton had wasted no time in cutting a wide swath among the feminine hearts of Boston.

"Oh, Elizabeth, wait until you meet him! He's simply divine," sighed Jane Davis as they entered the spacious anteroom outside the ballroom that took up most of the mansion's third floor.

"Doubtless you'll have him under your spell by the end of the evening, just like all the others." Plump, dark-haired Caroline Inman gave her a sour glance.

Although it was still early, the crowded room was already warm. Employing her ivory fan to cool her cheeks, Elizabeth drawled, "Faith, but I've already met him, and I haven't the least interest. He's all yours."

They greeted her words with squeals of disbelief and teasing objections. But to her considerable relief, after several minutes they deserted her to flutter off in a flurry of whispers and giggles. She was left standing alone just inside the anteroom door.

Intently she scanned the faces of the guests who crowded the room. All the prominent Tories of the town appeared to be present, some clustered together on the chairs that lined the walls, others hovering near the tables that stretched down the room's center, where they traded speculations while sampling the cakes, fruit, and other delicacies piled high on silver trays. Through the double doors opposite her, she could see groups of dancers gliding across the polished ballroom floor in the graceful patterns of the minuet.

Her parents stood just outside these doors, part of an animated group that included the spare, wasted figure of Earl Hugh Percy, commander of the First Brigade and colonel of the Fifth Foot; John Pitcairn, the handsome Scottish major of the Royal Marines assigned to Percy's brigade; and Major Edward Mitchell of the Fifth.

Apparently oblivious to the dancers who swirled past a few feet away, the group surrounded a familiar figure. Everyone appeared to be talking at the same time, the object of universal attention the tall officer who occupied the circle's center.

Even from several yards away, it was impossible to mistake the glance of keen liking that passed between her father and Carleton. They appeared to be engaged in a vehemently contested, though good-humored, argument.

Talking politics, Elizabeth reflected ruefully. It was her father's favorite subject, and he had evidently found an agreeable opponent, one he would doubtless find excuse to invite to Stony Hill often.

As she watched, a howl of laughter rose from the group. Lord Percy clapped Dr. Howard on the back, and smiling, the latter threw up his hands in a gesture of defeat.

Still chuckling, Carleton turned halfway to throw an idle glance in Elizabeth's direction. When his gaze met hers, he sobered, and his eyes darkened with a warmth that brought the color flooding to her cheeks.

Her blush wasn't lost on him. Instantly one eyebrow arched up and laughter tugged at his lips, a smile that was all the more galling because it was so disarming. He made a slight bow, pointed approval in his glance.

She acknowledged him with a bored inclination of her head, polite, but chilly. This brought a grin in response . . . then he returned his attention to the admirer draped seductively on his arm.

Elizabeth gritted her teeth. Lydia Ellsworth, who at the age of eighteen was rapidly becoming Elizabeth's most serious rival, possessed a brilliant beauty that Elizabeth had to admit perfectly complemented Carleton's blond good looks. And he was certainly being more than attentive.

For the first time in her life Elizabeth found herself wishing she were tall and statuesque, with blond hair and blue eyes. Vexed, she reminded herself that her only interest in Carleton was the intelligence she might elicit from him. His romantic involvements were no concern of hers.

Her reflections were interrupted by a slender, sunburned young cap-

tain who outpaced his companions to intercept her. Laughing at the officers who quickly surrounded her, she allowed herself to be swept into
the ballroom. Although they passed near the group that included
Carleton, she made it a point to act as though he were invisible.

To her relief—and a disappointment she refused to acknowledge—
Carleton made no attempt to seek her out, and for her part she deliberately kept her distance. She caught occasional glimpses of him during
the short intervals between dances when one of her partners escorted
her to the anteroom for a few minutes of rest and a cooling glass of
punch. Each time she found herself watching Carleton as he held court
over a party as animated as her own.

Her mother had joined Mrs. Gage and the ball's other chaperons,
who were seated along the wall where they could keep watch over who
went in and out through the door. From time to time others in the group
drifted off to join the dancers, only to return later as though drawn by
an irresistible magnet. Her father, Lord Percy, and Major Pitcairn, however, didn't leave Carleton's side until dinner.

Even though Carleton took no part in the dancing, a widening circle
of ladies fluttered around him like so many colorful butterflies. With a
twinge of irritation Elizabeth observed that he was generous with his
attentions.

At dinner she sat at a table that included Lieutenant Andrews and a
couple of the loose-tongued younger officers. But in spite of her best
efforts and the officers' free indulgence in the wine served with each
course, she learned nothing beyond what she already knew. There was
much speculation but no hard facts concerning the "new evolutions"
assigned to the light infantry and grenadier companies.

Carleton was seated at a table some distance from hers, along with
Lord Percy and a number of the ranking officers. With reluctance she
came to the conclusion that if she intended to gain access to the intelligence she urgently needed, she was going to have to join his party.

When they returned upstairs she gaily took the arm Andrews

offered. He was slightly drunk, and it was an easy matter to steer him on a path that took them near enough to Lord Percy to attract the earl's attention. As she had calculated, he greeted her and bent low over her hand. Pitcairn, in turn, did the same, and with no further effort, she and Andrews were drawn into the circle.

"Jonathan, ye've not met Miss Elizabeth Howard," Pitcairn began.

"As a matter of fact, I have." Carleton smiled down at her. "I was beginning to think I was permanently in your bad graces and that you never intended to speak to me again."

She returned his smile with a frigid one. "Don't be silly, Captain Carleton. In order to consign you to my bad graces, I'd be forced to think about you."

Percy snickered. "It seems your charm isn't having its usual effect, Jon."

"Evidently not," Carleton admitted, wincing. "It looks as if I'm going to have to do penance for my sins after all."

Relenting, Elizabeth said, "You haven't danced tonight, captain."

"Shall I take that as an invitation, *enfant?*"

She tapped him on the arm with her folded fan. "Don't be impertinent. I just meant to point out that you've neglected these ladies who've been waiting so patiently for your favor all evening."

"Tonight I intend to wait upon you," he countered. "I told you I meant to claim you for the last dance—by way of doing penance, of course."

His smile was infuriatingly confident, and she returned a discouraging one. "Then I fear you're going to wait all night, sir. My dance card is . . ." she gave an elaborate shrug, "lamentably overfull."

Andrews raised an eyebrow and drawled, "The host of us standing in line are fervently praying that one of our luckier rivals will trip and break a leg in the course of the gavotte."

Everyone laughed, including Carleton. Before he could respond, however, Lieutenant Colonel Francis Smith plowed through the crowd to join them, dabbing a large handkerchief at the copious moisture that dewed his forehead and jowls. When he lurched to a halt at the edge of the circle, Carleton greeted him with a bow.

"Colonel Smith, I've been waiting with bated breath for you to finish telling me about this spy of yours—Oriole, I believe you called him."

Elizabeth came instantly alert. Smith snorted, his full lips and deep-cut nostrils quivering with contempt.

"Nothing to worry about, captain. Merely one of this Yankee rabble who fancies himself a smuggler and passer of his little gleanings of information."

"His little gleanings o' information would seem to include knowing our plans before we do," Pitcairn put in, his tone sober.

Percy nodded agreement. "Oriole is the most daring member, perhaps the mastermind, of a band of rebel spies and smugglers. We first became aware of him last fall when he and his crew spiked all the guns in the North Battery. As if that weren't insult enough, they carried off four militia fieldpieces we'd secured in the gunhouse."

"They simply walked off with four fieldpieces?" Carleton looked from one to the other with astonished amusement.

Percy nodded, his narrow, fox-like face grim. "They cut through the outer wall of the old gunhouse and made off with them under the noses of a double guard. The next day, the general ordered the remaining field-pieces removed from the new gunhouse and placed in the middle of the camp. When the officers went to execute the order, they discovered the guns already gone."

Carleton guffawed. "But gentlemen, the new gunhouse stands directly across from the Common."

"Opposite the Fifth Foot's encampment, as a matter o' fact." Pitcairn directed a meaningful glance at Percy.

"As I recall, John, you reported a large number of muskets missing just three weeks ago," Percy rejoined equably.

"That I did."

"Oriole again, I take it," Carleton said with a smile.

Smith grunted. "Muskets, cartridges, gunpowder—all in the broad light of day. From the reports we pieced together, they were received by a squad of soldiers who carried very authentic-looking orders."

"And over thy signature, Francis." Pitcairn chuckled.

Smith grimaced. "I saw the orders myself. If I hadn't known better, I'd have sworn I really signed them."

"Clever. But once he has the goods, what does he do with them? I'd think it practically impossible to smuggle out any quantity of munitions without being detected."

Percy's features reflected the strain of prolonged frustration. "We've tried to stop every possible bung hole, Jon, but this place is as airtight as a sieve."

"Isn't it possible everything's still hidden here in Boston? For that matter, how do you even know this Oriole fellow is involved?"

Smith regarded Carleton with a contemptuous smile. "We have our own informants, in case the thought hadn't occurred to you."

"Then why don't you find out Oriole's identity and arrest him?"

The three officers exchanged uncomfortable glances. It was Percy who finally answered.

"We've tried for months, but it seems only a tight circle know who he is, and we haven't been able to break into it."

"Why is he called Oriole?" interjected Andrews.

"That's what the Yankees call him," Pitcairn explained. "And our guards always hear the distant call o' an oriole just before discoverin' a lack o' gunpowder or muskets."

"The bird's common in the area," Carleton pointed out.

"In late fall or winter? In the dead o' the night?"

Carleton stroked his chin. "I see what you mean."

"We almost had him last night," Percy said. "One of our informants learned he was riding circuit for the rebels, so we posted a mounted patrol on the other side of Brooklyne. They managed to intercept him, but he jumped his horse over a wall no mortal creature should have been able to hurdle and disappeared into the night like a phantom. One of our men tried the same jump and would have died if your father hadn't managed to save him," he added, turning to Elizabeth.

"I was shocked when my father told me of it," she agreed earnestly.

"A daring rascal. But the soldiers did get a look at our impudent friend?"

Smith dabbed at his brow, then stuffed the moist handkerchief into the pocket of his uniform coat. "It was cloudy, and all they could make out was that he rode a dark-colored horse and wore a dark cloak and broad-brimmed hat. He looked to be but a half-grown boy."

"Not much to go on, is it? There must be hundreds of black or dark bay horses in the area," Carleton noted.

"I own a black stallion myself," Pitcairn pointed out.

Elizabeth gave a muffled laugh. "I have a black mare, and Papa's gelding that pulls my phaeton is a dark bay."

For a moment, Carleton studied the fat colonel with a thoughtful expression. "But tell me about these informants of yours, colonel. Do you mean to say you employ the rebels' own people to pass information on to you?"

"I assure you, captain, these Yankees aren't all as loyal to the rebel cause as the so-called Sons of Liberty would have everyone believe." Smith paused to make sure he had everyone's undivided attention before continuing. "And gold has a way of persuading even the staunchest patriot of where his true interests lie."

"I know so little of these matters," Carleton said, his manner humbly self-deprecating. "Tell me, how does a spy go about . . . spying?"

As Elizabeth watched, fascinated, Carleton proceeded to play the perfect foil to the plodding, vain officer. With seemingly innocent, admiring, or dryly witty comments and questions, he prodded Smith to make ever more boastful remarks about his part in wringing crucial information out of the patriots. All the while he gave every evidence of astonishment at the colonel's brilliance.

"Deucedly clever," Carleton purred at length. "And you have these spies planted in the very midst, as it were, of the rebel camp."

"At Dr. Warren's elbow. He has hardly to sneeze but we know of it."

The others laughed appreciatively, all except for Percy and Pitcairn, who appeared to be more disgusted than otherwise.

With Carleton shaking his head in admiration, Smith continued, "As you can imagine, the role of informant requires a closed mouth, a cool head under pressure, and the ability to react quickly in unexpected circumstances."

Carleton bowed in acknowledgement. "All qualities you've so eminently exhibited."

Smith inclined his head uncertainly as muffled snickers tittered behind upraised hands and fluttered fans.

"Well," Lord Percy drawled, "if I do recall correctly, Francis, you were caught out at Brewer's Tavern a couple of weeks ago in spite of your laborer's getup by—wasn't it a Negro maid?"

Carleton swung to face the colonel as though he hung on every word.

Flushing, Smith blustered, "A fluke. It could have happened to anyone."

"Umm," Carleton conceded. "But of course, all this collecting of intelligence is carried out in the utmost secrecy."

"Well . . . naturally."

The colonel had at last gained some dim awareness of the precipice on which his feet tottered. But when Carleton allowed his innocent gaze to wander from face to face around the circle of eager listeners with a skeptical, though diplomatically faint, smile, the hot color flooded up Smith's neck and into his plump cheeks.

Elizabeth tried hysterically to think of anything but that the enraged officer looked for all the world like a fat turkey shaking his wattles in impotent fury at the one who held the ax. Lord Percy laughed openly.

Pitcairn was convulsed, as were the rest. But although a peculiar taut-ness tugged at the corners of Carleton's mouth and his eyes were alive with mirth, he continued to face the older officer with perfectly con-trolled gravity and the air of one who waited humbly to be instructed.

Realizing he'd been made a fool of, Smith drew his loose, untidy fig-ure up to his full height. "I believe I may speak in perfect confidence before each of these ladies and gentlemen," he huffed, quaking with anger.

"I dare say," agreed Carleton, "that it would never occur to these rebellious rustics to plant a spy at *our* elbows. Even this Oriole, whoever he is, couldn't have the audacity to invade His Excellency's ball—though he does seem to be an exceptionally cheeky devil," he added wryly, as an afterthought.

Elizabeth sobered as did several of the others in the circle. An icy thread of dismay crept through her veins.

Enraged, Smith appealed to the others for support. "If you mean to accuse any of these excellent ladies and gentlemen or the officers of the crown of collaborating with that despicable band of malcontents, I think you overstep your bounds, captain."

Carleton raised his hands in protest. "You mistake me, sir. It's just that it did occur to me—and if I'm wrong, please correct me—that if I were to undertake such an assignment, I might, perhaps, be inclined to avoid discussing it with anyone who wasn't directly involved."

Smith opened and closed his mouth several times like a fish out of water, but the only sound that came from his lips was a choked wheeze. After an awkward pause he managed to excuse himself. Giving a stiff bow, he lumbered off across the room—to lick his wounds and plot revenge, Elizabeth guessed, wavering between amusement and alarm.

"You're quite good, you know." At Carleton's quizzical glance, she added with a smile, "It would seem you've made Oriole's task a little more difficult."

Rubbing his prominent, high-arched nose, Lord Percy directed a frown after Smith's haughtily retreating back. "You've given us consider-able food for thought."

"My warning will be forgotten by tomorrow morning at the very lat-est."

"You're probably right." Percy gave Carleton a playful punch in the arm. "But you're our brightest star, Jon. Surely you have some ideas on how to go about trapping this gadfly Oriole."

"I'll give it some thought."

One by one the others deserted them, many going to join the dancers. Elizabeth noted that all the higher ranking officers seemed to have disappeared. After securing her promise of a dance, Percy also took his leave with the excuse that he had to speak to Gage.

Before she had time to consider what their business might be, she glanced up to find Carleton looking down at her with a light in his eyes that increased the pace of her heartbeat. Overcome by a reckless impulse to test her power over him, she allowed her lips to curve into a smile that promised everything while giving nothing away, one that invariably elicited an ardent response.

Carleton, however, returned a hard, calculating look that sent a shiver up her spine. Involuntarily she dropped her eyes from his, then, vexed, quickly raised them again. This time there was mocking, cynical amusement in the depths of his smoky eyes.

She was instantly furious with herself. Knowing every feminine wile, he would, of course, expect nothing more from her.

"Faith, captain, you've got to be the most exasperating man I've ever met," she snapped, saying the first thing that popped into her head.

He laughed easily, fine lines crinkling at the corners of his eyes. To her annoyance, she couldn't help thinking how attractive it made him, how she liked the sound of his laughter. Even more irritating was the realization that he read her thoughts.

"Then we're a fine match for each other." He glanced toward the dancers in the other room. "It seems you haven't been claimed for the jig, ma chère, or perhaps I've succeeded in scaring off your suitors. Shall I at last be favored with the dance you refused to promise me?"

"I'm not in the mood to dance right now, particularly not with you."

"Then come outside."

"With you? Alone?"

"You're not afraid of me, are you? Or is it that you're afraid of what people might say?"

Biting her lip, she threw an involuntary glance toward her mother who was seated a little distance away. He saw it, and his grin broadened.

"A proper young lady, after all." His sigh was heavy with regret.

She flushed. "The fact of the matter is I haven't the least desire to be gossiped about on your account."

He choked down a guffaw. While she tapped her foot indignantly, he struggled to compose himself enough to speak.

"I must say, I am disappointed in you," he managed at last. "If you had any spirit at all, you wouldn't give a fig for anyone else's opinion. But don't worry. I promise you won't be compromised by me."

"You're utterly insufferable. I don't know why I bother speaking to you."

His gaze became intense. "Because I'm nothing like the usual run of young bucks who fall all over themselves at your slightest smile. I don't play that game, so stop arguing and come outside with me. I want to talk to you without interruption, and that's impossible with this cloud of besotted admirers constantly buzzing about your ears." Grinning, he added, "I dare you."

The challenge exceeded her power to resist. "Wait a few minutes before following me. I'll meet you downstairs."

She didn't give him time to reply. Both her parents were occupied, and none of the chaperons was looking in their direction. Her head held high, she strode to the door and out into the deserted hallway. Ignoring the knot in her stomach, she marched downstairs, determined to get the best of Carleton yet.

The first floor appeared deserted except for the servants clearing the tables in the dining room. They took no notice of her, however, and within a short time Carleton came down the stairs. Before she could stop him, he caught her by the hand.

His expression was very serious now, and instinct urged her to pull away from him. As before she found it impossible to do so. Her heart began to pound, sending the blood into her cheeks. She looked hastily away to avoid his probing gaze.

"I've been devoured with curiosity since this afternoon," he said in a low voice. "Tell me, my sweet, who is the charming Mr. Hutchins? I assume he's one of the bewitched legion, but he seemed an extraordinarily surly specimen."

She stared at him blankly, taken off guard. "I . . . we'd pledged to marry," she blurted out, "but my father broke it off when David joined the Sons of Liberty."

As soon as she said it, she bit her lip, wishing the words away. Carleton released her, instantly contrite.

"I'm so sorry. That wasn't any of my business. I only meant to tease you, and I've ended up hurting you. Please forgive me."

He said it with a tenderness she didn't expect. In spite of herself, her eyes filled with tears.

Seeing them, he murmured, "So you still love him."

For a long moment she remained silent, rethinking the scene with Hutchins in the carriage that afternoon—and too many other painful scenes during the course of their relationship. At length she shook her head, relieved that she could finally mean it.

"No. That ended long ago." In spite of her resolve, the words trailed off as she fought vainly to blink back tears. "When we first met, David was so attentive, so ardent that I couldn't resist him. But once we were betrothed . . . it seemed as though he thought he owned me body and soul. He insisted he loved me, yet nothing I did pleased him. By the time Papa intervened, David had killed everything I ever felt for him."

She couldn't continue. The too-familiar wave of misery, shame, and guilt swept over her.

Why was she confiding all this to Carleton? Surely he had no interest in knowing what secrets she harbored in her heart of hearts. Or if he did, would he use the knowledge to control and humiliate her as Hutchins had done?

Fearfully she raised her eyes, afraid of what she would read in his. To her surprise, Carleton's face had clouded, and he was staring off into space. After a moment he drew in an uneven breath.

"I had a similar experience," he admitted in a husky voice. "Mine, however, was entirely my own fault."

He returned his gaze to her, and she saw in his eyes the same pain that twisted like a sharp dagger in her breast. "How old were you when you and Hutchins met?"

"Seventeen." She could hardly speak.

He took her hands in his, brought them to his lips. "So young. You could not have known. To my shame, I did not have that excuse."

Before she could ask him to explain, he nodded toward the double doors at the end of the hallway and said briskly, "I believe escape lies that way. Come along."

His touch gentle but insistent, he drew her outside with him onto the rear terrace of the house and shut the door behind them. She found it a distinct relief to be out of the warmth and babble of voices—and away from the disturbing memories their exchange had evoked. He also seemed determined to abandon the confidences they had shared, as though nothing had happened.

The rain had stopped, and she raised her face to the cool, damp air, wanting it to wash away the taint of the past. For both of them. She shivered as she drew in a deep breath.

"We should have stopped and gotten your cloak." Removing his uniform coat, he wrapped it around her.

It was warm from his body, and she pulled it gratefully close around her bare shoulders and neck. As he bent over her, she realized that the moment was again becoming too serious for comfort and gave her head a defiant toss.

"Are you really the army's brightest star, as Lord Percy seems to think?"

"A veritable Venus."

"That's a planet, idiot!"

"You see how far Percy was from hitting the mark?"

"I expected a little more vanity from you," she teased.

"Oh, but I am incredibly vain, *enfant*. In fact, I'm afflicted with so many vices a mere child like you shouldn't be left alone with me."

He was no longer smiling. The bitter cynicism in his tone made her wonder what he had been about to confide moments earlier before he had cut their conversation off.

"Nonsense," she faltered. "I think you're really quite harmless. All bluster."

"Do you? Then I'm afraid you'll end up being quite disillusioned."

They were standing close to one another in the darkness just outside the bars of light from the mansion's rear windows, their bodies almost brushing. And though he didn't touch her, something in his face, pale in the dim, reflected light, caused her to tremble.

She knew absolutely in that moment that he longed to kiss her, that she had no business out there, alone in the dark with him. Yet she was powerless to obey the insistent prodding of conscience that warned her to flee temptation before she gave in to it.

Urgently she wanted to feel his arms around her, to taste his kiss, the desire so intense it paralyzed her. The emotions that flooded through her she had experienced with no other man, not even in the beginning with Hutchins, and she was hungry to find out where surrender would lead them both.

As she stood there, frozen, her face upturned to his, he jerked away and stepped to the balustrade at the edge of the terrace. It felt as though she had been slapped. The breath was knocked from her lungs, and she stared blankly at his back.

Several seconds passed before she realized that the doors behind them had creaked open, spilling a shaft of light across the steps. His movements casual and unhurried, Carleton turned to face the officer who stood on the threshold.

"Eh, there ye be, Jonnie." It was Pitcairn's gruff voice.

Before she could pull away, Carleton caught her hand and forced her to step with him into the light. Pitcairn stared at her with a start, then smiled.

"Does thy mother know ye be out here alone with the captain, lass?"

Her cheeks burning, Elizabeth shook her head. "It was so hot inside, I felt faint," she lied quickly. "Captain Carleton kindly volunteered to escort me outside until I felt better. You won't tell anyone?"

Pitcairn looked from her to Carleton, then shook his head. "O' course not. But ye'd better come back inside a'fore you're missed."

The instant they reentered the house, Elizabeth returned Carleton's uniform coat with cool self-possession. Looking suspiciously as though he was working hard to maintain a sobriety appropriate to the circumstances, he pulled it on.

Pitcairn put his hand on Carleton's arm. "The general wants to see ye," he said in an undertone.

Turning to Elizabeth, Carleton made a graceful bow. "Please call on me anytime you decide to feel faint. My specialty is reviving swooning young ladies."

Elizabeth couldn't think of a reply scathing enough. Furious, she could only glare after him with outraged pride as he followed Pitcairn into the general's study.

Chapter Seven

ACCEPTING THE GOBLET of Madeira Pitcairn poured for him, Carleton threw a casual glance around the elegant room crowded with officers.

"For once keep control o' thy tongue, laddie," Pitcairn growled under his breath. "I know how ye love to play the devil's advocate, but Gage won't be in the mood tonight."

"I'll try to behave myself," Carleton promised with a smile.

The major retreated as Gage moved to the sideboard to greet Carleton and offer him a hand-rolled Cuban cigar. When the general had lit it for him, Carleton took a sip of wine, drew deeply on the cigar, and noted the fact that although there weren't seats enough for all the officers, two had been left unclaimed.

These faced each other on opposite sides of the blue delft-tiled fireplace. After introducing each of the officers in turn, Gage went to sit in one of the chairs and motioned to Carleton to take the other, which happened to be flanked by Percy and Pitcairn.

So it's to be an inquisition, Carleton thought. *How delightful.*

His smile faint, he sat down and slouched back, one booted ankle propped across the other knee. Ignoring Smith's glower, he lifted his glass to his commander. "To your health, sir."

"And to yours." Gage diminished his drink by half. "I hope you've had a chance to settle in by now."

"We're quite comfortable, thank you."

Carleton realized with amusement that the others were sizing him up, some, like Smith, with obvious resentment. Admiral Graves, a crusty old salt with a sneer of universal disdain so longstanding it had become permanently stamped on his features, watched him with undisguised malice.

"Hugh and John have filled me in on your background and qualifications," Gage said, nodding toward Percy and Pitcairn. "I've called you here because they tell me you have intimate knowledge of this region, its citizens, and the political situation. And of course, your record in the Dragoons speaks for itself. Your superiors all recommend you as having excellent judgment and a cool head. They say you know how to lead men and inspire their loyalty—all qualities we can put to good use right now."

Carleton considered the glowing end of his cigar, surprised by the open compliment. "You honor me, Your Excellency. I'll do my best to deserve your regard."

"I have every confidence you will."

Carleton noted that while Percy and Pitcairn were pleased, a number of the other officers seemed less so. Gage's favor, he decided, was likely to make his assignment more difficult than otherwise.

"I believe Hugh explained that my intent was to attach you to my staff as a special advisor and aide-de-camp until the Seventeenth arrives from England. I've changed my mind, however. I'm going to make the assignment permanent."

Carleton straightened, ignoring Pitcairn's restraining hand on his arm and Percy's warning frown. "I'm honored, sir, but with the Seventeenth being posted here, I'm finally in line for the field command I've been wanting, and—"

"I know that, and I'm sorry."

Carleton opened his mouth to protest, but this time Percy cut him off, his voice too low for anyone but Carleton and Pitcairn to hear. "It's a plum assignment, Jon. So shut up and consider your good fortune."

"He's right, laddie," Pitcairn growled from his other side. "Besides, you're not bein' given a choice."

Carleton drained his glass, staring straight ahead as he tried to come up with a tactful refusal. As one didn't present itself, he finally conceded, "I'm at your disposal, sir."

Gage smiled. "I trust you won't find it such unpleasant duty. And by the way, the assignment carries the rank of major, effective immediately."

"Thank you, sir."

The earl looked particularly pleased with himself.

"Why do I get the feeling I have you to thank for this?" Carleton demanded in an undertone.

"Because you do." Percy's tone held satisfaction. "I warned the general you'd object to the assignment, and I also advised him how to handle you."

"You're such a friend."

"The latest communication from Dartmouth, gentlemen," Gage was saying, "is that the Ministry wants an immediate move against the rebels, which means we'll march to Concord as soon after the Sabbath as the weather permits."

"The best time for a march is the Sabbath, when the ruffians will be occupied with their prayers." Admiral Graves's expression reflected contempt.

Gage held his hand up to silence the murmur of agreement. "I'm trying not to stir up a hornet's nest, gentlemen. In case you hadn't noticed we have four thousand troops fit for duty. That's not enough to counter a general insurrection, which is what's likely to happen if we violate their holy day, especially since it's also Easter. So we'll march Monday or Tuesday—Wednesday at the latest. Your orders are to proceed with caution, but to act firmly, and to avoid a confrontation if at all possible. Is that clear?"

It was, but Pitcairn's face hardened. Grabbing Carleton's wine glass, he stood up and went to pour them both another drink.

His voice stern, Gage continued. "The directive of the rebels' so-called Committee of Safety stated that an alert will be called if we march out of Boston with baggage and artillery. You won't be taking either, so there won't be any justifiable provocation. Just go out, find and destroy their military stores, and come back. It's as simple as that."

Carleton exchanged a skeptical glance with Pitcairn as the major resumed his seat and handed him his brimming glass. "Somehow I doubt the patriots will submit so gracefully," he observed under his breath.

"I have the same feelin', lad," Pitcairn returned, his expression gloomy.

Overhearing their exchange, Gage turned to Carleton. "What do you think the colonials' response will be?"

Carleton chose his words with care. "Sir, every time you've marched out of Boston, the militia has raised an alarm. The only way you're likely to avoid one this time is to move in absolute secrecy, get to the stores before the Committee of Safety can be alerted and the militia mustered, and be well on the way back before they gather a large enough force to oppose you."

Gage nodded in agreement. "That's my intent."

Thoughtfully Carleton drew on his cigar. "The trouble with that plan, of course, is that in just walking down the street this evening I overheard discussions on every side of how soon we're likely to march. The patriots know our objective is Concord. They're certain we'll move in a few days, and they're already on the alert.

"I must warn you, sir, that the likelihood of carrying out this mission with any secrecy is negligible, while the probability that the expedition will face a large force of hostiles by the time they reach Concord is, in my opinion, a dead certainty."

A clamor of derision greeted his words. Shaking his head, Pitcairn protested, "Ye're daft, Jonnie. There's no doubt the miserable bandits will make a show against us—and even less that we'll have but to draw our swords half out of their scabbards to send the ruffians running."

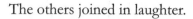

The others joined in laughter.

Percy put down his pipe. "Even if the rebels do muster their militia, they're so poorly trained they hardly know which end of a musket to aim. And they have no officers who have the first idea what to do in battle—"

"You're making a fatal mistake if you believe that," Carleton cut him off. "There are many good men among them who fought with bravery at Louisbourg and who know tactics and how to lead men. They can hit a target accurately, something our troops aren't trained to do. And they know the terrain and how to fight in this country, as they proved during the Seven Years War."

Pitcairn and Percy threw one another dismayed glances. The rest of the officers shifted uncomfortably, except for Smith, who was reveling in what he conceived to be Carleton's self-destruction.

To everyone's surprise, Gage's response was mild. "I don't deny the colonials' ability to fight. But I suspect their courage and resolution will be found wanting when they face a battle line of seasoned troops."

Carleton leaned forward in his chair. "The colonists believe they're protecting their homes, their families, their livelihoods—any one of which is a powerful inducement for a man to fight. They're used to governing themselves and consider it their birthright. Like any Englishman, the one thing they'll fight to the bitter end is the imposition of laws they've had no voice in making."

"It sounds like you're on their side, Carleton," Smith sneered.

Carleton rounded on him. "My concern is for England. I've seen enough of war to know that a conflict with our own countrymen will benefit neither side."

Gage waved Smith to silence. "I agree with you on that score, major, and I intend to do everything that's reasonable to avoid a conflict. But if the colonies refuse to submit to the authority of the crown, our sworn duty is to enforce obedience."

Breaking the tense silence that followed his words, Gage went on to detail his plans. The expedition would be composed of the flank companies of each regiment, the grenadiers and the light infantry, led by Smith with Pitcairn his second in command. They would take the northern route through Lexington, which scouts had determined to be the better road. The troops would leave Boston by boat, crossing the Charles River to Lechmere's Point to avoid the eyes and ears of the outlying towns while gaining valuable time.

He ordered Admiral Graves to have his ships lower their longboats at once to have them ready. Major Mitchell was assigned to ride out with a mounted patrol the afternoon before the troops embarked to keep watch on the roads and prevent any rebel couriers from reaching Concord. Some hours after the initial force left Boston, Lord Percy would lead out a sizable relief column equipped with artillery to act as a deterrent to any rash action on the part of the colonials.

After cautioning the officers to take every precaution to keep the expedition secret even from their own men until the moment of departure, Gage dismissed the officers, apologizing for keeping them away from the dance so long. He intercepted Carleton at the door.

"Do you have plans for tomorrow?"

"Dr. Howard invited Andrews and me to join his family for worship and dinner."

"You'll find the Howards delightful company," Gage approved as he accompanied Carleton back upstairs to the ballroom. "Enjoy your day, but report to me first thing Monday morning. I'd like to hear your thoughts on how we might go about putting a tighter leash on the rebels and perhaps even intercept this spy Oriole who's been plaguing us."

THE SIGNIFICANCE OF CARLETON'S ENTRANCE with Gage several minutes after the rest of the officers returned wasn't lost on Elizabeth. The room was soon buzzing with the news of his promotion, and for the rest of the evening he was surrounded. She could not have gotten close to him even if she had wanted to.

After their encounter downstairs and on the terrace, she found herself unexpectedly adrift on a tide of confusing and treacherous emotions. Longing to be near him, she was at the same time overwhelmed by the desire to put as much distance between them as possible.

Neither option was possible, however. She had been so lavish with her promises that she had no choice but to dance every dance, which left her no time to waylay any of the senior officers involved in the meeting with Gage. She had judged the risk too great to hover at the general's study doors in hope of overhearing the officers' discussions, and now, in spite of every attempt, the information she most sought to uncover still eluded her.

The final measure of the last dance came to an end, and the musicians began to put away their instruments. After bidding their hosts goodnight and reminding Elizabeth not to be tardy in following them home, her parents took their leave. Elizabeth watched them go unhappily, knowing she had no plausible excuse to linger.

The rest of the guests were already drifting in chattering clusters toward the doors, when she noticed Carleton making his way through the crowd to the musicians. He plucked a violin from the hands of its surprised owner, and putting the instrument under his chin, drew the bow across the strings. The lively tune he played stopped everyone in their tracks and brought them gathering around him.

Laughing, he said with mock outrage, "My friends, I'm astonished! I thought the good citizens of Boston—and certainly His Majesty's soldiers—knew how to make merry! Why, the night has hardly begun, and you're off to burrow in your beds before you've enjoyed the highlight of the evening." Turning a wicked smile on Elizabeth, he swept her a bow. "Miss Howard has graciously agreed to help me teach you a reel we dance in Virginia."

She gasped in dismay, then in spite of herself began to laugh. So he intended to make good his promise after all, and in a way she couldn't refuse.

His smile was infectious, and she decided that, although he was annoyingly perverse, it was impossible not to admire his audacity. She took her time going to take the hand he held out to her. He said nothing, only gave her fingers a quick squeeze before turning to demonstrate the reel for the musicians, but she could tell he was pleased.

He played so rapidly and with such skill that before he finished the first measure the listeners were tapping their feet and clapping their hands in time to the music. One by one the musicians picked up his lead. When he was satisfied with their mastery of the tune, he returned the violin to its owner.

After directing Andrews to call the reel, he offered Elizabeth his hand, and she followed him to the head of the line as the dancers eagerly took their places. An excellent teacher as well as dancer, he soon had Elizabeth breathless and laughing.

When the figures of the dance brought them together, she said, "It seems congratulations are in order, major."

His fingers tightened over hers, but although he smiled down at her, his eyes were serious. "I'm surprised you're still speaking to me. If it hadn't been for your quick thinking, I'd have landed you in hot water after all. Please forgive my thoughtlessness."

Suddenly she felt light as air. "You did tempt me, villain, though I've no one to blame but myself. At times I feel as if there's a little devil sitting on my shoulder whispering into my ear."

He grinned at her across the heads of the other dancers as they were swirled away from each other. When they met again he said, "I'm acquainted with that same devil. I'm afraid we're too much alike for safety if you mean to keep your virtue intact."

"My virtue is one thing I'm quite capable of protecting, sir," she retorted. "Make no mistake of it."

"The deuce, woman! You're as prickly as a hedgehog."

"How sweet. I'll have to remember that. I remind you of a hedgehog."

"Why is it I'm always getting off on the wrong foot with you?"

"I can't guess, sir," she said sweetly. "Won't you enlighten me?"

They were carried away from one another once more amid a laughing circle, then back again. "Truce?" Carleton tried.

"Never! It's much more fun to keep you guessing."

The exhilarating sensation of holding the advantage lasted through the end of the reel and the breaking up of the party. Carleton and Andrews escorted her through the crush of departing guests to her carriage.

It wasn't until she waved a gay good-bye and felt the phaeton roll forward that she realized with dismay how completely she had been diverted from the urgent mission that had been her sole reason for attending.

❋ ❋ ❋

It was almost midnight when Carleton and Andrews walked up Beacon Street in companionable silence, wrapped in their scarlet cloaks against the piercing east wind and spitting rain. As Andrews turned up the walk to the house, Carleton hesitated, staring out across the black silhouettes of the trees and hillocks on the deserted Common.

Without warning he was overcome by the same bleak emotions he had experienced on returning to Virginia. Little appeared to have changed outwardly, but he had changed.

The passage of years had done little to dull the deep ache inside, the yearning to return home to the man who had been a father to him. And now that he had returned, the one he had longed the most to see was gone.

He had felt strangely lost on his arrival in the colonies, as abandoned and alone as that frightened, rebellious three-year-old sent away by a gruff, uncommunicative father and a dying mother. The same feelings of rejection and loneliness cut through him now, as sharp as the bitter pangs of a guilty conscience.

He became aware of Andrews's questioning look.

"You go ahead," he said, keeping his voice flat. "I'm feeling too restless to go to sleep right now. I think I'll take a walk before turning in."

Andrews yawned. "Suit yourself. I'm going straight to bed. It's been a long day."

Carleton grinned. "How many times did you dance with the exquisite Miss Howard?"

"Once or twice more than you did," the lieutenant drawled.

"Sweet dreams, then, but don't oversleep. We'll have to be up with the dawn to meet the Howards in time for worship."

"You'd better make that walk a short one then, or you'll be snoring through the sermon, not I," Andrews retorted.

Laughing, Carleton waved his friend off and strolled to the corner. As he turned onto Charles Street, he looked back to make sure that Andrews had disappeared inside the house.

The deep shadows of the cloudy night intensified his pensive mood. He wandered along the gentle curve of the Back Bay, past Tramountain's steep incline on his right. Skirting the edge of the Mill Pond, he headed toward Copp's Hill, just beyond which Admiral Graves's flagship, *Somerset,* tugged against her anchor on the rising tide.

Chapter Eight

"Good morning, Papa. Happy Easter morn."

Dr. Howard turned from surveying his domain with proprietary pride to greet his elder daughter. She tiptoed to give him a quick peck on the cheek.

The steady rain of early morning had given way to thinning clouds and an occasional misty ray of sunshine that brought the fresh colors of the landscape into vivid focus. The air was still raw, however, and Elizabeth tugged her woolen cloak around her shoulders.

Dr. Howard nodded in the direction of the road. Turning, she caught a flash of color through the branches, heard the muffled plop of hooves and lazy murmur of voices. The two officers emerged from the trees, riding up the carriageway at a walk, their helmets catching the glint of the sun.

Carleton rode half a length in the lead astride a sleek, powerful bay stallion with black mane and tail and four black stockings. At his side, Andrews was mounted on a light bay with white markings. The bold, black XXVII L.D. of the Seventeenth Light Dragoons emblazoned the snow-white, silver-tasseled housings under their saddles.

The two officers drew up next to the Howard's landau at the foot of the steps and dismounted as Mrs. Howard and Abby emerged from the house. Trailing down the steps behind the rest of her family, Elizabeth stood slightly apart from the others through the exchange of greetings.

After introducing his wife and younger daughter, Dr. Howard said, "My sister, Teresa, will be joining us for dinner. I'm eager to have you meet her as well."

Feeling uncomfortably self-conscious, Elizabeth caught hold of the bay stallion's white bridoon and stroked his velvety nose, receiving a playful nudge in return. "What is his name?" she asked when Carleton turned to her.

"Devil." At Mrs. Howard's frown, he laughed and apologized. "I'm afraid I called him that so often and so adamantly while I was training him that he began to answer to it. He's spirited, but I'd trust him with my life."

Dr. Howard appraised the stallion. "I own some fine horseflesh myself. Perhaps after dinner you'd like to take a look at them. I warrant Elizabeth's mare is as excellent an animal as your Devil, if not better."

"I'd be more than happy to wager Devil against any horse on this continent."

"And Night Mare would win."

Carleton regarded Elizabeth with one eyebrow raised. "Night Mare?"

"Well, she is black . . . and a mare."

"Perfect," he returned with a laugh. "But if you're so confident, may I propose a race to settle the matter. I'm willing to take on whatever course you choose."

"Major Carleton, please don't encourage my wayward daughter in her willfulness," Mrs. Howard protested. "It's quite improper, not to mention far too dangerous for a young lady to—"

But Elizabeth had already stuck out her hand to shake Carleton's. "Agreed. There's a path behind the stable that's perfect. It's a little more than a mile, uphill then back down to the meadow. There are three or four jumps depending on which way you go. One's a little high—Devil might balk at it—but it's wonderful fun."

To Mrs. Howard's horrified objections, Dr. Howard soothed, "Now, calm yourself, my dear. Elizabeth's an experienced rider."

It was obvious he relished the idea of a race, and his wife drew him aside, trying without success to keep her voice too low for the officers to overhear. "I won't have our daughter riding in a race like a . . . a man! It's bad enough that you have her assisting on your rounds and in the surgery like one of your students, and now she's learning midwifery from Sarah. If you persist in indulging her, she'll turn out like your sister. While I have the greatest affection and regard for Tess, it's because she's so headstrong that she's never married."

"And she's all the happier for it!" Elizabeth burst out with more heat than she'd intended. "Excuse me if I can't view Aunt Tess's independence as quite the calamity you seem to, Mama. I refuse to believe that the entrapment of a husband is the sole measure of a woman's worth or that everything she does should be bent toward that aim!"

Carleton exchanged an amused glance with Andrews, obviously struggling to keep from laughing. When Elizabeth glared at him, daring him to make a teasing comment, he discovered a profound interest in the matched dapple greys that waited patiently in the landau's traces.

"A race on the Sabbath is out of the question," Mrs. Howard insisted.

"Speaking of the Sabbath," Carleton intervened, "if we don't hurry, we're going to be late for worship."

Dr. Howard consulted his pocket watch, then shooed the women toward the carriage. As the men mounted their horses, Isaiah clucked to the two greys.

The landau's top was folded back that morning. Elizabeth had taken the seat facing the rear, opposite her mother and Abby, and after they turned onto the road, Carleton brought his mount up beside her. Without speaking, she followed his gaze across the town and harbor that lay below them, wreathed in early morning stillness.

In the distance the green hills were robed in a light, pearly mist, and gauzy streamers of fog melted into the air off the surface of the water.

Looking out across the bay, his face grave, Carleton began softly to sing in a clear, true tenor. One by one the others joined in the hymn, their voices mingling sweetly on the cool wind.

When I survey the wondrous cross,
On which the Prince of glory died,
My richest gain I count but loss,
And pour contempt on all my pride.

Forbid it, Lord, that I should boast,
Save in the death of Christ, my God;
All the vain things that charm me most,
I sacrifice them to His blood.

See, from His head, His hands, His feet,
Sorrow and love flow mingled down;
Did e'er such love and sorrow meet,
Or thorns compose so rich a crown?

Were the whole realm of nature mine,
That were a present far too small;
Love so amazing, so divine,
Demands my soul, my life, my all.

As the last notes drifted away on the light breeze, Elizabeth glanced up, tears blurring her eyes. To her surprise, Carleton also blinked back tears, an expression of such intense sorrow on his face that she suddenly longed to know what wounds he concealed deep inside and to find a way to heal them. Just then he looked down, and the instant his gaze met hers, his expression was wiped clean as though he had put on a mask.

"Easter has always been my favorite holy day," she faltered. "There's no comfort more precious than remembering the price our Lord paid to redeem us."

His answer was gruff. "Sweet comfort, indeed, for those who haven't placed themselves beyond all hope of forgiveness." Spurring the bay forward, he rode off to the head of the procession.

There was no time to wonder at the bitter pain of his words. They had come within yards of the fortress outside the town gates, and as she glanced again in the direction of the harbor, she stiffened, everything else forgotten at the sight that met her eyes.

Tethered to the sterns of the men-of-war riding at anchor on the sparkling water were the ships' longboats.

Turning to Andrews, who had drawn up beside her, she indicated the scene. "It would seem our suspense is about to be broken, wouldn't you say, lieutenant?"

"What do you make of that, Jon?" Andrews called to Carleton.

He came riding slowly back. Isaiah had pulled the horses to a walk, and Dr. Howard rounded the rear of the carriage to join them.

"Perhaps we'll finally see some action, eh, major?"

"More than likely Admiral Graves is putting his men through routine exercises," Carleton returned with apparent lack of interest.

"I'll wager he's getting ready to transport troops for a march to Concord," Elizabeth persisted. "Isn't that what you gentlemen were discussing with General Gage until so late last night, sir?"

He regarded her, eyebrow raised, a glint of amusement in his eyes. "Surely such a charming young lady as you has far more interesting diversions to occupy her pretty head than military maneuvers."

It was an unmistakable rebuff. She gave a soft laugh and with a casual movement of her shoulders allowed her cloak to slip back, revealing a ruffling of lace, a flash of peach satin, and the creamy skin of her throat.

"Sewing, I suppose you mean . . . or perhaps . . . cooking."

His gaze lingered on her, the expression in his eyes causing the pace of her heartbeat to increase. "That's not exactly what I had in mind."

They said nothing more to each other until they reached the North End and drew to a halt in front of the simple brick facade of Christ Church, affectionately dubbed Old North by the citizens of Boston. The carillon of bells in its tall steeple had just begun to peal the hour of worship.

As Elizabeth stepped down from the carriage, her attention was arrested by a familiar figure astride a long-legged grey that was weaving his way toward them through the throng of worshipers. Sturdy in build, the rider had plain, square features characterized by a high forehead, a decisive mouth and jaw, and a direct, probing gaze.

Slowing his mount, he tipped his broad-brimmed hat, his gaze drifting past Elizabeth to the others. Mrs. Howard looked apprehensively toward her husband, but Dr. Howard turned a stiff back, his lips tightening with suppressed anger.

The rider's gaze sharpened as he looked Carleton up and down. "We'd heard some rumor of your return, sir—in uniform this time. I can't say I approve the change, but it appears to suit you."

"Mr. Revere," Carleton returned as though their meeting were unremarkable. "Your business must be urgent to call you out on the Sabbath. I trust you'll convey my respects to Dr. Warren, Mr. Adams, and Mr. Hancock."

"They'll be delighted to receive them." Resettling his hat on his head, the silversmith bowed himself off.

Elizabeth and the others listened to their exchange with astonishment. As soon as Revere disappeared in the direction of the town gates, Elizabeth demanded, "And how do you know Mr. Revere—not to mention his famous associates?"

"Sir Harry and I did some business with Revere and Hancock from time to time. I have a number of Revere's pieces at Thornlea, in fact. As for the others . . . " He shrugged. "I lived in Boston for several years, and our paths inevitably crossed."

"So that's Paul Revere!" Andrews exclaimed. "His name was brought up several times in our briefings yesterday. I must say, he appears very mild for his reputation."

Cutting off further discussion, Mrs. Howard led the way into the church. The expansive sanctuary with its high, darkly gleaming box pews and graceful galleries was alive with the rustle of bright fabrics and the murmur of hushed greetings, although even on this high holy day no more than half the pews were filled. Reverend Mather Byles, Jr., one of the few Loyalist clergymen left in the colony, presided over the pulpit. At a time when the majority of ministers preached openly against British policies, his outspoken views in favor of the crown had become a lightning rod for the townspeople's resentment, and the congregation showed a steady decline.

Yet as Elizabeth followed her family up the central aisle toward the front, Abby's hand tucked in hers, a sense of deep peace filled her as it always did. At the door of their pew she looked around to make sure Andrews and Carleton followed, and as she turned, her gaze fell on the pew that belonged to General Gage and his family.

The sense of peace and safety shattered at once. The Gages were faithful in their attendance, but this morning their seats remained empty.

HER ELEGANT ATTIRE providing striking contrast to her garb on the previous day, Tess joined them for dinner, as was her custom each Sunday. Pleading the convenience of attending her own parish church within walking distance of her home, she continued to attend Roxbury's First Church, covertly enjoying the minister's fiery preaching against the policies of the crown while pretending to object to his views. It was a constant irritation to her brother, one he once again gently chided her for during the meal.

As they rose from the table, Tess apologized to Carleton. "You'll have to forgive us, major. We colonists do cling stubbornly to our provincialism and the habits of years. You're an oddity in having traveled so widely and experienced so much of the world.

Carleton moved to pull back Elizabeth's chair before Andrews had time to get to his feet. "Sir Harry's business took him to all the major ports on this continent as well as in Europe. It was a better education than sitting in a classroom."

Leading the way into the drawing room, Mrs. Howard shooed Abby off to play. Pouting, the child walked with dragging feet toward the door, but when Carleton grinned and winked at her, she giggled and skipped outside.

Normally Abby kept her distance from the officers her father invited to Stony Hill, but she had taken an instant liking to Carleton and Andrews, with Carleton quickly becoming her favorite confidante. She had insisted on being seated between the two officers and on serving them from the generously filled bowls and platters. Carleton had brushed off her mother's remonstrances and entered into the child's play with an unforced good nature that convinced Elizabeth he found genuine enjoyment in the company of children.

Watching him now as he went to join her father by the fireplace, she couldn't help smiling at the thought of the attractive scene he and Abby had made at dinner, the officer's blond head bent to the child's as they laughed over a secret. Reluctantly she admitted that Will had been right in his advice to guard her heart. The more contact they had, the more she realized just how difficult it was going to be to heed her cousin's warning.

Throughout dinner Carleton had entertained them with humorous stories of his travels throughout the colonies and abroad. Now, as Andrews joined the two men, he urged, "Tell them about your adventures among the Indians when you were a boy, Jon."

"Sir Harry took you among the savages?" Dr. Howard exclaimed.

After a brief hesitation, Carleton admitted with perceptible reluctance, "I assure you, my encounters with the Indian tribes were initially without Sir Harry's knowledge or consent."

Tess settled herself on the sofa. "You mean you just strolled off alone into the wilderness without anyone finding out?"

"Well . . . I was supposed to be hunting with friends, but somehow I always managed to get lost."

Mrs. Howard shook her head incredulously, but Elizabeth considered Carleton with renewed interest. It was beginning to dawn on her what attracted her to him. She noted that Tess appeared equally intrigued.

The doctor poured brandy for both officers and himself. "Dangerous business, I should think, what with the Seven Years War raging and most of the tribes allied with the French."

"*Mais pour tous ils ont su, j'étais français,*" Carleton responded with a smile.

Doctor Howard chuckled. "And you didn't bother to inform them of your English parentage."

Carleton raised an eyebrow. "Ah, but that's only on my father's side, dear sir."

Andrews took a sip of his drink. "I'd say the lust for adventure runs on both sides of your family tree. Didn't Sir Harry fight in the rebellion of the Scottish clans at Sheriffmuir in 1715 when he was just a lad? I've heard that following their defeat he found it advisable to seek his fortune in the colonies and that your father subsequently became a staunch supporter of the Tories and George II to save your family from ruin."

"Oho!" Tess exclaimed. "Sir Harry was a rebel, eh?"

"The experience taught my uncle the futility of youthful idealism. As a result, he turned his talents to making a handsome profit at the expense of his former enemies. A much more agreeable and less dangerous occupation than waging war."

"How extremely cynical." Elizabeth plopped herself without ceremony on a footstool, her elbows on her knees, her petticoats billowing around her.

Leaning against the mantelpiece, Carleton returned her challenging gaze with a mild one. "When you reach my advanced antiquity, *enfant,* you come to realize that cynicism has definite advantages."

"There's nothing wrong with a man looking after his own interests," Dr. Howard pointed out.

"Everyone for himself, and the Exchequer for us all," Andrews noted, giving a short laugh as he strolled over to claim the chair behind Elizabeth's footstool.

Dr. Howard frowned. "You've been in the colonies too long, Charles. You're beginning to sound like those infernal rebels."

"I can't say I totally disagree with them."

"Be careful of their rhetoric," the doctor advised, "or you'll end up like my brother-in-law, an active and tireless champion of insurrection. Here is a man of prominent family who was given every advantage wealth and education can provide. And what did he make of it? Why, sirs, he threw over a promising law practice to become the proprietor of an unprofitable tavern in the insignificant hamlet of Lincoln so he could become a colonel of their militia and join the Sons of Liberty."

Elizabeth threw a swift glance at her mother, a familiar irritation shooting through her at sight of Mrs. Howard's head bent over her embroidery. They had been close until Elizabeth's ill-fated betrothal to Hutchins, which her mother had so eagerly pursued. The unhappy end of the relationship had driven a wedge between them, and so often now, where her mother was concerned, Elizabeth felt annoyance—and something more: the uncomfortable, subtle rivalry between a mother and grown daughter living in the same household.

Did she feel nothing when her husband criticized her brother, or was she simply too timid to defend him? She had not objected when Dr. Howard cut off all contact between the two families. Most of the time she acted as though nothing in the world existed outside her home, husband, and children. Even the political conflict that was tearing the colony apart did not seem to concern her apart from how it affected them. And currently her greatest preoccupation seemed to be to get Elizabeth married.

When Elizabeth opened her mouth to protest, Tess's warning look and the slight shake of her head stopped her.

With an abrupt movement, Andrews sprang to his feet and took a restless turn around the room. "I admit before coming here I saw the issues as black and white. But I can't anymore. The colonies have brought too many grievances before the king over the last two decades, and they've received no relief."

"I don't deny there are legitimate grievances," Dr. Howard answered, his tone stiff. "But in the end we have no choice except to submit to our legally and divinely appointed government."

"Why, I'd refuse to live under such oppression!" the lieutenant exploded. "You're denied trial by jury, homes and businesses are searched without warrant, and goods are seized without the possibility of appeal. You're forced to quarter in your own homes the very soldiers sent to oppress you. Why, there's not an Englishman on earth who'd submit his neck to such a yoke!"

A triumphant look passed between Elizabeth and Tess, while an angry flush darkened the doctor's face. Finding a vacant chair, Carleton slouched into it.

"I apologize for my young friend's rashness. The effect of too much youth . . . and too much brandy."

"You, of all of us—"

Carleton's wintry stare cut the lieutenant off. Gritting his teeth, Andrews struggled to contain his emotions.

"When we were in Richmond a few weeks ago, I noticed you listened with considerable interest and no protest to Mr. Henry's defense of his resolutions to strengthen Virginia's militia."

Elizabeth sat bolt upright, almost tumbling from the footstool. Turning pale, Dr. Howard swung to face Carleton.

"You don't mean Patrick Henry?"

Carleton regarded him with amusement. "I thought Charles should have the chance to hear a real orator. Whatever Mr. Henry's opinions, there isn't his like in either England or France."

"By the time he finished, I swear I had a hard time restraining the urge to take up arms myself," Andrews agreed with fervor. "I'm as loyal to England as any of you, but the fact is that all the pleas for justice the colonies have brought before the king have been ignored or denied outright."

Tight-lipped, Dr. Howard folded his arms across his chest. "Forgive me if I feel it a disgrace to your uniform to be seen at such an infamous affair."

"My dear sir, we weren't in uniform, but if we had been, we would have been in good company," Carleton protested. "The audience was liberally tinged with scarlet."

Partially mollified, the doctor conceded, "Well, I suppose it's useful to know what one's enemies are about. So what was Mr. Henry's theme this time? The same old lyric sung to a new tune, I trust."

"As I recall, he ended with the words 'Give me liberty or give me death.' "

"A fate I pray he may meet without delay."

"Are you acquainted with Mr. Henry?" Tess was unable to hide her eagerness.

Again Carleton hesitated before admitting, "Yes, I am."

"And what is your opinion of him?"

"That he's an outstanding demagogue."

"I'm surprised to hear you say so," Andrews cut in acidly, "considering that your relations with him appeared to be excessively cordial."

Carleton turned a level gaze on the lieutenant. "I don't recall expressing any opinion of him to *you* one way or the other."

A hot flush crept up Andrews's neck. "I seem to remember several occasions on which the two of you were closeted alone at some length."

At the others' questioning looks, Carleton answered, "My meetings with Mr. Henry were never secret. He was the executor of Sir Harry's estate, so I could hardly avoid dealing with him."

The answer, which appeared to satisfy her father, intensified Elizabeth's interest. Before she could ask any further questions, however, Carleton made an impatient gesture.

"Forgive me. I'm afraid politics is a subject I have little interest in and less knowledge of."

"But you grew up in these colonies," Dr. Howard insisted. "You own property here, you have wide contacts. You must hold your own private opinions about these issues."

Carleton shrugged. "As long as a government exists, its subjects owe obedience to its laws."

"If that's true, then unjust laws are written in stone, and the power of government can never be checked."

There was more of despair in Elizabeth's tone than she wished to reveal, and it drew Carleton's keen glance, though he made no reply. His face animated, Dr. Howard answered as though he had not heard her.

"Exactly right. If the colonies were to realize their foolish goal of independence, the result would be anarchy!"

"But, Papa, aren't they already governing themselves—and quite well, it appears—through the various provincial congresses and the Continental Congress?"

Once more Elizabeth became aware of Carleton's interested scrutiny. He was thoughtfully stroking his chin, his smile half hidden by his hand. Everyone else in the room stared at her as though she had taken leave of her senses, and Tess had gone completely white.

Yawning, Carleton stretched his long legs in front of him. "My observation has been that most young ladies wisely adopt the charming habit of leaving the dull business of politics to men. As a consequence they generally live longer and more agreeable lives."

The others laughed, and the tension in the room was relieved. Although Elizabeth seethed inwardly, she forced herself to give

Carleton a sweet smile.

"I'm sure we've all had enough of politics for one day. If I remember correctly, you did challenge me to a race, major."

The change of subject was agreeable to everyone except Mrs. Howard, whose objections had no effect on the general interest in the contest. In the end she was forced to give in to the inevitable, and Elizabeth hurried upstairs to change into a riding habit.

The temptation to don the breeches hidden beneath the false floor of her trunk almost overcame her, but there was no question of her transgressing propriety that far. She compromised by pulling on the riding boots under her moss green riding habit. As she walked out to the paddock, she couldn't help giggling at the thought of the others' expressions if she did appear in masculine dress. But since, hampered by petticoats, she would give Carleton enough of an advantage, she decided to ride astride instead of sidesaddle regardless of her mother's protests or whether the petticoat of her habit was full enough to ensure proper modesty.

Leaning on the top rail of the paddock fence, Carleton turned at her approach to look her boldly up and down. "You're going to find that petticoat a deuced nuisance. If I were you, I'd wear breeches."

She colored then laughed. "I was sorely tempted," she admitted as she poked a stray curl back into the chignon that bound her thick hair, "but I thought it wiser to resist any further mischief."

He grinned. "I'd be glad to lend you a pair. Start a new style."

She stuck out her tongue at him. "Mother would never recover from an indiscretion of that magnitude. I'm wearing riding boots, though. See." She pulled up the hem of her petticoat to show him. "And I'm not riding sidesaddle."

"Good girl."

Just then Elizabeth's mare charged out of the stable, satin coat gleaming, long, silky mane and tail rippling in the light breeze. Lifting her small, fine head with a snort as she caught wind of the stallion, she half reared then came down to tear at the turf with her hooves.

Carleton let out a low whistle. "She's a beauty! And fast, too, I'll wager. It looks like Devil has his work cut out for him."

Elizabeth laughed, pleased. While Isaiah saddled the mare, they walked the course she had chosen. After returning to the paddock, Carleton adjusted the stallion's saddle girth and shortened the stirrups. Removing his sabre and uniform coat, he swung into the saddle.

In shirtsleeves and waistcoat, he seemed younger, his body charged with tension. Vexed by the sudden turmoil of her emotions, Elizabeth forced herself to concentrate on her own preparations.

The mare's girth was sufficiently tight, the stirrups shortened to the length she preferred for her secret nighttime rides. Without waiting for assistance from Isaiah, she was astride in a flash of petticoats, pretending not to see her mother's tight-lipped disapproval.

It was obvious Isaiah had his own misgivings about the contest. For a moment he paused beside her, his hand on the ankle of her boot as he gave her a warning frown.

"This be foolishness," he said in a low tone. "Make sure you lose."

"Nonsense," she answered airily. "I have every intention of winning."

Approaching them, Tess overheard their exchange. As Isaiah stalked off, she took hold of the mare's bridle, amusement and concern mingling on her face.

"Isaiah makes a good point," she murmured. "Don't press this too far or you'll reveal more than you ought."

Elizabeth tossed her head, the familiar thrill of anticipation boiling in her veins. "Let the best man—or woman—win."

Dr. Howard had brought along a pistol from his collection. He handed it to Andrews, who drew a line in the dirt, then climbed astride the fence rails at the corner of the paddock.

Elizabeth brought her mare to the line alongside Carleton's bay, returning a frown to his confident grin. At the pistol's report, both horses leaped forward.

They charged up the sloping path through the lush meadow grass and in seconds were in the trees. Where the path narrowed the stallion muscled his way past her mare. Elizabeth ducked to avoid the slapping branches of the scrub pines that crowded close on either side, several times came close to being torn from the saddle. But she clung to the mare's back like a burr, keeping her eyes on Carleton just ahead of her.

Bent close to the bay's neck, he guided him to the shortest path around each obstacle. There was no need for her to direct her own mount. The mare knew each foot of ground and would have strained to overtake the bay even on the upward slope if Elizabeth hadn't kept a firm hand on the reins.

The blackened, mossy trunk of a fallen pine materialized in front of them, and both horses tore over it without urging. Seeming tireless, the bay lengthened his stride still more on the level.

Within a short distance, the jagged remains of a stone wall loomed up. The bay was over, then the black, hard on his heels, dirt and decayed leaves spraying from their hooves as they landed on the other side. They lunged into the first turn, treacherously close, their mounts' lather-streaked flanks all but touching. Pulling abreast of the bay, Elizabeth caught a glimpse of Carleton's face, white and intense, his jaw set in a determined line.

The marshes were a blur off to the left as they rounded the last turn and plummeted back down the slope toward the stable, invisible below them on the other side of the trees. The next jump was the most danger-ous, a high, tangled windfall on the other side of which the ground sloped treacherously. Stallion and mare flew over it side by side, but the stallion stumbled on landing, and the black shot like a rocket through the fringe of trees, a half length in the lead as they burst onto the meadow.

The paddock fence in the hollow below was a white streak sweeping irresistibly closer. Then without warning, where the path narrowed to pass between two low outcroppings of rock, Carleton brought the bay stampeding around her, cutting so close to the mare that his knee ground into Elizabeth's thigh.

There was no time to calculate the risk. As they brushed together, mad excitement exploded in Elizabeth's breast, and with a cry, she drove her mount recklessly into that narrow, closing space.

One of them had to give way if they were to avoid a disastrous collision. At the last instant, Carleton jerked hard on the reins. The bay faltered for no more than a fraction of a second, but it was enough.

Streaming past the paddock fence like quicksilver, they sent the watchers scattering out of their path, their shouts inaudible in the thunder of their charge as neck and neck they rounded the corner where Andrews teetered precariously on the top rail, whooping and waving the pistol above his head.

It wasn't until they were well beyond the stable that they managed to bring their mounts to a trot. Elizabeth's cheeks were flaming, her bosom heaving in shallow pants. With trembling hands she pushed her windblown curls out of her face, realizing only then that her chignon must have been dragged off her head by the low-hanging branches.

Carleton brought the bay around in a tight circle and threw a questioning glance at Andrews. They had been so close at the end that neither was certain who had crossed the line first.

With a triumphant whoop, Andrews shouted, "Night Mare by a nose!"

Trying to read the conflicting emotions that passed over Carleton's face, Elizabeth wondered what he would do. To her surprise, he rode over to her and took her hand. As he gazed at her, a light came into his eyes, then his fingers tightened over hers, and he bent to kiss them.

"Both Night Mare and her owner possess the heart of a lioness," he murmured. "You deserve the triumph."

She laughed up at him, for the first time liking him unreservedly.

Chapter Nine

"IF THESE FIGURES ARE ACCURATE, the rebels have managed to put together a substantial arsenal."

Looking up from the papers he was holding, Carleton stared through the window of General Gage's office. It was early Monday morning, and a cold wind blew a misty rain against the panes. Outside, the trees and gardens on the lawn appeared distorted and colorless, reflecting his emotions.

"Our sources are quite reliable."

Carleton transferred his gaze to the general. "Colonel Smith mentioned you're employing some of the patriots' own people to spy for you."

"That's right, though I'd have preferred to keep those contacts a secret," Gage replied.

"That's not easy to do around here. At any rate, it occurred to me they may also be the source of some of the intelligence that's leaking out of Boston."

Gage stared at the younger officer. "What do you mean?"

"How do you know these spies are trustworthy? If they're selling out their own people, why would they be loyal to England?"

"They both have impeccable credentials," Gage insisted. "And as you can see, their reports are in general agreement."

Then there are only two, Carleton thought. "That wouldn't be surprising, if they were working together. How do you communicate with them?"

"They come here—secretly, of course."

"So they pass in and out of Boston, they have access to Province House, they see and hear a great deal of what goes on."

Gage got to his feet to take a restless turn around the room. Carleton followed his movements, his gaze brooding.

"How can you be certain this information is accurate?" he asked. "Their purpose might be to lure us into a trap. It's even possible they're selling intelligence to both sides."

Gage turned perceptibly pale. "You've raised some disturbing questions." He thought for a moment, then said, "With your knowledge of the people and the area, you'd be able to move around in disguise without arousing suspicion, unlike the other officers I've sent out. After the march to Concord, I want you to pursue this, find out what kind of game these agents are playing and whether the intelligence they've provided checks out."

"I'll need their names."

"You'll have them, but for the moment we have more pressing concerns to deal with. If the weather cooperates, I'm going to order Smith to move out late tomorrow night, so for the time being I want you to stay available. Hugh asked to have you attached to his relief column, but I'm more inclined to send you with Smith and Pitcairn.

"Once this mission is accomplished, however, I'll expect you to actively pursue this assignment. Now what ideas do you have about capturing Oriole?"

Carleton stared down at the reports, careful not to show his disappointment. "On his own turf he has a thousand routes and dodges by which to slip through our fingers," he said, feeling his way. "However, if we present him with a piece of bait that's tempting enough, he'll walk straight into our hands. It'll take some thought to set up an irresistible lure, but I'll work on that angle. First I want to talk to the men who almost captured him the other night. They might have noticed some small detail that could help us identify him."

Gage eagerly agreed, but reminded Carleton to hold off on taking any action for the time being. Directing him to confer with Smith and Pitcairn about preparations for the march to Concord, the general dismissed him.

✳ ✳ ✳

SHIVERING, ELIZABETH THREW AN APPREHENSIVE GLANCE up Cornhill Street. The morning was dreary and lowering. Rain clouds hung over the dripping roofs of the shops, and a numbing, damp wind blew in off the sea. The few pedestrians on the street moved along without lingering, hooded and cloaked against the chill.

Overhead, the sign above the London Bookstore swung back and forth on its brackets with a dismal screech. Pulling the door open, Elizabeth stepped gratefully into the shop's warmth and pushed back the hood of her cloak.

Behind the counter, Henry Knox, the rotund proprietor of the establishment, was waiting on his customers with the genial attentiveness that had made his bookstore a fashionable meeting place for the young ladies of Boston and the British officers who made a habit of congregating there. Although he didn't make a secret of his patriot sympathies, neither did he wear them on his sleeve, and his recent marriage to the daughter of the former royal secretary of the province hadn't hurt his business. Everyone seemed to like and trust young Mr. Knox.

As usual, the shop's cluttered interior was crowded with red coats. At the front counter several officers were engaged in a good-humored argument over a partially unrolled map on which they furiously scribbled diagrams. Among them Elizabeth recognized Lieutenant William Grant, senior officer of the Royal Artillery. An almost daily visitor to the shop, he delighted in arguing points of theory with Knox, who was a serious student of gunnery. With him was Captain John Montresor of the Engineers, while Captain Laurie of the Forty-third and Captain Evelyn of the King's Own made up an amused and vocal audience to the debate.

Unhindered by the hand shattered in a gunning accident, which he kept wound in a white silk scarf, Knox stood at the other end of the counter wrapping the order of an elegantly dressed man whose back was to Elizabeth. Even so, she recognized Knox's customer before he turned around. As he strode in her direction, swinging his stout walking stick by its solid brass knob, the soldiers followed his broad shoulders to the door with stares that were, without exception, hostile.

There was nothing in the doctor's handsome, open countenance that would have indicated any reason for the soldiers' animosity. Everything about him, from his fine, black suit and silver-embroidered waistcoat to his flawlessly dressed tie wig, identified him as a man of culture and refinement.

There was about Dr. Joseph Warren, in the thirty-fourth year of his life, an immensely attractive vitality, a physical and mental energy that seemed to leap from his sturdy frame to engulf everyone he encountered, friend and foe alike. The most powerful patriot leader in Massachusetts with the possible exception of Samuel Adams, the foremost physician in the area as well, he had proven to be a formidable adversary in a fight, a compelling orator, and a propagandist who by instinct went for the jugular.

He was the close friend and mentor of Paul Revere and the unsuspected motive force behind Boston's unruly mobs. Since the death of his young wife two years earlier, he had given himself to the patriot cause with even greater intensity. First as a member of the Boston Committee of Correspondence, then as chairman of the provincial Committee of Safety, a member in addition of every important committee of the Provincial Congress, he had become the prime maker and effecter of policy throughout the colony.

As the primary author of the Suffolk Resolves the previous fall, he had urged armed resistance to Parliament's intolerable policies at a time when few of the patriot leaders except Patrick Henry in Virginia had recognized that this was the last recourse that remained to the colonies. That document had shaken the very roots of the First Continental Congress and drawn the unfavorable attention of the British establishment. Along with Adams and Hancock, Warren's name headed the list of subversives Gage was empowered to arrest at his discretion and ship off to England for trial. Yet Warren continued to move fearlessly in and out of Boston, so far unhindered by the British general.

As he came toward her, Elizabeth stepped out of his path. Since he was known by sight to most of Boston, Whig or Tory, he and Elizabeth avoided public contact of any kind. But this morning he came to a deliberate halt where he blocked her path.

"Miss Howard! It's been a long time since I've had the honor," he said in a voice that carried to the rear of the shop.

Looking up into his laughing blue eyes, she was hard pressed to keep her tone and manner frosty. "Not long enough, sir."

She fixed her gaze on a point behind his shoulder as though he were invisible. His genial smile broadened to a grin.

"You're looking exceptionally well, if you'll allow me the liberty of saying so."

It was all she could do to keep from laughing back at him, and she shot him a suspicious look. The officers at the counter nudged each other and exchanged meaningful glances, their interest in the proceedings keen. It occurred to her to wonder if Warren had planned this scene for the benefit of the onlookers.

She gave him a discouraging frown. "I'm not inclined to allow you that liberty or any other, sir. If it were up to me, you'd be cooling your heels in gaol."

The officers guffawed. Holding her petticoats as though contact with him would sully them, Elizabeth moved to step around Warren. He gave her a surreptitious wink and touched his fingers to his hat.

"A pleasant day to you too, Miss Howard." His smile rueful, he started out the door.

At that moment the threshold was blocked by a burly grenadier coming through in the opposite direction. Recognizing the doctor, the man attempted to force his way past, his shoulder gouging into Warren's.

Warren neither flinched nor moved aside. Immovable as a brick wall, he continued along his path as though the taller, heavier soldier were of no more consequence than a flea. A deft, apparently accidental movement of his elbow and forearm knocked the grenadier off balance and shoved him into the door jamb.

The grenadier regained his footing with a grunt of fury. His swarthy face contorted with hate, he whirled to face the doctor, his fist clenched and drawn back.

Warren measured his adversary with a level gaze, the light in his eyes daring him to attempt the blow. At the same time, his hand tightened noticeably around his walking stick. As sturdy as a shillelagh, it would clearly be a devastating weapon in a determined hand. And there was no hand more determined than the good doctor's.

For a tense moment the grenadier weighed his odds, then sullenly swung away. With a smile and a shrug Warren stepped out into the street and strolled out of sight, the mockingly whistled notes of "Yankee Doodle" lingering on the air behind him. Elizabeth let out her breath and went to join the officers clustered at the counter.

"The devil take that scoundrel and all his seditious friends to perdition!" fumed Captain Laurie. "I can't think of any employment I'd like better than to face the rascals on a battlefield."

Elizabeth shook droplets of rain from her cloak. "If the rumors I've been hearing are accurate, you'll soon have the opportunity to do just that."

"In which case we'll be treated to an excellent view of the ruffians' hindquarters as they disappear over the nearest hill," snickered Lieutenant Grant.

"You don't think they might stand and fight like men?"

"Don't worry about that," Captain Evelyn comforted her. "Those villains are the most absolute cowards on the face of the earth."

She allowed her glance to drift to the scowling grenadier who leaned on the opposite end of the counter. "As our friend over there can attest." Before any of them could respond, she went on in a plaintive voice, "But I do hope you're right. I can't bear to think that any of you might get hurt if His Excellency were to send you to Concord or some such dismal place."

They hastened to reassure her, and by degrees she brought them around to a discussion of the proposed maneuvers. They were all certain that, if not tomorrow, then by the next day at the latest, the grenadier and light infantry companies would be on the march, with Concord as the most likely goal.

Concluding that the officers still had no hard facts to offer, she excused herself. Knox was harder to dislodge, but she assured him she knew what she was looking for and took refuge behind a high bookshelf at the rear of the shop until he and his customers were again absorbed in their diagrams.

"Gentlemen, I disagree," she heard Knox say. "You've forgotten Dorchester Heights. If I place my batteries here, Boston becomes untenable."

Lieutenant Grant laughed. "But, Henry, you don't have any artillery that's heavy enough or that has a long enough range."

"Not yet," Knox reflected. "But you never know what might turn up."

Biting her lip to keep from laughing out loud, Elizabeth slipped between the rows of shelves at the back of the shop. In its usual place on a top shelf in the far corner, she found the small volume of poetry through which she and Warren had passed countless messages over the past months. Tiptoeing, she reached to pull it down.

"Here, let me get that for you."

She jumped as a hand went over hers to pull down the book. Whirling round, she found herself face to face with Carleton.

"Where have you been lurking?" she demanded, annoyed. "I didn't see you when I came in."

"I prefer it that way. You learn more."

"I didn't realize you'd taken up spying. It seems Colonel Smith underestimated your talent in that regard."

He raised an eyebrow at the coolness of her tone. "Did that little run-in with Dr. Warren put you in a bad mood, or did you get up on the wrong side of the bed this morning?" he inquired solicitously.

"Don't tell me you know Dr. Warren too."

"He treated me for a concussion once when I was thrown from my horse during a race."

"Well, it doesn't appear to have daunted you. And, by the way, how many other questionable associations do you have besides Dr. Warren, Paul Revere, and Patrick Henry?"

"As many, I would guess, as you do."

She studied him, frowning. He couldn't have helped overhearing her probing conversation with his fellow officers. Worse, he might have seen the conspiratorial wink Warren had given her.

"I apologize for my ill humor," she said with as much sincerity as she could muster. "I think you're right about Dr. Warren. I can't bear the man's smug attitude."

He gave her the searching look she was beginning to dread. Then he glanced down and noticed the book he still held. Before she could stop him, he opened it. As he scanned the first page, his expression softened.

"Love poems," he murmured. "Do you have anyone specific in mind?"

In a panic she grabbed the slender volume out of his hand. "Forgive me, major, but I'm in a bit of a hurry. There's an errand I promised to take care of, and I'm late."

"Being in a rush seems to be a chronic condition with you," he complained, but he returned her smile and ushered her back to the front of the shop without further protest.

She had no option but to buy the book. While Knox wrapped it, she exchanged pleasantries with him, but her mind was on Carleton's conversation with Montresor and Grant.

Bending over their diagrams, Carleton made several additions and corrections to Knox's notations. "As I recall, Foster Hill up on Dorchester Heights should give the right elevation," he said, marking the spot. "If you placed a battery of twenty-four pounders there, you could take out the *Somerset* at her current position."

Montresor gave a nervous laugh. "That's getting a tad close for comfort, isn't it, old boy. No use giving the rebels too much of a hand, eh?"

"Anything else you can think of, major?" Knox intervened happily. "We'll take all the help we can get."

Halfway between amusement and vexation, Elizabeth tapped her foot. "Faith, sir, is there no subject you aren't an expert in?"

"Just one," Carleton returned, looking up. "The mind of a woman."

The other officers grinned, and even Elizabeth couldn't resist a smile. Taking the package from Knox, she allowed Carleton to accompany her outside.

As he helped her into the phaeton, he said pleasantly, "I do hope you won't be late taking care of your urgent business. Please give my regards to your family."

Gritting her teeth, she wave good-bye. But when the phaeton turned the corner out of his sight, she sank back into her seat, overcome by annoyance and another emotion that left her strangely uncomfortable.

Alone in her room at last, she tore the wrapping from the small book and flipped it open to page ninety-nine. A folded scrap of paper had been stuck between the pages. Thin as tissue, it was yellowed with age, stained with damp, and wrinkled as though it had been crumpled to be thrown away. On its surface, a bold hand had copied the first few lines of the sonnet at the head of the page.

Her hands shaking, she lit a candle, smoothed the scrap, and held it close to the flame. As the paper began to warm, other words emerged between the written lines, the ink so faint they were barely legible. To her practiced eye, however, the words leapt off the page.

11:00 p.m. Brindley's Meadow lone elm above Stony Brook.

When she was certain of the message, she touched the fragment to the flame. It began to scorch and curl, then a blue tongue leaped upward toward her fingers. Dropping the burning paper among the embers in the fireplace, she watched until it had crumbled into fine ash indistinguishable from the rest.

THAT NIGHT AFTER EVERYONE HAD GONE TO BED and silence wrapped the dark house, Elizabeth donned her disguise and slipped outside. Stealthily crossing the dewy lawn, she crept past the stable where Night Mare waited already saddled. Behind it, she found the steep, hidden path to the meadow below Stony Hill.

There was no sign of movement as far as she could see. Staying low to reduce her visibility, she hurried toward where the marsh encroached upon the solid ground, feeling her way through the shadows. At the top of a slight rise fifty yards beyond her, the great elm stood alone a dozen paces back from the edge of the marsh, the black webwork of its branches barely visible against the clouded sky.

Every sense heightened, she crouched motionless for long moments behind a bank of scrub brush. But no matter how intently she searched the far reaches of the indistinct landscape, shivering in the damp cold, all she could hear was the sigh of the wind.

Softly she whistled the clear, sweet song of the oriole. Once. Twice.

Of a sudden she sensed that someone passed near her. Whirling around, startled, she squinted into the night, but she saw nothing. When she glanced back at the elm, she made out the darker shadow of a figure where there had been none before, leaning against the flat, black line that was the elm's trunk. At the same moment, the soft, answering notes of the oriole's call reached her from beneath its branches.

Patriot.

A chill went through her. Where had he come from? It was as though he had risen out of the earth.

She approached with caution. In spite of her attempt at stealth, her boots made soft squelching noises in the mud. As she came up the slope the shadow straightened, and even in the almost complete darkness she could feel the tension in the dim figure.

He was muffled from chin to mid calf in what seemed to be a voluminous great-coat. The wide brim of his slouch hat threw his features into even deeper shadow.

It was impossible to make out any details except that he was tall, though stoop-shouldered. She had the impression he was middle-aged or older. When he came toward her, he moved stiffly, dragging one leg as though it was crippled. Slightly more than a yard away, he halted.

"You're bloody late," he growled. "You've kept me waiting."

His voice was low, raspy. She could detect nothing familiar in it. He spoke with a strange accent, and while she did not recognize that either, there was no mistaking the curt arrogance of his tone.

"I was told eleven o'clock." She kept her voice flat, deeper than normal.

He waved her protest away, thrust a thin, tightly wrapped packet into her hands. "Just see you deliver these safely into the right hands."

"I ain't never failed o' that, sir."

Without answering, he turned and limped back up the rise, where he melted into the deeper shadows under the elm. Impulse drew her several steps after him, but it was already impossible to make out his form against the gloom. For a moment she hesitated.

It occurred to her that any attempt to determine his identity would give him the same opportunity in regard to her. Thinking better of the impulse, she returned to the scrub growth where she had first hidden.

She studied the brow of the wooded heights that beetled out over the meadow some distance inland. By daylight the roof of Tess Howard's barn was visible from where she crouched, but in the dark-

ness the headlands were a uniform smudge of indistinguishable char-
coal bulges.

No sound reached her, nor was there any further sign of life. After
waiting for some minutes she made her way back to the faint path that
led to the stable at the top of Stony Hill.

She reached her uncle's tavern in Lincoln shortly after midnight.
Unwrapping the packet Elizabeth handed him, Stern scanned the papers
inside, his expression becoming grim. "Just as we suspected. They're
going to move tomorrow night, unless it rains. Gage's objective is the
militia stores at Concord. Grenadiers and light infantry will be under
Smith and Pitcairn—they'll cross the Charles once it's full dark. Mitchell
is to ride out with a detachment early in the day to make sure no couriers get through, so we'll need to be on the lookout."

Will's eyes narrowed. "Effectives of the flank companies should add
up to around eight hundred men. That's a large enough force to justify
our calling out the militia."

Stern shuffled through the papers as Elizabeth watched over his
shoulder. "According to Patriot, Gage knows almost to the last musket
ball how much munitions we're storing, and his spies have provided him
a map of the town on which they've marked where they're hidden."

"Thank God Barrett's men have been hard at work all day moving
everything to a safe location," Will broke in. "By the time Smith arrives
most of our supplies should be secured."

"Was Patriot able to find out who these spies are?" asked Levi.
"They must be high up in our organization."

Stern shook his head. "He doesn't mention them." He swung to face
Elizabeth. "How available are you going to be the next few days?"

"I'm staying with Aunt Tess from tonight on through the end of the
week, supposedly to help with her spring cleaning. So I'll be able to
move in and out of Boston as needed. I'll keep an eye on things and
alert Warren at the first sign the Regulars are starting to move."

They were silent for a moment. "Well," Stern said at length, "all we can do now is watch and wait."

Will tipped his chair back against the wall, his hands behind his head, his intent gaze resting on Elizabeth. "By the way, how is my old friend?"

"Quite as you remember him, only more so. Your Jonathan Carleton has to be the most insufferable, annoying, exasperating man I've ever met. Gage has already promoted him to major, if that tells you anything. I haven't been able to get a thing out of him, and I doubt he's going to be of any use to us at all."

Will regarded her with a wry expression, but before he could reply, his father handed Patriot's report to him and got to his feet. "You'd better head home and get as much sleep as you can," he said to Elizabeth. "I suspect you'll be doing some hard riding before this is all over."

Levi accompanied her outside, his hands stuck deep in his pockets, his shoulders hunched against the bite of the wind.

"I hear your company elected you lieutenant," she ventured as she unwound the black's reins from the rail.

Levi reddened. "I had in mind to turn it down, what with Will bein' captain and Pa colonel."

"The men voted for you because they like and trust you. You'll make a fine officer."

"Sometimes I wonder if I'll ever amount to anything. Pa's made it clear he has his doubts."

"Levi—"

"Well, it's true!" the youth cut in with some heat. "He's always pinned his hopes on Will 'cause he's so perfect."

"Will's older than you are. He's had time to prove himself, and you haven't. Give yourself a chance."

Levi shrugged. "You're the same age as me, and look at all you've done. And you're a girl."

"Exactly. In my line of work, that's an advantage." Laying her hand on his arm, she added, "I know your father loves both his sons equally. He just doesn't express his feelings very well, and he's been preoccupied, as all of us have. Besides, Will can whip you into shape if anyone can," she added, smiling.

Levi gritted his teeth. "He's givin' it his best shot. If he keeps on lordin' it over me like he has been, I swear one of these fine days we're goin' to have it out."

"Will's a good officer, better than the majority of the redcoats I know. We need more like him. Heed what he's trying to teach you just in case we end up in a war."

She mounted and reached to grasp his hand. "I'm glad you're going to be at his side when we face up to the Regulars. I know you'll keep a cool head, and so does he."

She was rewarded with his reluctant smile. Squeezing her hand, Levi released it and waved her off into the night.

Chapter Ten

IT WAS SHORTLY AFTER ELEVEN Tuesday morning when Carleton finished his meeting with Pitcairn and came down the steps of the North End warehouse that served as headquarters and barracks for the marine battalions. The air was still cold, but the sky was cloudless, and the sun warmed the muddy cobbles and the worn bricks of the buildings.

Although the day seemed deceptively peaceful, there was no mistaking the tense expectancy that gripped the town this quiet April 18th. Lost in thought, he pulled the bay's reins free from the hitching post. Before he could mount, however, Major Mitchell rode up and drew to a halt beside him.

"I've prevailed on Gage to send you along with me. We're off on patrol right away."

Carleton hesitated. "I'll need to stop by my billet for my pistols."

"Andrews is coming with us and he's bringing your weapons. Let's get moving—we're due to meet the rest of the detachment at the fort before noon."

While he was still speaking, a thin, ragged youth wearing a battered hat with a floppy brim and carrying an oversized wooden bucket came toward them down the street. "Oystahs! Fresh oystahs! Git yer oystahs!" he called.

Mitchell waved him off with a growl. "We've no need of your wares today."

Whistling cheerfully, the youth continued on his way. Carleton watched him, frowning, until he turned the corner at the next street and passed out of their sight. There was something familiar about the boy, something in his movements and the way he held his head, but Carleton couldn't quite place it. Brushing the incident aside, he mounted and spurred the stallion after Mitchell.

From her vantage point in the alley behind the shuttered sailmaker's shop at the corner, Elizabeth watched the two officers ride off. As soon as they disappeared from sight, she gave a muffled laugh. The thrill of fear and excitement that bubbled through her veins each time she tempted discovery was as heady as wine.

With every daring encounter she became more confident that her disguise was virtually impenetrable. All of them, Carleton included, were blinded by the fact that she was a woman. Clearly it did not occur to them that she had a mind and a heart equal to that of any man. All that was necessary was for her to continue to weave her spell over them, and that she knew quite well how to do.

Whistling once more, she hefted her bucket of oysters and moved off in the direction of the wharves. She would make another round, check in with the members of her secret band, and see what else she could learn.

Carleton and Andrews made up the eleventh and twelfth officers of the mounted patrol, which also included ten sergeants. They formed up at the fortifications outside the town gate, a significant majority, to Carleton's considerable amusement, armed heavily enough to advise any passerby that something serious was afoot.

Andrews had brought along not only their holster pistols, but their carbines as well. Holding his exasperation and his tongue in check,

Carleton strapped the weapons to his saddle.

They rode across the Neck at a leisurely pace and passed through Roxbury and Brooklyne without incident. Taking the road to Cambridge, they crossed the Great Bridge that spanned the Charles River and at the crossroads turned west toward Lexington.

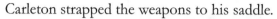

BOSTON'S CHURCH BELLS were chiming noon when a sudden flurry of activity began around the longboats moored beneath the stern of each man-of-war riding at anchor in the harbor. For a quarter of an hour Elizabeth watched the goings and comings of the sailors across the water before leaving her post in the shade of a dilapidated warehouse. She walked down North Street past Town Dock and Faneuil Hall, at regular points along her circuit stopping for a brief, guarded conference with one or another of her band of spies. Youths about her age or slightly older, none of them knew her real identity.

Finding a vantage point that gave her a wider view of the docks, she patiently waited and watched as boatloads of seamen came ashore for a quick visit to the local taverns and prostitutes. Before the bells tolled two o'clock, Elizabeth and her band had picked up every detail of the gossip spreading through the town like wildfire.

Convinced that a move by the Regulars was imminent, she hurried to Joseph Warren's Hanover Street home. She found the doctor in his surgery surrounded by a cluster of the local Sons of Liberty, all of whom appeared to be in a high state of excitement.

Warren motioned her into the parlor and shut the door behind them. "Everyone seems to think the Regulars will march tonight."

Elizabeth repeated the gossip picked up from the sailors to the same effect, then detailed the intelligence she had received from Patriot the previous night. "I saw Major Mitchell come for Major Carleton outside Pitcairn's this morning," she added. "Reports are they joined a fair-sized company riding out in the direction of Brooklyne that was later seen on Lexington

Road."

Warren considered this news for several moments. "Once I order out the militia there'll be no turning back. I have to be certain of Gage's intentions before I take that step. There's only one person who will know every detail of his plans."

Elizabeth paled. "Is there no other way? If I go to her now, her position will be most horribly compromised."

He regarded her with sympathetic concern. "If we miscalculate, all of us may lose our freedom, and many of our countrymen may lose their lives. Your own uncle and cousins might pay for our hesitation. Can you live with that? I can't."

She had no argument to counter his. Her heart heavy with foreboding, she returned to the deserted rooms above a long-closed printing shop in the North End, which she used as a secret rendezvous with her band and where she often assumed her disguise as Oriole.

With reluctance she began the retransformation from ragged fisher boy to elegant lady, her fingers fumbling with buttons and ribbons and hairpins in her haste. All the while she tried not to think of the destruction she was about to wreak in the life of a friend, tried equally not to think of her uncle and cousins, who were preparing for war. Or of Carleton and Andrews and the other officers she flirted with so carelessly, who in the coming hours might well face them at the point of a gun.

It was almost four o'clock before she completed her metamorphosis. Wrapped in a heavy, dark cloak, she slipped unnoticed through the shadows of the narrow alley to the stable on Salem Street where she had left her mare, grateful that she was a common sight in that neighborhood bringing medicine to some poor patient.

At Province House Margaret Gage received her in the drawing room. Although the older woman greeted her warmly, Elizabeth noted that her face was drawn and pale. For what seemed an eternity they made small talk until the maid finished serving tea and left them alone.

Elizabeth stared into the tea leaves at the bottom of her cup. "Dr.

Warren asked me to see you."

Mrs. Gage pressed one hand to her bosom, struggling with her emotions. "He promised he would not send to me except in case of emergency."

"This is an emergency, a very great one. If our countrymen are to save their lives and property, he must know with certainty whether the troops indeed march tonight."

"My husband has confided the full details of his plan to no one else. If I tell you, he will know I betrayed him."

Elizabeth set down her teacup and reached for her hand. "Do what your heart tells you is right. Whatever your decision, you'll receive no blame from me."

Mrs. Gage sprang to her feet and began to pace the floor, her clenched hand pressed hard against her lips. "I keep thinking of Blanche's speech in Shakespeare's King John just before the battle. It keeps going through my head. Do you remember it?

> *The sun's o'ercast with blood; fair day, adieu!*
> *Which is the side that I must go withal?*
> *I am with both; each army hath a hand*
> *And in their rage—I having hold of both—*
> *They whirl asunder, and dismember me.*
> *Husband, I cannot pray that thou mayst win,*
> *Uncle, I needs must pray that thou mayst lose.*
> *Father, I may not wish the fortune thine.*
> *Grandam, I will not wish thy wishes thrive.*
> *Whoever wins, on that side shall I lose,*
> *Assured loss, before the match is played.*

She stopped, turned back to Elizabeth. "You've suffered because of this division as much as I. We've both had our hearts torn in two by our love for those on either side, yet you've had the courage to help Dr. Warren."

Elizabeth made a swift, dismissive gesture. "I don't know how much help the little information I've passed along from time to time has been."

"But you've acted on your beliefs. I can't do any less, even if it costs me my marriage. Yes, the march is set for tonight. Smith's detachment is to cross the Charles to Lechmere's Point at ten o'clock, then march to Lexington. Mr. Adams and Mr. Hancock are known to be staying at the home of a Reverend Clarke, and they're to arrest them, then go on to Concord to search out and burn the militia stores."

Elizabeth got to her feet, and for a long moment they clung together, their tears mingling. At last, promising to do everything in her power to protect her friend from exposure, Elizabeth took her leave.

AFTER RESUMING HER DISGUISE and reporting back to Warren, Elizabeth haunted the streets while twilight gathered over the town, taking note of every movement of troops and officers and keeping in constant touch with her circle of contacts. Although the wind fell with the coming of night, the clouds had drifted away to the west, and the air remained piercing. At last she returned to the warmth of Warren's hearth, relief mingling with trepidation.

"Companies are forming up in the streets and moving onto the Common," she reported. "The navy has brought the longboats up. It looks as if they'll embark within the hour."

Illumined by the flickering light of the fire on the hearth, Warren leaned against the parlor mantel, his arms folded across his chest, his clear blue eyes revealing no sign of inner turmoil. Hearing the muffled tramp of innumerable footfalls moving down Hanover Street past his doorstep, he cocked his head, then nodded to the young boy crouched beside him.

"Run to Mr. Revere's house. Tell him I have need of him at once."

The boy sprang to his feet and slipped out of the room. With the closing of the door, the mantel clock began solemnly to toll nine o'clock.

Warren turned to a stocky man of about thirty years of age who stood in the shadows near the window, turning his hat nervously in his hands. Elizabeth had encountered him before. A local tanner, William Dawes on occasion served as courier for the patriots.

Indicating Elizabeth, Warren said, "Will, this is James Freeman. I want the two of you to ride to Reverend Clarke's in Lexington at once and warn Adams and Hancock that the Regulars are coming out with orders to arrest them. On the way, alert any militia members you know of along your route. Just remember, there's a patrol wandering around out there somewhere.

"James, I want you to take the southern route through Lincoln while Will takes Lexington Road. As another precaution, I'm going to send Revere across the bay and through Charlestown. With luck, at least one of the three of you should get through."

Dawes glanced at Elizabeth with mild curiosity as he jammed his hat on his head. Drawing her cloak around her, she followed him from the house without speaking, mentally thanking Warren for the appropriateness of the name with which he'd just christened her.

As they rode toward the Neck, Dawes cautioned, "Let me do the talkin'. I know the guards since I go by there purty often."

Elizabeth agreed without protest. As luck would have it, the bars that normally blocked the town gate at that hour had been removed to allow a relief detail to pass through to the blockhouse outside.

Dawes joked easily with the sergeant on duty, and to Elizabeth's relief the man gave them no more than a cursory inspection by the fitful light of his lantern before waving them on. To avoid exciting suspicion, they held their horses to a walk as they rode past the outer fortifications and into the concealing darkness beyond the derelict gallows. Before they reached the black shadow of the windmill a short distance up the road, however, they heard shouts coming from behind them and turned to look back.

As they watched anxiously, an officer rode up to the gate. A brief commotion followed, then the bars were put back in their place across the road. Although no one made a move to come after them, they urged their horses to an easy canter.

They passed through Roxbury without stopping. Throughout the town every light had been extinguished, nor had the moon yet risen above the trees on the eastern horizon. They met not a soul along the abandoned street.

Just past Tess's house, as they crossed the bridge over Stony Brook, where Pierpoint Mill loomed up close on their right, without warning four riders burst out of the shadows beneath a stand of oaks immediately ahead of them. By instinct, Elizabeth reined her mare hard to the left into an open, rocky meadow and spurred her to a gallop. Dawes veered to the right. His horse took off like a shot between the trees, closely pursued by two of the riders, while the remaining two came after Elizabeth.

Behind her, she briefly heard pounding hoofbeats, accompanied by shouts and curses. But with the mare's greater speed, Elizabeth's knowledge of the terrain, and the cover of darkness, she eluded her pursuers well before reaching the outskirts of Brooklyne.

Cautiously she returned to the road to cross the bridge over Muddy River. There was no sign of Dawes. In the sleeping hamlet and all down the road that led through Watertown and on to Lincoln, she stopped to rouse the inhabitants of every house belonging to members of the local militia. A short while before midnight she finally reached her uncle's tavern.

"The Regulars are on their way!" she gasped as she burst into Stern's office.

Will sprang to his feet. "You've seen them yourself?"

She nodded, struggling for breath. "Warren sent me and Dawes to warn Adams and Hancock. He's sending Revere out too." Speaking rapidly, she described her meeting with Margaret Gage.

His movements deliberate, Stern knocked the ashes out of his pipe, then clamped his hat on his head. "Will, hightail it over to Concord and find Barrett. Tell him I'm sending couriers off to alert Sudbury, Waltham, Framingham, and on south."

Grabbing his musket, Will sprinted out the door.

"Get to Lexington as quick as you can," Stern told Elizabeth. "Find out where the patrol is posted and warn Parker. If Revere or Dawes haven't gotten through yet, alert Adams and Hancock, then stay put and make yourself useful until you hear from me or Will."

Levi listened to their exchange, crestfallen. "What about me, Pa?"

"Get your company together now!" Stern barked. "I want to be on the way to Concord within the hour!"

His grin broad, Levi snapped a salute. "Yes, sir!"

Chapter Eleven

CARLETON EASED HIS BACK against the rough trunk of the gnarled hickory, at last gave up trying to get comfortable. Tipping his helmet a little farther over his forehead, he let his eyes drift shut.

A light breeze had sprung up. The silver moon rode high in the clear sky, just past the full, casting the grassy meadow in melting brightness against the hazy shadows of the woodland that surrounded it on three sides. In spite of the fresh sharpness of the air, the night had turned quite pleasant.

With the exception of the soldiers guarding their four despondent prisoners, the rest of Mitchell's patrol huddled together for warmth within several paces of where Carleton lounged, their breaths pluming onto the frosty air as they talked in low tones. From time to time, one or another of them clapped his chapped hands together to warm them.

Vaguely Carleton wondered what time it was. Past midnight, he guessed drowsily.

He could hear an occasional stamp or snort from the horses tethered out of sight in the trees. Each small sound seemed to intensify the hostile silence that brooded over the indistinct landscape. At the sound of boots crunching on dry dirt, he came alert.

It was only Mitchell who approached up the deserted road toward them. A short time earlier he had walked back in the direction of Lexington three miles to the east. Now as the officers turned toward him, their faces reflecting anxiety, he shook his head.

"Quiet as a graveyard."

"A trenchant image," Carleton noted. "But hopefully not a prophetic one."

Stopping in front of him, Mitchell nudged the recumbent officer's boot with the toe of his own. "We aren't putting you out, are we, Carleton? Keeping you from your beauty rest?"

Carleton yawned. "Not at all."

His comrades regarded his relaxed form with expressions ranging from resentment to amused envy. All of them had a keen awareness of their vulnerability posted alone on an isolated road directly between the patriots' headquarters at Concord and the village where two of their most powerful and respected leaders were staying. The oncoming column had to be miles away still, and with the passage of time Carleton's unruffled composure had begun to grate on nerves grown raw.

Andrews gave a muffled laugh. "Jon could sleep soundly in the middle of an artillery barrage."

"Let's just hope it won't become necessary to put your theory to the test," Mitchell responded.

With catlike swiftness, Carleton was on his feet, listening intently as he stared into the distance toward Lexington. When Andrews started to question him, he motioned the lieutenant to silence.

"Someone's coming."

Mitchell ran out onto the road, Carleton, Andrews, and several others at his heels. By now they could hear the patter of horses coming on at a rapid trot.

There were three of them, one riding well in front of the other two.

At the first sound of approaching hoofbeats, four of the officers had raced for their horses. As the first two of them appeared on the road, the leading rider called a warning to his companions, who spurred their mounts forward to join him. Together the three rode forward as though to break through the roadblock by main force.

"Stop!" bellowed Mitchell. "An inch farther and you're dead men!"

Pistols drawn, the dismounted officers swarmed around the three riders. "Blast you! Turn aside or we'll blow your brains out!" Captain Cochrane shouted.

With the path forward blocked, the riders had no choice but to follow orders. The rails of the gate into the meadow had been taken down, and they allowed the officers to herd them through it. The first two were no sooner inside, however, than one of them called to the other, *"Put on!"*

With that he turned to the left, sailed his mount over the stone wall that ran along the side of the meadow, and in seconds was lost in the darkness among the trees. At the same time, the trailing rider whipped his horse back down the road in the direction from which he had come and also quickly disappeared.

Taking advantage of the momentary confusion, the remaining rider raced for the trees at the foot of the meadow, the two mounted officers on his heels. Before he could reach safety, six more of the patrol rode out of the darkness into his path. Surrounded, with pistols pointed at his chest, he had no choice but to pull to a halt, and the reins were torn from his hands.

By now Carleton and Andrews had reached the group. Cursing the loss of his companions, the other officers forced the rider to dismount and shoved him without ceremony into the center of the circle.

Carleton hastened to intervene. "May I ask your name, sir?"

"Revere," the rider answered with obvious reluctance.

"What? Paul Revere?" Captain Lumm exclaimed.

Disgruntled, the rider acknowledged his identity.

"Are you an express rider for the rebels?" demanded Lieutenant Baker.

This time Revere's answer was bold. "I am, and you've missed your aim, gentlemen."

"What do you know of our aim?" Lieutenant Thorne said harshly. "We're looking for deserters, if that's what you mean."

"Ah, but I know better," countered Revere, "and I've alerted every village and farm this side of Boston. Colonel Smith was just beginning to embark his men when I left, and they were taking their fine time about it. I wouldn't expect to see them before daylight—if our militia doesn't get them first."

"You're bluffing." Lumm's tone was noticeably uncertain.

"The countryside has been aroused for fifty miles around. We'll have five hundred men at Lexington before another hour has passed."

Enraged at his impudence, the officers began to curse more violently and to threaten their prisoner until Andrews protested in outrage. Realizing the situation was slipping out of control, Carleton stepped between them and the silversmith, ordering them to leave him alone.

With a resentful glance at Carleton, Cochrane mounted his horse and rode off. In moments he returned with Mitchell, who leaped off his horse and ran over to Revere.

He pressed the barrel of his cocked pistol to the silversmith's head. "You'd better tell me the truth, or I swear I'll splatter your brains across this pasture."

Carleton and Andrews exchanged disgusted glances. Revere, however, appeared far from daunted.

"I don't need your threats to speak the truth. I'm glad to tell you whatever you want to know."

"First, tell us where Clarke's Tavern is."

Revere frowned. "I'm not familiar with any establishment by that name."

To the major's further questions, he repeated in greater detail the same information he had already given, emphasizing the size and temper of the force he claimed was gathering at Lexington. From what Carleton could make out of the others' expressions in the bright moonlight, Revere's words were having a marked effect.

There was no more cursing now as they absorbed every detail the silversmith related. After a brief consultation with the other officers,

Mitchell ordered everyone to mount. They rode out onto the road, keeping their prisoners in the center of the column, with a soldier leading Revere's horse.

"If you try making a run for it, or if we receive any insult whatsoever, I'll personally put a bullet through your head," Mitchell warned Revere.

Carleton said nothing. With a wordless jerk of his head, he sent Andrews to ride in front of Revere while he followed directly behind him. Exercising considerable caution, the patrol moved back down the road toward Lexington.

They were within half a mile of the Common when they heard the report of a musket firing. This was followed moments later by the reverberating explosion of a volley and the loud ringing of the town bell.

"The town's alarmed, and you're all dead men!" exulted one of their prisoners.

Noting the dismay and anxiety on every face in the patrol, Carleton pointed out to Mitchell that Revere had obviously told the truth. "Since our mission has been discovered, it would be less than wise for us to be found holding prisoners. It's almost two o'clock. If we let them go, we can move more quickly—head back to find out where the deuce Smith's column is."

With reluctance, the major agreed. Ordering the prisoners' release, but confiscating their horses, he formed the patrol into column and led them in a wide detour around Lexington. They left Revere and his companions staring after them in a state of jubilant satisfaction at the success of their night's work.

BY LUCK, LESS THAN A MILE from the village center, Elizabeth saw Mitchell's patrol before they saw her. Threading the wooded ridges and fields, she reached the burying ground undetected. In the darkness she all but rode over Revere.

The moon had sunk from its zenith in the direction of the western treetops. In spite of the early hour the triangular Green just ahead of them was a scene of activity unusual even by day. Candlelight flickered in the windows of Buckman's sprawling white frame tavern near the Green's southeast corner. Every house showed at least one light, while here and there along the pathways, torches and lanterns bobbed along, casting wavering circles of illumination under the trees.

Revere gave her an abbreviated account of his capture and release. With the silversmith perched behind her, they went to find John Parker, the captain of Lexington's militia company. The tall, gaunt officer was preparing to dismiss the company he had mustered after Revere brought the alarm three hours before. Since he had not received any word back from the scouts he had sent out, he told them, he had concluded that the alarm was either in error or exaggerated.

Their report convinced him otherwise. After a hasty consultation with his company, Parker advised the weary men to return to their homes if they lived nearby, otherwise to seek shelter and refreshment at Buckman Tavern until they were summoned by the report of the alarm gun or the ringing of the Meeting House bell.

With Revere again sharing her mount, Elizabeth turned the mare onto Bedford Road. Within a quarter of a mile they came to the home of the Reverend Jonas Clarke, the undisputed political leader of Lexington and cousin of John Hancock. An armed man stepped into their path as they approached.

"Sergeant Munroe!" Revere called out. "We need to see Adams and Hancock at once."

Short, plain-mannered William Munroe, the leader of the eight men who loomed up out of the darkness behind him, peered into Revere's face with suspicion. "You're making too much noise, sir! In case you hadn't noticed, the people within are trying to sleep."

"Noise!" cried Revere as he slid from the horse's back. "There'll be noise enough 'ere long! The Regulars are on their way!"

Elizabeth hurried to dismount as Revere strode to the door. Apparently in no mood to wait for an invitation to enter, he threw the door open and strode across the threshold with Elizabeth at his heels. To their left, they entered what appeared, in the faint glow from the hearth and the hazy shafts of moonlight slanting through the carved light holes in the shutters, to be a bedroom.

"I have every intention of staying to fight," a petulant voice was saying from the shadows opposite them. "Don't bother trying to persuade me otherwise."

The speaker, a slender, elegantly attired, and flamboyantly handsome man in his late thirties, stood in front of a dresser between the front windows loading a pistol. In spite of his attempts to appear in complete control of his emotions, his hands trembled noticeably, and his eyes glittered with excitement.

Shaking back the delicate white lace that fell over his wrists, he cocked the pistol, leveled it in the direction of the doorway they had just entered, and smiled coolly down the barrel at Revere. "You're back. What took you so long?"

"I was waylaid," Revere returned, his tone dry. "Do you mind putting that thing down? I've had a pistol pointed at my head quite often enough tonight."

With a grimace Hancock returned the pistol to half cock and tossed it onto the dresser, almost overturning the powder flask and scattering lead balls and wadding.

"It's as well you're back, Paul. Try to talk some sense into this madman, won't you?" a second voice chided mildly.

Elizabeth had never seen Samuel Adams up close, but she knew him by sight as well as by reputation. Although he was slight and kindly in appearance, his self-effacing manner was deceptive.

Wispy white hair crowned his balding head like a halo, making him seem much older than he was, an impression that was strengthened by the palsy that caused the continual trembling of his hands and head. At the moment, wrapped in a threadbare banyan with his balding pate uncovered, his appearance was so undistinguished that few would have guessed his pivotal role in the present crisis.

Nodding at Elizabeth, he asked, "Who's your young friend?"

"I believe you may have heard of Oriole," Revere answered.

A third man Elizabeth hadn't noticed until that moment levered himself out of the depths of the wing chair from which he had been observing the scene. She found the Reverend Jonas Clarke's burning gaze unsettling.

"Indeed we have," he acknowledged, his deep voice resonant. "The cause of liberty is in your debt, young man."

Elizabeth made a slight bow, unsure what was expected of her. The unrelieved tension of that day and night made the scene in the darkened bedroom seem incredibly fantastic. In her exhaustion and heightened state of excitement, she felt disembodied, as though she were dreaming or watching actors perform on a stage.

Before she could think of anything to say, Revere broke in to describe his arrest and release, adding that his captors had asked for directions to Clarke's Tavern in Lexington. "Since no such establishment exists, they can only have meant this house, which persuades me that both of you are in considerable danger. It would be wise for you to make an early start for Philadelphia."

Adams and Clarke vigorously supported Revere. Hancock, however, shrugged their warnings off.

"I'm not afraid to fight, or if need be, to die."

Adams sighed. "It isn't our business to fight, John. We belong to the government and must leave this battle to those who are fitted for it."

The others' arguments seemed to make no impression on Hancock, and at last Elizabeth broke in. "Forgive me, sir, but it seems to me that if our enemies were to hold our most respected and active leaders in their power, they would indeed triumph in their aims. We don't have such a surplus of men of vision and determination that we can afford to spare even one. If you refuse to leave while you can still reach safety and are taken prisoner by Gage, undoubtedly to be deported to England for trial and public humiliation, our cause must suffer, if not be ruined altogether."

For a taut moment the room was silent. All eyes were fixed on Hancock, who stood motionless, staring at her.

"I bow to the weight of your argument," he said at length, suiting his action to his words. "You persuade me of my greater duty."

Revere glanced at Elizabeth, and although he said nothing, she read the relief in his eyes. Explaining that he had to help Hancock's aunt and Dolly Quincy, Hancock's fiancée, to hide their valuables and finish packing to leave, Clarke strode out of the room. As he passed Elizabeth, he gave her shoulder a grateful squeeze.

When he had gone, Adams asked for an account of the preparations that were moving forward on the Green. Revere obliged.

"By now, the redcoats must have heard our signal guns," Adams mused. "And if they were to find a company or two of armed militia drawn up on the Green waiting for them, who knows what they might do after a fatiguing, frustrating march through a countryside that must seem quite hostile."

"I'm as anxious as you to pepper a few redcoated hides. But if we begin the conflict, we stand to lose many of our friends," Revere cautioned.

"Of course," Adams agreed. "We must not seem to begin it. The presence of a company on the Green should be all that's required. The king's officers know better than to turn their flank to an armed force, no matter how insignificant it appears."

Taken aback, Elizabeth stared at the rebel leader whose unimposing appearance gave little hint of the fires that smoldered within. A smile of anticipation wreathed Adams's pale features.

"Oh, what a glorious morning this is!" he exulted, rubbing his hands together with sudden glee.

✱ ✱ ✱

IT WAS PAST THREE O'CLOCK in the morning before Mitchell's patrol met up with the advance column of light infantry. The tall bearskin hats of the grenadiers were nowhere in sight.

Finding Pitcairn near the column's center, Carleton reined his bay around to keep pace with the major's rangy black. "Where's the rest of the column?"

"Ye'll find them back a ways," growled Pitcairn, disgruntled. "Smith ordered me to advance with the light infantry as fast as possible to secure the bridges at Concord. And from the sound o' the church bells and the muskets we've been hearin', these cursed Yankees seem to have gotten the word that we're comin'. I think Smith's gettin' a mite nervous. He's already sent a messenger back to the general to speed the relief column on its way."

Keeping his voice low so he couldn't be heard by the soldiers surrounding them, Carleton filled Pitcairn in on their encounter with Revere and what the silversmith had told them. Pitcairn threw him a sharp look.

"Ye see any evidence o' that many men gatherin' at Lexington?"

"You'll understand we gave the town a slight berth. The place did seem to be crawling with militia, though I can't testify to there being five hundred—yet. Any problems getting out of Boston?"

Pitcairn snorted. "None at all—unless ye count a total foul-up gettin' the men embarked, or the fact we ran aground in knee-deep water and had to wade ashore so everyone could start out soakin' wet. That part took a mere two hours, mind ye. Then after all the units finally got sorted out, we had to wait another hour for the navy to deliver rations, never mind we'd brought our own with us. All in all, we wasted a mere four hours before we got underway."

As he finished his account, Mitchell rode up. "Has Carleton told you that we captured Revere?" he said, his voice carrying to every soldier in the vicinity. "The scoundrel told us they have a thousand men waiting to stop us at Lexington. The militia units we saw heading in that direction were armed to the teeth, and there's a signal fire on every blasted hill. We were lucky to escape with our lives."

In little eddies of whispered conversation, Mitchell's words rippled outward through the ranks like tongues of flame through a field of ripe wheat while Carleton reflected soberly on the wisdom of sowing even greater anxiety among troops already on edge.

IN UNBROKEN FORMATION the light infantry stepped along to the measured tap of the drums. After three hours on the road most of them moved as though sleepwalking. Carleton also struggled with the numbing effects of fatigue intensified by the monotonous sway of his horse, and he noted that beside him Andrews was losing the same battle. But as the first long rays of the rising sun spilled over the lip of the wooded horizon to gild the wet, mossy, green-black trunks of the maples, oaks, and pines, he came fully awake, the foreboding he had felt since leaving Boston tightening around his chest like a steel band.

The strengthening light lit up the pink mist of buds that frothed the limbs of the trees, and glittered in miniature fires on each dew-wet blade of grass. A long rise in the road ahead of them still cut off the first view of Lexington, but they were within the town's boundary now and less than a mile from its center.

With every forward step, Carleton's unease deepened, intensified by the activity of the platoon Pitcairn had sent out to scout ahead of the column.

Loping on some distance ahead, the young officers leading the detachment had managed to capture each of the scouts the Lexington militia had sent out to determine the whereabouts of the approaching British force. The crestfallen rebels had been sent to the column's rear under guard while the platoon ranged on down the road, as tautly eager for action as spaniels on the scent of game.

The column reached the crest of the rise just as day broke. From this vantage point they could see between the greening groves the rooftops of the village half a mile off. Substantial bodies of men were visible in urgent motion across the Green, and they could hear a drum beating "To Arms."

Just then a small party of riders appeared along a crossroads below them at the base of the hill. Lieutenant Sutherland, who led the platoon, reached the intersection at the same moment.

Watching from the brow of the hill, Carleton drew in his breath sharply as the lieutenant sprang at the nearest rider. There was a brief flash of light, then the horses shied and bolted back down the side road and out of sight. Sutherland and his companions came racing back up the road to rejoin the column.

"One of them shot at us," Sutherland gasped, out of breath. "Luckily, his pistol misfired."

Drawing the column to a halt, Pitcairn ordered his men to prime and load their weapons. Fingers fumbling in their haste, the men began to ram ball and wadding down their musket barrels.

"Do you think that's wise under the circumstances?" Carleton cautioned. "If there's a confrontation, some of the men might be tempted to take matters into their own hands."

Pitcairn threw him a glowering look. "I've no intention o' walkin' my men into a hornet's nest without the means to defend themselves."

After a moment, however, he turned to the troops and shouted, "Mind, now, you're on no account to fire or even attempt it without orders."

As the steady tramp of the column resumed to the insistent tap of the drums, Carleton spurred his horse down the slope. Staring ahead into the village rapidly diminishing yards ahead of them, its houses and lawns lit by the melting hues of dawn, he felt the cold fingers of a sickening fear grip his heart.

❋ ❋ ❋

ELIZABETH JERKED AWAKE to find Revere shaking her. Fighting off an overpowering weariness, she glanced around the low-ceilinged room with its damp-stained plaster. She had left the Clarke house for Buckman's Tavern not long after Dawes's arrival. Sometime after three o'clock she had followed several weary militia members upstairs to collapse onto one of the inn's communal beds, lying head to foot with one of the men.

Her companion was gone and the other beds were empty as well. She had a vague memory of an alarm bell ringing an indefinite time ago, and for an instant she was afraid the Regulars had already come and gone, and she had missed the action. Then, becoming conscious of the faint, rhythmic rattle of drums, the high pipe of fifes still at a little distance, she directed an inquiring glance up at Revere.

"They should be in sight by now."

He sounded as tired as she felt. Sliding off the bed, she stumbled to the nearest window and yanked at the sash. The worn wooden frame was swollen with winter damp, but with some effort she succeeded in prying it open. She flung it wide and leaned far out into the cool morning air.

"I can see their uniforms through the trees!" Grabbing pistol and powder horn, she started for the door, only to find Revere blocking her path.

"You can see better from up here."

She was around him and out the door before he could prevent her, her feet barely touching the steps as she flew down the steep, narrow stairway. Bursting through the tavern's front door and onto the Green, she stopped dead in her tracks.

In the strengthening light of dawn, every detail of the scene stood out with an unearthly clarity. Directly in front of her the triangular strip of emerald turf was alive with the rapid movement of men. A haze of mist muted the outlines of the houses and trees in the middle distance, while between darker bands of shadow the grass was streaked with long spars of light cast by the fiery edge of the rising sun that had just burst above the horizon.

The light breeze felt sharp and clean on her skin through the rough fabric of her clothing. It carried the smell of wet earth from newly plowed fields, trodden grass, damp leaf mold, and, overlying it, the acrid tinge of wood smoke that curled in thin wisps from the chimneys of the houses.

At every house, from the doorways of the smithy across the Green and the tavern behind her, along the stone walls that bordered the road, onlookers craned their necks to catch the first glimpse of the long, crimson column that snaked down the slope of the hill, pacing off the last fatal yards toward them. Young children peered from behind their mother's petticoats, their rosy faces fearful of what they could not comprehend. The upper windows of each building were also filled, and even the Meeting House that stood at the Green's leading point harbored its share of curious or defiant watchers.

As the seconds ticked away, armed men continued to straggle across the fields to swell the numbers on the Green. One group raced past the detached belfry that sat on the ground at the back of the Meeting House to take up a post behind the stone wall just east of the tavern. They leaned their muskets against the wall at an angle that would keep the weapons out of sight of the approaching troops.

The sound of rapid hoofbeats approaching along Concord Road brought Elizabeth around. As Will's horse pounded onto the Green, she ran to him.

Jerking so hard on the reins that his lathered, wild-eyed mount sat back on its haunches, Will vaulted from the saddle to catch her arm in a painful grip. His set face drained of color and hard as marble, he took in the pistol clenched in her hand.

"What do you think you're doing?" He followed her quick, guilty glance toward Parker's company, now formed up in a wavering line straight across from the road where the oncoming Regulars would have to pass, and his fingers tightened around her arm until she winced. "You get out of the way and stay put!"

Before she could protest, he gave her a hard shove in the direction of a large, white frame house behind the militia's line, next to the smithy on the northwest side of the Green. Then he took off at a run to join Parker.

Chapter Twelve

FOUR FIFTY-SIX A.M. WEDNESDAY, APRIL 19.
The liquid trill of awakening larks and robins fell silent. Somewhere off beyond the houses and outbuildings a rooster crowed then stopped, its harsh cry cut off as though by an ax.

Around the rear of the smithy darted a half-grown boy braver than his fellows. As he cut past Elizabeth and across the near end of the Green, he flung a shrill taunt in the direction of the moving glimmer of crimson just visible through the trees on the other side of the Meeting House. Parker swung on him, the color rising to his cheeks, and the child scuttled to the safety of a dense hedgerow on the other side of the road.

Into the hush that followed crept another thread of sound, rapidly swelling in volume: the tramp of hundreds of feet in the powdery dust of the road. The foreboding rattle of drums grew louder, and now they were answered by the drummer of Parker's company, his cadence echoing the pulse that throbbed in Elizabeth's temples.

Beneath these sounds ran a low, sullen murmur that came from the clustered knots of grim-faced men behind stone wall and Meeting House, at the blacksmith's forge, in front of the tavern, on the Green.

Like a wave breaking onto a rocky shore, the scarlet flood surged around the side of the Meeting House, and the first ranks of the light infantry advanced onto the Green. They were coming on more rapidly than Elizabeth had expected, the regimental flags of the Tenth Foot fluttering in the van.

Only Parker's company stood between her and their determined forward sweep. Between the heads and shoulders of the men separating her from the oncoming troops, she could see the steely glint of sunshine rippling like a river of liquid fire along the bayonets that bristled over the shoulders of the soldiers, the brilliant, bloody upblaze of light on each uniform coat, the muted sheen of close-fitting leather helmets, the blur of white faces as they flooded toward the militia.

"Let the troops pass by," Parker commanded, his voice sharp. "Don't molest them without they begin it."

Slightly in advance and anchoring the British left flank rode a party of officers. With a shock, Elizabeth saw two scarlet-crested helmets of the Light Dragoons among them.

Carleton rode a length in front of the others, just ahead of Mitchell and Andrews, holding his drawn sabre outstretched across the detachment's path as though to slow the soldiers' forward rush. But catching sight of Parker's company, the troops increased their pace.

While Elizabeth watched, the breath choked in her throat, Carleton turned in the saddle to shout a command. His voice was blotted out by Parker's stern one closer at hand.

"The first man who offers to run shall be shot down. Stand your ground, men. Don't fire unless fired upon, but if they mean to have a war, let it begin here!"

She became aware that Will had moved off to one side. A few steps in advance of the militia, he faced the oncoming column, pale and intent, his lowered musket clenched in his hands.

She noted all these details within one heartbeat, with an eerie, detached clarity. There was no time for thought or feeling as the moment unraveled toward disaster.

Without warning, in the absence of any command, the soldiers wheeled from column into line and spread out to full company front across the width of the Green in front of the Meeting House, creating a battle line facing Parker's men. Each succeeding company coming onto the Green instinctively followed their example. It was an awesome display of power.

CARLETON THREW AN ANXIOUS GLANCE over his shoulder, relieved to see Pitcairn's high-spirited black stallion gallop around the opposite side of the Meeting House. The rear companies had halted on Concord Road, and as Pitcairn caught sight of the armed colonials at the far end of the Green, he rode toward them, pistol drawn.

"Throw down your arms, ye villains!"

The militia was hopelessly outnumbered, and it was fast becoming obvious that to hold their ground would be equivalent to suicide. With obvious reluctance Parker ordered his men to comply. Resentment and defiance mingled with apprehension on the men's faces as they lowered their muskets. Although they refused to lay their weapons down, most of them began to file off toward the stone wall that bordered the Green.

"Soldiers, form and surround them!" Pitcairn snapped.

The response was immediate and shocking. Shouting *"Huzza! Huzza! Huzza!"* the front ranks broke into a run to intercept the retreating militia.

Carleton sucked in his breath. At Pitcairn's unwitting command the light infantry, trained to take the initiative on a battlefield, now perceived this Green to be just that, Carleton realized with horror. In reckless determination, he reined his bay across the path of the leading companies, shouting for them to halt and reform. For an instant he bodily blocked their advance, then the front ranks surged around him with a frenzied roar.

Behind him he dimly heard Pitcairn screaming again and again, "Soldiers, keep your ranks! *Don't fire!* Form and surround them!"

But the order had no effect. Ignoring a small cluster of colonials still holding their ground at the Green's far side, the British vanguard gave a wild yell and converged, muskets upraised, on those who retreated.

Before Carleton could again reach the front, the sharp, metallic report of a pistol shot cracked above the excited shouts of men on both sides, its echo reverberating between the houses.

STARTLED, ELIZABETH SWUNG TO STARE in the direction from which the shot had come. She had only enough time to see that a puff of white smoke hung in front of the mounted officers who had halted off to one side, when a scattered crackle of musket fire from the light infantry split the stunned silence.

A ragged volley answered from the colonials posted behind the stone wall, causing a momentary tangle of panicky confusion among the light infantry. With Parker's company now scrambling to abandon the Green, Mitchell, at the far end of the line, pointed his sword in the direction of the retreating militia and shouted hysterically, *"Fire, curse you! Fire!"*

Instantly a jagged sheet of flame and oily smoke rippled from one end of the British line to the other. Bedlam followed: the terrified screams of onlookers at doorway and window, the shouted commands and curses of the officers, the din of massed gunfire as the light infantry fired repeated volleys into the rapidly thinning ranks of the militia.

Even now, a few colonials still refused to give way. Feeling as though she were trapped in a nightmare, Elizabeth watched in horror as a short distance in front of her a British soldier ran one man through with his bayonet, spurting blood into the air.

With a shock she realized that Will was also still on the Green. Kneeling on one knee, he fired, coolly reloaded, fired again. Squinting down his musket barrel, he took careful aim, appearing oblivious of the balls that scoured the air all around him like a horde of angry hornets.

A movement in the grass in front of her drew Elizabeth's appalled gaze to where one of Parker's men dragged himself in her direction. A bright crimson stain crept across the man's chest. He fought for breath, and bloody foam rattled in his throat as he scrabbled in the dirt, struggling to crawl onto the doorstep where she stood.

Behind her she heard a shrill shriek, then a woman pushed past to kneel at his side. Elizabeth saw that his face had already turned grey. As she watched, his eyes rolled back in his head.

"No—no! Dear God, no!"

The woman's moans sounded like the whimper of a tortured animal. Moving like a sleepwalker, Elizabeth knelt beside the mortally wounded man, ripped open the front of his shirt, and groped for his neck. For an instant she felt the faint throb of his heart. Then it ceased.

She stared down at her hand, at her fingers sticky with blood, and beads of sweat broke out across her forehead. She felt sick to her stomach, as though she was going to vomit. A killing rage choked the outcry in her throat.

Tears streaming down her cheeks, her face contorted, she scrambled to her feet. Tearing free the loaded pistol she had stuck into the waistband of her breeches a lifetime ago, she aimed it in the direction of the jubilant scarlet lines just as Colonel Smith rode up at the head of the grenadiers.

Her finger tightened over the trigger, then she stopped, her attention caught by two figures on the opposite side of the Green from where she stood. They were too far away for her to make out what they said, but there was no mistaking the angry defiance on Will's face. And Carleton's stunned dismay.

FOR A TAUT MOMENT neither could speak, each shocked at their unexpected meeting. Then Will lowered his musket and raised his eyes from Carleton's drawn sabre to meet his tortured gaze.

"I'd thought better of you," he spat out. "Once I called you my friend—you even shared my family's table. Now you're one of Parliament's butchers."

A shudder went through Carleton. With a painful gesture he indicated the fallen, bloody bodies scattered across the grass.

"I came here to try to stop this," he answered in a low, choked voice. "I haven't changed, Will."

"Haven't you?" Will shot back, his voice thick with contempt. "The color of your coat gives the lie to your words."

Carleton returned his bitter look with a hard one. "Things are often different than they seem." Reining his horse around, he dug his spurs into the bay's flanks and rode back to where the light infantry had been brought under tenuous control.

Will stared after him in puzzled fury. After a moment of indecision he raced to Elizabeth's side. Grabbing her by the arm, he dragged her past the few members of Parker's shattered command still remaining on the Green, urging her to a run toward Buckman's Tavern, behind which their horses were tethered.

"Come on! We've got to get to Concord before they do!"

RESTLESS AND ILL AT EASE, Carleton pushed his way between the tables and chairs and stopped at the front window of Wright's Tavern. Outside, a detail of grenadiers was hauling several gun carriages out through the doors of Concord's Towne House. As he watched they gleefully set about burning them, adding to the pile the liberty pole they had chopped down from the summit of the hill behind the building.

After a number of false starts they succeeded in kindling a modest blaze, although Carleton estimated it would be some time before the wooden timbers caught fire in earnest. A thin pall of smoke drifted up from the smoldering wood. It began to collect beneath the lower branches of the trees, but for the time being rose no higher.

He shook his head in disgust. A dangerous amount of time had been wasted by Smith's inexplicable insistence on holding a full dress review of his entire force before taking any action to achieve the purpose for which they had been sent out. It had been only after an inexcusable delay that the colonel had at last set up a command post—in the tavern—and then only, in Carleton's cynical estimation, to give himself and his staff opportunity to consume the establishment's entire stock of wine and ale before lunch.

They had arrived in Concord well before eight o'clock, escorted all the way into town by a scouting party of Concord and Lincoln Minute companies that had marched ceremoniously ahead of them to the music of "Yankee Doodle." It was now half past nine, and Carleton had begun to chafe at every further delay.

Mentally he counted the reinforcements he was certain must be swelling the militia units gathered on Punkatasset Hill above the North Bridge a half-mile outside the town. He forced himself to hold his tongue, however, determined to offer no advice or opinion unless it was solicited. And that was unlikely to happen, as Smith had made a point of refusing to speak to him since ordering Carleton to remain in the tavern.

The colonel's single flash of inspiration had been to send a messenger posthaste back to Gage even before they reached Lexington with an urgent appeal for Lord Percy to hurry along with any artillery that could be spared. Carleton thought sardonically that, in view of Smith's foot-dragging, the precaution was undoubtedly prudent.

With the passage of time, Smith had lumbered to the conclusion that it might be advisable to seize the town's two bridges just in case the rebels decided to cut them off. In due course a single company of light infantry was idling away its time at the South Bridge, a mile to the west.

Six more companies under Captain Parsons had been dispatched to secure the North Bridge and to keep an eye on the rebels massing on the heights above it. They had just marched out of sight when Smith had changed his mind and sent the Twenty-third to join them. They brought orders for Parsons to divide his force, leaving three companies to secure the bridge while the other four proceed to the farm of a certain Colonel Barrett two miles farther on, where it was rumored a quantity of militia stores lay concealed.

In the meantime, the grenadiers had been set to ferreting out whatever could be considered military stores in the town center, a task they had so far accomplished without antagonizing the inhabitants of the town any more than was inevitable. But to Smith's growing chagrin and annoyance, little had been unearthed beyond the gun carriages, some sacks of flour, a modest quantity of musket balls, and a few shovels and picks.

Carleton tried to keep his thoughts occupied with anything other than the incident on Lexington Green. Despite all effort, however, he was haunted by the vivid image of the broken bodies sprawled across the grass and the confrontation with Will.

"Sit down, Jon. You're makin' me nervous with your pacin'."

Without answering, Carleton returned to take the chair across from Pitcairn.

"You're right gloomy, laddie. That bit o' fun back in Lexington doesn't seem to have improved your mood."

"Excuse me if I don't find it very amusing to shoot down men who haven't fired on anyone," Carleton returned, his tone icy.

"Our men will disagree with ye on who fired first." Pitcairn considered his wounded finger, injured at Lexington by a militia musket ball, then grimacing, dipped it into his brandy. "Personally, I'm hopin' to stir some Yankee blood before nightfall."

"It would appear you've already stirred it," Carleton drawled.

They were interrupted by the entrance of a rotund young lieutenant. Mopping the sweat from his forehead, he gave Smith a hasty salute.

"Lieutenant Robertson reporting, sir. Captain Laurie respectfully requests that reinforcements be sent to the North Bridge right away. The rebel force on the hill above us keeps growing, and it's beginning to look like they're forming up for a move on our position."

Staring at him with disdain, Smith considered his options. "Where's Parsons?"

"He isn't back from Barrett's farm yet, sir. We have only three companies, and we're facing at least four times that number, if not more."

Sighing, Smith levered his corpulent bulk out of his chair, adjusted his sword, and began to move ponderously in the direction of the door. Passing a group of the younger officers at one of the tables, he waved his thick hand at one of them.

"Lumm, get your tail over there and see what the fuss is all about. Tell Laurie to keep his shirt on—I'll personally bring along a couple of companies just to keep him happy."

Carleton threw Pitcairn a pleading look, which the major pretended not to see. Before the colonel reached the door, however, Pitcairn spoke as if the thought had just occurred to him.

"How about Jonathan ridin' along with the lieutenants, Francis? It'll keep him out of mischief for a while, and he can keep them in line."

Smith directed Carleton a long, freezing look, then unexpectedly his features contracted into an unpleasant grimace that Carleton took for a smile. With uncharacteristic affability he allowed as how he'd be delighted to have Carleton make himself useful by applying his varied talents to the salvation of the besieged companies. Ignoring his insulting tone, Carleton gratefully deserted the tavern with Lumm and Robertson.

"It appears you've made an impression on the colonel," Lumm snickered as they mounted their horses.

Carleton reined the bay around and led the way down the road. "The problem with Smith is that his activity and expertise as an officer are exceeded only by his intelligence and imagination."

Lumm and Robertson guffawed. Together they rode out of town, not noticing that on the square behind them the smoldering gun carriages had at last burst into flame.

ALL DURING SMITH'S PONDEROUS PREPARATIONS for action, while the sun burned the spring coolness out of the air and turned the day unseasonably warm, Elizabeth watched the ranks of the colonial militia swell at an astounding rate. In a steady stream, armed men straggled up the hill, appearing in twos and threes, singly, entire companies together marching in disciplined formation. They came mostly on foot, a few mounted, even an occasional company well turned out in uniform.

From Bedford, Lincoln, Woburn, Lexington, Carlisle, Waltham, Acton, Chelmsford, Littleton, Billerica as well as small towns far to the west, they came. Roused from their beds by signal guns, Meeting House bells, and express riders, they had delayed only long enough to pull on boots and grab musket and powder horn before taking to the road.

Within the past hour, the rebel force had moved down from its initial post on the summit of Punkatasset Hill to occupy the old muster field on a rise behind Buttrick's farm, a position considerably closer to the bridge. The details of the skirmish at Lexington, along with the names of their neighbors killed and wounded, buzzed from mouth to mouth and were repeated to every new arrival. And the anger and the determination, like runaway wildfire, intensified with each repetition.

From her post behind the stone wall that bordered the field, where she waited with the rest of the Lincoln militia, Elizabeth had an unobstructed view of the North Bridge. Drawn up on the high ground on the near side of the river were the Tenth and the King's Own commanded by Captain Laurie, with the Forty-third guarding the bridge itself.

Through her uncle's spyglass she watched the captain pace up and down between them and the bridge. From time to time he glanced anxiously down the road after the messenger he had sent a back into Concord when the militia companies had filed down to the muster field.

Lieutenant Sutherland was also there. With him was Andrews, who had accompanied the Twenty-third and had remained behind while that company continued toward Barrett's farm to join Parsons. Leaning against a tree this side of the river, Andrews shook his head to a remark Sutherland emphasized with a furious gesture in their direction.

Just then three riders arrived at a gallop: Carleton, Lumm, and the officer Laurie had sent into Concord a short while before. They dismounted and walked across the bridge to confer with Laurie. Sutherland and Andrews joined them.

Elizabeth passed the spyglass to Levi. While he squinted through it, she glanced around at the impromptu army gathered on the hill behind her.

For some time now she'd been aware that Major Buttrick and a majority of the officers, among whom her uncle and older cousin assumed a vocal part, had been trying to persuade aging, lame Colonel Barrett of the Concord militia to order an attack now that they owned the advantage of numbers. Clustered in an animated huddle in the shade of a tall pine, they were still engaged in passionate debate on the issue.

As she turned to glance back down at the bridge to see if the conference below had resulted in any change in the enemy's disposition, she drew in her breath sharply.

"Levi—look!" She pointed at the thick plume of smoke that spread like an evil omen across the serene, cloud-dotted sky above the rooftops of the town. "They're burning Concord!"

Everyone within earshot swung around to look in the direction she pointed. A murmur of outrage rippled through the groups of men, interspersed with cries of disbelief and fury.

Will was quickly at her side, Stern on his heels, then Buttrick, Barrett, and the rest of the officers.

"God help us!" Will choked on the bitter words. "They didn't carry out their threat to burn Lexington to the ground, but it looks like they mean to make it good here."

CARLETON TOOK STOCK of the companies' dispositions, then swiftly surveyed what he could see of the rebels' formation behind the stone wall at the top of the rise. One glance convinced him that Laurie had not been crying wolf in pleading for reinforcements.

With as much tact as possible he suggested to the captain that under the circumstances it might be prudent to remove the advanced companies to the Concord side of the bridge, where they could maintain a stronger defensive position until Smith's arrival. Relieved, Laurie agreed.

Before he could order the withdrawal, however, they were stopped in their tracks by a roar of fury from the rebels.

Swinging around to follow the direction of the colonials' stares and angry gestures, Carleton cursed under his breath. "It's only the grenadiers burning some gun carriages, but they must think we've torched the town."

"We're in for it now," Andrews said.

Carleton returned his gloomy look, but kept his response too low for the others to hear. "After what happened at Lexington, I can't say I blame them."

Too distracted to pay any attention, Laurie sent Robertson galloping back into town to find out why the reinforcements were still nowhere in sight and to prod Smith to some haste. As soon as the lieutenant was on his way, Laurie ordered the retreat to the other side of the river. By now, however, it had become obvious to every man among them that the choice was no longer an option, but a very real necessity.

THE VOICES FAVORING AN IMMEDIATE ATTACK on the British position had changed from urgent pleas to indignant demands. Still Barrett hesitated, unwilling to be the first to break the peace. The decision was taken out of his hands by his adjutant, Joseph Hosmer.

With an enraged gesture toward the plume of smoke, Hosmer demanded, "They've set the village on fire! Will you let them burn it down?"

Scanning the circle of livid faces that surrounded him, Barrett at last conceded. The officers ran to order their men into formation, and within moments the long column was moving.

Fife and drum took up the tune of "The White Cockade," an old march dating from the Jacobite rebellion and calculated to incense any loyal Hanoverian. As the column snaked down the footpath and turned onto the road to face the bridge, the men kicked up a thin skein of dust that hung over their heads like a grey shroud.

WITH THE COLUMN OF MILITIA spilling down the rise, Laurie ordered his advanced companies headlong back across the bridge. Carleton and Andrews had crossed over ahead of them to order the Forty-third away from the well at a nearby house, where they were lounging, and into a defensive position near the bridge. Pausing by the stone wall that ran along the road, the two officers watched the infantry's retreat.

Too much confusion, Carleton thought unhappily. *Just like at Lexington.*

He could feel the soldiers' anxiety as they glanced uncertainly from the unfamiliar officers who commanded them to the approaching rebel force coming on at a quick march. As the column continued to pour down the path without apparent end, they began to recognize the weight of the odds stacked against them.

In trying to clear the bridge, the soldiers jostled into each other, blocking those who shoved at their backs to get through. The maneuver was rendered doubly difficult because the troops of the Fourth, still in the process of coming over, had to push their way through the ranks of the Tenth as that company hurried to form up in the narrow road on the Concord side of the bridge. Further complication was added by the Forty-third, which filed over from the well just in time to force its way into the middle of the confusion.

The fatal ingredient to this disastrous brew was Laurie's sudden inspiration to order the Fourth and Tenth into column four abreast for street firing, a maneuver Carleton quickly surmised the troops had not been drilled in. The result was chaos.

By the time Laurie belatedly made a desperate attempt to untangle his command and get them into correct position, the rebels had closed to within musket range. The last of the Regulars raced over the bridge's gentle arch. Among them was Lieutenant Lister, who turned to glance back at his friend bringing up the rear a few yards in advance of the militia.

"I say, Sutherland, pull up those planks, will you?" he called with a nervous laugh. "That'll slow the Yankees down a tad."

The irrepressible subaltern flashed his friend a grin and dropped to his knees on the bridge. As everyone watched in amazement, he proceeded to tear loose several of the broad planks.

Another roar of protest came from the rebels. "That's town property he's destroying!"

"Shame! Leave off, ye cursed lobster!"

In the lead, Major Buttrick led his men forward at an increased pace. "You there, leave our bridge alone!"

Looking up, the lieutenant saw that the rebels were well within range, with himself as prime target. Apparently deciding on the virtue of strategic retreat, he jumped down onto the riverbank and shouted for the Forty-third to follow him as he readied his fusil.

The next moments seemed to Carleton part of a monstrous, recurring horror. Again, nervous, disoriented soldiers took aim, jittery fingers stroking the triggers of cocked muskets while the rebel force came doggedly on to the defiant music of drum and fife.

They were within a few short feet of reaching the bridge. At Laurie's command, the men in the first rank of the British column dropped to one knee to squint down their musket barrels.

Springing forward, Carleton screamed, *"No! Don't shoot!"*

His words were drowned out by a scattered popping, a high, random firing that for the most part splashed musket balls into the water. It was followed by a full, deafening volley that reverberated between the ridges.

Elizabeth had barely time to realize that the Acton fifer had dropped to the ground when she saw Buttrick leap into the air. "Fire, fellow soldiers, for God's sake, fire!" Taking aim, he pulled the trigger of his musket.

From mouth to mouth the cry rose, "Fire! Fire!" And instantly a hail of musket balls tore into the Regulars.

Amid the confusion created as the rear ranks tried to push forward to take the place of those who had already fired, officers and men staggered or sank on the spot, clutching at wounds, blood running between their fingers. Some hobbled off, screaming in pain. Within seconds, four of the eight British officers were wounded, one soldier near Carleton lay dead, and another close by was dying.

Carleton could not see what was going on at the rear, but he heard shouts of alarm as those at the back of the column broke. Panic was contagious. Before the officers could intervene they were swept aside by a melee of shouting, swearing, sweating soldiers, who took to their heels in a mad, unstoppable rush back down the road to Concord, abandoning the dead where they lay and leaving the wounded to fend for themselves.

All but knocked down by the press of fleeing troops, Carleton fought his way to the bay and grabbed the reins before the stallion could bolt. Clawing into the saddle, he looked around desperately for Andrews.

The lieutenant was near what remained of the column's van, pinned against the stone wall and in danger of being trampled underfoot by the jostling backward flood. Red-faced, he waved his sabre, screaming at the retreating companies to halt.

Forcing his way through the stampede, Carleton caught his hand and dragged him up behind him. The surge around them was so irresistible that he was forced to spur the bay down onto the river bank to avoid injury to the animal and themselves.

Not until the road was clear did he urge his mount back up the bank. There he stopped, and after a glance in the direction of the detachment in full flight back to Concord, he turned to face the militia drawn up on the opposite side of the bridge. Muskets held ready, they waited as though to see what he would do.

For a long, tense moment, Carleton stared earnestly at them. Then he pulled off his helmet, and sweeping the astonished victors a graceful bow, he drew his mount around to follow the fleeing Regulars at a slow walk.

He had only a fleeting glimpse of a slim youth who stood on the riverbank, openmouthed, watching him go with an expression of astonished wonder.

ARRIVING ON THE SCENE moments later, Smith sized up the situation and concluded that it was too risky to do anything about it. So he about-faced his command and marched them all back into the town on the heels of the demoralized detachment, to all intents and purposes abandoning Parsons and his four companies to whatever fate the enraged militia might have in store for them.

He retreated to Wright's Tavern, where Pitcairn, Mitchell, Carleton, and very nearly every other officer pleaded and cajoled, to no avail. Their ponderous commander refused to be moved. Even to Carleton's desperate offer to attempt the ride alone to Barrett's farm to warn Parsons, he turned a deaf ear. It was, he maintained, the captain's responsibility to manage the safe return of his small force through what was now actively hostile territory, even though he had no way of knowing just how dangerous his situation had become.

Some time later, Parsons' detachment marched unscathed back into Concord, speeded on by the distant sound of firing and by the appalling sight of their comrades' bodies at the bridge. They had been allowed to pass under the barrels of the rebels' muskets.

The enemy, Parsons reported nervously, had taken up a post on a hill at the edge of the town. And while the detachment had uncovered no militia stores at Barrett's farm, they brought another report that stirred consternation and fury.

One of the wounded men, who still showed signs of life, had a deep cut in the skin over his eyes, and the top of his ears had been chopped off. Scalped by the Yankees, Parsons concluded in outrage.

At this Carleton snorted contemptuously. "That isn't how you scalp someone. If there's a man this side of the Berkshires who has the vaguest idea how to lift a scalp, I'll dare him to take my own."

Smith's smile was sour. "So you're an expert on scalping too, are you?"

A dangerous light glinted in Carleton's eyes. "As a matter of fact, I am. I lived among the Shawnee as a youth, and at one time I owned a belt of scalps longer than your arm."

With a deliberate movement, he drew from beneath his waistcoat a leather sheath richly decorated with wampum. Gripping the knife it by its carved handle, he bared it for all to see. Smith's eyes widened as he stared at the gleaming, razor-sharp curve of the blade.

The room had become deathly still. The other officers regarded Carleton with amazement mingled with grudging respect, but as though unaware of their reaction, he brought the blade horizontally through the air in a casual, liquid movement that caused everyone to shrink away.

"If you'd like a demonstration," he said, "I'd be happy to oblige."

Swallowing hard, his eyes fastened on the blade, Smith flushed darkly. "Is that a threat, major?"

With a slow, meaningful smile, Carleton drawled, "*Pardon, Colonel.* I am not fool enough to threaten a superior officer—at least not in front of witnesses. I was merely . . . offering enlightenment."

Smith was clearly too shaken to reply. Shrugging, Carleton sheathed the blade and returned it to its concealment. Then he put on his helmet and strode to the door, ignoring the officers who scrambled out of his path.

Leaving Smith to stew in his humiliation, he went outside without a backward look, letting the door bang shut behind him, defiantly satisfied even as he cursed his stupidity.

Chapter Thirteen

"Y E NEVER LEARN YOUR LESSON, do ye, laddie?"

Carleton gave Pitcairn a wry smile. "Smith's such an easy target I can't resist the urge to skewer him."

"Was that true about ye owning a string o' scalps?"

"Well . . . I didn't actually lift them myself. But don't tell Smith that."

Pitcairn grimaced. "The colonel will be lookin' for a way to even the score, so be on your guard. Today'd be a bad day to hand him the opportunity, if ye get my meaning."

Carleton followed his uneasy glance in the direction of the formidable body of colonials who swarmed across the Great Meadows below them, moving parallel to the road the Regulars were following as though they intended to head the column. He said nothing, but the knot in his stomach tightened.

It had been almost eleven o'clock before Parsons had led his four companies back from Barrett's farm. But instead of setting out on the return to Boston before the militia's numbers could swell even further, Smith had marched and countermarched his detachment in apparent indecision, to the frustration of officers and troops alike.

The skirmish at the bridge had cost them three killed, with nine wounded, four of them officers. Abandoning the dead, Smith had insisted on hiring carriages to carry the wounded. Consequently, more time had been taken up in making the necessary arrangements before the column had finally moved out a short time after noon.

The instant the Regulars set foot on the road, the militia units crouching in the hills gathered on their flanks like cougars stalking prey. Now, as the troops quick-stepped east along Lexington Road, where a high, prow-shaped ridge loomed on their left, they darted anxious glances to each side.

As a precaution Smith had sent a flanking party of light infantry to sweep over the ridge. When the detachment rejoined the main column, they brought disquieting reports that they had been shadowed by a force of alarming size. Anxiety swept through the column like wildfire, enlivened by the rumor of the scalping at Concord Bridge.

The ridge ended at Meriam's Corner, where a narrow bridge spanned a sluggish rivulet called Mill Brook. At the rear of the column the grenadiers bunched up in crossing, taking much longer to clear the short span than made anyone feel comfortable.

Off to the north the British found ample cause for concern. Old Bedford Road was inundated by a moving sea of men, which, at sight of the scarlet column, rolled out like a monstrous breaker to surge around the tavern at the crossroads and crowd right up to the stone wall that bordered the road. To the south, the flats were equally alive as companies of men emerged from the direction of Sudbury and Framingham.

It was there, as the last of the grenadiers shoved their way across the constricted bridge, that Armageddon exploded. Riding with Pitcairn near the front of the column, Carleton didn't see the frustration and fear of the soldiers who turned on their stony-faced tormentors and fired wildly. But he heard the report and the maelstrom that answered it.

This time the militia's response was immediate and lethal. Two previous encounters, brief though they had been, had irrevocably stripped away the tenuous restraint the colonists' waning loyalty to a distant king had so far provided. Now, as though they had waited for this signal, they swarmed to within point-blank range of the king's troops, heedless of their own safety and intent on exacting retribution.

At the first roar of musket fire, Pitcairn and Carleton reined their mounts around hard and galloped back down the line. Before they could reach the column's end, the rear guard was already on the verge of disintegration, the air thick with lead, the action obscured by greasy smoke. The soldiers who had worked their way into the clear were blazing away like madmen at targets they couldn't see, their volleys of minor effect against the deadly marksmanship of the colonials, while the troops trapped in the center milled about in confusion amid the chaos. From all sides came the shrieks of the wounded and the dying.

For an appalling interval it seemed to Carleton they would never be able to restore any semblance of order and that the entire column would be lost. Many of the officers were shot down in the first few minutes, leaving to those who remained an all but impossible task. Seasoned troops shoved their mates aside to run, oblivious of the furious commands of the officers who galloped back and forth, cursing and striking the runaways with the flat of their swords. Up and down the road a rapidly growing number of soldiers crumpled to writhe in widening pools of blood or to lie motionless in unnatural postures, trampled underfoot in the stampede.

To ELIZABETH, who watched from the prominence of the ridge, it seemed that the road itself ran blood. The breath choked in her throat, she searched the chaotic scene below for the distinctive helmet of the Seventeenth Light Dragoons.

She couldn't erase from her mind the image of Carleton placing his life in danger to save his friend, his fearless confrontation with the oncoming militia, his eloquent, gallant salute. And in spite of her passionate belief that her countrymen had no choice left but to defend themselves against tyranny run amok, cold fear gripped her heart at the thought that he might be killed.

As she stared out across the plain in wordless horror, Levi appeared at her side. "The others have gone ahead," he shouted over the roar of musket fire. "We're to join Parker's company this side of Lexington."

Her heart throbbing wildly, she scrambled down the ridge after him.

THE FEW MILES TO LEXINGTON were a nightmare without respite, a protracted struggle that continued past the point of physical and mental collapse for men already exhausted. By desperate effort Carleton and the other officers succeeded in forming the column up under heavy gunfire. At last the detachment forged on from Meriam's Corner, with difficulty bringing off as many wounded as they could, but forced to leave a distressing number to the mercies of their enemies.

Behind them, under the relentless sun that baked the dust-choked road, a great many lay dead.

Before they reached the crest of Brook's Hill a half mile east of the bridge, every one of the volunteers and unattached officers had been pressed to duty. Carleton had his hands full keeping tight rein on the orphan company of light infantry he and Andrews inherited when the last of its officers took a musket ball through the head.

The parched road's numerous turns dipped repeatedly into small ravines lined with trees and dense brush that concealed parties of snipers, while the open road was commanded by militia units hidden on the heights above them. Individuals, companies, entire regiments dogged every step of their route, falling out whenever ammunition or stamina were exhausted, only to be replaced by even greater numbers of fresh combatants.

The continuous, deafening gunfire and the drone of musket balls frayed raw nerves to the breaking point. The sharp smell of gunpowder and the choking haze of dust stirred up by hundreds of tramping feet clogged their nostrils, burning throat and eyes. By the time the soldiers staggered across the Lincoln boundary, their ammunition was beginning to run dangerously low.

Even under the most intense assault, Carleton felt a certain black humor at his predicament. It didn't take long for him to realize that Smith ordered his company out as flankers more often than any of the others. The colonel's malicious glare made it clear he wouldn't be incapacitated by grief if Carleton were not to return from a foray.

Each time, he and Andrews were forced to dismount and fight their way through the densely wooded, rocky terrain at the head of their detachment. Every boulder and tree trunk concealed pockets of militia. Twice a musket ball grazed his helmet and another furrowed along the outside of his knee and thigh, searing through his breeches and leaving a raw, stinging welt that oozed a steady trickle of blood.

The only concession he made to the danger was to carry his sabre unsheathed. No matter how heavy the rebel fire or how close they were forced to advance to drive the stubborn colonials off, he refused to draw pistol or carbine and insisted that his men advance with bayonets leveled instead of firing. Although Andrews plainly struggled to conceal his fear, he followed Carleton's example without comment, encouraging the frightened soldiers and joining the van without complaint or hesitation.

Several times during the day the thought of Elizabeth had crossed Carleton's mind with a curious, unfamiliar poignancy. They had just driven a strongly armed contingent of militia off the column's right flank when without warning the desire for her stabbed through him once more, this time with an urgency that caught him without defense.

How would she feel when she learned of the day's events? If he didn't return, would she care?

For the first time he admitted how deeply he longed for the comfort and security of a woman's arms. And for a fleeting instant he allowed himself to wonder what her body would feel like pressed against his, how her lips would taste . . .

He brushed the treacherous thoughts away and wearily led his detail through the trees back to the road. So exhausted they moved as though drugged, they walked straight into a vicious fire that had pinned the column below a rocky bluff at a sharp bend, where the road began to

202 ❋ J. M. HOCHSTETLER

wind uphill.

Pitcairn was riding up and down the line, sword drawn as he urged the disoriented, terrified soldiers to form up. Just then a sizable body of militia barricaded behind a stack of fence rails fired at almost point-blank range. Pitcairn's horse reared, then bolted, throwing the major to the ground.

Ordering Andrews to take over command of the company, Carleton fought his way to Pitcairn's side. The major had already scrambled to his feet and was dusting himself off by the time Carleton reached him, and they watched as several of the colonials jumped over the barricade and caught the skittish black gelding's reins.

"Are you all right?"

Pitcairn nodded in disgust. "If ye don't count the loss o' a good horse and a pair o' excellent pistols."

Over the din they heard a bellow of pain. There was no mistaking Smith's voice. They found him lying on the ground, bleeding from a wound through his thigh and in danger of being trampled by the crush of panicked troops.

With some effort, the two officers managed to heave the corpulent colonel to his feet and drag him to the side of the road and under cover of a growth of brush. Carleton knelt to examine the wound, then tore off the sash at Smith's waist and wound the length of silk around his leg to staunch the copious flow of blood.

"That's too tight, curse you!" Smith whined. "I feel faint—I'm going to bleed to death."

"No ye aren't, Francis," soothed Pitcairn. "You're just lucky the ball went all the way through. Now ye won't have to have one of our expert surgeons dig it out for ye."

Smith glared at Carleton. "We all know who's responsible for this disaster."

Carleton raised an eyebrow. "If you mean me, I'm flattered. While I do have many talents, I've never claimed the ability to stir up a general insurrection single-handedly."

"You managed to weasel your way in tight with Gage before you'd been here a day," Smith snarled. "If you're genius enough to do that, you could have talked him into sending artillery with us and giving me a large enough force to teach these villains a lesson they'd never forget. Instead, you took their part. I wouldn't be surprised if you were in league with them."

Pitcairn snorted. "Ye've gone daft, Francis."

"If I am on their side," Carleton answered politely, "then explain to me what the deuce I'm doing out here getting shot at."

Turning on his heel, he stalked away. Pitcairn threw Smith a contemptuous look then followed, leaving the colonel to fend for himself.

Before Carleton could rejoin his company, the entire column splintered once more into a shouting, sweating, shoving horde. He and Pitcairn, along with as many of the other officers as could reach them, rushed to the van. All of them together formed a line across the road, blocking the forward stampede with their bodies and brandishing bayonets, swords, and pistols to warn the hysterical mob back.

"Advance, and ye die!" Pitcairn screamed as he prepared to make good his threat.

Carleton grabbed the nearest drummer by the arm and dragged him forward. Placing the quaking boy in front of him where the child would be shielded by his body, he ordered him to beat "To Arms."

The terrified youth obeyed. Automatically the troops stumbled into line and followed the officers forward. In a mercifully short time the outlying houses of Lexington came into view.

Carleton had to shout to be heard above the musket fire. "I wonder what kind of reception they'll give us this time."

Pitcairn's face was set in grim lines. "If Percy doesn't show up to relieve us soon, we won't have any choice left but to surrender the entire command."

Just then they heard the explosion of cannon fire. A blazing ball arced through the sky high above them and dropped to earth, sending the closest militia regiment scrambling for cover. Within seconds, a second shot blasted a hole through the Meeting House, where some of the colonials had scurried to find shelter.

"Speak of the devil," Carleton said, his tone dry.

A ragged *huzza* rose from the Regulars, and laughing and shouting in hysterical jubilation at their imagined salvation, they staggered forward to find Lord Percy in possession of the town and waiting for them in a state of singular astonishment.

PERCY HAD SET UP TEMPORARY HEADQUARTERS in Munroe Tavern on the eastern edge of town. His face reflecting frustration and impatience, he explained that Gage's orders to move had been sent to his major, who happened that night of all nights to be out late. When the major had finally returned, his servant had neglected to give him the message; consequently it had been six o'clock before Percy had received his orders.

Another hour had been wasted in waiting for Pitcairn's marines to show up before Percy discovered that their orders had been addressed to Pitcairn and sent to his billet. It had been almost nine o'clock before Percy's column had gotten underway, and by then Boston was buzzing with rumors of a skirmish at Lexington.

Pitcairn filled the earl in on the morning's events, to which Mitchell added lurid details. Taking a deep draught from his foaming pint, Pitcairn concluded, "Ye haven't arrived a minute too soon."

His expression reflecting distaste, Carleton shoved away the mug in front of him. "We still have fifteen miles ahead of us before we reach Boston. Now that they've tasted blood, the rebels aren't likely to slink tamely away."

"I'd feel a bit easier if you'd brought a couple more cannon with you," Smith complained, nursing his wounded leg.

Percy frowned. "I hate to tell you, but the only ammunition we brought is what's in the side boxes. I was afraid another wagon would slow us down too much, and I didn't think we'd need it. So much for my estimation of these colonials."

Smith groaned.

"Our combined strength is around eighteen hundred men plus artillery, which should prove some deterrent to even the rashest of the rebels." Percy got to his feet in a gesture of dismissal. "We'll move out in half an hour. I want all officers dismounted. There's no use presenting a better target than we already do."

Carleton followed the others outside. As he stepped out the door, he saw Stowe walking toward him. Pleased that the servant had taken it on himself to come as a volunteer with Percy's brigade, Carleton sent him to make sure his and Andrews's horses were watered before they moved out.

For several moments Carleton studied the heights that surrounded the town, where several large units of militia were visible moving between the trees. Then he went to find his company, reflecting grimly on the twisted path that had led him to that day and to that hour, and wondering if it were blind fate—or something more.

HER MOVEMENTS SLUGGISH WITH FATIGUE, Elizabeth rubbed the sweat off her powder-streaked face with her dirty shirt sleeve, then bent to fill the waiting private's empty powder horn. Beside her on the wagon bed, Levi passed the man a handful of lead balls.

To all sides of the wagon on which Elizabeth and Levi stood, companies and regiments passed at a run. Many detoured long enough to replenish their stock of gunpowder and ball from the wagonloads of ammunition Warren had sent along from Tess's stores on his way out of Boston.

Suppressing a yawn, she raised her eyes from the line of hot, dusty men who waited impatiently for their ration. A short distance away, near the brow of the low hill that offered an unobstructed view of Lexington, a number of officers crowded around Warren and fat, balding Brigadier General William Heath.

As usual, Will and her uncle formed part of the inner circle, all of whom were talking and gesturing excitedly. Even though she couldn't pick up much of what he said, from the expressions of the other officers she judged that they were finding Heath's suggestions to their liking.

Waving off the rest of the men lined up to receive the salt pork, hard biscuit, and ale he'd been doling out from the wagon next to them, Isaiah jumped down and sauntered over to lean against the side of the ammunition wagon.

"What did Warren and Heath decide?" Elizabeth asked him. "Will they let you join the militia?"

Isaiah broke into a wide grin. "They say they take no slaves, but any man that be free can join up."

"What am I going to do without you?"

Before he could answer, the cluster around Heath broke up. Most of the officers hurried off to rejoin their regiments, but Stern and Will started toward them, accompanied by Warren. Hastily Elizabeth and Levi distributed the last of the ammunition and scrambled off the wagon in time to intercept them.

Smiling, Warren took in the streaks of dirt across Elizabeth's face and her dusty, sweat-stained clothing. "It looks as though you've done a good day's work."

Grudgingly, Stern conceded, "She's turning out to be a fine soldier. We could use more men with her spirit."

She could feel Levi stiffening beside her. Whether his father meant the remark as a slap against him, as usual Levi took it that way.

Before Elizabeth could think of a comment to smooth over the undercurrent of tension, Warren fixed her in a keen look. "It's time we sent you home, I'm afraid." He cut her off as she opened her mouth to protest. "Your family has likely discovered your absence by now and will be wondering where you are."

"I don't care! I'm not going back."

"And what do you plan to do? Join the militia?" Stern demanded.

"A woman can fight as well as any man—"

"You have talents that are more valuable to us just now," Warren broke in. "After today, there'll be no further possibility of compromise. Gage must be driven out, and that will mean laying siege to Boston while we build an army. We're going to need someone on the inside."

"What about Patriot? He'll be able to provide you more detailed information than even Elizabeth can."

"After today his situation may change, Joshua. In any event, the ability of Oriole and his band to carry on sabotage, create diversions, and smuggle out munitions may soon become as crucial to us as gathering intelligence."

Turning away, Elizabeth clenched her hand over the rough wood of the wagon's side and let her head droop onto her arm. "I don't see how I can keep on after today," she said as much to herself as to Warren. "There has to be an end sometime."

Warren put his arm around her shoulders, forcing her to face him. "You can do it. You *must* do it. Your role is more vital now than before."

His face contorted with anger, Will stepped between them. "Look, Joseph, she's worn out with all this intrigue. There's a price on her head, and you keep sending her back into the lion's den. I don't blame her for wanting to stop."

Stern patted Elizabeth on the shoulder. "You don't have to go back if you don't want to. Will, Levi, and I will be staying with the army, and Martha will need someone at home to keep her company if you don't want to go back home."

Ignoring the others, Warren kept his intense gaze on Elizabeth. "You know how important this is and how desperately we need your help. Besides, how will your parents feel when they learn of your involvement with the Sons of Liberty?"

He'd played his ace, and Elizabeth cringed, feeling as though each one of them was tearing off a piece of her heart. "I don't have a choice, do I? All right, then. I'll go back."

Warren's relief was obvious. "Get back to Tess's house as quickly as you can. If I know your father, he'll be setting up a hospital for the wounded. He'll undoubtedly send for you soon—if he hasn't already."

"Levi, take her back to Roxbury," Stern snapped, tight-lipped.

Swinging on his heel, he stalked away, his back stiff with anger. Throwing both Elizabeth and Warren a disgusted look, Will strode after his father.

AT MENOTOMY, the Regulars faced the severest test yet. The fighting raged from house to house in the small village, and not even Percy could restrain the rampaging troops. Without discrimination they put to death every man, woman, and child they encountered, slaughtered the unlucky animals they chanced upon, and set fire to the homes after looting them of valuables.

Since setting out from Lexington they had been galled front, rear, and on each flank by the deadly sniping of a constantly moving circle of skirmishers. Now the militia was joined by mounted units that galloped ahead of the British line of march, dismounted long enough to shoot at them, then rode off again before they could be engaged.

Expecting the heaviest attack on his flanks and rear, Percy had placed a small vanguard ahead of the column, with the strongest force of fresh troops as flankers and rear guard. Between these he placed Smith's broken command and the carriages that carried the wounded.

Relieved of the necessity of flanking, Carleton's company ended up directly behind the vanguard. Contrary to Percy's estimation, however, the pressure of the rebels was almost as severe in front as at the rear, and their casualties mounted steadily.

Smith managed to keep up with his detachment, limping along with a stout branch as a crutch. Carleton could feel the colonel's malignant gaze boring into him.

Not long after they passed Black Horse Tavern, Percy and Pitcairn moved off in the direction of the column's rear. As soon as they were out of sight, Smith pushed his way through the lines to intercept Carleton. Ordering him out of the line of march, he snarled at Andrews to keep moving.

The lieutenant threw Carleton a worried, questioning look, before hesitantly moving off at Carleton's gesture of dismissal. Although Stowe hovered at Carleton's elbow, Smith made a point of ignoring him.

A sneer twisted the colonel's lips. "I have an assignment that's tailor-made for a man of your talents. We've received a report that the rebels have taken up the planks of the Great Bridge to keep us from crossing. If that's true, we'll be trapped once we turn onto Cambridge Road. So I want you to ride on ahead, check the condition of the bridge, then report back on the double."

Carleton paled as he looked from Smith to the road ahead of them. Several sizable bands of militia were scurrying through the underbrush to post themselves in the woods along each side of the road. As he watched, a strongly armed company of horsemen appeared over the far rise.

"It's a fool's errand. I'll never make it back. But that's what you want, isn't it?"

"You have my order, sir. Do you refuse to obey it?"

Carleton stared into Smith's cold, unforgiving eyes for a long, tense moment, then involuntarily glanced toward the rear of the column. Percy was still nowhere in sight.

"What's the matter, Carleton? Looking for Percy's skirts to hide behind? It's just as I thought—your brave talk is nothing more than a cloak for cowardice."

He knew it was foolish pride, but a bolt of rage surged through

Carleton with the force of lightning. Not allowing himself time to think, he tore the stallion's reins out of Stowe's hand.

"No, sir, ye can't do it!" Stowe protested vehemently. "It's bloody murder."

Gritting his teeth, Carleton put his foot in the stirrup and swung into the saddle, ignoring the balls that swarmed through the air around him. The bay danced nervously amid the deafening crackle of musket fire, but Carleton dug his spurs into the trembling animal's sweat-darkened flanks, bent over his neck, and coaxed him forward.

Oblivious to the astonishment of the troops he passed, he wove a reckless path through the marching ranks, shot past Andrews in a blur, only faintly hearing his friend cry out his name, and charged through the van. The riders on the hill had pulled up to watch him, and for agonizing yards he thought they might let him pass after all.

Then he saw the officer in the lead raise his pistol.

He gave a hard jerk on the reins. As the bay swerved to the right, the ball hissed past his ear. But at the same instant he spurred his mount in a desperate attempt to recover his course, the second rider fired.

There was an instant of blank shock as though someone had struck him hard in the chest, knocking the breath out of his lungs. As the bay reared under him, he lost the reins, clawed at the animal's mane in a desperate attempt to keep from falling, only to realize in dismay that the strength had gone out of his hands and arms.

A vicious jolt of agony seared through him then, as if he had been impaled upon the red-hot point of a spear. This was followed by a great tide of pain that melted the hot sunlight into a suffocating, darkening sea that sucked him down and down into its swirling depths.

Chapter Fourteen

IT WAS HALF PAST SEVEN that Wednesday evening by the time Elizabeth entered the dimly lit, echoing warehouse. Picking her way around the rows of thin straw pallets strewn across the stone floor, she reviewed the alibi she and Tess had worked out while she bathed, then dressed in a plain blue linen gown and white apron.

It wasn't far from the truth. It just didn't include quite all the details.

She'd gotten back to Tess's house shortly before five o'clock that afternoon, only to discover that her father had shown up three hours before to take her with him to the hospital the army surgeons had begun setting up in a large, vacant warehouse near the North End wharves. In spite of Tess's best efforts to smooth things over, he had guessed at once where his daughter had gone and had returned to Boston more angry than Tess had ever seen him.

Now, in the wavering light of scattered lanterns and the few torches hung in rusty iron sconces along the rough brick walls, Elizabeth made out her father's familiar form across the vast hall with several of the army surgeons. Their conversation didn't appear to be agreeable, not surprising since most of them resented her father because so many of the officers preferred his services to theirs.

Her steps lagged as she moved toward him, but before she had advanced far, he turned in her direction. As their eyes met, his narrowed. Excusing himself, he strode to meet her.

"So you went to Lexington. Do you mind giving me an explanation?" His voice was as cold as his stare, and there was a hardness in his look that sent a chill up her back.

"We'd been hearing rumors," she began humbly, "and I was worried. I didn't think I'd be in any danger—"

"That's right. As usual, you didn't think." He stopped, gave her a piercing look. "I suppose you went to find your uncle and cousins."

She bent her head, tears welling up in spite of her attempts to blink them back, her carefully rehearsed story forgotten. "Yes, Papa. I was afraid . . . "

The unrelieved tension and anxiety of the past twenty-four hours got the better of her, and the words ended in a ragged sob. As the memory of the broken, bleeding bodies on Lexington Green, at Concord Bridge, and beside Mill Stream flooded over her, hot tears spilled down her cheeks.

After an awkward hesitation, he pulled her against his chest in a rough embrace. "They're all right?"

She nodded, unable to speak.

"We've been hearing horror stories all day. Did you get close enough to see how bad it was?"

There was no way to tiptoe around the truth. "A great many are dead. They're going to be bringing in a lot of wounded." Again the tears flowed.

"I'm sorry you had to see it, Beth," he said gently, calling her by the pet name he had not used since she had grown up. "I apologize for my anger, but it never occurred to me you'd run off into the middle of a battle. All I could think was that you'd get hurt—or killed. There are times I want to spank you, grown up as you are. You don't—or won't—stop to think how your carelessness hurts those who love you."

She buried her face against his chest and began to cry in earnest. "I'm sorry, Papa. You have every right to be angry. Can you forgive me?"

She could feel his chest raise and lower with a sigh, then he kissed her on the forehead. "You're a grown woman, after all, and you have the right to make your own decisions. I only wish you wouldn't worry your mother so. I won't tell her about this, if you won't. It would put her in her grave."

In spite of herself, Elizabeth giggled in response to his crooked smile. As she wiped away her tears, he cocked his head. She heard it also: the boom of a cannon firing in the distance. Together they ran for the door.

Outside, shadows stretched in long shafts across the cobblestones. On the other side of the bay, behind and above the clustered houses of Charlestown, the molten edge of the orange sun was just sinking below the western hills.

Flashes of cannon and musket fire sparkled like fireflies through the darkness that shrouded the near side of Bunker's Hill. They could make out the frantic movement of troops pouring down from its summit toward the docks, where longboats already waited to bring off the shattered detachments.

Within a half hour the wounded began to arrive, crowded into commandeered carriages, carried by friends, hobbling along painfully on their own. In half an hour more, Elizabeth's mind had grown numb at the devastation that met her eyes.

In a short time the air in the vast, unventilated room had become rancid with the stench of blood, stale sweat, and vomit. Surgeons and nurses had almost to shout to hear each other over the groans and pleas of the critically injured and the shrieks of those undergoing crude, hasty surgeries without anesthetic. But it was the ones who lay still and without complaint that Elizabeth dreaded most, for she knew they would not live to see daylight.

Her respect for her father deepened as she watched him minister to the wounded, soothing pain and fear while dispassionately judging who would benefit from his attention and who would not. By taking him as her example she found the chaotic hour that followed easier to bear.

Trying not to give way to feeling, she concentrated on obeying his orders with practiced efficiency as she hurried along at his heels, all the while pretending not to hear the disdainful comments of the surgeons and the soldiers' wives and older matrons who assisted as nurses. The latter made no effort to hide their opinion that a young unmarried woman had no business trying to care for wounded men. Several even ventured crude, suggestive assessments of Elizabeth's motives.

Dr. Howard had finally had enough. Fixing a particularly vocal matron in a cold stare, he silenced her by saying in a voice that everyone in the vicinity could hear, "My daughter knows how to care for the wounded and sick, and she does it without wasting time in gossip. I wish the same could be said of everyone here."

Smith was brought in with the first great wave of wounded. With a petulant gesture the heavy-bodied colonel waved away the surgeons who clustered around him and demanded Dr. Howard.

Elizabeth had to struggle to stifle her contempt for the man, but her father patiently calmed him while he unwound the blood-soaked sash from around Smith's thigh. Motioning Elizabeth to slit the leg of Smith's breeches, he sat back on his heels while she exposed the wound, then applied steady pressure to control the bleeding.

They worked swiftly, shoulder to shoulder, Elizabeth instinctively anticipating her father's directions. Absorbed in cleansing the wound, by degrees she became aware of a commotion at the door, and glanced up.

She saw Andrews first, and her hand faltered, her first, terrified thought that he had been wounded. His face was smudged with grime, drawn with fatigue, and his uniform was in several places darkly stained with blood. Then her eyes fell on Stowe and Briggs who followed him into the hall, and she started to her feet, her heart constricting.

Between them, supported with difficulty in their arms, sagged Carleton. His clothing was streaked with dirt and his tangled hair fell loose across his face. Under his uniform coat, which had been taken off and thrown over his shoulders, his waistcoat was unbuttoned, the shirt torn open to reveal the rough bandages that bound his chest.

His left arm hung limp in a makeshift sling. All down his left side, waistcoat, shirt, and bandages were saturated through with blood.

Even at that distance she could make out the greyish pallor of his skin. The expressions of his companions reflected panic as they looked urgently around for aid.

Glancing up, Dr. Howard followed her gaze. He took a quick breath, then his mouth tightened.

"Find out what his condition is. I'll finished here as quickly as I can."

In heedless haste she made her way across the hall, stepping over and around pallets, shoving past clusters of surgeons, nurses, soldiers. When she reached Andrews's side he showed no surprise at her presence, just clutched her by both arms.

"Thank God you're here! Your father—?"

"He's coming. When—how long ago—?"

"I don't know. Hours. I didn't think he'd make it."

She pushed past him to cup Carleton's chin in her hands. His skin felt burning hot to her touch, and he made no resistance as she forced his head up until she could look into his eyes.

"Major Carleton, can you hear me? Do you know where you are?"

He looked at her with dull disinterest, his eyes glazed with fatigue and pain, no sign of recognition in them. She threw a swift glance around her, then motioned to Stowe and Briggs to follow. Directing Andrews to fetch a basin and a pitcher of water, she helped the soldiers ease Carleton onto the nearest unoccupied pallet. In spite of their care, his face contorted as they lowered him to the floor, and he groaned through gritted teeth.

Andrews hurried back to set the basin and pitcher on the floor beside her. While Stowe and Briggs hovered helplessly on either side, Elizabeth sponged the sweat and dirt from Carleton's face, then moistened his parched lips with the wet cloth. After a moment he roused, and she held the pitcher to his lips.

He swallowed the water thirstily, but she let him have only a little for fear it would make him vomit. As she set the pitcher back down, his eyes focused on her face, and wincing with pain he reached his right hand to brush her cheek with his fingertips.

"Am I . . . dreaming . . . or are you . . . really here?"

"I'm here, Jonathan. Don't be afraid."

"You won't . . . leave me? I don't think I . . . can bear it if . . . you go away . . . again."

"I'm not going anywhere. I'll stay right here beside you."

With a barely perceptible sigh, he closed his eyes, his head drooping to one side. For an instant of blank terror, she was certain the battle was lost before it had begun. Praying wordlessly, she pressed her fingers to his neck below his jaw. Though it was dangerously faint, she could feel the reassuring throb beneath the skin.

Relief flowed through her. Wasting no more time, she pulled a pair of surgical scissors from her apron pocket and began to cut through his sodden waistcoat and shirt, ripping the stubborn cloth where it resisted her haste as she stripped away the ruined clothing. After showing Andrews how to apply pressure on the edges of the wound to control the bleeding, she carefully cut through the makeshift bandage that bound Carleton's chest and shoulder, then steadied herself before peeling back the blood-stiffened cloths as gently as possible.

She had to bite her lip hard to keep from crying out at sight of the raw, shredded flesh just below his left shoulder. A steady crimson pool oozed from the ragged, blue lip of the hole.

The blood was dark, and she breathed a prayer of gratitude. At least the ball had hit a vein, not an artery. Of course, if it had torn through the latter, he would not have made it this far.

With trembling hands, she tore off a length of clean bandage and folded it into a thick pad, pressed it firmly against the wound. Almost immediately a red stain spread outward across the white surface, but to her relief, after a moment it slowed, finally stopped.

While Andrews held the bandage in place, she laid her head on Carleton's chest and listened to his breathing. By a miracle, his lung had escaped damage. Springing to her feet, she ran to find her father.

He had just finished bandaging Smith's thigh. "How bad is he?" he asked as he took in the expression on her face.

"Come right away," she pleaded, her mouth dry with fear. "The wound is deep, and he's lost a good deal of blood. I'm afraid he may die."

"If you don't take care of my leg, I'll end up a cripple!" whined Smith.

Dr. Howard patted his shoulder. "Your leg's going to be fine, Francis. You need to rest now. I'll check on you in a little while."

Only one who knew her father as intimately as Elizabeth would have read the disdain in his tone and look. Catching up his surgeon's case, he hurried after her.

The moment he bent over Carleton, she saw the closed, emotionless look come over his face that she often noted when he attended someone who had no chance to recover. It was as if he consciously distanced himself from his patient as a defense against the ultimate impotence to hold death in check. Seeing it now, she felt the cold fingers of dread tighten over her heart.

Without speaking, he reached to feel the pulse at Carleton's throat, checked his eyes, laid his ear against his chest. When he lifted the edge of the bandage to examine the wound, Carleton stirred briefly, but did not open his eyes. Dr. Howard straightened, and seeing Elizabeth's stricken expression, pulled her aside.

"He's lost too much blood, and the ball's done considerable damage. If that were all, it would be a miracle if he survived the night. But that fever indicates infection has already taken hold. He's too weak to fight that too."

"The ball missed his lung. If we can get it out and stop the bleeding, he may pull through. We've got to try, Papa—we can't just sit back and watch him die!"

His eyes softened at the passion of her plea. For a moment he hesitated, then he took the probe she held out to him.

"If I can't get the ball out right away, we'll have to leave it or we'll kill him by trying." He sighed. "Of course, if we don't get it out, the infection will worsen."

Hardly hearing him, she nodded, began to rummage through his case, pulling out scalpels, a needle and ligatures, bullet forceps, her fingers fumbling in her haste.

There was no time to lose. Carleton had drifted into consciousness, and she forced a twisted length of bandage between his teeth. Drawing aside the now saturated bandage on his chest, she applied firm pressure on the edges of the wound while Dr. Howard began to probe the torn flesh with delicate precision. At the first touch, beads of sweat broke out across Carleton's forehead. A groan escaped his lips, and he writhed in helpless agony, gagging on the cloth.

Elizabeth motioned to Andrews and Stowe. Hastily the two knelt to hold Carleton steady, Andrews at his head, Stowe at his feet. Dr. Howard glanced up, sweat trickling down his brow.

"The ball's just between the ribs. If you can control the bleeding, I think I can get it out."

Forcing herself to concentrate, Elizabeth increased pressure at the site of the wound. With her other hand she doggedly sponged away the crimson flow while Dr. Howard again probed for the ball.

Carleton was drenched with sweat, his skin clammy. With each passing second he grew perceptibly weaker. And although she struggled to blot out consciousness of the anguish on Stowe's and Andrews's faces, the fear in her own heart tightened until it formed an agonizing knot in her breast.

When she was certain Carleton could not endure more of the torture, Dr. Howard located the ball deep within the torn muscles and between the bones. It took only a second longer for him to loosen the flattened, slippery piece of lead with the probe and pluck it out.

By then blood-soaked cloths littered the floor around Elizabeth's knees. Glancing toward him as she reached for needle and ligatures, she saw that Carleton had mercifully lost consciousness.

RUBBING HER BURNING EYES, Elizabeth jerked awake at the light touch on her shoulder. Lord Percy bent over her. Behind him stood Pitcairn. It was past midnight, but the last of the wounded were just now being carried in through a cold rain.

She scrambled to her knees and bent over Carleton's pallet, uncertain whether he was unconscious or sleeping. His face and hair were wet with sweat, and his forehead felt dangerously hot to her touch. His breathing shallow and irregular, he rolled his head restlessly from side to side.

Stretched out beside him on the floor, Andrews had surrendered to exhaustion. A couple of yards away, Stowe and Briggs sat with their backs propped against the wall, snoring, heads drooping onto their chests.

"Is he going to make it?" Pitcairn asked, his voice gruff.

She checked the bandage that bound Carleton's shoulder. No more blood had seeped through. With a light and gentle touch she laid her hand on his brow, feeling, as she did so, a familiar, quiet peace flow out of her to him. After a moment his breathing steadied and deepened, and he lay still.

Looking up to meet Pitcairn's gaze, she smiled. "I can't say for certain, but the bleeding has stopped. That's a good sign. At least he has a fighting chance now."

"If it were up to me, I'd have Smith's hide for this." Although Percy kept his voice low, it shook with anger. At her questioning look, he explained, "The fool waited until I was at the rear of the column, then he ordered Jon to ride on ahead to Cambridge to make sure the Great Bridge was passable. Jon made it a quarter of a mile, if that."

The color drained out of Elizabeth's face as she stared at Percy in disbelief. Awakened by their voices, Stowe crawled over to Carleton's side.

"The major protested the order, sir, but Smith called 'im a coward, knowin' no man'd bear that. If ye ask me, it's pure, bloody murder."

They were interrupted by Dr. Howard, who looked as worn out as Elizabeth felt. He had his coat off, his shirt sleeves rolled back to the elbow. Blood streaked his shirt and waistcoat.

The two officers conferred with him for several minutes before leaving. After they had gone, Dr. Howard gave Carleton a cursory examination, then straightened, frowning.

"He's holding his own, but this fever worries me. As much as I'm loath to move him, I'm certain his chances would improve a thousand percent if we could get him away from here and any further infection."

He didn't need to persuade Elizabeth. They woke the others and sent Stowe hustling outside to bring her phaeton around while Elizabeth fashioned a sling for Carleton's left arm and wrapped a blanket around him. Together they were able to rouse him, get him to his feet and into the carriage, delirious, but conscious. Promising to stop by as soon as he could get away, Dr. Howard saw them off.

Keeping a firm hand on the reins, Stowe eased the phaeton over the cobbled streets with the gentleness of a mother rocking her child. Even so, they had to stop three times while Carleton was racked by vomiting. But although he shivered with chills by the time they reached the town house, Elizabeth was encouraged to see that he was more alert than when they had left the hospital.

They managed the stairs without too much difficulty. Once Carleton was seated on the edge of the bed, Stowe and Andrews worked at prying off his boots, while Briggs built up the fire. Pulling the blanket from around Carleton's shoulders, Elizabeth reached to undo the buttons of his breeches.

"I think . . . I can manage that," Carleton said, his voice hoarse, but steady.

She looked up to meet his gaze, and hot color flooded her cheeks.

"I'd like some water," he added with an effort. "I'm deuced thirsty."

"I'll bring some right away."

Ignoring the grins the others exchanged, she went to the door. On her way out, she glanced back and said sweetly, "To set your mind at ease, major, I have seen more than a few men undressed in the course of my work, and I can't imagine you're equipped any differently."

SHE STRUGGLED TO SUPPRESS A YAWN, but it was no use. She wasn't going to be able to stay awake much longer.

She eyed the bed longingly. Some time ago, Carleton had finally sunk into a restless sleep. Briggs had crept away to get some rest, and Andrews had also given in to fatigue and retired to his own bed across the hall, leaving the doors open so he could hear her call if she needed him.

Stowe alone remained, curled up on the rug next to Carleton's side of the bed, fitfully asleep like a faithful dog guarding a beloved master. All her efforts to persuade him to go to bed had been futile.

She felt confident that Carleton was in no immediate danger. The first crisis had passed, and with luck his fever would not worsen.

The unoccupied half of the bed beckoned her insistently, and she finally gave in to physical necessity. Tiptoeing around Stowe, she blew out the candle on the dresser. In the faint illumination of the moonlight that slanted through the shutters and the dying firelight from the hearth, she found her way around to the opposite side of the bed.

After pulling out the pins that held the chignon at the back of her neck, she shook her long hair loose over her shoulders. With a sigh, she took off her apron and loosened the waist of her gown and the stays beneath before gratefully creeping onto the wide bed, careful to avoid disturbing its occupant. For a moment she bent over Carleton to reassure herself that his condition hadn't changed, that he still slept.

Earlier, even as she had worked with desperate haste to save his life, she hadn't been able to help but notice how well proportioned his body was, how smoothly taut the tanned skin of his chest and arms stretched across the bulging contours of muscle and sinew. On impulse she lightly touched the hard muscles of his arm, brushed her fingertips across the rough, golden stubble on his jaw. A shiver ran through her at the masculine feel of his beard.

At her touch, he turned his head on the pillow, but didn't open his eyes. Studying his face, shadowed with the suffering of that day, she asked herself what it would feel like to kiss him. If she did and he awoke, what would he do?

Hastily she pushed the betraying thoughts away. Sliding back toward the edge of the bed, she lay down and curled up on top of the covers facing him. Briggs had lit the logs in the fireplace just after they first arrived, but by now the fire had died down and the room was becoming chilly. Her cloak lay across the foot of the bed, and she pulled it up, wrapped it around her.

The sensation of the mattress bearing up her aching muscles and of the down pillow beneath her head was too seductive to resist. Promising herself she would sleep no more than a couple of hours, for the first time in almost two days she allowed herself to relax.

Her last conscious awareness was of Carleton's nearness, of the sound of his labored breathing, and of wondering what it would be like to lie beside him each night and to wake each morning in his arms.

Chapter Fifteen

Pᴀɪɴ sᴏ ᴀʟʟ ᴇɴᴠᴇʟᴏᴘɪɴɢ it pinned him to the bed with the weight of a white-hot anvil dragged him back from merciful insensibility, scattering the fever-induced dreams that possessed his mind. As each time before, it was the first sensation he became aware of, then nausea flooded over him and a sense of dread.

Gradually he became aware that someone lay beside him. He began to open his eyes, quickly squeezed them shut again to ward off the sensation of the room spinning crazily.

When he was at length able to force his eyes open, he lay for a long time motionless, staring at her, suffused with relief to find her beside him, afraid he was dreaming again. The first blush of dawn tentatively lightened the room, and he drank in the fine, regular features of her delicately modeled face, beguiling in repose with the unself-conscious innocence of a child.

The passion and sweetness in the curve of her mouth had made him hungry to kiss her ever since she'd tumbled into his arms at that first, accidental meeting. In spite of the pain, he found himself longing to bury his face in the lustrous curls that tumbled across her throat and breast in a glorious cascade, to seek redemption in her love.

If only he could touch her, reassure himself that she was indeed flesh and blood—but it hurt too much to move. His whole body felt raw, heavy, unresponsive as stone. He had neither the energy nor the strength of will to fight against the bone-deep weariness that kept sucking him beneath the surface of that dark swamp he feared so much, felt himself slipping back into suffocating heat and sapping agony. All he could do was cling to the hope that she would still be beside him the next time he awoke.

An indeterminate period dragged by with torturous slowness, then he became conscious that it was day and that someone was bathing his face and body. He started to call Elizabeth's name, but stopped himself, remembering there was danger in giving in to his desire for her, although he had forgotten the reasons why.

From time to time someone held a glass to his lips. Often the fluid it contained tasted bitter, but thirst drove him to drink it. And each time, to his relief, the pain soon lessened, and he felt as though he drifted weightless in space.

For long periods he wandered through a desolate land of shadows and drifting fog, alone and frightened. He was distantly aware that people came and went, that they called his name, changed his bandages or bathed him, forced him to drink warm broth or thin gruel. But he recognized no one. All he knew was that he wanted none of them. He wanted no one but Elizabeth.

Over time a deeper longing took the place of his need for her. The memory of the nightmarish hours during the retreat from Concord swam through his mind like the residue of a hellish dream, although the pain that riveted him to the bed testified to its reality. And he remembered that at some point, well before they'd made the turn onto Charlestown Road, he'd given up hope of enduring long enough to reach the safety of Boston. Yet he had, and now he began to ask himself why.

That he wasn't going to die after all, even though he knew he was very ill, was a certainty he began by degrees to rest in. He didn't know the answer to that why either. What was he doing there safe on that bed when so many others had died? What—or who—had brought him through when his own strength had given out? Who watched over him now?

Was there some meaning to his life, a larger purpose he couldn't yet see? He had stopped believing that years ago, and now he was afraid to consider the possibility that it might be true after all.

Each time he floated up just below the surface of consciousness, the questions, more painful than his wounds, began to circle through his mind, tearing at him like ravenous wolves. But with the tortured passage of time, he became aware of another presence in the room, an unseeable Spirit that hovered above him on mighty wings. The sense of *someone* was so real it sent a thrill through him—not of fear, but of welcome, safety, infinite peace.

He'd searched all those years without its ever revealing itself to him, and though he'd all but given up hope of finding it, now when he needed it most it unexpectedly enveloped him, bore him up above the sea of agony and turmoil. He didn't have the strength to question who it was or why it had come. All he could do was to surrender himself to its arms in mute gratitude.

And resting in that loving presence, he slept like a little child.

"YOU'RE A LUCKY MAN, JON."

Carleton grimaced. "I don't feel especially lucky."

Dr. Howard closed his medical case. "Well, you should. The ball missed your lung by a hair, and if it had gone an inch higher, it would have destroyed your shoulder and crippled you for life, if you hadn't bled to death. I'd say someone was looking out for you."

Carleton sighed and laid his head back on the pillow. Closing his eyes, he said in a muffled voice, "I can't argue with you on that score. My question is—why?"

Elizabeth came into the room carrying a bed tray, on which were a covered plate and a glass of milk. She was dressed in deep rose, her hair swept back into a chignon from which beguiling strands escaped to curl at her temples and ears.

Setting the tray on the table by the window, she pulled back the curtains to admit a flood of morning light. He couldn't keep his eyes away from her, and when she turned she blushed at what she must have read in his eyes before he could avert his gaze.

An hour before, Stowe had bathed him as though handling a newborn infant, gotten a clean nightshirt on him without too much pain, and promised him a shave later that morning. The sheets on the bed, bloodstained and soaked with sweat, had been changed for clean ones, and he'd been comfortably propped up against a pile of soft pillows. A short time ago Elizabeth had settled herself on the bed beside him to brush and tie back his hair, an unconsciously intimate gesture that had made it necessary for him to concentrate on shoring up the fragments of his defenses.

Looking around the room now, he noted the small touches only a woman would have thought of. The personal possessions he'd brought with him from Virginia had been disposed so that his surroundings felt familiar and welcoming. His books lay in a casual stack on the table, and his woven plaid in the deep blues and greys of the Carleton tartan, which he had stuffed into his kit on a whim before leaving Thornlea, was draped across the wing chair next to it. Somewhere she'd even found several cushions that echoed the plaid's colors and had propped his violin case in the corner of the window seat amid a pile of them.

On the dresser across the room a vase of daffodils and narcissus reflected their vivid colors in the mirror, while a smaller vase of deep purple violets brightened the breakfast tray. Everything his eyes lighted on was fresh and welcoming.

He had lived in the world of men too long, he realized with a pang of regret. A woman had a way of bringing grace and beauty to her surroundings without conscious effort. Where Elizabeth was concerned, however, he wished mightily those feminine virtues were not quite so alluring.

He had realized early on that in flirting with her he was playing with fire—as too often before. He had a penchant for it, in fact. It amused him to do so. But he'd assured himself that he'd not get burned, not allow himself to get sucked in by her charms and fall in love with her.

That, however, was an endeavor that was becoming more daunting by the day.

Coming to his side, she placed her hand on his forehead. "You look much better this morning. The tinctures of laudanum and cinchona have helped—your fever's almost gone. By the way, Lord Percy and Major Pitcairn stopped by yesterday and the day before, but you were asleep both times. They promised to look in again today. Oh, and General Gage sent word he intends to call to see how you're doing."

Carleton rubbed his beard with his good hand. "What day is it?"

"Monday."

He threw her a searching look. "Where've I been?"

She laughed. "Far away." Sobering, she added, "Several times I thought we were going to lose you. If you hadn't been so fit, I'm afraid you wouldn't have pulled through."

Dr. Howard put his arm around her shoulders and gave her a quick hug. "The credit is due to Elizabeth. I couldn't have done a better job of looking after you myself."

Carleton looked at her with an expression she couldn't read. "I thought you'd gone away. Were you here all the time?"

"I promised I'd stay."

He looked away, frowning.

Dr. Howard cleared his throat, then picked up his case. "I need to get back to the hospital. Not all our casualties are going to be as fortunate as you. Many of those who survive are going to end up crippled or invalids for life."

"What's the military situation?" As Elizabeth set the tray across his lap and removed the cover from the plate, Carleton regarded the single poached egg and sliver of toast with distaste. "That isn't all I get, is it?"

She tucked a napkin around his neck. "You aren't ready to handle much solid food yet, and I don't relish the thought of cleaning up after you if you throw up."

"So you intend to starve me as a precaution."

She put her hands on her hips. "Drink your milk and don't grumble—you'll have more later." As he complied sulkily, she amended, "Actually, I'd better not make any promises. The rebels have pulled together a fair-sized army and occupied the heights from Dorchester on past Cambridge. So many regiments are coming in every day that it looks as if they'll soon be able to extend the lines all the way to Charlestown. We're already having trouble getting fresh provisions. It appears they mean to starve us out."

Dr. Howard snorted. "If I know our brave patriots, the realities of warfare will soon wear thin, and they'll begin to fight among themselves. Mark my words, they'll all have melted away before summer—if they last that long."

"My experience with the Yankees has been that they're as stubborn as they are resourceful," Carleton countered through a mouthful of egg.

"I would feel more comfortable if the general hadn't ordered the evacuation of Charlestown peninsula," Dr. Howard conceded. "I can't conceive why he's given away such a valuable strategic position, especially since Montresor had already begun to fortify it."

"Isaiah and his oldest son joined the rebel army," Elizabeth told Carleton. "Only Sarah, Pete, and Jemma are still with us."

Dr. Howard went to the window and stared outside, his face tense. "Stony Hill has become virtually a no-man's land, with the rebels breathing down our necks from Roxbury Heights. The cannon at the Neck saved us from being taken over, but I don't know how long we'll be able to hold out. Needless to say, Mrs. Howard is quite beside herself."

Carleton nibbled on a slice of dry toast. He didn't want to admit that Elizabeth had been right, but the nausea was beginning to return, and the thought of lying down seemed suddenly very appealing.

Giving him a sharp look, Elizabeth removed the bed tray. "That's enough for now. If you don't get some rest, you'll have a relapse."

"Where's Charles?"

"Lord Percy lost so many officers that he's put him to work until your troop arrives. When he gets back later this afternoon, he'll fill you in on everything you're bursting to find out. Right now, you're going to take a nap."

She wouldn't be persuaded otherwise, and when Dr. Howard had gone, she made sure Carleton was comfortably settled, then pulled the curtains half closed. He watched her with drowsy interest.

"Did you sleep here beside me that first night, or was I dreaming?"

She came to the bedside, the color deepening in her cheeks in spite of her matter-of-fact reply. "I was pretty worn out, but I wanted to stay close by in case you got worse."

"I didn't mind. I was glad you were there." He stopped and looked away. "You said you've . . . been here all the time."

She smiled at the implied question. "When I was a little girl that bedroom on the other side of the dressing room was mine. With the doors open, I can hear if you call."

He grinned. "Won't the whole town be scandalized at your staying unchaperoned in a household of men?"

"Not in the least, since I had Stowe bring up a cot for Mrs. Dalton. She's been staying every night too."

"I'm relieved—for the sake of your reputation."

Giving him a sour look, she retrieved the bed tray from the table. "Your concern for my virtue is very touching, sir."

"Are we going to remain on formal terms forever?" he snapped in sudden irritation. "After all this, I should think we could be a little more familiar with each other."

This time she couldn't suppress a smile. "I don't mind, if that's what you'd like, Jonathan."

With his good arm he yanked loose the covers she'd tucked around him and settled himself into a more comfortable position. "That's better. Put that tray down and come here, Elizabeth."

Puzzled, she returned the tray to the table and came to his side. To her surprise, he took her hand and kissed it, then pressed it to his cheek.

"Abby calls you Beth."

"When she was little it was easier for her to say than Elizabeth." She hesitated. "You may call me Beth if you'd like." Despite every effort, she couldn't quite keep her voice steady.

"You'll find me a cantankerous sort, Beth," he said in a muffled voice, "but I do appreciate everything you've done. I owe you my life. So no matter how difficult I may be at times, never think I'm ungrateful."

Squeezing his fingers, she blinked back sudden tears, angry at herself for again allowing him to so easily move her. Each time it became that much harder to build up the barricades.

She had the disconcerting sensation that she was falling, didn't have the first idea how to stop herself, wasn't certain she wanted to. But after a moment she forced herself to disengage her hand from his, though her heart yearned to leave it there forever.

"You'd better sleep now. I'll check on you in a little while." Picking up the tray, she fled from the room.

"SEE HOW HARD you can squeeze my hand."

He tightened the fingers of his left hand around hers. Every movement of his arm sent a stab of pain through his shoulder, but he was relieved to see he could clench his fingers without great difficulty.

"We'll have you playing the violin again before you know it."

"I'm relieved. It's turned out to be a handy talent for persuading certain stubborn young ladies to dance with me."

Wrinkling her nose, she laughed down at him, then pretended to concentrate on adjusting the sling that bound his arm. This time she was confident that her unpredictable emotions were under strict control.

Carleton had slept the rest of the morning, and after he had awakened she and Stowe had settled him in a chair at the table to eat his lunch. She was pleased to see that even after a short visit from Percy and Pitcairn, he showed little sign of tiring.

Downstairs, someone knocked at the door. After a few moments Mrs. Dalton ushered General Gage upstairs. He greeted Elizabeth with affection.

"The major is doing very well this afternoon," she assured him. "If he continues to improve, I expect him to be fit for light duty in three or four weeks."

"A week," Carleton insisted. "Less, if I have anything to do with it."

Smiling, Gage shook his head. "You're under doctor's orders, and I won't hear of insubordination on the part of one of my officers. You'll return to duty when you're released and not a moment before."

"That settles the matter," Elizabeth said smugly.

Carleton made a wry face. "No fair—you're plotting against me."

As Elizabeth started to excuse herself, the general motioned to her to stay, explaining that his visit would be brief. Pretending a lack of interest she was far from feeling, she busied herself stacking the dishes from Carleton's lunch and tidying the room, while remaining as inconspicuous as possible.

Gage pulled a side chair next to the bed and straddled it, giving Carleton a probing look. "I'm relieved to see you looking so well."

"I understand we're under siege."

Gage sighed. "That's what the rebels are calling it. Our most immediate problem, however, is that all the Loyalists in the area are seeking refuge in Boston. We haven't enough food or housing to supply the people who are already here, but I don't feel I can turn away anyone who is in danger of reprisals."

"Any sign the rebels might try to storm the town?"

"If they do, they're even bigger fools than I think they are. They'd have to brave the Neck against our cannon or hazard crossing the bay under the navy's guns."

Carleton stared out the window. "Their best strategy is to try to starve us out."

Gage shifted in his chair, his expression growing strained. "Well, I'm not sitting idly by. I've ordered the townspeople to turn over all their weapons as a precaution against insurrection. I'm also sending circulars to all the colonial governors to counter the vicious propaganda the rebels are spreading to the effect that we're the ones who fired first. Plus, my report to Parliament about the engagements at Lexington and Concord is going out on the *Sukey* tomorrow."

Carleton jerked his eyes to Gage's. "That should get some action."

"The reinforcements we've been promised should arrive before too much longer, then we'll see about breaking this siege." Gage stopped and placed a hand on Carleton's shoulder. "Now, I didn't stop by to trouble you with this, but to have a frank talk with you. Smith gave me his report, and while I commend your bravery under fire and your concern for the men's safety in volunteering for such a hazardous assignment, I also have to reprimand you for taking such an enormous risk."

Carleton stared at the general, his expression neutral. "Sir?"

"Francis explained that when he mentioned the reports that the rebels had pulled up the planks of the Great Bridge, you insisted on riding ahead to find out if it was passable, and that you refused to be dissuaded in spite of his warnings."

Astonished, Elizabeth opened her mouth without thinking, but before she could blurt out a heated protest Carleton threw her a look that withered the words on her tongue. Swinging away, she crossed to the far side of the room.

Gage glanced at her, then leaned closer to Carleton, his voice low. "It's a miracle you weren't killed. I must insist that you avoid taking such foolhardy risks in future. When you recover enough to take on that assignment we spoke about, you'll have to promise to tread carefully. We can't afford to lose a man of your caliber."

As she strained to hear their conversation, Elizabeth came alert. What assignment was he talking about?

"You're right, of course," Carleton answered in a voice that suddenly sounded weary. "Rest assured I'll be more cautious from now on."

Gage smiled and squeezed Carleton's arm. "I'm sure you will. Judging from my conversations with Percy, Pitcairn, and Mitchell, you've already more than justified my confidence in you. Depending on how our situation develops over the next few months, I may be able to put you into that field command you've been wanting, after all."

"Thank you, sir. I'd appreciate that."

When Gage had gone, Elizabeth returned to the bedside. "According to Stowe, Smith ordered you to ride to Cambridge, though he must have known there was no chance you'd make it alive."

Carleton shrugged, but said nothing.

"Why didn't you tell the general?"

"It would be my word against Smith's."

"Percy, Pitcairn, and Stowe would all back you up—"

"Percy and Pitcairn weren't there. The only witness was Stowe, and he's my servant."

She folded her arms across her chest, anger flooding over her. "You knew the odds. Why didn't you simply refuse?"

"Smith was in command. He would have had me court-martialed for disobeying a direct order."

"That isn't the reason," she shot back. "He called you a coward, and your masculine pride won't bear that."

The muscles in his jaw hardened, and he returned her angry gaze with a smoldering one. When he didn't reply, she snapped, "It's all a game to you men, isn't it? 'I'm the bravest'—'No, I am!' Well, you're the perfect example of why I refuse to ever fall in love!"

Not waiting for an answer, she whirled on her heel and stormed out of the room.

✳ ✳ ✳

Rolling over, she jerked the covers up around her chin. No use trying to sleep. She felt permanently awake.

The evening had dragged by on leaden feet. The memory of Carleton's conversation with Gage and the angry confrontation that had followed kept returning to her mind with the monotonous regularity of the waves slapping against the shore outside her window.

All evening she had been afire with the urgency of reporting Gage's plans to Warren. Unable to come up a plausible excuse for leaving Boston that night, however, she had been forced to keep a tight curb on her impatience.

Andrews had done his best to entertain her, in the process dropping helpful details about the fortification of Copp's Hill by Admiral Graves's marines. But although he had been charming, attentive, and funny, his good humor had grated on her nerves. She had been hard pressed to disguise her irritation, and it had been a relief when it was at last late enough that she could excuse herself on the pretense of retiring for the night.

From the cot across the room she could hear the housekeeper's soft, regular breaths. For the thousandth time she glanced toward the shadowed rectangle of the open dressing room door. As usual, Stowe had insisted on bedding down at the foot of Carleton's bed, and the muffled sounds of his snores were audible from that direction.

The wavering light of the candle at Carleton's bedside had reflected across the planks of the floor for a long time after he had retired. Several times she had heard the creak of his bed and wondered if he was having as much difficulty falling asleep as she was.

A short time ago the candle had been snuffed out, however. Only the glimmer of starlight falling through the half-opened shutters softened the darkness, and against her will the treacherous emotions she had wrestled with all day ensnared her in a clinging web she couldn't seem to break through.

It was an unsettling sensation to realize that Carleton lay a few feet away. She sensed that he also was still awake and as aware of her presence as she was of his.

During his fight for survival it had seemed quite natural for her to sleep near him. But now that he was regaining some strength, her feelings were becoming increasingly bewildering. Could it be the same for him?

The rest of that afternoon and evening had been strained. They had spoken very little to each other. Still brooding over their argument, furious at herself for leaving him with the undoubted impression that she was on the verge of falling in love with him, Elizabeth had made a point of keeping her distance.

She wasn't exactly sure what she was angry about, to tell the truth. For his part, Carleton had made no attempt to bring the subject up. Although he had talked at length with Andrews and she'd heard them laughing from the other room, he had remained withdrawn and wary in her presence.

As she thought about it, tears welled into her eyes. She had come so close to being invited into the well-guarded stronghold of his soul, but her thoughtless words had slammed the door shut between them. Now that the door was once more bolted and double locked from the inside, she found herself desperately wanting to open it again.

At last she sat up, determined to go to him. If he was awake, she would find a way back to that moment when he had taken her hand and asked to call her by that intimate childhood nickname.

Just as she swung her legs over the edge of the bed, the housekeeper muttered in her sleep and rolled over so that she was facing her. Elizabeth lay back down and burrowed beneath the covers, her heart beating hard.

In a state of abject misery, she clenched her teeth and pounded the pillow. It felt as unyielding as rock beneath her head.

No, she decided. Things were safer left as they were. She couldn't risk an entanglement with a British officer, no matter how deeply she longed to learn what secrets lay hidden in his heart. She must never forget even for an instant that absolute secrecy was for her a matter of life and death.

Carleton's condition had improved enough that Stowe could take care of him quite as well as she. And so she decided that when her father stopped by in the morning, she would return with him to Stony Hill. But instead of feeling relieved, she felt even more unhappy than before.

Curled into a tight ball, she heard the mantel clock downstairs strike the second, then the third quarter after two o'clock. At last she heard no more.

Chapter Sixteen

D R. HOWARD CLUCKED TO THE HORSE, and with a jerk the light chaise rolled forward. Releasing a sigh, Elizabeth settled back in the seat. Her head ached and her eyelids felt heavy as lead. It took all her strength of will to force them to remain open.

She directed an appraising glance toward the top of Beacon Hill, rising above the roofs of the houses to her left. Just below the steep crest a company of soldiers labored to construct a temporary redoubt. The lush grass was gouged and the earth scarred where casks filled with earth had been dragged into place. All along these makeshift walls, pointed stakes were being driven into the ground.

An exploratory walk early that morning had revealed that Gage was also fortifying Barton's Point just northwest of Mill Pond. At the same time Admiral Graves's marines were making rapid progress emplacing a battery of twenty-four pounders on the summit of Copp's Hill in the North End at a height equal to that of the looming bulk of Bunker's Hill straight across the water.

Possibilities, however, still lay along Boston's entire west side below the Common, where the bay was too shallow for any of the men-of-war to anchor. Even though the Regulars had begun to set up their white tents all across the wide, grassy field in preparation for the summer's encampment, they had so far posted only a few small batteries along the waterfront, hardly sufficient to protect Boston's vulnerable underbelly.

Her father broke the silence. "Is everything all right?"

Elizabeth forced a smile. "Of course."

"You're unusually quiet this morning. I thought something might be bothering you."

"I'm just tired."

Dr. Howard guided the grey gelding around the fisherman's barrow that blocked the narrow street. Turning the chaise onto School Street, he said, "I'm pleased the major has improved so much that you're able to leave him this soon. I must say, I couldn't have cared for him better myself."

"Thank you, Papa." It took an effort to focus on his words.

"You haven't quarreled, have you? I noticed you hardly spoke to each other."

She gave an elaborate shrug. "I find Major Carleton insufferable, and I'm sure the feeling is mutual."

"That wasn't my impression at all," Dr. Howard returned, his smile diplomatically faint. "Not on either side."

Elizabeth made no reply, but she couldn't help remembering the searching look Carleton had given her when she had told him that she was returning to Stony Hill. By the time she had returned from her walk, Stowe and Andrews had gotten him up, dressed, and established downstairs in a comfortable chair in the parlor. He had seen her come in the door, so to forestall any questions about where she had been, she had blurted out that she would be going home that morning.

His expression had revealed nothing of what he thought or felt. "I'm surprised you've stayed so long," he had said. "Stowe is perfectly capable of taking care of me from now on, so you needn't be bothered. I thank you for all your trouble on my behalf."

Something in his tone and look had left her feeling uncomfortable, and she had made a quick excuse about needing to pack her things. Yet when the moment had come, leaving had been harder than she had thought it would be.

Unexpectedly, in those few days the house had begun to seem like home to her again. Carleton's presence had been in large part responsible for the contentment that had grown stronger in her with each passing day, she admitted reluctantly.

An ache deep in her heart had urged her to turn around and go back to him, but she had refused to give in to it. Tilting her chin to a resolute angle, she had marched after her father without a backward look.

"Your mother is quite taken with him," her father was saying. "She feels the two of you are well suited to each other and that I ought to approach him concerning his intentions toward you."

"Papa, you can't!" Elizabeth cried, horrified.

"Well," he hedged, "I have to admit I like Carleton immensely. I wouldn't mind having him as a son-in-law, and I agree with your mother that you couldn't make a more advantageous match."

Her back ramrod straight, she burst out, "I won't be married off just to satisfy you and Mama. If you try to make me marry him, I swear I'll go live with Aunt Tess—or with Uncle Josh, if necessary."

Angry color flamed into Dr. Howard's face. "If it turns out the major is agreeable to the match, you'll do as we say, young lady. Considering that you'll have a substantial inheritance, I shouldn't think it at all difficult to arrange mutually satisfactory terms."

An unaccustomed wave of terror turned Elizabeth cold inside. She wasn't sure which prospect was worse: being forced to marry a British officer who, if he discovered she was Oriole, would be duty bound to have her arrested; being bound for life to someone who was inimical to her most passionate beliefs, even if her role remained undiscovered; or being offered to him and rejected.

"I can't believe you and Mama would treat me like a . . . a piece of property to be sold to the highest bidder!" she sputtered.

His voice rose in outrage. "You will not speak to me in that tone of voice! Your mother and I have your future security and happiness at heart—"

"Oh. And that's why you mean to force me into a marriage I despise—"

"You're a young, headstrong girl, and you haven't the least idea what's best for you," he returned, in a high state of dudgeon.

"But you and Mama do, of course." Waving away her angry words, she tried another tack. "Papa, I've known Major Carleton barely a week—"

"Your mother and I knew each other for no more than a month before we married, and we've been exceedingly happy these twenty-two years. Love develops over time, as yours will for him."

Her jaw set with defiance, Elizabeth stared straight ahead, her expression reflecting a determination equal to her father's. For some moments, they rode in silence.

At length, Dr. Howard signed and said more quietly, "If this is all because of what Hutchins did—"

"Papa!" Making a quick gesture of protest, she glanced over at him, then away.

"After what happened, I can't blame you for being frightened of marrying. I wish you had told your mother and me everything that was going on between the two of you."

Her head bowed, she stared down at her clenched hands in her lap, tears scalding her eyes. "I couldn't. I was so ashamed."

"It wasn't your fault! You had no experience with a man like that. Even your mother and I thought well of him."

"That's one thing David is very good at—deception."

Dr. Howard hesitated before saying, "I apologize for my harshness at the time. I simply could not bear to see him ruin you."

Elizabeth stared at him, taken aback. "I . . . I thought you were angry because he had joined the Sons of Liberty."

He gave her a wry smile. "Well, that was part of it, of course. I refuse to see my daughter married to one of these detestable rebels. But I was more concerned about the way he treated you when he thought no one was around."

"Oh." They were approaching the town gates, and she frowned, pretending a great interest in the guards who stepped into the road to block their way. "I never thought you suspected," she said in a muffled voice.

He reached over to give her hand a quick squeeze as he drew the carriage to a halt. "Where my daughters are concerned, I see more than you think I do."

After careful scrutiny of the doctor's pass, the guards allowed them to proceed. Just beyond the fortress outside the gate, squadrons of soldiers were digging a triple row of *chevaux de frise* and erecting additional batteries to command the marshes. The sight renewed Elizabeth's fever to reach Warren, and she set aside further thought about the exchange with her father for another time. It took some effort to suppress her impatience until the chaise turned onto the drive at Stony Hill.

Hearing the carriage, Abby came running outside, eager to fill her sister's ears with chatter about the past days' events. Mrs. Howard joined them on the lawn. Following on the argument with her father, her mother's solicitous questions about Carleton's health set Elizabeth's nerves on edge, but she answered calmly and pretended not to see the meaningful look that passed between her parents.

As they turned to go inside, Dr. Howard pointed out the rebel outposts visible on the heights above the estate. They were close enough, Elizabeth noted, that with a spyglass the sentries could surely see into the mansion's windows.

All that held them at bay was the British cannon trained on them from the fortifications at the Neck. Elizabeth reckoned that as long as the gunners on both sides were exceedingly well trained and disciplined, Stony Hill was probably not in too grave a danger of sustaining more than a few stray shots in case a fight developed.

The most pressing of her parents' concerns was the fact that since the skirmishes the previous Wednesday, they had received no word from Tess. By now they were almost sick with worry about her safety.

Although Elizabeth suspected that her irrepressible aunt was in the thick of the action and enjoying herself immensely, her parents' concern gave her sudden inspiration.

Pointing out that sentries on both sides were passing people through the lines for humanitarian reasons, she added, "I should think the safety of a close relative would qualify. They're not likely to pass either of you through since you're known to be staunch Loyalists, but I might have a chance."

Her mother protested that the rebels would undoubtedly shoot her if she approached the lines. But after a lengthy discussion of the risks and appeals to concern over Tess's welfare, her parents' objections wavered. With reluctance Dr. Howard at last agreed to allow Elizabeth to make the attempt.

Sending young Pete to saddle the black, Elizabeth ran up to her room and pulled on her riding habit with trembling fingers, excitement pulsing through her veins with every heartbeat. She took extra care with her hair and clothing, calculating that her appearance might help over-come the objections of even the most suspicious sergeant.

While her anxious parents watched from the carriageway, she rode at a trot up the steep incline toward Roxbury Heights. At her approach the soldiers lounging in the shade of a gnarled pine got to their feet. As she came closer, four of them walked out onto the road to intercept her. Although their expressions were uniformly stern and they carried their muskets with them, they made no move to raise their weapons.

Extending to either side of the road and down toward the low hills of Dorchester off to her left, earthen breastworks marked the rebel army's advanced line. As she drew the black to a halt, heads poked up all along the works to watch the action.

She gave the reception committee a dazzling smile. They didn't appear to be impressed.

"What be yer business?" their leader demanded gruffly.

"You see, sir, we haven't had any news about my old aunt since the battle last week, and we're very worried about her." Elizabeth did her best to look concerned and frightened at the same time. "She's been ill for several months and hasn't been able to get out much. She lives just up the road in Roxbury. Please, sir, won't you let me go see her and make sure she's all right."

The look she gave him would have melted an iceberg, and she saw that her appeal did have some effect. The two younger soldiers showed a definite thaw, and their middle-aged companion shifted from one foot to the other, scratching his chin. However, the one she took to be their sergeant continued to squint up at her with suspicion.

"Ye come from that house down thar, didn't ye? I 'spect ye be that Tory doctor's daughter."

When Elizabeth admitted she was, he fixed her in a calculating stare and allowed as how, since her father was known to be in Gage's pocket, she had to be a spy. Elizabeth's most creative protests and pleas could not convince him otherwise.

Within moments, a number of the soldiers had left their posts behind the breastworks to form a semicircle around Elizabeth and the sentries, taking a lively interest in the proceedings. "Aw, now, Seth, let the little lady through," drawled a strapping farm youth. "She's no more a spy than your aunt Millie, and she's a durn sight purtier."

The others guffawed. Grinning widely, several of his companions shouted encouragement to Elizabeth while the rest expressed their disapproval of their leader's unwarranted hard-heartedness. Elizabeth took full advantage of every opportunity to whet their enthusiasm for her cause, but at length, it became clear she was getting nowhere.

Realizing there was no recourse left but to play her trump card, she told the sergeant sweetly, "If you'll be so kind as to take me to Dr. Warren, I guarantee he'll vouch for me. So will my uncle, Major Stern of the Lincoln militia, and his sons, Captain William Stern and Lieutenant Levi Stern."

This occasioned further heated debate among the guards. Throwing an anxious glance over her shoulder, Elizabeth was alarmed to see her father hurrying up the road to her rescue. Convinced that the game was up, she turned back just as a familiar lanky figure came striding across the open fields in their direction.

Waving her hand, she cried out merrily, "Levi! Hey, Cuz, come vouch for me. These fine gentlemen are convinced I'm a spy!"

Laughing, Levi detoured to her side. "Well, they're probably right. What nefarious business have you been up to? And what took you so long to come over?" Waving the others off, he grabbed the black's reins and vaulted up behind her. "It's all right, boys. I'll make sure she doesn't get into any trouble."

As he guided the mare through the passage between the earthworks, Elizabeth looked back past the astonished soldiers standing in the road to where her father had come to a halt. Pretending not to understand the meaning of his vehement motions for her to return, she gave him a reassuring wave and turned quickly away.

"I'm on my way to deliver a message to General Thomas," Levi told her as he turned the mare toward the outskirts of the small village, "but afterward I'll take you on to Tess's house. She's fine, by the way. Pa, me, Will, and the rest of our officers are all stayin' there so nobody'll bother her for bein' a Tory."

He winked at her. Relieved, Elizabeth laughed.

She looked around her with interest. It was a bright, clear day, warm with little wind, and the smoke from the campfires and the chimneys of the village houses drifted skyward, the scent of wood smoke mingling with the fresh springtime odors of damp earth and greening grass.

Everywhere she saw evidence of the impromptu army that had gathered in haste. Village and field were alive with the movements of thousands of men. Rough entrenchments were rapidly being extended on all sides, and contingents of soldiers, stripped to the waist, sweated over the walls of the fort they were straining to carve into Roxbury Hill.

Many homes appeared to have been taken over by officers and their staffs in the absence of their owners, who had either fled into the country or to Boston, depending on their politics. On both sides of the road, sprawling encampments crisscrossed the open fields. Depending on their commander's discipline and attention to detail, the tents of the various regiments were either scattered haphazardly across hillock and hollow or laid out in precise rows on cleared, leveled ground.

By now it was almost noon, and men were beginning to straggle in for the noon mess. From what Elizabeth could make out, few companies sported uniforms. Most of the men wore their usual daily garb of loose homespun coats over shirts and waistcoats, breeches, and hose in muted colors, along with broad-brimmed hats and buckled shoes.

In answer to a rapid fire of questions, Levi explained that General John Thomas and General Artemas Ward had split the rapidly growing army between them. Thomas had established his command south of the Charles River, while Ward had set up headquarters in Cambridge and spread the regiments under his command northeast toward Charlestown.

At the moment, finding enough housing for all the regiments pouring into the sprawling camp was the most pressing problem the rebel army faced. Many of the companies were weathering the damp, chilly nights in the open.

After Levi delivered a report from his father to General Thomas's aide, they rode on to Tess's home. The Lincoln encampment surrounded the house on two sides, its orderliness a welcome contrast to many they had passed.

Will and Stern were just sitting down to lunch with Tess when they arrived, and she and Levi didn't have to be asked twice to join them at the massive dining room table. After reassuring Tess that her parents were in good health, Elizabeth gave a humorous description of her adventure at the guard post.

"You'd better go see Joseph right away," Stern observed. "He'll give you a pass so you can get through to see your 'old aunt' without running into any more trouble."

Elizabeth looked startled. "In person? Is that wise?"

Will snorted. "You won't be the first Tory to apply for a pass. Joseph has been besieged by a constant stream of folks with every imaginable excuse to be let through the lines, so no one will think twice about you showing up."

Since Stern had a meeting with General Thomas that afternoon and Levi was on guard duty, Will volunteered to take her to Cambridge. When they had passed through Brooklyne, he took a slow breath and plunged in as though he dove into deep water.

"Cuz, I've been thinking a lot about your involvement with us and everything you've done. You've put your life on the line and taken a lot of risks, some, like Pa says, that maybe didn't need to be taken. It's as if you're trying to prove yourself somehow, and that's mad because you don't need to prove yourself to anyone.

"I know—you're a grown woman, and you can make your own decisions," he continued, before she could break in. "You're not the little girl I used to ride around on my shoulders and take fishing. But I worry about you. I don't want you to get hurt, and I don't want you stepping outside God's will either because that's the surest way to get hurt."

She stared down the road, finally said in a muffled voice, "I feel I have to do everything I can, Will. I have access that no one else has. And if I stand by and we fail, then I'll be responsible, at least in part."

Will nodded. "I feel the same way, but I'm not rubbing elbows with British officers every day. I don't know everything that goes on, but it's a pretty good bet you're flirting with them a lot to get the information you do, and maybe more than would be pleasing to the Lord. No amount of intelligence is worth putting your reputation or your life in jeopardy. It may seem like a game to get what you want, but some men don't take no for an answer. I just want you to be careful."

Smiling, she urged Night Mare alongside her cousin's rangy chestnut. Leaning sideways, she kissed Will on the cheek. He put his arm around her, drew her into a quick hug before releasing her again.

"I'm glad you care, and I appreciate your good advice. But I care too. When I saw you on Lexington Green, I was terrified you were going to be killed. So you be careful too, all right?"

Will grinned. "I have four good reasons at home to be careful."

They had reached the outskirts of Cambridge. The town was also the scene of urgent activity, with every rise of ground undergoing fortification. All along the graceful curve of Watertown Road, the luxurious houses of Tory Row, vacated in haste after last week's battle, housed officers and units of the rebel army. Even Harvard's gracious old brick buildings had been pressed into service as barracks, with the students dismissed for the duration.

They found Warren just finishing a conference with Ward at the general's headquarters in the comfortable residence belonging to Jonathan Hastings. The doctor was preparing to ride to Watertown five miles west, where the Provincial Congress had set up shop for the time being.

As Will ushered Elizabeth into the room, Warren looked up in surprise, delight twinkling in his clear blue eyes. "Why, Miss Howard, what an unexpected pleasure! What brings you here?"

She gave him a chilly nod. "Major Stern assured me you would provide me a pass through your lines so I can visit my aunt, Tess Howard. If you please, I'll need one for her to come visit my parents as well."

She threw a surreptitious glance from Warren to the general, who heard her plea out silently, disgruntlement furrowing his brow. Forty-seven years old, Ward was of average height and heavyset, an imposing figure in powdered wig, long coat with silver buttons, and fine riding boots. Elizabeth had heard enough about him, however, to know that his apparent physical energy disguised mental processes that were both sluggish and unimaginative.

Warren excused the three of them and led the way into the library. As soon as he had closed and locked the doors behind them, he took Elizabeth's hands in his, smiling down at her.

"I expected you to come by night as Oriole. I should have known you were more likely to stroll into camp at high noon."

She laughed up at him, then blushed as, to her surprise, he bent to give her a light kiss on the cheek. Although he quickly dropped her hands and motioned her and Will to take a seat, his pleasure at her presence was evident.

As always, he was impeccably dressed, although the strain and overwork of the past days had left their stamp on his features. In the week since the battle, control of an undisciplined, contentious body of men three times the size of Gage's army had dropped into his lap. In spite of the consequent burdens and his obvious weariness, he looked to be in high good humor.

In some detail, he outlined the progress the Committee of Safety was making in organizing what was essentially a mob into an army capable of effective resistance. The process was painfully slow, and since it was the season to plow and sow crops, men had already begun to trickle away. The discouraging, but understandable, reality was that the majority of them had families to care for.

When he finished, Elizabeth described the measures being taken to strengthen the fortifications in Boston and on the Neck, adding that Gage had ordered the townspeople to turn in all their weapons. Gage's report on the battle accusing the rebels of firing first, she told them, was already on its way to London.

"We've been taking depositions from every eyewitness we can track down," Warren said. "Most didn't get a clear view of what happened, but we've found several who insist that the Regulars fired first, both at Lexington and at Concord."

"Then we'd better get that information to Parliament before Gage's report can do us serious damage," Will interjected.

Warren rubbed his chin. "I know a man with a fast ship who just might be able to do us some good."

Elizabeth hesitated before asking, "What about our British contact,

Patriot? The intelligence he can provide will be crucial now, but his position must be even more precarious. Do you think he'll continue to work for us or decide to lie low?"

"The night I met with him in Boston, he made it clear he'll continue to help us in any way he can." Lines of worry creased Warren's brow. "He was to have contacted me as soon after the expedition to Concord as possible, but it's been almost a week now, and I've heard nothing from him."

"Do you want me to try to contact him, find out what his situation is?"

Warren shook his head. "He was adamant that any attempt to do so could place him in even greater danger, and that he would find a way to contact me. In fact, he insisted I give my word of honor never to divulge his identity to anyone, nor Oriole's to him. It was the condition he set for his assistance to us, so that if either of you were captured, it would be impossible to betray the other under pressure."

When she began to protest, he added, "Please don't ask any more questions, Elizabeth. The less anyone knows about Patriot, the safer he is. All we can do is to wait for him to contact us."

He had a way of speaking in a gentle but firm manner that made it clear further attempts at prying information out of him would be useless. She bit her tongue, but questions buzzed through her mind like a swarm of hornets while Warren wrote out a pass for her, another for "James Freeman" that she could use when in disguise, and one for Tess.

"I suppose you've talked to Jon since the battle," Will said as she tucked the papers into her reticule. "What's his assessment of the British situation?"

"We haven't discussed it," she answered, her mind still on their secret British contact. "He was badly wounded on the road back from Lexington, and Papa and I had quite a fight to save his life. That's the reason I didn't try to get through before—today is the first day I've been able to leave him. But he's out of danger now, and I expect him to be back on light duty by the end of next month.

"That reminds me—yesterday I overheard Gage say something to him about a special assignment, but they didn't go into any detail. However, Gage all but promised him a field command, and he appeared delighted at the prospect."

She directed an idle glance at Warren as she spoke and saw, to her surprise, that he was staring out the window, his face pale and set. "Is something wrong?"

Looking up, he made a dismissive gesture. "I was just thinking about the men who have died and all those who will sacrifice their lives before this is ended. I've spent my life healing the sick, and now it all seems so futile. If only there were another way . . . " His words trailed off.

After an uncomfortable silence, Elizabeth admitted, "The reality is much different than the theory. I didn't expect war to be so personal, but I've found I care a great deal about the safety of those I know on both sides."

Warren forced a smile. "Our medical training doesn't make it any easier."

She turned back to Will, remembering. "What did Jonathan say to you on Lexington Green?"

At her casual use of Carleton's first name, Will raised an eyebrow and gave a faint smile that brought the heat flooding into her cheeks. He sobered, his gaze piercing.

"I accused him of participating in the murder of his own countrymen, and he told me he'd come back here to prevent that very thing."

Leaning forward, his body tense, he continued, "What struck me later was that he said it as if he'd deliberately chosen to come, as if Gage's orders didn't have anything to do with his decision. There was an emotion in his eyes that made me think what was happening was tearing him apart inside.

"I've been doing a lot of thinking since then. Do you remember right after the skirmish at Concord Bridge, how before he rode off he pulled up and saluted us. The more I think about it, the less I believe he's indifferent to our cause."

"By his own words, he's a professional soldier, not a politician," she countered. "He's made it clear to me more than once that he'll do his duty to England regardless of any private doubts."

Frowning, Will shook his head. "The man I knew would wager everything he owned on a toss of the dice without giving the risks a second thought. And he'd stare death in the eye before he'd go against what he believed in. I'm beginning to wonder if, after all, he's changed so very much."

Chapter Seventeen

PERCY PUSHED HIS PLATE AWAY with a sigh of satisfaction and indicated the platter of roast beef in the center of the table. "Tess, you've made life worth living again. If I were single and a few years older, I'd be tempted to ask you to marry me."

"And if you were a few years younger, I'd be tempted to consider it." Tess's response prompted a laugh from the others seated around the dining room table of the Howards' town house.

In the three weeks since the battle, the rebels had made no attempt to interfere with Elizabeth or her family as they traveled back and forth between their home and Boston. Every attempt by members of the British garrison to approach Stony Hill, however, had provoked a sharp skirmish, and Gage had put an end to any further excursions so near the rebel entrenchments. Consequently, because he was still too weak to venture out, Carleton had issued a standing invitation for dinner following Sunday services, and Tess and Mrs. Howard insisted on taking charge of all the arrangements.

"I don't see the problem, Hugh," Carleton said. "A fine wine isn't fit to drink until it's had a chance to mature."

Tess leaned back in her chair and winked at the others. "In that case, Jon, I'd be delighted to take you on."

Andrews elbowed Carleton. "Let's see you talk yourself out of this one."

"I'm sorely tempted, Tess, but you're too young for me," Carleton protested. "Why, at my creaky age, I doubt I'd survive the wedding night."

"Once you're fit again, I'd be willing to test your mettle, if you change your mind," Tess retorted with a mischievous smile.

By now their audience was convulsed. Chuckling, Pitcairn reached over to ruffle Abby's hair as she leaned on Carleton's arm.

"If ye ask my opinion, this wee lass is the one ye should be waitin' for."

Giggling, Abby squeezed between table and chair to climb onto Carleton's lap. She took his face between her small hands and boldly gave him a kiss full on the lips. Engulfing her with his good arm, he returned her kiss with a hearty one.

"Now this one I can handle. Abby, will you marry me?"

She looked up at him through her long lashes, her lips pursed. "I'm too little. But if you married Beth, you'd be my big brother."

Elizabeth could feel her face turn scarlet as a delighted whoop went up from Lord Percy and Pitcairn. She was uncomfortably aware of the pointed glance that passed between her parents and that Andrews had discovered an intense preoccupation with his dinner.

Carleton grimaced. "Oh, Beth is far too prickly—we'd never get along. I'd much rather have you."

"Don't I have a say in the matter?" Elizabeth intervened with more heat than she intended.

Carleton's cool gaze countered her own. "We're waiting with bated breath, *enfant.*"

Flustered and furious, she answered loftily, "Faith! I wouldn't marry you if my life depended on it. There's enough misery in this world without our adding to it."

Pitcairn held his wine glass up to the light to assess its ruby contents. "If I were ye, Jonnie, I'd try a different tack. Ye seem to be meetin' a little less than full success with all your sweet talk."

Percy guffawed, and Andrews choked on a mouthful of bread. Tess bit her lip to keep from laughing outright and concentrated on rearranging the food on her plate, ignoring Elizabeth's glare from across the table.

Unruffled, Carleton returned equably, "As a matter of fact, it's all part of my master plan. At this rate I'll have her eating out of my hand before the meal's over."

Elizabeth opened her mouth to make a cutting retort, but when her eyes met Carleton's she saw that his were full of merriment and he was struggling to suppress a grin. Her irritation evaporated as quickly as it had come, and throwing back her head, she laughed until tears came to her eyes.

Percy, however, sobered. "Considering the unhappiness of some marriage bonds, I'd advise treading with caution in that direction." At the others' puzzled looks, he explained, "The Gages are hardly speaking, and rumors are it's because Mrs. Gage betrayed our march to Concord."

Shocked, Mrs. Howard protested, "Margaret would never do anything to hurt her husband."

Percy pursed his lips. "Some members of the staff are convinced she's been passing intelligence to the rebels for months. And the general himself told me that early on the day we marched he confided to her—and to no one else—the exact time Smith's detachment would embark. By nightfall, the rebels knew every detail."

In the strained silence Dr. Howard said in a hoarse voice, "What has the world come to if the women of our own households are spying for our enemies?"

Feeling sick to her stomach, Elizabeth threw a tentative glance in the direction of her father, only to intercept Carleton's steady gaze. He was studying her with a still intensity that caused her to go cold through to her bones.

Dr. Howard gave a short laugh. "But perhaps we can turn the

tables on the rebels. Now that Tess and Elizabeth have managed to persuade Dr. Warren to provide them passes through the lines, we'll enlist them as spies for our side."

Percy sat bolt upright. "What?" He looked from Tess to Elizabeth. "You've obtained passes from Dr. Warren?"

Pitcairn and Andrews followed the earl's astonished questions with their own, and oblivious to her daughter's dismay, Mrs. Howard recounted every detail Elizabeth had confided of her adventure into the rebel camp. While Elizabeth had realized the news must come out at some point, this was not the time or the place she wanted it to happen. Particularly not when Carleton was watching her with that cool, assessing glance that dissected her like a surgeon's lancet.

Leaning back in his chair, his long, slender fingers caressing the stem of his wine glass, he made no comment, asked no questions. But it was equally clear he did not miss even the slightest nuances of the conversation. And while his expression gave nothing away, each time their eyes met she had the unsettling impression that his keen mind continued inexorably to calculate numbers on a balance sheet, and that each detail, seemingly negligible in itself, brought him a step closer to the correct sum.

Pressed by Percy, Pitcairn, and Andrews to tell them everything she had observed in the rebel camp and during her meeting with Dr. Warren, Elizabeth forced herself to answer calmly. "They took me straight to Aunt Tess's house, then to Dr. Warren, and afterward escorted me directly back through the lines. A guard stayed with me every minute, and I was never allowed to get close to any of the camps. All I could tell was that there were an awful lot of them, and they appeared to be entrenching every rise of ground in sight."

"Now one of ye must have noticed something that would help us," Pitcairn scoffed when Tess protested almost equal ignorance. "How many regiments—?"

Laughing, Elizabeth threw up her hands. "The truth is, Aunt Tess has only been allowed to leave her property to come to Stony Hill, and I was too frightened to notice anything that might be helpful."

"As frightened as a lioness, I'm sure," Carleton drawled.

Elizabeth threw him a veiled glance, remembering, as she was certain he meant her to, the comment he had made to her on Easter Sunday barely three weeks earlier when she had bested him in their race. How she wished now that she had taken Isaiah's and Tess's advice and lost! Thankfully, her father saved her from the necessity of a reply by making a sarcastic comment about Warren's generosity in issuing her and Tess passes considering the harsh treatment many of the Loyalists were receiving.

Percy was more interested in whether they had caught wind of any plan on the rebels' part to attack Boston. Answering in the negative, Tess countered that she had overheard some of the rebel officers discussing rumors of an imminent attempt by the British to break the siege. Percy's reaction convinced both women that, at least for the time being, the rumor remained simply that.

It was a relief when they left the table and withdrew into the front parlor. Percy and Pitcairn stayed only a short time longer before excusing themselves to attend to pressing duties, but her parents showed no inclination to leave. Carleton and Andrews were clearly enjoying their company as much as they enjoyed visiting with the officers, and as Tess also appeared content to extend the visit, Elizabeth gave up any hope of an early escape.

Seated on the sofa next to Andrews, she was vexed to find her eyes continually attracted to Carleton in spite of her determination to pretend he didn't exist. Out of uniform, thinner, and with his arm in a sling, he seemed younger, appealingly vulnerable—at least when he wasn't weighing her in the balances with that uncomfortably piercing look. But for the moment he was immersed in conversation with her parents and aunt and appeared to be as oblivious of her as she wished she were of him.

That day he was clad in elegant simplicity in a coat of fine char-coal grey wool, with dove-grey satin breeches, and a waistcoat of smoky blue brocade that echoed and intensified the color of his eyes. Abby stood at his side, and as he talked to Dr. Howard, he reached absently to lay his hand on the child's head. When she lifted her rosy face to give him a conspiratorial smile, a stab of pleasure went through Elizabeth, accompanied by a flood of warmth that took every ounce of resolution she possessed to fight down.

In spite of her impatience to get away, the afternoon passed pleas-antly enough. Since the day was warm and sunny, Carleton suggested they walk on the Common, where they could enjoy the fresh breeze. Strolling arm in arm with Andrews, Elizabeth kept her distance from Carleton. If he noticed, he gave no indication and seemed more than happy to be entertained by Tess, Abby, and her parents.

They wandered as far as Fox Hill, well past the last rows of the Regulars' encampment and near the rhythmically lapping waves of the bay before Elizabeth and Andrews came up to the others. By then the westering sun threw long amber rays across the salt grass at their feet.

Giving Carleton an appraising look, Elizabeth said firmly, "We'd better head back. You need to rest, and besides, it's almost time for tea."

"I am tired." Grimacing, he readjusted his sling where it chafed his neck. "This business of getting well seems to involve a deuced amount of time."

Dr. Howard clapped his hand on Carleton's good shoulder. "You're making marvelous progress, Jon, so don't complain. Just leave yourself in Elizabeth's capable hands, and she'll put you right in no time."

Elizabeth could feel the color rising to her cheeks at her father's fervent recommendation. Carleton's quick smile deepened her blush.

"I'm not complaining about that part." He accompanied the words with a look that contained unmistakable warmth.

Hastily, Elizabeth pulled Andrews around, and together they led the way back to the town house. Tess insisted that she and Elizabeth take charge of preparing tea, and Elizabeth eagerly followed to help the housekeeper carry trays of delicacies from the kitchen to the dining room.

When Mrs. Dalton returned to the kitchen, leaving them alone at the sideboard, Elizabeth pulled several folded sheets of paper from the pocket beneath her petticoat and pressed them into Tess's hand. "For Joseph."

Tess gave her a searching look. "I hope you're not too troubled by what your father said."

"I hate the deceptions we practice too, but what alternatives do we have if we're ever to be free?"

"Stand firm," Tess told her fiercely. "We must never lose sight of our goal."

She broke off, raised her eyes to a point above and behind Elizabeth's shoulder, at the same time with a casual movement sliding the papers she held through the opening in her petticoat and into the pocket she wore beneath. Even before she glanced around, Elizabeth felt the hair on the back of her neck stand up.

Five yards behind her in the doorway stood Carleton.

He leaned against the door jamb, massaging his wounded shoulder as he watched them through narrowed eyes. Had he seen her pass the papers to Tess?

As usual, she could read nothing in his expression. But she had the uneasy suspicion that he had seen enough to further fuel his suspicions.

"I thought you were going to rest." She managed to keep her tone brisk and unconcerned.

"I decided I was more hungry than tired."

If Tess was concerned about how much Carleton might have seen, she showed no evidence of it. "You men are so predictable. As long as your stomachs are full, all's right with the world."

Carleton grinned and threw a glance at the sideboard, which by now was groaning under an assortment of delicacies. "Isn't tea about ready? I'm starved."

"Your appetite has certainly improved." Elizabeth pretended to concentrate on finding room for a plate of scones next to the tea cakes, but she was hardly aware of what her hands were doing.

"That's a healthy sign, isn't it?" For a moment he watched them without speaking, then he said, "It's amazing that you've been able to stay in Roxbury, Tess. The Loyalists coming into Boston tell horror stories about being taunted, threatened, even tarred and feathered and driven out of their homes. But the rebels haven't disturbed you?"

For an instant Elizabeth froze, her eyes flying to Tess's. Tess returned her look with a warning one, then laughed and put her finger to her lips.

"I'll tell you my secret if you promise not to breathe a word to Samuel. He'd be furious with me, but the truth is I'm not about to watch everything I've built over the years go up in smoke. You see, the rebel officers need headquarters, so I offered to take in the staff of one of the regiments if they'd promise to protect me and my property. I'm not thrilled at having a houseful of rebel soldiers, but so far they've left me alone."

She was interrupted by Mrs. Dalton, who came in carrying the steaming teapot. Taking it from her, Elizabeth set it on the tea cart, astonished that her hands remained steady in spite of the tightness that constricted her chest. Looking up, she found Carleton watching her with that faint, enigmatic smile instinct warned her to distrust.

"It sounds like an eminently practical arrangement to me," he said without shifting his gaze from her. "How's Will doing? He wasn't wounded in the battle, I hope."

The question was obviously directed to Elizabeth, but there was no possible way she could speak just then. She prayed that nothing showed on her face. Before her silence could become noticeable, Tess answered as matter-of-factly as Carleton had spoken.

"Thankfully, he was not. Joshua stopped by just yesterday and assured me they all came through unscathed."

Carleton gave Tess a slight bow. "I'm sorry. I assumed it's the Lincoln regiment that's staying with you—a natural enough mistake considering your ties." Again he returned his probing gaze to Elizabeth. "I thought you might have seen your uncle and cousins when you went over the other day. I know how much you've missed them."

He said it with such innocence that if she hadn't known better she would have been touched by his apparent concern. Taking a steadying breath, she shook her head.

"Whether fortunate or unfortunate, I didn't run into them," she lied.

Giving Elizabeth a meaningful look, Tess excused herself and followed Mrs. Dalton out to the kitchen. Carleton ambled over for a closer inspection of the tea cakes. When he reached to test the icing, she slapped his hand.

"You're worse than Abby! No tastes—you're just going to have to wait until everything is ready."

"You're no fun at all."

The moment her back was turned, he dipped his finger in the icing and stuck it into his mouth. "Umm."

When she rounded on him in mock annoyance, he grinned. "I couldn't resist." Smiling down at her, he said, "Will has a younger brother, doesn't he? Levi, as I recall." When she nodded warily, he continued, "He must have been around ten years old when I knew him—that would make him about the same age as you. He was an engaging youngster, small for his age, with a mop of white hair."

"He's as tall as Will now—or he was the last time I saw him," she amended hastily.

He was silent a moment before saying idly, "I imagine Dr. Warren is delighted at the turn of events. Where did you say he's set up headquarters? Cambridge, wasn't it?"

She managed to keep her tone unconcerned. "I don't recall mentioning it."

He yawned and stretched. "I could have sworn you did. But then, I have a terrible memory for details."

She knew better than to believe him. But she gave him her most charming smile, which he returned with an apparent lack of guile.

He was standing very close to her. Looking up into his eyes, she felt her heart turn over and her pulse quicken.

"Who has taken over command of the rebel army?"

Dangerous seconds passed before she could gather enough control over her scattered wits to realize that he was, in fact, interrogating her. Stiffening, she stepped away from him.

"I don't know. Why are you asking me when all you have to do is talk to His Excellency's spies?"

The change in him was immediate. "You don't know?" he drawled, ignoring her question. "You went to the headquarters of the rebel army to meet personally with the head of their Committee of Safety, and you didn't have occasion to learn who their commander is? I find that impossible to believe."

The icy edge of sarcasm in his tone took her breath away. His eyes had shaded to that wintry grey she by now knew to dread, and, as swiftly, the camaraderie of the afternoon was ended, replaced by a deadly steeliness that sent a thrill of fear through her.

She felt as though she stood on the very brink of disaster, with what had been solid ground crumbling beneath her feet like sand sucked away by an outgoing tide. But the sensation brought the familiar, heady sense of exhilaration bubbling up in her.

Instinct took over, drew her closer to him. Looking up into his eyes, she laid her hand on his arm.

"I'm sorry you don't believe me, Jonathan. But the truth is I have little interest in military matters, and I didn't think to ask those kinds of questions. I wish I could help you, but unfortunately I can't."

For a long, breathless moment, he looked down at her, and gradually the warmth came back into his eyes. And something else.

Admiration. Respect.

Reaching to touch her throat and cheek, he let his fingertips trace the line of her jaw, brushed his thumb across her lower lip, finally tilted her chin up so she couldn't turn her eyes away from his. She caught her breath, in a state of panic at the realization that he wanted to kiss her as much as she longed for him to.

"I'm beginning to realize how very little I know of what's in that beautiful head of yours—and in your heart," he murmured, his voice husky. "But I mean to find out if I must—"

"If you don't stop pestering the ladies, we'll starve before we get anything to eat."

There was a sharp edge to the lieutenant's tone in spite of the attempt at humor. Carleton dropped his hand away from Elizabeth, and both of them started round to find Andrews in the doorway, looking from one to the other with a smile that was obviously forced.

Laughing, Carleton went to join the younger officer. "It does appear I'm having the opposite effect to my intention."

Turning back to Elizabeth, he grinned and made a graceful bow. Then throwing an affectionate arm around Andrews's shoulders, he dragged him out of the room.

"Patience, Charles, patience. All good things come to those who wait."

Elizabeth stood looking after them, trembling, her head held high. After a moment, she raised her hand to touch the place where his fingers had caressed her, wondering what he would have done if Andrews hadn't come in just then.

There was no longer any use denying to herself the intensity of the attraction she felt toward him. That there was an equally powerful force on his side was becoming more apparent each time they were together.

But he'd also made his suspicion of her very clear, had made it equally clear that he intended to find out what she was most determined he should not learn. And she couldn't help wondering to what lengths he would go to find out, and what use he would make of the knowledge if he succeeded.

TUESDAY MORNING, MAY 16, Carleton reined the bay to a halt outside the gate of Province House. Lifting his face to the warm sun, he took a deep breath of the salt air, overwhelmed by a flood of gratitude and humility.

From the moment he had drifted back to consciousness a little more than three weeks ago, he had chafed at the restrictions his wound and the infection that had accompanied it had placed on his activities. An oppressive sense of urgency kept nagging at him, but in his anxiety to be well again, he had heeded Elizabeth's warnings to avoid taxing his fragile strength.

That morning impatience had gotten the better of him. He still tired easily, but the worst of the weakness and pain had passed. Deciding he had played the invalid long enough, he had put aside his sling, even though his shoulder was still stiff and ached with every movement, and had donned his uniform for the first time since the battle.

It felt good to be back in the saddle. But as he glanced up at the mansion that crowned the top of the rise before him, his face clouded. For some minutes he appraised it through narrowed eyes.

He had come on the off chance he could get in to see Gage, but he almost hoped the general would be too busy to meet with him. He had given his word, however, and there was no turning back. Reluctantly he urged his mount up the carriageway.

To his surprise, the ensign stationed outside the door of the general's office returned immediately upon announcing him and ushered him inside. With Gage was Lord Percy.

The general rose from his chair to greet him with a smile. "You're looking fit this morning."

Percy rose and stretched, yawning. "I thought the lovely Miss Howard had given orders you weren't to report for duty for another week."

Carleton grinned. "If I'm forced to spend another day watching your brigade stumble though their maneuvers in front of my window, I swear I'll go mad."

"You're more than welcome to have a go at drilling them any time you feel the urge." Returning his grin, Percy excused himself.

When they were alone Gage motioned Carleton to a seat. "You're not thinking of reporting for duty so soon?"

"I'm feeling stronger every day, and some activity would do me good. This assignment you mentioned has been on my mind ever since we talked, and it wouldn't be strenuous. With your permission, I'd like to take it on."

"Unfortunately, our situation is considerably changed." Gage leaned back in his chair with a sigh. "My spies haven't been able to get through, so my most critical need right now is for intelligence as to what the rebel dispositions are, the names and quality of their commanders and where they're headquartered, how many effectives they have, how well they're trained and equipped, how many reinforcements they're receiving. Are you up to that?"

"On condition I have your guarantee that no one except you and me will ever know about my role in this."

"You have it."

Carleton thought a moment. "I'll need to make several trips behind the lines. Any absence during the day would be questioned, so I'll go at night. If you'll provide me a pass through the town gates, once I'm outside I'll . . . disappear."

"I'll trust your prudence in handling this any way you choose." Writing out a pass, Gage handed it to him. "All I ask is that you keep us supplied with a steady flow of intelligence. I'm going to wait until Clinton, Howe, and Burgoyne get here before making any decisions about an assault on the rebel lines. But once they arrive we'll want to act quickly, which means we'd better be prepared."

"As long as I'm over there, I may be able to dig out some information on those spies of yours."

"I want you to leave that for the time being," Gage cut him off. "The more you nose around, the more you risk exposing yourself and them. This will be dangerous enough. Concentrate on getting the information we need and returning safely, nothing else."

Carleton was careful to keep his disappointment from showing. "I'll do my best, sir. With your permission, I'll go across tonight, but I'd rather not give any further details even to you. Just a precaution."

Gage nodded. "I respect your caution—and I trust your judgment. One more thing, though. If the opportunity should arise to get a line on Oriole, by all means pursue it."

A GUST OF WIND OFF THE OCEAN set the limbs of the trees creaking overhead in the dense blackness. Lounging at ease around their smoky campfire at the edge of the woods, the small cluster of men shivered and tugged their tattered coats around them as the firelight flickered across their spare, gaunt faces.

The day had been warm, but with the sun's disappearance below the western hills the air had taken on a keen edge. Rousing, one member of the outpost reached a sinewy arm to drop another half-rotted branch onto the dying embers, releasing a shower of red-gold sparks that swirled upward into the indigo sky, blinking like a swarm of fireflies.

Suddenly one of his fellows jerked erect and grabbed for his musket. Before his fingers could connect with the steel barrel, a moccasined foot kicked it out of his reach.

"Now, y'all jest let yore weapons lay," drawled a steely voice.

On the fringe of the firelight, a tall figure materialized out of the night.

The sentries stumbled to their feet to find themselves staring down the long barrel of a rifle held in the steady hands of a lean, tanned stranger clad in dusty buckskin. A faded woven band in a rainbow of colors circled his head, tying back the long blond hair that fell loose over his shoulders. From the belt of wampum knotted at the waist of his fringed tunic hung a powder horn, a hunting knife in a leather sheath, and a leather pouch. Fringed ankle-length leggings and moccasins completed his wild look.

"Who be ye," demanded the sergeant, "and what be yer business here?"

"If I stood guard like y'all," the stranger returned with dry amusement, "my scalp'd sure bin decoratin' some redskin's war belt long a'fore now."

A couple of the men gave a nervous laugh. Steely blue-grey eyes left no doubt as to the stranger's reaction if anyone was foolish enough to reach for his weapon.

"Ye come to jine up?" one of them asked suspiciously.

"That I have."

"Where ye hail from?" demanded the sergeant.

"Kaintuck," was the slow reply. "Soon's we heerd there ben fightin' I took off. Ben walkin' north ever since."

With an exclamation, the sergeant pressed the stranger to join their circle. The offer of tobacco and coffee was eagerly accepted. Laying his rifle across his lap, the lean frontiersman sat down cross-legged just within the circle of the firelight while the others resumed their positions.

For some moments they were content to sit in companionable

silence, watching their guest savor hot, bitter coffee from a battered tin mug. As he packed tobacco into the clay pipe he took from the pouch at his waist, one asked, "What be yer name?"

The stranger drew a smoldering stick out of the fire and applied it to the tamped tobacco. "Rawlings," he returned laconically at length, releasing a stream of smoke into the night.

"With thet there rifle, I'd bet yer a crack shot," the sergeant spoke up. "If'n ye come alone, ye'll be wantin' to jine up with a good fightin' company. We're with Gen'l Putnam's regiment, and we'd be right proud to hev ye."

The stranger considered him in thoughtful silence before answering, "I hear Gen'l Ward's in command."

One of the men confirmed the information and volunteered that Ward had made his headquarters in a house in Cambridge, a mile and three quarters up the road, where the Committee of Safety also held its meetings. Knocking the ashes out of the stained bowl of his clay pipe, the stranger grasped his rifle and in a lithe movement was on his feet.

"I thank y'all for yore hospitality."

With that, he melted back into the shadows and was gone before any of the soldiers could move, leaving them to stare after him in open-mouthed astonishment.

Chapter Eighteen

ELIZABETH LOWERED TO HER KNEES in front of the window. Wiping her sweaty forehead with her apron, she laid her cheek on her crossed arms. The day was unusually hot for mid-May. Although it was already past noon and the east side of the house lay in shadow, the windowsill still felt warm against her skin.

She yawned. The night had been a long one. Much of it she and Sarah had spent at the bedside of Felicity Whyte, who had given birth to a daughter earlier that morning, following a long and difficult labor.

They had arrived a little before three o'clock. On examining her patient Elizabeth had gone cold with fear at the discovery that the young mother's labor was making no progress because the baby was in breech position. Although she had never encountered this complication in any of the births she had attended, she had heard heartrending stories of mothers and infants enduring intense suffering or even dying during such a delivery.

Felicity's mother had added to her daughter's fear and pain by wailing out loud at the news. To Elizabeth's intense gratitude, Sarah had wasted no time in maneuvering the woman out of the room, then with reassuring calmness had knelt at Elizabeth's side before the birthing stool and had shown her how to turn the baby. It had taken several fearful, unsuccessful attempts while Sarah held the young mother from behind, but at last Elizabeth had felt the miracle of the tiny body under her hand sliding around into the correct position.

In two more hours the child had been born kicking and wailing, healthy and perfect, her small, red face creased with outrage at the indignity of her entrance into the world. In mute wonder at the unceasing miracle of new life, Elizabeth had cleared the infant's airway and wiped the tiny, puckered face before placing the newborn into her mother's anxious arms.

Later, after she and Sarah had bathed and wrapped the child, she had stood for a moment clutching the sweet-smelling bundle to her breast. Without warning, she had been overwhelmed by the same surge of fierce maternal protectiveness she had felt the previous week at Tess's house when Will's wife had come for a visit with her husband, bringing their three young children.

At last Elizabeth had been able to hold her newest cousin. Then also, as she had cuddled the plump, wiggling infant at her breast and smiled into his wide blue eyes, she had been pierced by a deep longing for a home and family of her own. Always before she had been able to repress those treacherous emotions, but later while wrestling on the floor with young Will and little Anne, the three of them convulsed with laughter, she had found it impossible to extinguish the hunger for nighttime romps with her own babes.

Her gaze pensive, she followed the male oriole's flight as he left the stately elm across the yard, swooping so low his bright orange breast skimmed the long grass. Fluttering upward into the spreading branches of the apple tree just outside her window, he came to rest on a twig above the pouch-like nest across from her, where his mate brooded her clutch of eggs. Hearing the beat of his wings, the female stuck her head out through the small opening to swallow the fat caterpillar he offered.

The cooling breeze ruffled Elizabeth's loose hair around her shoulders and brushed the lacy curtains against her cheek. As she gratefully lifted her face to it, another image stole into her thoughts: the memory of a lean, lazy figure, of blue eyes laughing at her with that irresistible light, of the way his glance would sometimes linger on her lips, and the heady rush of excitement that throbbed through her veins when he was in the same room with her, that caught her breath away on a tide of desire and sent shivers up her spine even now at thought of him.

Disgusted and angry with herself, she sprang to her feet with a soft outcry and began to pace up and down.

The weekly Sunday dinners at the town house following worship were a continual hazard to her heart, despite the defenses she struggled to maintain. And although social engagements had dwindled in number and extravagance due to the siege, during the past fortnight she had attended a tea, two dinners, and a dance at which Carleton and Andrews had been present.

Each time she had encouraged the younger officers to monopolize her attention. For his part, Carleton had made no effort to approach her. He had given every evidence of being very agreeably occupied by the admirers who hovered over their wounded hero.

She had, however, found it impossible not to be aware of his every movement. He was capable of being so charming that he invariably attracted a large circle. And to her dismay she endured many a sharp pang of jealousy at his attentiveness to the young women who flocked around him. In particular, to Lydia Ellsworth, who, Elizabeth sourly noted, draped herself across his arm like a shawl. Worse, Carleton made no effort to detach her.

She could be mistaken in his feelings, Elizabeth reminded herself. Yet feminine instinct told her that flirtations were nothing more than a diversion as far as Carleton was concerned.

The tension that charged the air whenever they were together had to be more than simple illusion. More than once she had surprised his glance upon her and read in his eyes an emotion she could not fathom, but which left her confused and troubled.

She had never met another man who so challenged her, excited her, claimed her heart and soul. In spite of all effort to banish it, longing to feel the security of his arms around her would not leave her. And for a long, hungry moment she indulged her imagination with the sweet vision of what life would be like if he were her husband.

Gulping back a ragged sob, she stopped in the center of the room. How could God have allowed this to happen? Why had he brought Carleton to Boston, knowing the attraction they must have for one another and yet that she could never surrender to it?

Could it be that Carleton had come into her life for some purpose she couldn't yet fathom? Did God mean to test them—or to mock them?

If there was a deeper purpose in the events of the past month, in the horror of war and broken bodies and agonizing death, it was beyond her comprehension. Equally incomprehensible was what possible good could come of her falling in love with a man whose duty and allegiance made him her enemy and must tear them apart from each other.

Yet in spite of every argument she could come up with, she found herself attracted to Carleton on every level. His self-deprecating sense of humor delighted her, his razor-keen mind challenged her, and the secret depths of his soul beckoned her to discover what lay hidden there.

Desperate, she pressed her fingertips hard against her throbbing temples. If only she could fall in love with Andrews instead. He was handsome, sweet, funny, charming, all that a woman could ask for in a life's companion. And over the past weeks he had begun to express increasing disillusionment with England's policies. The confrontations at Lexington and Concord had been a revelation to him, and he no longer made any attempt to conceal his sympathy with the colonials for trying to protect their families and property.

She was certain he could be swayed to join the patriots. In contrast, every time she thought she detected the slightest chink in Carleton's armor, he said or did something that shattered her trust and proved that his allegiance to England was unchanged, reminded her of the danger into which he could so easily place her, and put her back on her guard.

Yet if he loved her and if she revealed her love for him, would that make a difference? Dared she trust him?

With pain she reviewed her conversation with Andrews late that morning. After leaving Sarah to care for Felicity, Elizabeth had encountered him walking down Cornhill Street. After congratulating him on his recent promotion to captain, she had offered him a ride. They had not driven far before she sensed that something was troubling him.

It had taken some effort to draw him out, but at last, sitting in the phaeton outside the town house, Andrews confided that a few days earlier he had awakened in the middle of the night and, restless and unable to sleep, had gotten up. Noticing that the door to Carleton's bedroom was ajar and thinking that he must also be awake, Andrews had glanced inside the room.

"He wasn't there or anywhere in the house. After sitting up for almost two hours, I went back to bed, but not to sleep. A short while before dawn I heard someone come up the stairs very softly, then Jon's bedroom door creaked shut. Every night since then, it's been the same thing. He disappears and doesn't come back until just before dawn."

Keeping his voice low, he confessed, "Last night I waited up and followed him when he left the house. I took every precaution to remain invisible, but I'm convinced he got wind that someone was on to him. Just when I began to think he was heading for the town gates, he turned down one of those infernal crooked alleys this place is infested with, and by the time I got there, he'd vanished."

Elizabeth glanced away, thinking of her own elusive maneuvers. "You tried to find him?"

"He was nowhere to be found. I even waited near the town gates for more than an hour, but he never turned up."

"Have you asked him about it?"

Andrews nodded. "He just said he couldn't sleep and that walking late at night clears his head. I asked what was bothering him, and he told me there's nothing wrong and that I don't need to concern myself."

"Perhaps Stowe knows something," she suggested.

"I thought of that too, though I didn't really expect him to tell me anything. And, of course, he pleaded ignorance. Jon has a habit of rescuing castaways, and Stowe is one of his recovery projects. He'd die before he'd betray Jon's confidence. And since I'm another bit of flotsam Jon's dredged up out of the sea, I'd do the same a thousand times over."

For a long moment, neither spoke, each preoccupied with troubling reflections. At length Andrews said, "It's strange, but as far as I can make out, Jon hasn't been assigned any specific duties and doesn't have any regular hours. But the past three afternoons I've found him at home writing some sort of report that he won't discuss and that he's careful not to leave lying about. This morning I saw him take the papers with him when he went to meet with Gage."

"What do you think he's up to?"

His reply had sent a chill through her. "The only thing that makes any sense is that he's spying for Gage. He's secretly crossing the rebels' lines at night."

If Carleton was indeed a spy and if he suspected her loyalties—and there seemed little doubt on either score—then he was very likely trying to use her as she had hoped to use him, Elizabeth concluded. Considering the role she herself played, she couldn't blame him for that, but her wisest course of action would be to find some excuse to keep as much distance between them as possible.

The trouble was that his close friendship with her parents and their weekly Sunday dinners made it impossible to avoid him. And hardest of all, the thought of living the rest of her life apart from him, of never hearing his voice or his laughter, never feeling his touch, never seeing his face or gazing into his eyes filled her with a desolation that came near to breaking her.

How could she go on loving a man who was working to destroy everything she held dear? Yet her heart refused to listen to logic.

There was no answer to her dilemma but to go on as she had been and to conceal her suffering as best she could. No one must ever guess her heartache, or if they did, the reason for it. And he, most of all, must never learn how utterly her heart belonged to him.

With a sharp intake of breath, Elizabeth stepped back into the shadows under the bushes at the corner of the Hastings house. Motionless, she watched as a slender, black-clad figure paused on the doorstep in the faint candlelight from the windows.

Squinting into the darkness, he drew on riding gloves, then swung to stride in her direction. She held her breath, eyes pressed shut, as he passed by her hiding place without pausing. Not looking around, he went straight to the lone horse tethered at the hitching post and leaped into the saddle. Whipping his mount to a gallop, he vanished into the darkness down the road.

The instant he disappeared from sight, she ran for the door and let herself in without bothering to knock. She came to a halt, surprised to see Will sitting at the writing desk squeezed into one corner of the foyer, scribbling rapid notations on the papers in front of him.

"What was David doing here?"

He glanced up, eyebrow raised. "Good evening to you too, Cuz. We weren't expecting you tonight. Is something goin on?"

"I didn't know I had to schedule an appointment. What was David's business with Joseph? Or was it Ward he was here to see?"

Will dipped his quill into the ink pot and returned to his writing. "Actually, Hutchins has been making himself useful to us while amassing a substantial profit for himself," he said as he sprinkled sand across the page, then carefully shook it off. "He's become a privateer. Right after the battle, he bought a couple of fast schooners and outfitted them with some heavy firepower. So far he's brought four British merchantmen into Marblehead. They've yielded a fair supply of gunpowder, muskets, cloth, flour, and a few other sundries that we've been able to put to good use."

"In other words, he's a pirate."

"That's what some folks call it. He does have letters of marque from the Provincial Congress."

"And that makes his piracy legal," she said dryly, frowning. "I don't know why, but I don't trust him, Will. Perhaps I'm overly suspicious because of what happened between us."

He stood up and came around the desk. "I can't say I like his methods or his manner, but we're in desperate need of everything he can supply."

"Does he hang about here a great deal?"

"More than I wish he would, but Warren seems to trust him."

Just then Warren threw open the library door and stepped out. "I thought I recognized your voice," he said, beaming down at her. "Come in. I have news for you, and I'm eager to hear yours."

He ushered her inside and closed the door behind them. "We received a dispatch a couple of days ago that Benedict Arnold, along with Ethan Allen and his Green Mountain Boys, captured Fort Ticonderoga on Lake Champlain last week. That heavy artillery Henry Knox has been itching to get his hands on is now under our control. If we can only find a way to transport the guns here, Gage won't be able to hold Boston with twice the number of troops he has now."

Elizabeth laughed, sharing his exuberance. "The end may be in sight!"

"I'm afraid it won't happen anytime soon." Smiling nevertheless, he held a chair for her, then pulled his next to it. "Since those four British companies came in from Halifax last week, Putnam, Prescott, and your hot-headed uncle have been pestering the committee to allow them to build a fort on Bunker's Hill before any more reinforcements arrive. Ward insists we have too many deficiencies that need remedy before we stir up the hornet's nest again, and I'm afraid I have to agree with him."

At Warren's urging, Elizabeth plunged into an account of her recent meetings with her secret band and their plans for carrying out an organized program of sabotage. Her intent was to spike as many British cannon as possible within the next two weeks, beginning with the emplacements on Copp's Hill, Beacon Hill, and below the Common along the Back Bay.

Meanwhile, she was working on a way to acquire more munitions for the rebel army. For this project, they would make use of a couple of sturdy skiffs one of the members of her band kept hidden in the marsh below Cambridge, across the Back Bay from the Common. They would employ, as well, the British uniforms secreted in Longworthy's attic that had been custom-made the previous winter for Oriole's more devious escapades.

"You're running too great a risk," Warren objected, frowning. "For the time being, it would be far wiser to keep your ears open, but do nothing to draw attention to yourself. Patriot hasn't been able to uncover our traitors—" He broke off.

Elizabeth jerked forward in her chair. "Patriot? You've been in contact with him?"

He waved her words away. "He has devised a way of getting intelligence to us without involving you."

"But how—?" She stopped. It was clear from Warren's expression that that subject was closed.

"Patriot and I both feel it's safer for the two of you to stay as far apart as possible."

Her thoughts raced through a list of every officer she knew, as they had so often before. But none of them came close to fitting the description of the man she had met on the marsh that night weeks earlier.

Disappointed, she changed the subject, knowing there was no point in pursuing the issue further. "Speaking of spies, this morning I talked to Captain Andrews." Outlining the substance of their conversation, she concluded, "He's certain Major Carleton is passing behind our lines."

For a long moment Warren said nothing, appearing to struggle for a response. He started to speak, reconsidered, finally said, "It's possible, of course, but even if it's true, he can't do us as much damage as the spies the general has planted inside our highest counsels."

"Major Carleton understands the military situation better than any of the other officers I've talked to," Elizabeth countered. "Once he discovers our lack of munitions and proper training, how our fortifications are laid out and where their weaknesses lie, he'll be able to—"

Warren made an impatient gesture. "Elizabeth, I understand your concern, but I have more pressing matters to deal with at the moment."

"If he were to stumble across Patriot's identity—or mine—our lives would be forfeit."

Warren regarded her with a frown. "That's true. Perhaps you're right, then. Nose around a bit, see if you can find out what he's up to. But whatever you do, be careful not to compromise yourself. Trust no one!"

Puzzled by his reaction, Elizabeth frowned and looked away, drumming her fingers on the curved wooden arm of her chair. As Warren watched her, his expression grew troubled.

"What's your relationship with the major?"

She looked up, startled. "We're acquaintances. He's a friend of my parents. Nothing more."

"No romantic involvement?"

His voice was unexpectedly gentle. Elizabeth flushed, but managed to keep voice and expression under control.

"I'm not that foolish, and neither is he." She couldn't help asking, "If Major Carleton were to be captured behind our lines in disguise, what would happen to him? According to the rules of war, spies may be hanged."

For an instant a smile tugged at the patriot leader's lips, then he substituted a studious frown and turned to the window, stroking his chin with long, graceful fingers. "He'd be brought to me, and I'd parole him back to England. I have no taste for hangings."

✳ ✳ ✳

"I won't go! This is my home, and I see no reason to leave it."

"There's no way of telling how long this war will last or what the result will be, Elizabeth," Dr. Howard answered, clearly struggling to remain calm. "It's unlikely, of course, but if the rebels should win the conflict, all ties with England will be severed and anarchy will reign supreme. No one will be safe."

The last thing Elizabeth had expected was her parents' announcement at lunch that Saturday noon that they had decided it was too dangerous for them to remain in Boston any longer. They had already engaged passage for the voyage to England aboard a ship scheduled to leave the first week of June, little more than two weeks away.

Caught unprepared, with no time to marshal her arguments in opposition, Elizabeth stared at her father, her heart hammering violently. She turned to her mother in appeal.

"I understand your reasons for wanting to return to England, even though I don't share them," she said, forcing her voice to remain calm. "But none of that applies to me. In fact, it makes much more sense for me to stay. If we abandon Stony Hill, the rebels will take it over, and everything you and Papa have spent all these years building will be lost. But if I stay here—"

"A young, unmarried woman living alone in a house between two warring armies?" Her mother's voice scaled upward. "Elizabeth, that is a plan of such extreme foolhardiness that even you can't seriously entertain it. When you are back in England—"

"How can I go back to England when I've never been there in the first place?"

Her logic caused her father to grit his teeth.

"All the more reason for you to go," her mother responded eagerly. "We'll be in London in time for you to come out this season, and you can attend all the splendid parties with the other young women of your station. With your beauty and accomplishments and your father's connections, to say nothing of your inheritance, who knows what suitors you'll attract—perhaps even someone from the nobility."

Elizabeth threw up her hands. "So that's what this is all about. You haven't managed to marry me off over here, so you're going to try to—"

His face brick red, Dr. Howard slammed his palm down on the table so hard that the dishes clattered and all of them started. Bursting into tears, Abby jumped up from the table and ran upstairs, sobbing.

"There now, see what you've done!" Dr. Howard thundered, ignoring the fact that it was his violence that had sent his younger daughter to flight. "No daughter of mine is going to speak to her mother and me with such impertinence in my own house."

Elizabeth stared straight ahead of her, her face gone chalk white. Of all the disasters she had faced thus far, this was the worst. She felt cornered, trapped, desperate, at a complete loss what to do.

The last thing she wanted was to defy the parents she loved so dearly, but she saw no alternative. To leave the country of her birth and the cause to which she had given herself with such passion to go with them to a land and a people that were foreign to her was beyond contemplation.

Her mother leaned over to stroke her arm. "For once, listen to us and be guided for your own good. Who knows what might happen if we left you here all alone. Why, we'd be sick with worry every minute."

"It would be different if you were married and had the protection and support of a life's partner," Dr. Howard pointed out.

Mrs. Howard brightened. "That's the best solution, of course. If you are opposed to going with us, then let your father talk to Major Carleton. I've seen the way he looks at you, dearest, and I'm certain he would be quite agreeable to a match. And if the two of you were married, I'd have no concern in the world at your staying behind."

For a suspended moment, Elizabeth stared at her mother, horrified that words of assent had almost slipped from her tongue. Indeed, the solution seemed so logical and so incredibly sweet.

Was her allegiance to her country dearer than her love for Carleton, her need for husband, home, and children? Had she not done enough? Did she not deserve to give up the weary struggle at last and drink of the blessings of peace and love?

"No." She forced the word through numb lips, feeling as though a white-hot brand seared her breast. "I forbid you to talk to him about this. I shall go live with Aunt Tess if I must, but I'll never go with you to England."

Getting unsteadily to her feet, she looked from one to the other. They regarded her with mingled anger, puzzlement, and hurt. Unable to bear their unspoken reproach, she turned and rushed from the room to prevent them seeing her tears.

Chapter Nineteen

SUMMONED IN HASTE by Dr. Howard to help find some solution to their impasse, Tess broke the strained silence at the dinner table that evening. "I have been thinking it might be best for me to move here to Stony Hill after all. I'd hoped my home would provide an inheritance for my nieces, but with my property occupied by the rebel army, my situation is well nigh intolerable. So I might as well admit the inevitable."

She pushed aside her plate. "If Elizabeth is determined to stay, we could live here together, with Sarah and the children to help us. I'd be glad of her company, and we could take care of your property."

Drumming his fingers on the table, Dr. Howard transferred his gaze from his sister to his wife. "That's an eminently sensible suggestion, Tess. What do you think, my dear?"

Mrs. Howard's eyes filled with tears. Several times she attempted to respond without success, finally conceded, "We can hardly drag Elizabeth aboard the ship if she has her mind set on staying behind." Her face lighting with hope, she turned to Elizabeth. "Won't you reconsider, my love?"

Elizabeth bit her lip and clenched her hands, fighting back her own tears. "I've thought and prayed about this all afternoon, Mama. It pains me greatly to think of your going so far away, but I cannot reconcile myself to leaving my home, perhaps forever. And with Aunt Tess here all alone, it would seem best . . . " She broke off, unable to continue.

"I'm going to miss you all so much," Tess said into the painful silence. "It would be a great comfort to at least have Elizabeth with me."

Abby jumped up out of her chair. "How can you talk about breaking up our family like it was nothing?" she cried, her face contorted with fury and anguish. "Either we all stay or we all go, Aunt Tess too!"

"Abby—!" Mrs. Howard began.

"If Beth's staying, then so am I!" the child cut her off. "I'm not leaving her!"

"You are too young to be separated from your parents, young lady! This is a matter for grownups to decide—"

"I'm almost ten, Papa! I'm old enough to make my own decisions!"

"There'll be no more insubordination, Abigail!" Dr. Howard snapped. "Sit down at once and be silent!"

Abby looked from him to Elizabeth, who sat watching her, her hands clasped over her mouth, tears streaming down her face. Stamping her foot, she wailed, "I hate you! I hate all of you! I won't go!"

Sobbing hysterically, she ran from the room. They could hear her running up the stairs.

Elizabeth and Mrs. Howard rose at the same instant, but, dabbing at her tears, Elizabeth motioned her mother to sit down. "Let me take care of this if I can."

Mrs. Howard nodded and sat down, her expression reflecting her misery. Elizabeth hurried upstairs and tapped on Abby's closed door.

"It's me, sweetie. May I please come in?"

All was silent inside for a long moment, but at last Abby pulled open the door and threw herself into her sister's arms. "Oh, Beth, if Mama and Papa insist on going, please promise you'll come with us. *Please!*"

Closing the door, Elizabeth led Abby to the bed and sat down beside her. "You wouldn't want to leave Aunt Tess here all alone, would you, dear? She would be so lonely."

"Then why can't I stay?"

Elizabeth smoothed the hair out of Abby's flushed face. "This is hard enough for Mama and Papa without losing you too. They would be brokenhearted. You need to be with your parents, and I need to be with Aunt Tess. I know it's hard to understand, but I promise I'll write you long letters and send you lots of presents. If at all possible, I'll come for a visit in a year or so. You'll have so many new things to do and make so many new friends that it won't seem like such a long time."

Abby pulled out of her arms. "You won't come!" she sobbed. "We'll never be a family again!"

ALL THAT NIGHT AND SUNDAY Elizabeth agonized over her decision to stay while the little sister who owned such a large share of her heart was taken away across a vast ocean. But every fiber of her being rebelled at the thought of abandoning her homeland amid a crisis of such proportions—one she had a role in resolving.

To her relief, their usual Sunday dinner at the town house was cancelled at the last moment when Gage precipitated a confrontation by sending an armed sloop to carry off hay for the garrison's horses from one of the numerous small islands that dotted Boston harbor. The rebels did not taken kindly to what they considered to be theft of their hay. In short order a force of almost two thousand men landed on one side of the island while the British detachment made a hurried exit from the other. Carleton and Andrews were tied up with the crisis all that day.

In spite of every attempt to sort things out, however, the events of the previous week continued to wear a monotonous circuit in Elizabeth's head. At last, on Monday, May 22, she determined to resolve one troubling issue, at least, by finding out whether Carleton was indeed spying for Gage. That afternoon she had Peter drive her into Boston. But on reaching the town house, she sat outside in the phaeton for several minutes, uncertain how to proceed.

Since her conversation with Andrews she had been trying to invent a pretext to drop by in hope of finding Carleton at home alone, perhaps writing one of the reports Andrews had mentioned. But she hadn't been able to come up with a single plausible excuse. At last she decided to walk boldly in and see what developed.

If he was there. To her disappointment, all the windows she could see were curtained. The house appeared to be deserted.

She had the key to the front door in her reticule, however, and she decided she might as well go inside and nose around. It was wrong, she knew, even though the house did belong to her parents. But although she felt guilty about doing it, the questions that nagged at her drove her to act.

She breathed a prayer, asking God to help her uncover everything she needed to know. As an afterthought, she added a request that his will be done, all the while trying to persuade herself that God's will was in agreement with her own.

The instant she opened the front door and stepped into the hall, she heard the muted strains of a violin coming from the library. Closing the door without making a sound, she hesitated.

Her presence there was a violation of Carleton's privacy. She could not pretend he would want an audience at that moment, and she knew she should withdraw as quietly as she had come.

But the deep emotion in the music held her, drew her irresistibly to it. After a moment of indecision she slipped into the parlor, intending to listen for a short while, then to escape without making her presence known. The inner library door stood ajar, so she tiptoed over to it, inched it open until she could just see inside.

Carleton's uniform coat lay across a chair, sword belt and scabbard thrown across it. His waistcoat unbuttoned and stock pulled loose, he stood in front of the far window, looking out across the bay, his back to her so she couldn't see his face.

She didn't recognize the piece he played so expressively, but the sad longing of the music touched a deep chord inside, drew her into the room without her being aware of what she was doing. Her eyes filming with tears, she sank into a chair near the door and listened, unconscious of the passage of time.

A last expressive measure sweeter than the rest faded to silence. Lowering the instrument stiffly, he rolled his shoulder as though its movement still pained him, then stood some moments longer, staring out the window, appearing to be lost in thought. At length he half turned to his left to lay violin and bow on the table next to him.

Stiffening, he stood still, his hand suspended in midair. Then he carefully placed the instrument on the table and turned to face her, his face wiped as clean of emotion as though he wore a mask.

"What are you doing here?"

There was no welcome or friendliness in his tone and look. She got to her feet, taken aback by the coldness of his greeting.

"I . . . I'm sorry, Jonathan. Please forgive me for intruding. You play so beautifully, and it moved me so much that I . . . couldn't help coming in."

His expression remained closed. When he made no reply, she bit her lip and looked down.

"The piece you were playing . . . I don't believe I've ever heard it."

"You haven't."

"It's your own composition?"

He inclined his head, but said nothing.

"Forgive me. I'll leave you alone." Trembling, she turned to the door and fumbled for the handle.

"Don't go."

His words were still abrupt, but more gently spoken. She stopped, struggling to regain control of her emotions. After a tense moment he crossed the room and took her hand. Leading her to the sofa, he sat down beside her.

Looking up, she met his piercing gaze. "Truly, I didn't mean to intrude. But as you played, I felt . . . pain, anguish, hopelessness. I feel it in you so often—that something or someone has hurt you terribly, that you hate yourself for some imagined offense, or—"

He made a quick, painful gesture, but she rushed on, "If you refuse to trust anyone enough to talk about it, you'll never be free of the burdens you carry."

"So you're a physician of hearts as well as of bodies."

She flinched at the harsh sarcasm of his words. "I make no pretense of that. But I do care, and I wish I could find some way to help you."

"That, no one can do."

He still clasped her hand, and looking down at their intertwined fingers, she lightly traced the network of veins on the back of his strong, tanned hand. "I well know how difficult it can be to trust when you've been badly hurt. But you seem to find it impossible."

"I've learned that no one is trustworthy. Least of all myself."

"Not even Sir Harry?"

The impulsive words brought a spasm to his face. "He was different. But he's dead."

There was such deep hopelessness in his tone that she took his hand between both her own. "What about God? Have you gone so far that you can no longer trust even him?"

He gave a short, hard laugh. "After the life I've lived, all I can expect from that quarter is condemnation."

"I can't believe you've been so wicked that you've placed yourself beyond all hope of forgiveness."

"A soldier's life isn't conducive to virtue. Quite the contrary."

She was at a loss what to say. He looked around the room as though searching for something, then back at her.

"You remind me of what I was at your age: vital and passionate—and innocent in spite of a veneer of sophistication. I dearly regret losing that young man."

"How do you know you've lost him? Maybe he's still there deep inside, waiting to be reclaimed."

He let out a deep sigh. As though speaking to himself, he said,

"Perhaps that's the real reason I came back. To redeem myself."

"We can never redeem ourselves," she protested. "You know that as well as I."

He released her hand and got up to move restlessly across the room. "How could you know what it feels like to go so far that no matter how hard you try you can't find your way back?"

"I understand more than you think I do. It might help if you confided in someone, and I'm willing to listen."

"I'd rather not lose your good opinion of me."

"Does that matter so much to you?"

He turned to face her. "More than you know. If you knew me as well as I know myself, you'd despise me as much as I do."

"Learning you're human being isn't going to change my good opinion of you."

Again he swung away and for a strained interval stood in moody silence. At length he said, "Well, you shall have the truth then, and we shall see if your opinion of me will not undergo a change."

Then, pacing up and down, he told her all of it in halting words, not meeting her gaze. It was not a pretty picture he painted of himself with harsh self-condemnation and cynical contempt.

He had just turned twenty-two when he had received urgent summons to return to England, where Lord Oliver lay dying. Reluctantly he had gone to fulfill what he believed to be his duty to the man who had sired him, a man whom he had seen only twice, briefly, since being sent away at the age of three.

He had arrived at his family's estate late one winter night to find Lord Oliver already buried. Exhausted by two months aboard ship and three days on the road from London, he had been unprepared for the interview with the elder half-brother he remembered distantly as his childhood tormentor.

Nineteen years had done nothing to erase the enmity between them, he had discovered at once. In taking possession of the vast majority of their father's estate, Edward had possessed himself also of the small stipend Carleton was to have inherited. When Carleton had demanded an explanation, his brother had produced letters written by Carleton's mother to her cousin, which detailed a love affair between them that had begun soon after she had married Lord Oliver and made it clear that this liaison had resulted in Carleton's birth. This proof Edward had used at their father's deathbed to persuade the dying man to disinherit his younger son.

Carleton had been staggered by the revelation. In his exhaustion he had not thought to question the authenticity of the letters, but had returned to London, shattered by the belief that the gentle young mother whose memory he had cherished in the years since her early death had lived a life of betrayal, that his birth had been a shameful one, and that he had been living, though unwittingly, a monstrous lie.

On reaching London he had realized that he had neither means of living nor enough money to buy passage back to Virginia. He carried a letter from Sir Harry to his factor authorizing Carleton to draw on his uncle's account, but now believing himself to be unconnected by any tie of blood, he had shrunk from accepting financial support under what he conceived to be false pretenses.

The only course available to him had been to live by his wits. Credit and entrance to the highest levels of London society had been easy to obtain, given his connections. He had soon discovered that he could make a handsome living through bluff and by gambling with his new friends, pursuits he had found himself exceptionally well suited to. Within a year he had purchased a commission in the Light Dragoons and had begun to think very well of his abilities.

There had, however, been a price for the life he had lived.

"She was thirty-six and beautiful, trapped, or so she told me, in an unhappy marriage. What I didn't learn until much later was that she had used the same line to seduce a string of young lovers before me while her husband looked the other way. I thought she was my friend, and I was so naive I didn't realize what she was after until I found myself in her bed.

"At first I justified my actions. Then I excused my weakness. At last I believed myself the true son of an unfaithful mother. But I couldn't stop. Each time, I swore I'd never see her again. But every time she sent for me, I went back.

"You tell yourself no one knows what you're doing, that you're being so discreet. But I discovered she boasted of her conquests to her friends, and our affair was soon common gossip in our circle. But far from bringing me under contempt, my fellow officers thought all the better of me for it.

"When in desperation I finally tried to walk out on her, she threatened suicide. I told her I didn't care, so she slashed her wrists. I got a doctor to her in time, but the news was all over London in hours, and her husband could no longer ignore the scandal. He challenged me to a duel to avenge his honor."

"What . . . what happened?" Elizabeth stammered, feeling sick.

He laughed coldly. "He died the following day."

She drew in a sharp breath, pressed her hands to her bosom. She could not meet his gaze. For a moment he regarded her with a bitter smile, then continued, his face like stone.

"I received a slap on the wrist from my superiors—and my reputation was greatly enhanced. It seems there is no debauchery or perversion so gross that my countrymen will not practice and esteem it."

"And the woman?"

"Oh, never daunted, she assumed we would marry. I couldn't stomach the prospect, but it took another year before I found the resolve to finally put an end to our relationship."

"But . . . you did break it off."

"And promptly turned to every vice and sin in the attempt to blot her and my own shameful birth and character from my memory. In short, I was a proper officer of His Majesty the King. I continued so until I couldn't bear to look at myself in the mirror any longer.

"The worst was when I received a letter from Sir Harry. He'd heard about the life I was living, and he was deeply grieved. From his factor he'd learned of the letters Edward had used to disinherit me, and he wrote that my parents had come to visit him in Virginia soon after they were married. Three months after their arrival my mother conceived me—while her cousin was far away in France. The letters were gross forgeries. I had believed a lie. And Sir Harry pleaded with me to return to a life worthy of my Savior.

"That's what ended my course of self-destruction. I knew I had to either end my life or stop. So I stopped. But I was too ashamed to write and tell him I was trying to change."

Shocked and repulsed, Elizabeth sprang to her feet and moved to the opposite side of the room. The air felt stifling. Her head bowed, her hand clenched and pressed to her mouth, she fought to regain her composure.

She was aware that he watched her with cold satisfaction at the effect of his revelation. Indeed, it was more than she had expected, and the thought of the life he had sunk into appalled her. Perhaps he had been right. Perhaps it would have been better had she never known.

And yet, their relationship ▪whatever it was or might become could not exist on a foundation of secrecy and lies. At some point they had to stop playing games and be honest with each other.

The thought stabbed through her, made her wince. Would it ever be possible for her to reveal as much of her heart to him when he held the power of life and death over her? Again she faced the question: What was God's purpose in bringing them together?

It was all too confusing. She could make no sense of it. But as she struggled with the revelation of his past, a pang of deep conviction cut through her. How could she judge and condemn him when she had been on the verge of being drawn into a sordid and abusive affair by a man she had chosen to marry? If God had not prompted her father to rescue her when he had, what might her end have been?

Another thought occurred to her. How could she minister to Carleton when the Holy Spirit was convicting her that there were corners of her being she had not yet surrendered to her Master? Yet she had chosen to come to him this day. She had been drawn there by a power other than her own, and she could not sidestep this moment.

Biting her lip, she turned to look at Carleton. His shoulders slumped, he was staring out the window, his face sad, the defiance all gone out of him.

Ashamed, she went over to him, feeling as if a force stronger than herself drew her. Taking his hand, she said, "You are made of human flesh, and it shocked you to learn that. Do you think God is disappointed in you for being human? Do you think he does not know what your heart is made of or that he has ceased to love you because of your weakness? If that were so, I too would be lost beyond hope of reclamation."

His expression tortured, he took a shaky breath. "I believed I had accepted him as my Savior. I was baptized, I pledged my life to him, then I betrayed every vow I'd ever made. How can God possibly forgive that?"

"We have nothing to cling to but the cross," she murmured, her voice unsteady. "Do you remember the hymn we sang on Easter day? We can boast in nothing but that Christ died for us."

He nodded, bent his head. "When Sir Harry died and I went back to Virginia to settle his estate, I felt like the prodigal son returning home. But I found that my father was no longer there to forgive me."

The words welled up from the depths her heart before she was conscious they were there. "Oh, Jonathan, your Father is waiting with open arms to restore you to your rightful place. He'll freely forgive all your sins and make you pure again if you'll only come home to him. He's been waiting all this time, loving you, his heart aching to have his son back again, grieving over your pain. But you've kept running from him."

With a clumsy gesture, he brushed away his tears. "I want to believe that," he said, his voice ragged, "and I keep asking myself if it can be possible that God could forgive me for the wicked life I've led. Could he truly make me clean again?"

She smiled through her tears. "Is anything impossible with the Lord?"

He made a gesture of frustration. "I don't want to deceive myself. I'm not worthy of his forgiveness."

"Am I? Are any of us? Christ died to do what we couldn't."

He looked away, at length said, "Maybe the truth is I can't forgive myself."

"Oh, how I understand that!" She gave a painful laugh. "But if you keep waiting for the day when you can somehow find the strength to forgive yourself, you'll never find peace. Do you remember when you were a little child and you trusted Sir Harry utterly, without asking any questions? You knew he loved you and would take care of you no matter what happened, even if you were naughty. That's the way our relationship with the Lord has to be too.

"Take him at his word. Ask for his forgiveness, then believe you have it and let go of the past."

"I can't go on this way, that's sure."

Taking his hands, she drew him to his knees beside her, tears flooding her eyes. "Just ask him, Jonathan."

He hesitated, then bowed his head, his hands gripping hers as though she were a lifeline. "Oh, Lord," he began, his voice trembling, "you know how wicked I've been. You know every evil thing in my heart."

He stopped then and began again with words that came from the depths of his soul. "Father, you know how sorry I am for turning my back on you and going my own way. I never want to live that kind of life again. I want to be the man you meant for me to be, but I can't do it no matter how hard I try.

"Please forgive me for failing you so miserably. Please forgive me for my pride and stubbornness, for blindly clinging to my own desires. I want to be worthy of the sacrifice you made for me. All that I am—all that I have—I surrender to you, Father. Make of me what you will. I'll fight you no more."

Seeking guidance, she tentatively placed her hands on his bowed head. This time, too, the words that came were not her words, but they were the right ones.

"Father, you have heard your son's prayer. May he be made whole again and restored to your love. Fill him with your peace, Father. Cleanse him of all sin and make him new. I ask this in Jesus' name. Amen."

When he raised his head, there was peace and joy in his face. Impulsively they embraced and for some moments clung to each other in mute gratitude.

At length he released her, and getting to his feet, helped her to rise. "I knew from the first moment I saw you that you were going to be my good angel. God sent you here today. Thank you. I feel as though every burden has been lifted from my shoulders and that I am whole again."

She reached up to touch his cheek. "You are, Jonathan. Now you can truly make a new start."

As she smiled into his eyes, the fleeting thought came to her that this vulnerable moment might yield valuable information if she approached it with care. But at the same instant she felt ashamed. She couldn't go that far. To try would be to violate a sacred trust that had been given to her without her deserving it.

The memory of the prayer she had whispered little more than an hour before came to her. Was this, then, God's will for herself as well as for him? For there was a place inside her that had been healed as well.

She had never felt closer to Carleton. They were bound now in a relationship as brother and sister in the Lord. And her heart warmed with the realization that, no matter what might come, this bond would remain between them.

Later as she drove down Beacon Street she thought of the moment when Carleton had embraced her. There had been no consciousness then for either of them of anything beyond the joy of his restoration. Yet now, remembering it and feeling again the warmth of his arms enfolding her, she longed to lay her head on his shoulder, to bare her heart to him, and to rest in the security of his love.

Something else kept nagging at her, and she knew she should face it too. Wasn't it time for her to surrender all of her life as Carleton had? The memory of the many chances she had taken, the rash plots she had conceived and carried out heedless of the warnings and advice of those who loved her rose up to convict her conscience.

All too often she didn't wait for God's guidance. Instead, she ran far ahead of him, following the path that seemed right at the moment. Too often she trusted her own judgment instead of God's and walked in her own understanding and strength.

Her passion insisted the patriots' position was right and the king and Parliament were wrong. But how could she know that for certain? And even if she was right, what if God didn't approve of everything she was doing?

What if God's plan was different from her own?

She had no doubt of her salvation, but she also knew that she was still holding back a part of herself that she didn't fully trust the Lord to control. The need to prove herself, the thrill of testing her skill, daring, and courage against impersonal events and human foes was too alluring.

Did the details matter to God as long as the motive and the goal were noble ones? Hadn't he made her as she was for a reason, after all? Wasn't it his will for her to act on convictions he had planted in her heart?

There were things she needed to do before she sorted everything out, she decided. And once more she drew back, putting off the decision for a more convenient day.

❋ ❋ ❋

WHEN ANDREWS RETURNED from duty later that afternoon he saw the difference in his friend. After dinner that evening he and Carleton had a long, serious talk for the first time since arriving in the colonies.

It was not a hard decision for Andrews to make, for he had been thinking of committing his life to the Lord since soon after they had begun attending services together at the small Virginia church Carleton had attended as a youth. That night before they parted to go to their beds, to his great joy, Carleton welcomed into the Kingdom a well-loved brother.

Chapter Twenty

H ER FACE BURIED IN THE DEWY GRASS, Elizabeth lay motionless a dozen yards below the summit of Beacon Hill, the blood thudding in her ears. She focused every sense on her mission as she waited for her breathing to slow to its normal rhythm. Reassured that they had not been detected, she cautiously raised her head to peer through the shadowy blackness.

Twenty feet off to her left and above her loomed the dim bulk of the redoubt. A lone sentry was visible from where she lay, standing as mute and motionless as a statue on top of the wall this side of the nearest cannon. Careful reconnaissance had revealed five more sentries posted around the other side.

Her fingers tightened over the shoulder strap of the leather bag she carried. It was filled with iron spikes. Seven members of her band hugged the ground to each side and behind her, all cloaked and masked, as she was, in black. Nearest was young Pete, who since the defection of his father and older brother to the rebel army had become her right hand.

The warbled notes of an oriole reached them from the direction of the bay below. The sentry in the redoubt whirled toward the sound, then his mates ran around the cannon to join him. Somewhere off in the darkness they heard a scuffle accompanied by muttered curses, then voices shouting.

"It's Oriole and his men!"

"After them! They're getting away!"

The instant the sentries took off at a run down the hill in the direction of the commotion, Elizabeth and her companions were on their feet. Scrambling over the walls of the redoubt, she leaped onto the gun carriage of the nearest cannon, tore one of the spikes from her bag, and shoved it into the touchhole. As quickly, young Pete was up beside her. Three times he swung his sledgehammer with every ounce of his considerable strength, forcing the spike deep into the hole.

The rest of their fellows were similarly occupied. Before the repeated clang of steel against steel had attracted cries of dismay from below, every cannon in the redoubt had been put out of service.

Signaling the others with a shrill whistle, Elizabeth leaped over the wall and led the race down the steep back side of the hill, their boots swishing through the wet grass as they scrambled and slid down the incline, their breath coming in shallow pants. Below them waited several of their compatriots who had been standing guard to keep clear their path of retreat.

The three who had carried out the diversion intercepted them at the narrow alley on the other side of Chestnut Street. On their heels came a substantial detachment of Regulars, while a second detachment poured down the slope of the hill, shouting and swearing in fury.

Waving her companions forward, Elizabeth took the rear to make sure everyone got away. In a dense phalanx they tore down the winding alley, more exhilarated than scared.

When they reached Mount Vernon Street they spread out, several detouring through a deserted warehouse while the rest veered off into the abandoned ropewalks on the other side of Pinckney Street or melted away into one of the numerous unlighted, narrow lanes that wound off on every side between the dark, closely crowded buildings. By the time the two patrols had traversed the first alley and paused to get their bearings, their quarry had vanished like the mist off the bay into the inscrutable maze that was Boston.

✳ ✳ ✳

HIS EXPRESSION GROWING STONIER with each page, Carleton read through the reports spread out in front of him on the library table at Province House the next morning. When he had finished the last one, he sat back in his chair and stared into space for some minutes longer. Coming to a decision, he grabbed the papers, stood up, and strode to the door.

Throwing it open, he stopped on the threshold as though struck by a bolt of lightning. A short distance down the passage, Gage was ushering a man out of his office. As he turned in Carleton's direction, he also stopped in his tracks, blanching.

For a suspended moment, each stared at the other, thunderstruck. Then the other man's eyes narrowed. His lips tightening to a sneer, he brushed past Carleton and went out the mansion's rear door without a word.

Carleton watched him go before turning back to the general. Answering his look of inquiry with a frown, Gage motioned Carleton into his office and closed the door.

Carleton indicated the sheaf of papers Gage held. "I take it Hutchins is one of your spies."

Gage handed him the report. "As long as you're evaluating the others, have a look at these."

Carleton scanned the pages. He saw at once that the hand that had written them had also written the reports he had just been studying. And as he read, an unaccustomed tightness closed around his chest.

He looked up to meet Gage's steady gaze. "What's this about a traitor?"

"Hutchins said he picked up a hint of it from Warren and direct confirmation from a new contact he considers reliable. The rebels have lately been receiving detailed military intelligence, much more than Oriole has ever provided them, so Hutchins is convinced he can't be the source. He's certain it must be coming from an officer on my staff, who's undoubtedly passing it on through Oriole. Consequently, our first priority is to find and stop our traitor before he can do us any further damage. Our second priority is to capture that blasted Oriole. You heard he spiked more of our cannon last night?"

"Andrews filled me in this morning after I got back through the lines."

Gage motioned toward the papers Carleton held. "Hutchins is convinced his new contact knows Oriole's identity and with some careful handling might be induced to share it. He believes he's using the name James Freeman, though that's probably a blind."

Carleton kept his expression neutral. "I'd be inclined to question Hutchins' sources—and his motives."

"So far I've found him reliable."

Carleton laughed softly. It wasn't a pleasant sound and Gage stiffened.

"Oh, he's reliable, all right—in treachery. I found out just last night that your friend is a privateer for the patriots. The four merchantmen we lost off Halifax were taken by sloops he outfitted for the purpose and personally commanded. It seems he made a handsome profit selling the cargo to the Committee of Safety."

Gage sagged into his chair, the color draining out of his face.

"And as for these reports," Carleton continued, flicking the papers with contempt, "considering what I've observed, Hutchins has underestimated the rebel strength by at least a third in both men and munitions, and I can vouch that there are new, well-equipped units coming in every day. Were we to attempt an attack on the rebel lines without substantial reinforcements, I guarantee we'd suffer heavy losses, if not be overrun altogether. But that's undoubtedly Warren's plan."

"You think Hutchins is working for Warren? If that's true, why would Hutchins inform on this traitor?"

"He's an invention meant to keep you from trusting anyone except Hutchins. One of the most effective means of overcoming an enemy is to sow the seeds of suspicion and dissension. I agree you're surrounded by traitors, sir, but they're on the other side of the lines, not on your staff. A witch hunt will do nothing but destroy us."

Gage got to his feet, his face contorted with rage. "We've got to stop him! Send a guard after him at once—"

"By now he'll be at the town gates. No, the best we can do is to post a warrant for his arrest. If you offer a large enough reward, someone in the rebel camp should be sufficiently tempted to turn him over."

"Do it then," Gage agreed through gritted teeth. "Take care of it personally. I want to see Hutchins hang for this."

Carleton fixed him in a moody gaze. "First you'd better tell me who your other spy is so we can find out what game he's playing as well."

Gage hesitated, then blurted out, "It's Dr. Benjamin Church."

Carleton started, then gave an incredulous laugh. "Dr. Church? Why, he's a member of the Provincial Congress and a close friend of Warren and Adams."

"Excellent situations, no doubt, but they pay nothing, and my experience has been that the good doctor is in need of regular transfusions of money. Do you know anything that might compromise him?"

Carleton shook his head. "Among the patriots his reputation is newly minted gold. But give me time, and we shall see what the good doctor is really made of."

Gage concurred. "Tonight, though, I want to go over these reports with you to determine where the errors lie. Then I want you to write a detailed report of your own observations."

"My notes are at my billet," Carleton answered, keeping his voice steady, though his heart sank. "This can't wait another day? There's a good deal of essential information I haven't had time to search out, and I expected tonight to—"

"This is too important to wait," Gage interrupted impatiently. "I depend on your counsel, Jon, especially with Howe and his coterie due to arrive at any moment. Secure the warrant for Hutchins' arrest, then fetch your notes and join me for tea and dinner. I'll expect you back here in an hour."

Without further protest, Carleton took his leave. But as he rode back to the town house, an increasingly oppressive sense of entrapment and danger hung over him. For the moment, the crisis had been averted. But he could summon no confidence that it had been entirely eliminated.

THE DAY WAS UNSEASONABLY HOT AND SULTRY, but invigorated by the success of the previous night's adventures and her stealthy return to the mainland aboard Captain Dalton's fishing sloop, Elizabeth returned to Boston. Assuming her disguise at the abandoned printing shop that was their usual rendezvous, she called together her band. They spent some time evaluating the results of their work and planning further strategies before breaking up late in the afternoon.

Resuming her normal identity, she headed home. As she passed Lord Percy's headquarters, she saw Andrews coming down the steps. He saw her at the same time, and she could not avoid answering his greeting.

"Won't you join me for tea?" he urged. "I was just on my way home."

Sensing that he had something important to tell her, she accepted his invitation. When they were alone in the parlor, he told her of his decision to accept the Lord.

Delighted, she demanded all the details, then ran to give him a hug. "Oh, Charles, I'm so glad. Now you're truly my brother too."

Holding her, he sobered. The emotion she read in his eyes caused her to draw out of his arms, the color flaming into her cheeks.

"I'd hoped I might be a little more than a brother to you. But I suppose it's Jon, isn't it?"

"Don't be absurd. Neither one of us has any interest in a love affair."

Andrews shook his head. "I've seen Jon flirt with a lot of women, but he has never looked at anyone the way he looks at you. I've never heard his voice soften the way it does when he says your name. And I see the way you look at him too when he isn't watching."

On impulse she put her hands on his shoulders and tiptoed to kiss him on the cheek. "You're imagining things, you silly goose!"

He laughed down at her. They were standing very close together, his hands encircling her waist, his forehead almost brushing hers, when both at the same time became aware of footfalls in the hallway. They looked round with a guilty start just as Carleton stepped into the room.

"Beth?"

He came to an abrupt halt, the welcoming smile erased from his eyes as he looked from one to the other. Releasing Elizabeth, Andrews took a hasty step away from her. For a suspended moment, Carleton stood as though he were frozen to the floor, his face expressionless.

Hot color flooding into his face, Andrews said, "Jon, we weren't—"

"It's none of my business what you were doing. Pardon me for interrupting."

Giving them a stiff bow, he turned and went out of the room.

Paralyzed, Elizabeth stared at the empty doorway Carleton had vacated. She could hear him going down the passage into the library, then the door closed and there was silence.

The humid air seemed to press in on her like a heavy weight. The light breeze that had brought some coolness to the afternoon had died away.

She felt like crying. It took all her considerable strength of will to excuse herself and leave with apparent calm, all the while feeling that she was running away.

All the way home the memory of Carleton's expression when he had found her in Andrews's embrace accused her. Actions that had seemed so innocently playful a moment before took on a much more serious hue when reflected in his eyes.

She had placed herself and Andrews in a position so compromising it was unthinkable. Worse, she had initiated a kiss, which must have appeared to any observer to have a significance quite different from what she had intended. She went cold at the thought of what Carleton would have thought if he had walked into the room a moment earlier.

Considering the part he had seen, what must he think of her now? At the very least, it must have appeared that she was trifling with the emotions of a friend who was dear to him. And at the most?

In that first instant of surprise, he had been unable to disguise his shock and pain at finding them in such intimate proximity. If he did not care a great deal for her, he would not have reacted so strongly, she realized with dismay.

She must find a way to put their relationship on a safer footing. They were too vulnerable after the closeness they had experienced just two days earlier, when Carleton had recommitted his life to God. Perhaps what had happened now was for the best after all.

By the time she reached Stony Hill, her emotions were at least outwardly under control. As she came in the door, however, her mother greeted her with suppressed excitement.

"Here you are at last! I was almost ready to start tea without you. But look—there's a note from Major Carleton. A messenger brought it not half an hour after you left this morning."

Taking the folded paper from her hand, Elizabeth stared down at the intertwined letters JSC pressed into the crimson sealing wax. Her mother was waiting for her to open it, and finally, with trembling fingers, she broke the wax and unfolded the page. It was dated the day before and had evidently been delayed on its way through the lines.

Beth—I had to tell you again how very much the kindness of my good angel means to me and how far her influence has already reached. Last night Charles also gave his heart to our Lord, so now you see, two more lives are greatly in your debt.

When I accused you of being a physician of hearts, I little realized the truth of what I said. But I know it now, and this heart is overflowing with gratitude.

It was signed simply, "Jonathan." With her finger, she traced the graceful scrawl, then folded the note and stuck it into her reticule, her face turned away so her mother wouldn't see the emotions that threatened to overcome her.

"It's nothing, Mama," she said with a careless laugh.

Excusing herself on the pretext of changing for tea, she escaped upstairs to her room.

WHEN THE PHAETON HAD DISAPPEARED from sight, Andrews went to the library door. After some indecision he knocked and without waiting for Carleton's response went inside.

Carleton sat at the desk, writing. He didn't look up when Andrews came in, but finished his task. Blotting the page, he folded it together with several others and slipped them into his pocket before meeting Andrews's troubled gaze.

"I'm meeting with General Gage this evening. I won't be back until quite late."

"Jon, what you saw a minute ago wasn't what you think."

"As I said, it's none of my business." Standing up, Carleton moved toward the door.

Andrews blocked his path. "The fact is I tried to tell Elizabeth how I feel about her, but she thinks of me as a brother, that's all. So I began teasing her because she wouldn't believe me when I told her that you're in love with her and because she refused to admit she's in love with you—"

Frowning, Carleton came to a halt. "What the deuce makes you think either of us is in love with the other?"

"For all your protestations, I haven't noticed you making any effort to avoid her."

"I won't deny I enjoy flirting with her, but that's as far as it goes. She's rather like a high-spirited little sister. I like to match wits with her."

His voice softening, he added, "And she's done me a good service, for which I'll always be in her debt."

"But you're not in the least in love with her."

"As I keep pointing out, I don't have the time or the inclination for a romance."

"That's not what I asked."

A disgusted look was the only answer he received. Folding his arms across his chest, Andrews persisted, "Can you look me straight in the eye and tell me you're not in love with her?"

The muscles in Carleton's jaw tightened, but he didn't meet the lieutenant's gaze. "Why are you so interested in what I may or may not feel for Beth?"

"Because we've been friends for a long time, and we've never told each other anything but the truth," Andrews shot back.

For a long moment, Carleton remained silent, then he sighed. "There are things about me even you don't know, Charles. Things that would make it impossible for me to offer myself to any woman, much less to her. Things that would make it impossible for her ever to accept me as her husband even if she were so inclined."

"What things? That scandal with Lady Randolph? But that's all in the past."

Carleton met Andrews's probing gaze with a tortured one. "Perhaps some day I'll be able to confide in you, but not now."

"Jon, you've been a brother to me when I had no one. I wouldn't have survived if you hadn't come along and taken me away from that drunkard who called himself my father. But lately, you've seemed different . . . remote, secretive. Until the other night I was feeling I hardly knew you anymore. It's the first good talk we've had since we left England."

Carleton stared at him, stricken. "My dear friend, I've had a good many things on my mind, that's all. It hasn't been intentional."

He reached out to the younger officer, and they embraced. His voice husky with emotion, Carleton said, "You're all the family I have now,

Charles. I pray you'll judge me kindly no matter what happens."

Andrews drew back, his hands tightening on Carleton's shoulders. "Nothing could make me think ill of you, Jon. Nothing."

Chapter Twenty-one

I T WAS AFTER ONE O'CLOCK Thursday morning by the time Carleton left Province House, almost two before he stretched across his bed. But even though he was mentally and emotionally spent, his mind refused to quiet, continuing to plod along the same endless path, seeking a solution that seemed farther off the longer he thought about it.

When he felt the most alone, his thoughts returned to his conversation with Andrews and to the sweetness of that hour when Elizabeth had prayed with him. He found himself hoping that his friend had been right about her feelings toward him.

Most of the time he simply tried not to think about her, but that night no amount of effort could keep the aching of his heart at bay. It seemed like such a long time since he had first yearned to tell her how dearly he loved her, how bleak his future seemed without her in it, how little desire he had to continue life alone.

Even if she did love him, he reminded himself in despair, even if she knew his heart and were still willing to accept him as her husband, he was in far too dangerous a position to ask her to share a future with him. That too, as all the rest, would have to be left in God's hands.

Coming so close to death had forced him to confront issues he had spent many years trying to ignore. Now, reflecting on his life, he saw how the Lord had covered him with a hand of protection every step he had taken along his own willful path. Even when he had felt the most abandoned, the least worthy of redemption, the stronghold of God's love had shielded him, and his sure hand had guided him back home.

Thinking of it, a deep assurance calmed the storm that raged inside, and he was filled with a peace that the peril surrounding him could not touch. At the same time, not knowing what the immediate future would bring, but realizing that the coming days would require every ounce of strength, discretion, and wit he could summon, he felt wound tight as one of his violin strings, on the verge of snapping in two.

He was up with the dawn and, shortly past eight o'clock, back at Province House, as ordered, to meet with Gage and his ranking officers to begin mapping out a strategy for breaking the siege. Since Clinton, Howe, and Burgoyne would not know about the engagements at Lexington and Concord until their arrival, Gage had decided on the prudence of first making sure that everyone involved with the expedition would appear to have acted with proper discretion and that there could be no criticism of subsequent actions.

Carleton tried to force himself to concentrate on the matters at hand, but his mind kept wandering. He had a raging headache, and as the meeting dragged on it became progressively worse. When they received the news at a quarter after ten o'clock that the ship *Cerberus* carrying the long-awaited generals had anchored in the harbor, his mood wasn't improved. Scanning the circle of glum faces around the library table, he noted that even Percy looked pained.

Gage sent aides scurrying to summon Pitcairn, Smith, Mitchell, and Admiral Graves; to order a carriage to bring the generals to Province House; and to take care of other necessary preparations. Percy huddled with another of the general's aides to gather copies of the reports filed after the battle by each of the officers involved. These he distributed to their respective authors as each came into the room, adding the wry advice that they might want to review their observations and prepare to defend them.

Watching the officers weighing the effect words written in the heat of the battle's aftermath might have on their careers, Carleton groaned inwardly. He knew he would be called on to corroborate their reports and was repulsed at the prospect of wrestling his opinions into a form palatable to a room full of generals who would be less than delighted to hear an honest appraisal of the debacle.

They were forewarned of the generals' arrival by the cheers of a large contingent of Loyalists who had followed them from the docks all the way to Province House in the profound certainty that their saviors had at long last appeared. Clustered behind Gage, the officers waited in the foyer to welcome what many of them suspected was to be the new regime.

Senior in rank, tall, dark William Howe was the first up the steps, his movements characteristically languorous. Carleton knew him both by casual acquaintance in England as well as by his less than savory reputation for living the high life, and he noted that Howe's military bearing was beginning to show the effects of a self-indulgence that suffered little restraint.

Strutting along behind him like a bantam cock came short, paunchy Henry Clinton, his deceptively cherubic face puckered in a sour attempt at a smile. The long trip across the ocean with his colleagues had been trying to his ego, Carleton suspected.

Junior in rank, although the oldest of the three, John Burgoyne followed on their heels, a flamboyant, dashing figure with an overbearing manner, with whom Carleton was more intimately acquainted than he wished. In spite of Burgoyne's reputation for enlightened treatment of the men under his command, Carleton knew him to be pompous, self-serving, and insufferably vain.

On their way from the docks the three generals had learned something of Boston's beleaguered situation, and Gage spent several minutes in sober conversation with them before introducing them to the rest of the officers in turn. When they reached Carleton, Howe and Clinton acknowledged their introduction with a brief nod, but Burgoyne stiffened as his glance raked over the younger officer.

"Why, Jonnie boy, what a surprise," he drawled. "I didn't know you'd been posted here."

"You're acquainted?" Gage asked.

"We go back a very long way, don't we, Jonnie?"

Carleton conceded the general a stiff half-bow, his expression neutral.

"Major Carleton has been an enormous help in the short time he's been with us," Gage volunteered.

"Oh, I'm certain he has been."

Burgoyne's smile held all the warmth of a hungry wolf's. Gage gave Carleton a puzzled look, but to Carleton's relief the others had already moved along and the matter was dropped.

The rest of the day crawled by in an interminable discussion of the battle and its aftermath, with Carleton called on only briefly to corroborate his fellow officers' reports. Gage's abundant praise of Smith for his conduct in leading the disastrous expedition and the announcement of his promotion to brigadier honed Carleton's cynicism to an even finer edge.

Friday brought no relief. Most of the day was taken up by an extended tour of the town's fortifications for the benefit of the new arrivals. Gage placed Carleton in charge of the outing, and every ounce of his patience was tested before it was done.

A meeting with Admiral Graves followed late that afternoon, during which the normally irascible seaman fawned over the visitors, who had brought his promotion to vice-admiral. Afterward the officers sat late at dinner, then spent the rest of the evening smoking, drinking, and gambling at hazard or whist for high stakes while Carleton struggled to maintain a tight curb on his tongue and his temper.

All that day he managed to keep his distance from Burgoyne, and except for a few obscurely malicious remarks, the general ignored him. It was past ten o'clock before he was at last free to return to his billet, but since Gage planned to meet alone with his guests Saturday morning, he looked forward to a few hours' reprieve.

He was summoned back to Province House a short while before noon. British sentries had noticed a large party of men spread across Noddles Island, half a mile off the North End, and Hog Island, just beyond. It soon became apparent that a rebel detachment was driving across to the mainland all the horses, sheep, and cattle the local farmers pastured on the islands' lush grass—to prevent Gage from commandeering them as provisions for his troops, Carleton surmised.

In due course, the schooner *Diana* tacked across the bay to cut them off. As she began to land a substantial party of marines, the rebel force raced for cover on Hog's Island. For several hours the crackle of musket fire reverberated between the hills, but neither side made any advance.

Given the unpleasant duty of keeping the generals informed of what was going on, Carleton spent the afternoon shuttling between Province House and Graves's flagship, *Somerset,* in a state of profound frustration. To make matters worse, at nightfall, with the ebbing of the tide, the *Diana* settled into the soft mud along the island's shore. Dispatched to her aid, a dozen barges and the armed sloop *Britannia* clustered at a safe distance from the stranded schooner, refusing to move any closer.

Raging silently, Carleton hurried to Province House to deliver a blunt assessment of the situation. For his trouble, Gage sent him back to the *Somerset* as twilight gave way to full darkness.

In the fitful light of the torches and bonfires that thickly dotted the shore of the farther island, it appeared to Carleton that the ranks of the original rebel force had swollen enormously. Graves sent a second marine detachment to protect his ships, and before long the starry sky was crisscrossed with fiery arcs blazed by solid shot from British and rebel fieldpieces, punctuated by the boom of cannon echoing across the harbor.

Carleton watched while the schooner heeled over at a progressively steeper angle as the tide continued its steady ebb, until at last her crew was forced to abandon ship. Around midnight, as the British withdrew to the waiting vessels, a resounding whoop went up, and the rebels swarmed in on their heels to overrun the helpless schooner. In minutes, she was ablaze.

Again Carleton notified the generals in person. He was still at Province House when, at three o'clock Sunday morning, the flames reached the schooner's magazines and she exploded with a roar and a spectacular geyser of flames that sent a tremor through the peninsula, rattling the chandelier above the officers' heads.

The incident erased any hope he had of escape. Sunday morning and afternoon were consumed in tense meetings that neither produced a satisfactory explanation for what had occurred nor determined who was responsible for the disaster. At last the matter was tabled.

Monday, May 29, brought a return to the pressing issue of giving themselves "elbow room," in Burgoyne's expansive phrase. It was during the morning's extended meeting, while the generals were scrutinizing the most recent intelligence, that Gage remarked casually to Howe, "Those reports you're holding are the most accurate and complete intelligence available. We have Major Carleton to thank for them. He has crossed the rebel lines in disguise several times these past weeks."

His words caused a sensation. The officers gathered around the table turned to stare at Carleton. For a moment of blank shock he sat paralyzed, too dismayed to come up with a response that might minimize the damage.

In mock salute Burgoyne raised the glass of wine he had been nursing. "So, you've added spying to your considerable list of accomplishments, have you, Jonnie boy?" he said, his voice dripping malice. "How very convenient for you, I'm sure—passing over to the rebel side whenever you choose. Pardon me if, knowing you as I do, I wonder when you intend to stab us in the back. Or if you already have."

He said the last with a nod toward the report Howe was still holding. There was an audible intake of breath around the table accompanied by astonished sidelong looks in Carleton's direction.

Regaining his self-possession, Carleton met Burgoyne's attack with a wry laugh. "I should have expected as much from you, John, though I'd thought by now you'd have finished grinding that ax."

"I insist you explain yourself," Gage said to Burgoyne, his face shading from dark red to livid.

"Gladly. Not only did the major debauch the wife of my good friend Lord Randolph, but after finally dropping the poor, misguided woman so that she attempted suicide, he murdered Lord Randolph for good measure, a man who had not only trusted him, but introduced him into London society."

Intercepting Percy's indignant glance, Carleton shook his head, but Percy ignored him. "You're hardly objective on this matter, John. Why don't you drop it?"

Gage cut the earl off with an impatient gesture and a cold glance that included Burgoyne and Carleton. "This is a private affair between the two of you, gentlemen. It has nothing to do with the matter at hand, and I don't care to hear any more of it."

"There are some of us here who beg to differ," Smith cut in malevolently. His eyes met Burgoyne's, and with foreboding Carleton saw a flash of mutual interest pass between them.

"It's a matter of character," Burgoyne insisted.

"And, of course, yours is impeccable." Carleton instantly regretted the words, but they were out before he could stop them.

Burgoyne laughed, a nasty sound. "Oh, very fine, coming from an adulterer and a murderer."

Carleton didn't move, but Percy and Pitcairn were on their feet. "Ye know very well that Lord Randolph insulted Jon and forced him into a duel after he'd tried everything he knew to avoid it," Pitcairn ground out. "Mayhap your friend should ha' stopped to reckon who was the better swordsman a'fore he sent his second to him."

"Everyone knew Lady Randolph was notorious for taking young lovers, except for a lad straight from the colonies," Percy added. "Jon was only one in a very long line that spider caught in her web, and certainly not the last."

"That justifies his actions, of course," sneered Burgoyne.

Carleton motioned the two officers to sit down. "Perhaps you have never fallen prey to any youthful indiscretion you've had occasion to dearly repent of, but I've not been so fortunate. My life, I hope, may in time prove some atonement for the great wrong I did."

Howe had been scanning another of the reports in front of him. As Gage cut off the conversation and returned to the issue at hand, he looked up.

"According to this, there is a traitor in our midst, quite possibly someone in this very room."

"Major Carleton found no evidence to support that claim, and in fact, he discovered that the informant who brought the report is a privateer for the rebels and has been selling intelligence to them as well," Gage said stiffly.

Their voices seemed to reach Carleton from a great distance. His vision was strangely blurred, and he felt breathless as though he had been running, at the same time as though he were bound to his chair by steel chains.

Triumphant, Burgoyne pounced on the revelation. "Charges that would make perfect sense if Jonnie here turned out to be your traitor. If I were you, Your Excellency, I'd consider all the intelligence he has provided to be tainted, and I'd put an immediate end to any further excursions across enemy lines until his reports can be fully substantiated."

"Jon was with us all the way to Concord and back," Pitcairn snapped, outraged. "He did a more than creditable job of commanding a company, and the wound he suffered and almost died of should prove where he stands. Any man who has the effrontery to question his loyalty will have to answer to those of us who fought with him that day."

Arms crossed, Burgoyne stared at Carleton through narrowed eyes. "Just before we left England, I had a visit from your old friend St. Claire. You'll remember him, I think."

Carleton went cold, but managed to keep the dismay out of his face and voice. "St. Claire is no friend of mine."

Burgoyne smiled. "I shouldn't wonder. But he told me how your uncle died."

"Did he?" Carleton responded icily. "I've never known him to tell the truth."

"He said a writ of assistance was issued against Sir Harrison Carleton on charges of smuggling. Not surprising for one in whose veins flows the treacherous blood of the Stuarts, who as a lad fought on the side of the Scots at Sheriffmuir and after their defeat fled to the colonies to escape arrest and execution for treason—"

"Jon's father was the personal friend and advisor of King George II," Percy broke in through gritted teeth, "and if you think we'll sit here and listen to this—"

Raising his hand, Carleton stopped him. Turning to Burgoyne he said, "You promised you'd have your revenge, and you've waited a long time. So let's hear all of it."

Burgoyne gave him a mocking half-bow. "It seems Governor Dunmore sent soldiers to seize one of your uncle's warehouses, which happened to be full of illegally imported goods. Sir Harry and a band of ruffians he'd raised attempted to prevent them, and in the altercation he was thrown from his horse and died of his injuries. The goods were seized, with a loss to you, as his heir, of near £20,000."

A murmur of astonishment filled the room. The color had drained from Gage's face.

"Is this charge true?"

Carleton got slowly to his feet. "Accusations were brought against my uncle by men who envied his wealth and wished to rob him legally. That much is true. But the charges were found to be false and malicious.

Among Sir Harry's papers is the proof that he paid to the last halfpenny taxes due on all goods he ever imported. If you wish me to send for them, I'll do so."

He stopped then, squared his shoulders. "If I no longer have your confidence, Your Excellency, if you believe me capable of treason as I stand accused by General Burgoyne, then you shall have my resignation immediately."

For a taut moment Gage stared hard at Carleton, who met his gaze without flinching. Finally the general said, "I require no proof of your loyalty, major, nor will I accept your resignation. But there will be no further excursions across enemy lines. You will return your pass to me on the conclusion of this meeting, and you will account to me personally for every movement you make from this hour forward. Now take your seat, sir."

Carleton bowed and resumed his seat with outward calm. But inside he felt shaky and lightheaded.

Tightlipped, Gage directed a stern glance at the strained faces around the table. "You will remember, gentlemen, that everyone in this room had access to the same information."

"Access," said Burgoyne. "But only one had motive and opportunity for treason."

Gage gave him a cold look. "Unless undeniable proof of treason is uncovered, I will hear no more of this matter. You will neither discuss it among yourselves nor mention it to anyone outside this room. Is that clear, gentlemen?"

Trading covert glances among themselves, the officers indicated that it was. The meeting continued in an atmosphere of tense distraction.

All during the discussion of the necessity to secure Dorchester Heights and Charlestown peninsula to prevent the rebels from seizing them and leaving Boston untenable, Carleton's mind continued to race, testing every possibility. He could find no crack in the walls that hemmed him in. The world had narrowed to the width of a tightrope, and each step he took led him farther from solid ground with no assurance that he would find a firm foothold on the other side.

For the rest of the day even Percy kept his distance, and except for a quick, sympathetic squeeze of Carleton's shoulder as he passed by, so did Pitcairn. Neither would meet his eye, and all of the other officers made a point of avoiding unnecessary conversation with him.

Burgoyne had at last gotten the revenge he had promised, Carleton thought, feeling numb, and it couldn't have come at a worse time. The bitter seeds of suspicion had been sown, and already their roots were twining deep into fertile soil.

That those seeds would bring forth fruit, he had no doubt. And the harvest, he feared, was destined to be an evil one.

In the days that followed he was rarely allowed far from Gage's side. Although the general made no more mention of Burgoyne's charges, it was very clear that the relationship between them had changed and that he no longer enjoyed his commander's complete confidence.

Equally serious, Burgoyne and Smith appeared to have formed an alliance. Several times Carleton found them huddled together in hushed conversation that ended the moment he entered the room. Each evening they left Province House together.

That Carleton's friendship with Lord Percy had also suffered irreparable damage was obvious as well. Saturday evening following dinner, when he had been dismissed to return to his billet, Percy intercepted him on the steps outside, his narrow, triangular face taut with emotion.

"I won't insult you by asking if you've betrayed us, Jon. As your friend, I believe I know you well enough to be certain that Burgoyne's charges are malicious lies. But you also know that if evidence of your involvement in treason should be found, I will do everything in my power to bring you down."

Carleton gave him a level look. "If you really believed me, Hugh, as you say you do, we wouldn't be having this conversation, would we?"

Not waiting for an answer, he touched his fingers to his helmet in a stiff salute, turned on his heel, and stalked off into the darkness.

Chapter Twenty-two

SHADING HER EYES AGAINST THE SUN, Elizabeth stared in bleak sadness at the ship that would take her family three thousand miles across the ocean. A film of tears blurred her vision. Now that the moment had come she was overwhelmed by the realization that she would not see her parents and sister again for many months, perhaps years. And by the equal possibility that she might never see them again at all.

It was Sunday, June 4. They stood in an unhappy cluster in the bright mid-afternoon sunshine halfway out on Long Wharf, opposite the shuttered, deteriorating warehouses and counting houses that lined its north side. Because it was the Sabbath, the area surrounding the docks was comparatively quiet. The chests and boxes that held the Howards' possessions had already been loaded into the ship's hold, and in a few minutes the vessel would put out to the open sea.

For Elizabeth the past fortnight had vanished in a blur of sorrow and anxiety. Torn between the desire to spend every minute with her family before they sailed and the urgency of the rebel leaders' need for intelligence, made more acute by the arrival of the British generals the previous week, she had crossed the rebel lines just once since the night of the raid on the *Diana*. Warren had been closeted in yet another of the endless meetings that had taken over his life, and she had entrusted the intelligence she brought to Will before returning home.

She directed an apprehensive glance back down the wharf toward the town. Her father had notified Carleton of the time of their departure, and he had replied that he would see them off. But she wondered if he would be able to get away after all. Security in Boston had been greatly tightened now, and the perimeter of the town bristled with constant patrols. He and Andrews had been on extended duty, and she had seen neither of them since the compromising scene with Andrews a week and a half earlier.

It seemed much longer. A nagging, aching need to see Carleton had taken permanent possession of her soul. She longed to explain what had happened that day and be reassured that nothing had changed between them. At the same time she dreaded a confrontation. But there was no sign of him, and she wasn't sure whether she was more relieved or unhappy.

When she turned back, her father drew her off to one side where they could talk without being overheard. She looked into his well-loved face, and seeing that his eyes were moist, her own tears overflowed.

"I want you to remember how much your mother and I love you."

She nodded, the tightness of her throat making speech impossible.

Glancing over at his sister, he said, "I've suspected for some time that Tess is in sympathy with the rebels, that she probably has been helping them." He returned his gaze to Elizabeth. "Do you support their cause too?"

He spoke matter-of-factly, without anger or judgment, and she answered simply, "Yes, Papa. I've tried to hide my feelings because I didn't want to hurt you."

It required visible effort for him to absorb the impact of her words. But at length he said, "Well, daughter, you have to follow your own conscience. I may not agree with you, but nothing will ever cause your mother and me to stop loving you. We'll never shut you out of our lives, no matter what may happen."

He drew a letter out of his coat pocket and handed it to her. "The

Lord has been convicting me about some wrong attitudes, and I want to ask Joshua's forgiveness. If you have occasion to see him, give this to him. I've judged him harshly, and I've refused to forgive him for some disagreements that seem quite trivial now."

After slipping the letter into her reticule, she threw her arms around his neck. "Oh, Papa. You are the reason I am the person I am. You have influenced my life more than anyone else, and I'll always remember the lessons you and Mama taught me. I'll always love you both with all my heart."

At the sound of hoofbeats, they turned to see Carleton ride up to the end of the dock. Dismounting, he strode down the wharf toward them. As naturally as though she were his own mother, he went to embrace Mrs. Howard. After receiving her affectionate kiss, he lifted Abby into his arms for a tender hug before turning to clasp Dr. Howard's hand.

"Thank you for your friendship, Jon. Watch over Elizabeth for her mother and me."

Carleton was clearly struggling with his own emotions. "You know I will. Please don't worry."

Elizabeth went to her mother, and Mrs. Howard enfolded her in a tender embrace. With her cheek against her daughter's, she whispered, "Promise me you'll be more careful from now on. You take far too many risks."

Elizabeth pulled back to look into her mother's eyes. "What . . . what do you mean?"

"You know what I mean. You're my daughter. I know what concerns you. Please be careful."

Stunned, Elizabeth struggled to speak. "How long have you known?"

"From the first time you climbed out your bedroom window in the middle of the night. Who else could Oriole be?"

When Elizabeth threw an alarmed glance toward her father, Mrs. Howard murmured, "He has no idea, and I'll never tell him. It would break his heart."

"But you wanted me to marry Jonathan. If you knew, then why?"

"Because you love him. A part of me hoped that if you married, you would have to give up these dangerous risks you take. I want you to be safe and happy, and I know he would take care of you."

"How could I be happy living a lie?" Elizabeth demanded, keeping her voice low so none of the others would hear.

Mrs. Howard stared into the distance, at length said, "Your father and I disagree on these issues, but all these years I've tried to keep peace between us. Sometimes I wonder—"

Breaking off, she cupped Elizabeth's face in her hand, brushed back the fine tendrils that curled against her cheek. "I am proud of you! I was like you when I was a young girl—adventurous, fearless. I love your father so, and I love my daughters. But I have missed that part of me. I can't regret that it lives on in you."

Elizabeth threw her arms around her in a fierce hug. "Oh, Mama! How I have misjudged you. Can you ever forgive me?"

Mrs. Howard brushed a soft kiss across Elizabeth's cheek. "There's nothing to forgive."

Feeling an insistent tug at her petticoat, Elizabeth looked down to see Abby reaching up for her. She fell to her knees to cling to the child, their tears mingling.

Behind them they heard the sharp cry of an officer's commands. The sounds of activity on deck increased as the sailors sprang to ready the vessel to set sail. When her parents took her little sister's hand to lead her, sobbing, up the gangplank, Elizabeth felt as though a large portion of her heart was being torn away.

Sensing someone beside her, she looked up to meet Carleton's sympathetic gaze. He put his arm around her shoulders, and she leaned against him, drawing a measure of comfort from his presence.

It was hard for her to look up at the three figures who clung together slightly apart from the crowd that pressed against the railing, but impossible to turn her eyes away. The sailors swarmed up the swaying masts as the anchor rattled upward on its chains. Then the boat swung away from the dock. Turning majestically as her sails unfurled, she caught the wind and slipped off with the outgoing tide.

As long as they could make out the three small figures at the rail, Elizabeth and Tess waved their handkerchiefs. Unable to speak, they watched the diminishing form of the ship as it slid past the islands in the harbor and headed out to sea.

When at last the ship's sails had melted into the hazy horizon and become indistinguishable, Elizabeth turned to bury her face against Carleton's chest. He did not speak, just held her as she let the tears flow. He felt as steady as a rock to her, his arms secure like a sturdy shelter against the bitter storm of grief. At length strengthened, she dried her eyes.

"Are you all right?"

"I will be," she answered, her voice choked. "But I already miss them terribly."

"I know." He glanced over at Tess who had moved off to a discreet distance. "I'm free for the rest of the day. Why don't the two of you come back with me and stay for dinner. It'll feel lonely at home right now."

"That's a wonderful idea." Tess glanced from him to Elizabeth. "I have to stop back at Roxbury first. There are still a few more things I need to bring down to Stony Hill. Why don't you take Elizabeth with you, and I'll join you for dinner."

Elizabeth agreed to the arrangement with dull disinterest. After giving her an encouraging hug, Tess left in the Howards' landau with Pete driving. Tying his stallion to the back of Elizabeth's phaeton, Carleton climbed in beside her and took the reins.

At the town house Elizabeth wandered into the library and stared out the window while Carleton directed Mrs. Dalton to serve tea. When he came into the room, she turned to face him, suddenly feeling very awkward.

"I hope what happened last week . . . I mean, Charles and I . . . we weren't . . . " Feeling her face heating, she let the words trail off.

"Charles explained everything."

Her blush deepened at what she read in his eyes, and she said the first thing she could think of. "Will he be joining us?"

"Hugh needed him for a while, but he'll be back before dinner."

His tone was so kind that she had to turn away to hide the tears that welled into her eyes. Crossing the room, he gathered her into his arms and rested his cheek against the soft curls on top of her head.

"I'm sorry. I'm not going to be very good company tonight, I'm afraid."

"I know how it feels, so go ahead and cry."

The tender understanding in his voice broke down the last of her defenses. For several minutes she gave way to grief.

At length he ventured, "Perhaps it would have been better if you had gone with them."

She dabbed at her tears with her handkerchief. "This is my home. Leaving it would feel like going into exile."

"I've had that experience twice. It isn't a happy sensation."

Disengaging herself from his arms, she forced a smile. "It must be hard to be so far from home. I don't see how you bear it."

He made no response and she could not read his expression. Feeling as though she had said something wrong, she blurted out, "I'll be all right, truly. Thank you for being here. Your friendship means more to me than you know."

They were interrupted by Mrs. Dalton, who wheeled in the tea cart, then quietly withdrew. He brought Elizabeth a cup of steaming tea and drew her down beside him on the loveseat. Wondering what to say, she sipped the tea without interest, wishing she weren't so conscious of his nearness.

"You accused me of being a physician of hearts," she said, keeping her tone light, "but today you hold that office."

He returned her smile, then sobering, for a long moment regarded her as though he searched her soul. Her heart pounding, she looked down, hoping he could not read her thoughts.

He took the cup out of her hand then, set it down, and drew her into his arms with a gentle insistence as natural as though he claimed what belonged to him. She could no more resist than deny the rising and setting of the sun or the flow and ebb of the tide.

She knew he was going to kiss her. Every part of her being ached for him to.

Catching his breath, he cupped her face in his strong hand and turned it up to his. It felt as though her body were melting into his, and then his lips found hers.

For a sweet eternity he held her as though all his life he had waited to kiss her, as though he would never let her go. By swift degrees tenderness and longing gave way to a rising passion that kindled in her also until she was no longer conscious of anything beyond his touch and a fierce hunger she had not known was sleeping in her heart.

At length he drew back, gazed deep into her eyes. "Beth . . . oh, my love—"

A confusing rush of emotions brought her back to herself, and she pressed her fingers against his lips. "Don't! Jonathan, please—"

He caught her hand, kissed palm and wrist with a passion that left her faint. His fingers tightened over hers.

"I've tried to deny my feelings, to hide them from myself and from you. But I can't endure this torture any longer, and I think neither can you."

She tore out of his arms, sprang to her feet, and retreated to the window, her back to him. He followed, and with tender desire that swept away every defense on an irresistible floodtide, enclosed her in his arms, bent to kiss her bare shoulder and the satin skin of her neck. Eyes shut, she leaned back against him with a soft gasp, trembling, her heart hammering in her breast.

"Don't say it. Oh, Jonathan, please don't."

"My love, I am as frightened as you are. I have wearied heaven on this matter, and always I'm given the assurance that it's not chance that has brought us together, but that God has meant us for each other."

She twisted around to face him, searched his eyes in anguish. But inevitably her glance was drawn to the blood red of his uniform coat, and with a ragged sob she turned her head away.

"I can't love you! *I can't!*"

He dropped his arms, let her go. For a long moment he stood motionless as though she had struck him.

"I understand. How could you love someone who has led the life I have?"

"No!" she protested, stricken. "You're no worse a sinner than I am. God has cleansed you. All that matters is that you've been forgiven."

He studied her for a moment, then comprehension came into his eyes. "Hutchins hurt you more deeply than you've ever admitted, didn't he? Beth, I'm not the man he is. I swear I'd never do that to you."

She bent her head. "I know you wouldn't," she whispered.

Hope lit his face. "Then marry me. I love you more than life itself, and as long as I live I will cherish you with my whole heart."

It required all her strength to force herself to answer his tender appeal with a shake of her head. Choking back a sob, she grasped at the first excuse that came into her mind.

"I won't marry a soldier! I've seen how military wives suffer from the separations, the uncertainty, the hardships and loneliness of that kind of life. I want more in a marriage than that."

After a taut moment he turned away, his expression blank, and retreated to the fireplace. "This isn't fair to you," he said in a choked voice as though talking to himself. "You don't deserve to be dragged into . . . " With an abrupt, dismissive gesture, he stopped.

Relief washed over her. Feigning a composure she was very far from feeling, she sat down on the loveseat across from him.

"No one can tell how long this conflict will last," she agreed, struggling to keep him from seeing the tears that kept welling up no matter how she fought them back. "Even if this siege is broken, the rebels will continue to fight, perhaps for years. Now that the generals are here, I suppose they're planning to attack soon, and we shall have full-fledged war."

She said it without any conscious plan. Carleton had remained close-mouthed when it came to military matters, and she expected nothing from him now.

To her surprise, he said, "Yes. The date hasn't been fixed yet, but the plan is to seize Dorchester and Charlestown peninsulas within a couple of weeks."

She stared at him, stunned. The sensitivity of the intelligence he had just handed her took her breath away. And then she became aware that he was watching her with a penetrating intensity.

"You wouldn't, by chance, know anyone," he asked, "by the name of James Freeman?"

The question was more than unexpected. With desperate speed she mentally counted everyone who knew that name. There were few, and of them only Warren and her uncle and cousins knew that James Freeman, Oriole, and Elizabeth Howard were one and the same. Surely they could never be induced to betray her.

How had he learned the name? And why had he asked her if she knew it?

"I don't believe so," she said carefully. "Should I?"

"There's no reason why you should. I just wondered if you might."

His steady gaze had become uncomfortable. Fully alert now, she fought to keep the dismay out of her face.

"Who is he?" she asked.

"That's just it—I don't know. I'd like to find out. I think he may have some information that might be useful."

"Intelligence for General Gage, you mean?" She gave a careless laugh.

"Perhaps." Still, his gaze did not waver.

She tossed her head. "Faith, I hope you find him, then. It's high time these infernal rebels were taught a lesson."

His smile was faint. "We'll do our best. I'm pleased that you're so staunchly on our side."

"These past few weeks have convinced me that the worst that can be said about these so-called patriots is absolutely true."

He made no reply, but she had the disconcerting feeling that the door that had once more been tentatively opened to her was now closed and barred, and that she had turned onto a path from which there was no turning back. But just then Tess came into the room, followed by Andrews, so she shrugged the feeling off. Grateful for escape from the deep waters that had come so near to sweeping her away, she gaily turned her attention to her rescuers.

The rest of the evening passed as though nothing had happened between her and Carleton. He seemed quite at ease and entertained his guests in apparently unaffected good spirits. She could read nothing in his look or manner to betray any change between them.

Yet she sensed that a barricade as impenetrable as a mountain rampart separated them now. And as the hours passed until she and Tess took their leave, the very constancy of his manner toward her tore at her heart more cruelly than if he had treated her with open scorn.

"They're planning a move against both Dorchester and Charlestown within the next two weeks."

Will threw her an astonished look. "How did you manage to find that out?"

"Jonathan let it slip last evening."

His laugh was incredulous. "Jon? You mean he just blurted it out?

Your feminine charms must be having quite an effect."

She took a restless turn around the parlor as a brilliant flash of lightning lit up the room, followed by a sharp clap of thunder. Outside the windows grey sheets of rain sluicing down in gusts obscured the view of the distant bay.

Storm clouds had been brewing and the wind rising when she and Tess had returned to Stony Hill late the previous evening. It was obvious her aunt sensed that something was very much amiss, but, unable to bring herself to confide the unhappy scene with Carleton, Elizabeth had retreated to her room.

There to spend the night racked by torment so intense she could not even begin to sort out her feelings, much less form any conscious plan. Adrift on a sea of anguish that carried her increasingly farther from shore, all she could do was to pray for dawn and the strength to face the new day.

With the first light she had risen to pace the floor until she could bear the need for action no longer. Pulling on her riding habit, she had gone downstairs. When Tess had intercepted her at the terrace door, Elizabeth had told her she had intelligence for Warren and had run out of the house before her aunt had time to ask any questions.

She was fleeing, she knew, running away from thought and feeling.

She had gotten as far as Tess's house when the storm hit. Judging it wiser to trust her uncle and cousins to carry the intelligence to Warren rather than trying to continue to Cambridge, she had turned in at the carriageway, determined to make her report without touching on any dangerous territory, and then leave as soon as the storm abated. She had found Will alone, and after giving him the letter from her father to his, she had relayed the information for Warren.

"I'll warn Joseph as soon as I can track him down," Will told her. "The Committee of Safety has so been so busy they've hardly come up for air."

"I'll be surprised if he hasn't heard the same thing from Patriot."

Will's face clouded. "I had a couple of minutes alone with Joseph yesterday, and he said he hasn't heard from Patriot for two weeks—since the night of your raid on Beacon Hill. Joseph's worried because he had been making contact every day or two."

"Gage has drastically tightened security since the generals' arrival," Elizabeth explained. "It's probably too dangerous for Patriot to try to contact us right now."

"You haven't heard of anyone being arrested or under suspicion?"

Elizabeth shook her head. For a moment she considered telling Will that Carleton had brought up the name James Freeman, but decided against it, fearing the evidence that a traitor was still active in their counsels would influence Warren to curtail her actions.

"Your parents sailed yesterday then?" Will asked, misreading the shadow that had come over her face.

"Yes." After a moment she added, "Jonathan came to see them off, and Tess and I spent the evening with him and Charles."

Her voice broke, making it impossible for her to continue. Will studied her troubled face.

"You're not in love with Jon?"

She forced a sarcastic laugh. "In love with Jonathan Carleton? Indeed not. Quite the contrary."

"Methinks the lady doth protest too much," he teased.

She swung away. Sobering, Will took her by the shoulders and forced her to turn around.

"You *are* in love with him."

"I can't be! I refuse to fall in love with a British officer."

He groaned. "I was afraid of this, but I told myself it wouldn't happen, at least not so fast. You know, Cuz, it's rare that I see you in anything other than breeches. I forget you're a woman, with a woman's heart."

Taking her in his arms, he held her tightly. This time she couldn't stop the tears.

"Oh, Will, I don't know what to do. I've tried and tried to tear him out of my heart, but all I succeed in doing is loving him more."

"Has he shown any feelings for you?"

"Yesterday . . . he asked me to . . . to marry him. It was all I could do to say no."

Will let go of her and leaned back against the wall. "Oh, Beth, I'm so sorry. I had no idea it would go this far."

She hesitated before adding, "He asked me if I know James Freeman."

Will stared at her in suspended horror, then swore. "You don't think he suspects?"

They both started at the sound of someone pounding on the front door. When the barrage did not stop, Will went to see who was there. Elizabeth began to follow but stopped on the room's threshold.

As Will threw open the door a man shoved past him and strode inside. Rain dripped from his black cloak and cascaded onto the rug from the drooping brim of the hat he pulled off with a violent gesture.

Elizabeth caught her breath at sight of his pale face drawn in rage. At the sound, Hutchins glanced up. His mouth hardened as his burning gaze raked over her.

"How fortuitous. But may I ask what you're doing behind rebel lines?"

Elizabeth drew herself up. "Aunt Tess has moved to Stony Hill, and I came to pick up a few things she forgot to bring with her—if it's any of your business."

Not removing his gaze from her, he shook the water from his hat. "They must be urgently needed to bring you out in a thunderstorm. But all the better you're here. You might be interested to learn the true character of the man I've heard your name linked with so frequently." His voice dripped sarcasm.

"I don't know whom you mean."

His smile became venomous. "Why, Major Jonathan Carleton, of course. But perhaps your faithless heart has been toying with more than one."

Will clenched his hands. "If you have something to say, Hutchins, spit it out."

Decisively taller and stronger than Hutchins, Will easily could have knocked him to the ground with a single blow. But Hutchins bridled as though daring Will to strike him. Pulling a piece of paper from his pocket, he thrust it under Will's nose.

"What's this?"

"A warrant for my arrest. You might be interested in who signed it."

Seeing the muscles in Will's face tighten as he scanned the page, Elizabeth hurried to his side. Meeting her anxious gaze, he handed the paper to her without speaking. As she read it, the color drained from her face.

> By order of His Excellency General Gage, a reward of £100 will be paid to the person who delivers Mr. David Hutchins of Cambridge to His Excellency's agent for arrest on charges of high treason and piracy.

For a long moment she stared at the damning signature scrawled at the bottom of the warrant. She didn't need to compare it to the one on the tender note she carried in the bodice of her gown against her heart. She had memorized every graceful curve and line, and she stared at its duplicate, feeling heartsick at the incontrovertible evidence of Carleton's ruthlessness.

Yet what had she expected? Had he not told her where he stood by word and deed many times over? In spite of it, she had foolishly continued to harbor the secret hope that now lay shattered at her feet.

Looking up, she met Hutchins' dark, triumphant gaze. "At least they place a high value on my head," he sneered.

"He must have been under Gage's orders to do this."

His eyes narrowed, and then he laughed with bitter mockery. "How do you think Gage found out I was the one who captured four of his ships?" He paused for a deliberate moment. "Your precious friend is spying for him, that's how. The warrant was issued last week, the same day Carleton just happened to see me at Province House. If he weren't a spy, how could he have known what my involvements are?"

At their startled looks, he explained smoothly, "Warren asked me to offer my services to Gage so I could feed him false intelligence. I was to meet with the general again early this morning, and if chance hadn't placed this in my hands first, I'd be swinging at the end of a rope by now."

The paper fluttered from Elizabeth's fingers onto the floor. Giving her a hard look, Hutchins caught her by the wrist and wrenched her toward him. She flinched at the pain, a soft outcry escaping her lips.

"You are in love with him, aren't you?"

Outraged, Will shoved him away from her. "You've had your say, now get out of here before I have mine!"

Hutchins shook free of Will's hand, livid with anger. His malevolent gaze turned from Will to Elizabeth.

"I shall have my revenge on all of you," he snarled. "Be very certain of it."

Turning on his heel, he went out the door, slamming it shut behind him.

Chapter Twenty-three

AFTER A LONG, BLEAK SILENCE, Will put into words the stark conclusion neither wanted to confront. "The dirty spy! I take back every
kind thought I ever had about Jon!"

"He hasn't done anything I haven't."

"He's betrayed his own countrymen—"

"He's British."

"So are we!" He stopped, then continued more calmly, "Hutchins is
a small fish. Jon's real goal must be to learn Oriole's identity, and even if
he doesn't suspect you by now, sooner or later he's bound to find you
out. If he's capable of doing this to Hutchins, then he's capable of putting a noose around your neck. You can't risk going back into Boston
now."

"There's too much at stake for me not to, Will! We have no way of
knowing when or if Patriot will be able to contact Warren again. If we
don't find out when the British plan to attack, many of our men will die
unnecessarily. And if the siege is broken, our cause may well be lost."

None of his arguments swayed her. Finally he said, "Warren will
have to know about this."

"If you tell him about Jonathan and me, he'll forbid me to go back,"
she protested. "Nothing can be allowed to jeopardize our getting the
intelligence we need. And besides, it's my personal affair. I forbid you to
tell anyone of it!"

He regarded her unhappily. "I'll respect your wishes then, though it's against my better judgment. But Warren must know about the warrant for Hutchins' arrest."

Relieved, she agreed. The storm had rumbled off to the west, leaving the air fresh and cool, and as soon as the old caretaker brought Night Mare up from the stable, she left.

The pain she had felt before was nothing to the torment that oppressed her now. Retreating to Stony Hill in hope of nursing her wounds in solitude, she met Tess at the door. Her aunt read the devastation in her expression.

There was no possibility of suppressing the tears any longer. She managed an explanation through bitter sobs, and the story of Carleton's declaration of love the previous day spilled out as well. When all was told, she broke down in earnest.

For some time Tess's tears mingled with hers. "This is all my fault," she said at last. "If I'd not encouraged your relationship with him in hopes of what we might learn—"

Elizabeth dabbed at her tears. "You're no more at fault than I."

Tess caught her into her arms. "You must stay as far away from him as possible. We don't know how much he already knows, and it may take little more for him to guess that you are Oriole. Will is right. You must not go into Boston again. If you were to be arrested because I drew you into this, I could not bear it."

Although Elizabeth returned her embrace without reservation, she remained unmovable. There was nothing Tess could say to dissuade her from her determination to learn when the British attack was planned.

In the days that followed, she passed by turns from a paralyzing anguish to a determined denial of any feelings for Carleton to angrily blaming God for bringing him into her life. No matter how fervently she pleaded to be relieved of the love she felt for him, he still possessed her heart and mind. Knowing what he was, she yet longed for the sweetness of his embrace with an unceasing intensity of despair she had

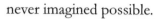

never imagined possible.

It was the first full week of June, and as though oblivious of the military crisis that hung over the town like a brewing storm, Boston and its environs reveled in the full glory of spring. Morning and evening a froth of white sailed across the sunny blue heavens like the spotless sheets of ships fully decked. Silken breezes caressed Elizabeth with their perfumed breath each time she went outside, and everywhere she looked a riot of flowers nodded joyously from each garden and window box and orchard, while the lush trees ruffled full emerald petticoats as she passed.

Yet the world might as well have been cloaked in the frosty silence of winter for all she cared. As though sleepwalking she went through the motions of meeting with her band and planning Oriole's next foray, watched and listened for any intelligence about the planned British move. But the officers involved in the strategy sessions with Gage were out of reach, and though she forced herself to flirt with the younger officers, all they had to offer were indefinite rumors of a possible action. Even Andrews had hardly seen Carleton for days and had no fresh information to impart, while her few casual meetings with Carleton on the street were painful and awkward, providing no opportunity she could exploit.

She delayed crossing over the rebel lines, even when Will sent Levi to Stony Hill with an urgent message that Warren needed to see her. She had no heart for a meeting with the rebel leader, and so she put off answering his summons.

Through it all, she felt as though a gaping hole had been torn through her breast and that in the place where her heart had once beaten was a great, aching void. In desperation she sought the peace and reassurance of God's presence, but all she found was her own misery and inability to understand.

✱ ✱ ✱

DURING THAT WEEK, his duties as Gage's aide-de-camp occupied Carleton from early morning until late in the evening. The few times he passed Elizabeth on the street, she was with Tess, and they exchanged only the most casual pleasantries. He was grateful for that.

Getting her out of his mind was another matter altogether. He had the unhappy suspicion that it would be a very long time—if ever—before he would be successful in that endeavor. Despite every effort to block it out, at unexpected moments the vivid image of her would rise before his eyes, and his coldest resolution was powerless to banish it.

He was possessed by an aching sense of loss that gave him no rest. All the sweetly seductive dreams the temptress hope had been so busily spinning in his heart had been torn asunder and revealed for what they were—fantasies impossible of fulfillment.

From the beginning he had been determined never to join the long list of Elizabeth's rejected suitors. He had assured himself that he would not allow himself to fall in love with her. Failing that, he had sworn that she would never guess how he adored her, that he would never be fool enough to ask her to marry him.

So much for pride.

What had happened had been as much of a surprise to him as it obviously had been to her. She had seemed so vulnerable in that moment of heartache that the desire to comfort and protect her and the love he had struggled so long to deny had welled up spontaneously like the waters of a free-flowing spring spilling through parched sand.

Thinking of it, he gave a short laugh at his folly. Once more he had run ahead of God's leading, and as a result he had come dangerously close to drawing the one who had become most precious to him into the maelstrom that threatened to suck him into its vortex. It was better that she was beyond his reach and would always remain so. He had to make peace with that.

Yet reliving the moment when she had come into his arms, he couldn't deny that she had done so willingly and without hesitation. Each time he tasted again the exquisite sensation of her lips against his and felt the passion of her response, he was overcome by the certainty that she loved and desired him as much as he loved and desired her.

What had she said? "I *can't* love you," not "I *don't* love you." That was what brought the endless, agonizing doubts to his mind.

How dearly he wanted to confide to her everything that was in his heart. But each time he found reason to hope that he might yet be mistaken, she said or did something to put him back on guard.

Impulse had caused him to bring up the name of James Freeman. In spite of her firm denial, it was clear the name meant something to her. The last thing he wanted was to know Oriole's identity, but he was curious about what she knew about the rebel courier and if she had any involvement with him.

Early on he had toyed with the idea that Oriole might be one of Elizabeth's cousins—either Will or Levi—but the details didn't add up. And the more he thought about it, the more the description of Oriole seemed to fit Hutchins: He was slender in build, wore black, and rode a black horse.

Since Oriole had made his appearance not long after Elizabeth's engagement to Hutchins was broken, if he was the rebel courier, then it was plausible she might know or at least suspect his role, hence her reaction to Carleton's question. And in that case, he could rule out any possibility of her involvement with a man who had violated her trust so completely. When Hutchins had appeared at Province House, however, Carleton had all but discarded that possibility, though from what he knew of the man, Hutchins might well be devious enough to carry on that level of deception toward both sides.

The question remained: Was Elizabeth more than a spectator on the sidelines? Could she be a go-between to Oriole?

Every instinct told him she was involved with the patriots on some level. The pass Warren personally had provided her was in itself far too suspicious to discount. When added to all the other seemingly minor details he had gleaned over the past weeks, the total was something other than a committed Loyalist.

At the same time he couldn't forget that she and her parents were on the most intimate, even affectionate, terms with the Gages and with many of the officers, especially Percy and Pitcairn. And every attempt he had made to trap, surprise, or frighten her into an admission had gained nothing except steady denial. She remained unvaryingly adamant in her loyalty to the government whose hated uniform he wore, whose stubborn course of destruction he despised, and whose designs to sub-jugate his countrymen he was determined with his whole heart to thwart.

In the end he concluded that unless he could find a way to make cer-tain of her beyond the shadow of a doubt, he dared not risk trusting her. His position, dangerous from the beginning, had since the arrival of the three generals become perilous. One unguarded word to the wrong person would mean the hangman's noose, a fate he preferred to avoid.

He revealed nothing of his mental turmoil, not even to Andrews. He knew he was being watched now, but he went about his duties as though unaware of the stealthy figures who shadowed him each night when he left Province House, taking posts on the Common across from his billet and in the shadows at the back of the property until he returned to duty in the morning.

In reality, he was always on guard. While his shadowers watched him, he in turn watched them without seeming to, taking careful note of their number and movements. He hoped that as the days passed the unvary-ing regularity of his routine would lull them into carelessness. But at the end of that week they remained as alert as they had at the beginning.

Observing them from behind the curtain of his darkened room, he thought how ironic it was that he had resisted the assignment as Gage's aide, fearing it would give him too much visibility and restrict his freedom of movement. At the same time he had been so certain of his precautions to avoid discovery. In fact, the position provided without any effort on his part had opened broad avenues to him, while his carefully thought-out precautions now walled him into a corner.

For the moment, Gage had no hard evidence against him. Only three men knew absolutely the whole truth, and two of them could not be gotten at.

The danger lay in Dr. Church, the traitor who lay like a serpent in Warren's bosom.

ON FRIDAY, JUNE 9, the generals set Sunday, June 18 as the date for the strike on Dorchester. A plan had begun to form in Carleton's mind, and that night and the following one he spent laying out a plan of attack with nerveless calculation, mapping out the vulnerable line of rebel entrenchments that extended out toward Dorchester Neck.

All day Sunday Gage was closeted with Burgoyne writing a rambling, pompous proclamation that castigated the rebels and declared martial law. As the officers met on Monday, however, discussion turned once more to the Dorchester attack.

Finding his opportunity, Carleton detailed how the entire rebel line at Roxbury might be easily flanked and attacked from the rear by disembarking on the mainland below Dorchester Point under cover of night. As he defended his plan with carefully reasoned logic, it was clear that Gage was intrigued by the merits of the proposal. Clinton and Howe opposed it, however, while Burgoyne remained silent, watching Carleton through narrowed eyes.

Dismissing Carleton with a languid wave of his hand, Howe yawned. "A very commendable little plan, major, but rather too much trouble. A direct attack on these dogs' front will not only save time and manpower, but will roll them straight back through Roxbury with their heels about their ears."

The consensus supported his assessment. Conceding Howe's point, Carleton dropped the matter, the tight knot in his stomach easing. It had been a dangerous gamble, but as he had calculated, Howe had remained true to form.

It was soon apparent that the throw of the dice had bought him breathing room as well. When the meeting broke up Gage intercepted him and drew him aside.

"Your plan was quite well thought out, though Howe and Clinton are right. Landing where you suggest would take too much time and put us at greater risk of discovery. However, I thank you for the input." After a brief hesitation, he added, "You've handled yourself well, Jon. Your bearing this past week has discredited Burgoyne's charges."

Carleton bowed. "My only intent was to be of service, sir."

To his satisfaction, he read in Gage's eyes that the general believed him.

It was late that afternoon before he arrived back at the town house. He found Andrews already at home and entertaining Tess and Elizabeth.

"Welcome, stranger," Andrews greeted him with a laugh. "We were just ready to sit down to dinner without you. Our lovely guests have brought a load of provisions for our table, and I thought it ungentlemanly to send them away without sampling the plunder."

"We were afraid your stores must be in sad case by now," Tess said.

Forcing a smile, Carleton took a deep breath of the savory odors coming from the direction of the kitchen. "It isn't chance that brought me home. I've been following the aroma all the way from Province House."

They all laughed. Sobering, Carleton excused himself for a moment to take the papers he carried into the library. Returning, he bowed to Elizabeth and offered his arm.

She tried to act as though nothing was out of the ordinary, but as she gave him her hand, the color in her cheeks deepened, then drained away. When she glanced up, she found him looking down at her with so much of his heart in his eyes that she had to drop hers, in that moment loving him and fearing him with equal intensity.

After they were seated and the first course had been served, Tess said, "You look tired, Jonathan. You've been working too hard."

"Not voluntarily, I assure you." Draining his wine glass, he refilled it.

"They're plotting some sort of secret action," Andrews offered. "Until today Jon hasn't been home until nine or ten every evening, and then he's locked in the library another hour or two, writing up notes."

Elizabeth found it difficult to direct her attention away from Carleton. She had never seen him drink more than one glass of wine, even during a long evening, and now he had finished his second and was once more refilling his glass.

"It won't be a secret after this Sunday." Carleton tossed down another draught.

"Sunday! Let me guess. Dorchester would seem a logical target."

Carleton raised his glass in Tess's direction before tossing off the contents. "Your talents are being wasted, Tess. You'd make a fine general."

Lightheaded with excitement that he had so easily revealed the exact information they had come hoping to discover, Elizabeth was at the same time dismayed at the realization that he was already slightly drunk and was determined to become considerably more so. The hard recklessness in him frightened her.

During the rest of the meal, his strange mood became obvious to the others as well. Inconsequential small talk became more awkward as the evening progressed. By the time they rose to go into the drawing room, Andrews was no longer able to conceal his concern, and Elizabeth was stricken by the certainty that she must be the cause of Carleton's uncharacteristic behavior.

At the drawing room door, Tess pulled her aside. "You've tempted fate long enough," she warned in an undertone. "We have what you insisted we must learn, and he's drunk enough now that we can leave without arousing suspicion. Before anything goes wrong, let us go."

Elizabeth shook her head. "Give me a few more minutes. He was carrying papers when he came home, perhaps a report on plans for the attack. He took them into the library and I want to see them. I won't have another opportunity."

"This is foolhardy!" Tess hissed. "What if he discovers you?"

"He won't. As you said, he's too drunk to suspect anything."

Pulling out of her grasp, Elizabeth followed the two men into the other room. "Oh, I almost forgot," she said breezily. "There's a matter I need to discuss with Mrs. Dalton. Please excuse me for a moment."

Not giving them time to respond, she went out into the passage and turned toward the kitchen. Slowing her steps as she passed the library door, she saw that Carleton had left it ajar. The murmur of voices from the drawing room remained reassuringly steady, and she slipped inside, her heart hammering.

A candle burned on the sconce just inside the room. Carrying it with her, she glided to the writing desk and eased down the lid. Inside were the papers she sought, turned upside down.

With careful haste, she flipped them over and scanned each, feeling as though a cold hand squeezed the breath from her lungs. In hardly more than a minute she had replaced everything as she had found it and retreated from the room.

She was shaken by what she had learned, in a fever to reach Warren. Thankfully, Carleton was nursing a glass of whisky and appeared to take little notice of her brief absence. Her nerves strained to the breaking point, she forced herself to endure the visit for another quarter of an hour before she and Tess at last took their leave.

❀ ❀ ❀

AFTER SEEING THEM OUT, Carleton returned to the drawing room. With relief he took off his uniform coat, unbuttoned his waistcoat, and loosened his stock. When Andrews came in, he was refilling his glass.

"Don't you think you've had enough?"

"Reversing roles, aren't we?" Carleton responded with a laugh, his tongue slurring the words.

"You're exhausted. You've been under too much strain. I'm going to bed—why don't you?"

"I'll be up in a little while. Now run along, my good fellow." Carleton gave an airy wave of his hand.

Directing a puzzled, hurt look at him, Andrews shrugged and left the room.

For some time Carleton sat motionless, staring moodily out the window into the night, his drink forgotten. When he heard no further sounds from upstairs, he rose and went into the library, taking care to make no sound.

He was quite drunk, but still sober enough to add up the details the evening had provided. That the papers he had deliberately left in the desk had been moved he saw at once, for he had laid one of his own blond hairs across the top sheet. In the glimmer of candlelight, he found it on the floor beside the chair.

One person alone had left their company the entire evening. And although Elizabeth had not been gone for five minutes, he calculated that that had been just long enough.

IN SPITE OF THE LATENESS OF THE HOUR, as soon as they reached Stony Hill Elizabeth donned her disguise and hurried to Cambridge, hoping to find Warren still there. Learning that he was meeting with Ward, she returned outside to wait. Almost an hour passed before he emerged from the house.

His stride was slow, and the weary droop of his shoulders reflected her own mental and emotional exhaustion. When she rose from the ground beside the hitching rail, he started, then gave a soft laugh of recognition and reached for her hand.

"You've been absent too long, dear friend. I hoped you'd come sooner. But you've spoken to Will?"

When she shook her head, he said in a hard voice, "What Hutchins told you about me sending him to carry false intelligence to Gage was a lie. Why would I ask him to do what Patriot is doing so much more effectively than he ever could? The only conclusion I can come to is that Hutchins is the one who's been betraying us all along."

Elizabeth gripped the hitching rail to steady herself. "But Gage issued a warrant for his arrest. I saw it myself. Major Carleton signed it, and—"

Warren's eyes narrowed. "I've suspected before that Hutchins is for sale to the highest bidder. It appears he was supplying Gage with intelligence with one hand while picking his pocket with the other, then selling us the goods at highly inflated prices. Obviously Gage found out about it. I've issued my own warrant, and in the meantime, I've ordered that Hutchins' schooners and other property be confiscated until he can be arrested and tried. Unfortunately, he has found it prudent to disappear."

The depth of Hutchins' treachery took Elizabeth's breath away. She stared at Warren, a dull fury seeping through her veins.

"What brings you here so late? Has Gage determined on the attack against Dorchester?"

"It's set for Sunday." Shaking off her anger, she summarized the details she had gleaned from Carleton's notes.

Warren nodded, his face taut. "I'll have to consult with Ward and the rest of the committee, but my feeling is that we must strike first. Bunker's Hill would give us an excellent lever with which to test Gage's mettle." He gave her a probing look. "How did you find this out? Your friend Carleton again?"

She couldn't stop a hot blush. Giving a brief description of their visit, she explained, "He was drunk and let some of it slip. I discovered the rest in his papers while Tess kept him and the captain occupied."

"There has been no sign that anyone on Gage's staff might be suspected of having turned over intelligence to us?"

"Not that I've heard, but Will told me you've had no contact from Patriot in some time, so he may be in a tight spot. Since the generals' arrival, every inch of Boston's perimeter is constantly patrolled. The only way in or out is with a pass, and there are few being given out these days. Perhaps it would be wise for me to try to make contact with Patriot, offer to bring him out."

For some moments Warren said nothing. She sensed that he was deeply troubled, but at length he shook his head.

"No. If you've heard nothing, then we must assume he's still safe. We'll talk in a few days. There's something important I need to tell you, but it will have to wait for now."

To her surprise, he again took her hands between his own. "One of the wisest decisions I ever made was asking you to work with us. You've found a place very close to my heart, my friend."

"I know your heart belongs to our cause, as does mine," she answered, trembling without knowing why.

"Sometimes I worry that you've sacrificed too much. You deserve the joy of a husband and children."

"There'll be time enough to think about that when our work is done."

Gently he said, "Your assignment is ended now. You know it, don't you?"

Her throat had become so tight she could only manage a nod.

With a quiet firmness that made his words a command, he said, "There's nothing more any of us can do now. Until the British have been driven out, you must not go back into Boston."

Chapter Twenty-four

THE FOLLOWING DAY several ships anchored in the harbor, bringing a sizable contingent of Parliament's promised reinforcements. The distraction proved a welcome one for Carleton. Gage assigned him to oversee arrangements for their landing and encampment, which made it easy for him to leave Province House for indeterminate periods of time.

He made immediate use of the opportunity. Uneasy over suspicions he could not yet completely define, he decided to learn everything about Oriole and his movements that could be discovered.

It took him a full day to determine that the soldier who had been injured the night of Oriole's near capture and his own arrival in Boston had returned to England and that the officer in charge had died on the road back from Concord. Still another day elapsed before he was able to discreetly track down the only member left of the patrol.

"He's nerveless as the devil—took his horse over that stone fence like a banshee," the corporal told him.

"You got a good look at him?"

"Scott and the captain got considerably closer than I did. All I could make out was that he was ridin' a black horse."

Carleton considered this information thoughtfully. "You're certain it was black."

"Black as the devil himself."

"Where did you intercept him?"

"On Watertown Road. We figured he was headin' for Concord."

"That road passes through Waltham, doesn't it, then north to Lincoln?"

The corporal shrugged. "I reckon."

Carleton got to his feet. "Thank you. You've been most helpful."

He left the tent that served as company headquarters and paused for a moment at the edge of the marquee, looking out across the neat rows of white tents that filled the Common. It was Thursday, June 15. Time was swiftly running out, he reminded himself, and he hadn't learned much more than he'd already known.

Suddenly it occurred to him that the guards stationed at the town gates might have noted something out of the ordinary the night Oriole had been intercepted. Wondering what their logs might show, he decided to find out.

IN THE REBEL CAMP supplies of guns and ammunition had run alarmingly low. Even the stores hoarded in Tess's barn had diminished to the point that Ward refused to release any more except in case of assault by the British.

On Thursday morning Tess brought Elizabeth the news that the Committee of Safety had elected Warren major general and was meeting that day to decide how to respond to Gage's planned attack. With Stony Hill in direct line of bombardment from both sides, Tess had already begun removing all the horses and other livestock as well as their personal effects to Roxbury, working after nightfall to avoid attracting attention from the British fortifications below.

Elizabeth watched the unfolding events with a curious sense of detachment, as though none of it involved her any longer. Instead of helping Tess, Sarah, Pete, and Jemma to pack and transfer their possessions to Roxbury, she spent long hours sitting on the terrace with her hands folded in her lap, staring out across the gardens, or curled up in a chair in the library pretending to read a book whose pages kept blurring before her eyes.

She had a vague consciousness of the frequent, troubled looks Tess gave her. When Sarah brought her food and coaxed her to eat, she forced herself to swallow what she could, but everything was equally tasteless.

Mental and physical exhaustion went so deep that she felt disembodied, though she could not sleep. At night she lay awake for hours counting the chimes of the tall case clock on the landing, too tired to get up, too distraught to drift off into healing slumber.

Her accusing conscience would not let her rest. In her pride and stubbornness she had believed her parents did not understand the deepest part of her. She had been so wrong about them, just as she had been wrong in loving Hutchins. And now Carleton.

Was she wrong about everything she believed? Where was solid ground? She didn't know anymore.

Somehow she had mistaken the purpose of her life, she concluded. And fighting back unaccustomed waves of panic, she wondered if she would ever find it.

IT WAS NOT UNTIL FRIDAY AFTERNOON that Carleton could shake free again. After making sure he was not followed, he went to the guardhouse at the town gates.

Leafing through the logbook, he saw that the entries were cursory at best, with few details and almost no names. On the fourteenth of April no one but the patrol had passed through the gates after dark, and none of those who had gone through earlier came close to fitting the description of Oriole. That meant he had to have come from outside the town, Carleton concluded, frowning.

Turning the page over, he read the entry for the eighteenth. Mitchell's patrol was noted as leaving around noon. Few entries followed, but when he came to one scrawled at nine-twenty that night, he stiffened.

A local tanner, William Dawes, was noted by name as leaving Boston. With him had been a companion, a youth who was not named.

Returning to the previous page, he found the signature of the sergeant in charge that night. Several inquiries led Carleton to the fortification outside the gates. He found the sergeant in the blockhouse that overlooked the road, and after Carleton had refreshed his memory about the night in question, the soldier acknowledged passing Dawes through.

"It seems a curious time to be setting out," Carleton noted. "He had a companion. Did you get a look at him?"

After some thought the sergeant admitted, "There was someone—a boy, I think. Didn't pay much attention to him. He didn't say nothin', just stayed back in the shadows."

"Would you say he was tall—say about my height?"

"No, sir. He was slight and about this tall, I'd guess."

As he held out his hand to illustrate, Carleton's gaze became fixed. "Did you notice his horse, by any chance?"

"Ah, now that you mention it, I did, sir. I'm a lover of good horse-flesh, and she was a beauty—a mare black as midnight without a mark on her, and she looked fast as the wind."

Carleton clenched his hand over the hilt of his sabre. "The youth—what color was his hair?"

The sergeant shrugged. "Like I said, I didn't pay much attention to him. Anyways, he wore a hat."

Carleton was already on his way to the door. "Thank you, sergeant."

He had to be at Province House within the hour, so he rode straight there, sorting through the possibilities in desperate haste, stunned at his incredible stupidity, exultant and terrified all at the same time. How often he had come so close to guessing the truth, only to allow himself—like everyone else—to be blinded by the fact that she was a woman! But every preconception he had harbored had now been shat-

tered, and he was certain of his conclusion.

Silently he prayed that Warren had understood his real intention in signing the warrant and had arrested Hutchins. If not, if Hutchins was still free and in the confidence of the patriots, then Elizabeth was in extreme danger. And unless she came into Boston—and he hadn't seen her since Monday evening—he had no way to reach her.

Entering Province House, he met Smith on his way out. The general had a look of satisfaction about him that tightened the knot in Carleton's gut.

"His Excellency begs your immediate attendance," Smith said in an oily voice before bowing himself off.

Every step Carleton took toward the door of Gage's office felt like a step on the road to the gallows. Something was very wrong. Whatever it was, he might as well face it head on, for all routes of escape had been obliterated.

He found the general writing at his desk. Wasting no time on pleasantries, Gage told him, "We've had some very interesting developments this afternoon. Our friend Hutchins made contact with Smith yesterday. He offered to turn Oriole over to us."

Carleton stared at him, astounded. "He knows Oriole's identity?"

"He insists he doesn't, but I suspect he does and that he figures he's safe from us so long as we need information he has to offer. He told Smith that Oriole is planning a raid for tonight. He and his band are supposed to rendezvous on Brindley's Meadow beneath a tall elm tree that appears to be some sort of landmark in the area. They'll go by boat to the base of the Common, with their objective the munitions in the gunhouse."

"Knowing Hutchins' treachery, you still believe him?"

"Smith seems to think he's telling the truth, and I can't take the risk of losing so valuable a prize."

Carleton made an impatient gesture. "Why is Hutchins selling Oriole out now after we've issued a warrant for his arrest? What does he stand to gain?"

"He denies that he's responsible for the capture of our ships. He wants to prove his loyalty to the crown."

"Do you believe him?"

Gage met Carleton's incredulous look with a hard one. "No."

Carleton took a slow breath, let it out. "If he does hand Oriole over to us, what will you do with Hutchins?"

Gage frowned as though he didn't understand the question. "Why, hang him, of course. Hang both of them."

Carleton had expected it, but he felt nauseated nevertheless. "I know the place where they plan to meet."

"You know the outlying areas better than anyone," Gage agreed. "That's why I want you in charge of this action. I'm going to put a company of Percy's light infantry at your disposal."

"That's too many to conceal on the marsh, especially from someone as canny as Oriole. His band doesn't matter—it's their leader we want. Give me half a dozen men, and if Hutchins' story is true, I guarantee we'll take that fox tonight."

The general's gaze became penetrating. "It's your call. Just don't disappoint me, Jon. There's a great deal riding on the outcome."

More than you know, Carleton thought grimly as he went out. But what concerned him most was the part *he* didn't know.

Chapter Twenty-five

NOTHING ABOUT THE ASSIGNMENT felt right. Hutchins' involvement alone jarred every instinct he possessed, and that Smith had a hand in it as well—with Burgoyne doubtless directing the play from behind the curtains—set him doubly on guard.

What were the odds, he reflected, that the story about Oriole was pure fiction, the tempting morsel baiting a cunningly devised trap impossible for him to sidestep?

He had tried to come up with a plan, but quickly had given up the attempt. There was no way to anticipate how the encounter would develop once all the players were on the field. He would have to trust his instincts when the time came to act.

His first move had been to secretly send Stowe to confirm that Hutchins was with Smith at the general's headquarters and that they were as yet making no move to leave the town. Then, notifying no one, he had ordered his detachment out well before the appointed hour, hoping to reach the rendezvous ahead of any interested parties. The last light had just been fading from the sky when he led his men through the town gates and onto the marsh.

Turning in the saddle to throw a calculating glance back in the direction of the Neck, he estimated that they had gone a safe distance from the outer British line. A blacker bulk against the backdrop of indigo bay and sky, the walls of the fortification were illuminated only by faint starlight and the fitful blink of an occasional lantern or torch.

Frowning, he evaluated the distance that still remained before the marsh gave way to the distant, hazy shadows of Brindley's Meadow and, rising above it, the looming, irregular headland that marked Roxbury and the rebel line. Every sense heightened, he strained eyes and ears for any sign of danger.

There was none that he could detect. The only sounds that reached him were the rhythmic lapping of the incoming tide's sibilant advance through the long salt grass and across the diminishing mud flats, the hoarse croak of frogs and occasional reflective hoot of an owl, the muted clink of metal and creak of leather from his horse and the men, the squelch of feet and hooves in the spongy earth of the bog.

They were out there somewhere, hidden by the night. He could feel it, and his uneasiness deepened. But even as the pale mist rising from the surface of marsh and bay blurred his surroundings and veiled his enemies, so it also provided equal concealment for him.

On the surface it seemed that Providence had unexpectedly opened up the opportunity for escape. For just such a contingency he had memorized the contours of the marsh, each hillock and mud bank and tidal pool. He was confident that in the darkness and fog, if he moved with extreme caution and carefully scouted the ground, his odds of slipping past a patrol were better than even.

In contrast, the odds that there would be another such opportunity were all but nonexistent. If the story about Oriole was true, however, to take the chance would be to abandon his beloved comrade to the fate that undoubtedly would be his own if he played the game out to the end.

So he pointed out to the soldiers Oriole's supposed rendezvous and where they were to lie in wait. Ordering them to intercept anyone who attempted to cross the marsh, he dispersed them to their cover, noting with satisfaction that even in the misty darkness the brilliant hue of their uniform coats was just visible enough to warn off an alert intruder.

He had wrapped himself in a voluminous, high-collared black cloak that concealed the buckskin tunic, leggings, and moccasins he had substituted for his uniform. By lucky chance they had encountered few people on the way out of Boston, and no one had appeared to note anything out of the ordinary.

Unknown to the soldiers, his own hiding place was at some distance, and once assured that they were in their places, he moved off nearer the water. As soon as he was out of their sight, he dismounted.

Pulling off his cloak, he reversed it so that the dull grey silk lining was on the outside, making him all but indistinguishable in the steadily thickening fog. His helmet he stowed in the tall grass beside a hillock, then covered his blond hair with the deep grey slouch hat he had concealed beneath his cloak, tipping it to shade his features.

All sound was damped by the mist. Leading his horse, he glided along the outer rim of the marsh, his moccasins making no sound on the spongy earth as he followed the gradual slope to higher ground. At last, at a short distance above him, the solitary elm that had been his rendezvous with Oriole two months earlier stretched ebony branches, full-leaved, into the starry, as yet moonless sky.

For some minutes he crouched in the shadow of a low sand bank, watching and listening. When he was confident there was no one in the vicinity, he dropped the bay's reins so they trailed on the ground, ran his hands along the animal's neck and withers, whispering soothingly to him. Then, staying low, with the marsh to his back to avoid offering a silhouette against the starlit waters of the Back Bay, he inched forward until he melted into the inky shadow beneath the tree.

From where he crouched he could make out the blunt shape of Stony Hill, a hazy shadow rising above the low-lying mist a third of a mile off. From that angle no buildings or points of light were visible on its summit.

The hill's slope was too steep and too exposed to climb without running the risk of detection. By now it was almost ten o'clock. If he took the time required to scout out a concealed ascent he might miss her.

Of course, she might not be there, might come from another direction altogether—if she came at all. Deciding to stay put, he prayed that she would not come from the direction of Boston and stumble onto his detachment.

His only certainty was that somewhere, hidden in the night, the steel jaws of a trap waited for the false step that would spring it, whether his, hers, or their betrayer's.

FRIDAY DRAGGED BY with such painful slowness that Elizabeth had almost given up hope it would ever end. That day was to be their last at Stony Hill, and shortly after nightfall Tess, with Sarah and her children, left to shepherd the last wagonload to Roxbury.

Instead of going with them, Elizabeth pleaded the need for exercise and fresh air and promised to walk up to Roxbury within the hour. She had kept her disguise to change into, but for some time after the wagon had gone she continued to sit motionless, staring into space.

She missed her parents desperately. She longed to lay her head on her father's shoulder, to pour out every ache of her heart and receive his wise counsel, to cling to her mother and let her soothe away the pain that knotted in her breast.

Becoming aware of the clock's chiming, she started as she counted ten strokes. Two hours had passed.

It was full dark outside. The candles in the room were guttering, and spectral shadows had gathered in the corners. A warm, humid breeze billowed the gauzy summer curtains, and she shivered in its breath, feeling very much alone.

As she rose, she heard the outer door open, then close. A step sounded in the hallway.

"Tess, is that you?" she called, sudden fear causing a tremor in her voice.

After a tense moment, the shadowed figure of a man appeared in the parlor doorway. As she shrank back, groping for the fireplace poker, he put out his hand.

"Don't be afraid—I won't harm you."

"What are you doing here?" she demanded, shaken.

"I saw the light and knocked, but no one answered. The door was unlocked, so I came in."

She drew herself fully erect, taking in his windblown attire and hair with a raised eyebrow. "What do you want, David?"

Hutchins gave her an ingratiating smile. "Just to see you looking so lovely is enough." When she continued to watch him with silent suspicion, he went on, "I was hoping we could resolve our differences, be friends again."

"I'm surprised you haven't been arrested. I understand the patriots are also after you now."

For an instant anger twisted his features, but he recovered quickly. "Warren has made a mistake he will pay dearly for. You see, I know who Patriot is."

"Patriot? You mean you've—what are you talking about?" she amended, the color flooding into her cheeks.

"Why, Warren's contact on Gage's staff, of course. Gage is paying a handsome price for the information, with immunity thrown into the bargain."

His smile caused her to shrink back. "Warren's contact?"

"If I didn't know better, I'd think you've heard of him. But, of course, only Warren's inner circle knows of his existence."

"The only traitor I've heard of is you."

Hutchins' malevolent gaze darkened. "We'll soon find out who the real traitor is. Fortunately, Patriot doesn't yet know he's been exposed. Gage requires absolute proof of the treachery of one of his most trusted officers, so I've devised a trap. Patriot thinks Oriole is going to meet him on the marsh tonight to bring him to safety behind the rebel lines. Their rendezvous is supposed to be set for eleven o'clock down by that big elm tree just below here—you know the one. What he doesn't know is that General Smith will be waiting with a sizable detail to arrest him. Clever, don't you think?"

She clenched her fists. "That's despicable! How could you believe that I'd admire you for betraying someone to his death."

He raised an eyebrow at her vehemence. "I'm astonished that you'd take Patriot's part."

"You've betrayed everyone on both sides! Do you believe in nothing at all?" She broke off, staring at him with suspicion. "Why are you telling me all this?"

"Why, to redeem myself in your eyes, my love. Besides, it has become obvious that this disorganized rabble the patriots call an army can never win the conflict they've so foolishly started. When I hand this traitor over to Gage, my loyalty to the crown will be unquestioned."

None of it made any sense. *He must be mad,* she thought. Yet she had no doubt that he was telling the truth about Warren's contact, and that in less than an hour Patriot would stumble into Smith's clutches.

"What you mean is that Gage can pay better than the patriots can," she spat out, stalling for time. "It's in his eyes you wish to redeem yourself, not mine."

"Believe what you will. I'm sorry I can't stay longer. I intend to ride along with Smith to see the fun." He swept her an elaborate bow. "I'll bid you farewell."

"Who is he?"

He straightened, his eyes glittering with a mocking light. "I'm afraid you'll have to find out when everyone else does, my love. I guarantee it'll be worth the wait."

He could not quite hide the malevolence in his look. A bitter, triumphant smile contorted his features. She swung away to keep him from reading the fear in her eyes, and by the time she turned back he had already swept from the room like an evil shadow. She heard his footfalls in the hall, the outer door open, and a few seconds later the sound of a horse moving off at a trot.

In panic she ran into the hall, slammed the door shut and bolted it against the night wind with trembling hands, then leaned her back against it, her heart hammering, her breath coming in ragged pants. On the landing above her, the tall case clock chimed the first quarter.

The shocking thought occurred to her that the trap might in reality be meant for her. Hutchins had sworn revenge, and if he had somehow learned that she was Oriole this might be just the ingenious means to accomplish it. But if Patriot was genuinely in danger, then she had less than forty-five minutes to come up with a plan to warn him away.

At first her mind refused to function. Distracted, she thought that she should pray, seek God's wisdom in such a perilous dilemma. But the clock continued to tick away the minutes.

Feeling as though she had been shaken out of a dream, she caught up the flickering betty lamp on the hall table and ran for the stairs.

SHE COULD MAKE OUT NEITHER FORM nor movement in the blackness beneath the elm. Squinting through the deepening fog that all but obscured the partial disk of the moon that had just cleared the tops of the eastern hills, she whistled the low, melodious warble of an oriole.

The sound was echoed instantly. Staying low, she left her concealment in the tall grass to run through the fog like a ghostly wraith. She had no more than reached the edge of the elm's dense shade when a hand caught hers and jerked her into the circle of shadow.

"Smith has men posted there . . . and over there." She had to fight for breath as she indicated the edge of the mud flats behind them and an area between Stony Hill and Roxbury Heights. "It's a trap . . . Hutchins . . . "

She could not see his face or make out more than the bulk of his cloaked form, but she could feel his dismayed comprehension. "Then we're both betrayed," he hissed. "Two birds in the same snare."

"They're already on the move. We've got to get out of here!"

The sudden low rumble of hoofbeats brought them both around. On each side hazy points of torchlight danced toward them like fireflies through the shifting streamers of fog. Closing fast, the riders fanned out to three sides, moving at a gallop to cut off the rapidly diminishing path of escape.

As Elizabeth stood paralyzed, her shadowy companion gave a sharp whistle. In seconds a horse burst out of the darkness and galloped up onto the rise. Grabbing the trailing reins, her companion jerked the animal to a halt, and before she realized what he was doing, he had swept her up and into the saddle.

Tearing the nearest pistol out of the holster, he snapped, "Take the other—it's loaded."

She pulled the pistol free and reached for his hand with her other. "Haste!"

"He'll never make it carrying two."

"I won't leave you!" She clutched for his hand to pull him up behind her.

"*Ride!*"

Before she could protest, he gave the horse a hard swat across the rump, at the same time again gave a shrill whistle. Her mount leaped forward.

She jerked hard on the reins, but without effect. The horse plunged down the slope toward the river. A short distance across the uneven, boggy terrain, three riders galloped into their path.

Her mount came up with a squeal, ears laid back, hooves tearing at the nearest horse and rider. With a shock they crashed together. Somehow Elizabeth managed to keep from being thrown, then the other rider grabbed her, trying to tear her out of the saddle. Bringing up her pistol, she fired, and he reeled backward.

By now the other two were on her. To all sides she heard shouts and curses, the crack of pistols firing. A ball tore past her ear, another ripped through the sleeve of her shirt.

Dropping the now useless pistol, she twisted past the second rider. Screaming, her mount charged the third, crashed into him, and sent him rolling into the greasy mud. She dug her heels hard into the animal's flanks and bent over his neck as he bolted forward.

There was time for a single, anguished glance back over her shoulder. But Patriot had already been swallowed up in the blackness behind her, and she caught only a fleeting glimpse of bobbing torchlight closing around the place where she had left him.

THEY WERE ON HIM bare seconds after she vanished into the night. He saw the advance rider raise his pistol in the direction she had taken, brought up his own and fired point blank, his heart in his throat. With a guttural cry, the rider gave a sharp jerk, his shot going off harmlessly into the air as he dropped from the saddle like a stone.

The rest of the patrol closed the last few yards so swiftly there was no time to take a single step before he found himself surrounded, the dull gleam of weapons pointed at his breast.

"*Hold!* One move and your brains will feed the fish."

He knew that voice all too well. Facing his captors with outward calm, he made no attempt at resistance as the riders slid from their horses and crowded around him.

One of them grabbed his pistol; another ran up with a tin lantern and pulled off the shade as he held it up to Carleton's face. Involuntarily Carleton flinched in the light of the flame.

Writhing on the ground where he had fallen nearby, Hutchins clutched at his breast, a bright red stream pulsing through his fingers. As his eyes met Carleton's in the wavering light, he gave a hoarse laugh, flecks of bloody foam staining his lips as he struggled to sit up.

"Speak . . . of the . . . devil," he rasped out.

"A term I'd think more fitting for you," Carleton returned. "Or perhaps snake would be more appropriate."

Hutchins gave a choked laugh. Then, shuddering, he fell back against the earth, and his eyes became fixed.

Looking up to meet Smith's triumphant stare, with an airy wave of his hand Carleton drawled, "My condolences. It seems that Oriole has once more flown the coop."

Smith flushed, but he returned a malevolent smile. "Ah, but we've snared an eagle in his stead. I don't think His Excellency will be disappointed."

It had been several minutes since she had heard any shots from the direction of the marsh. Where the ground began to rise, she pulled up, not knowing what to do, staring back in the direction from which she had come.

After long moments of indecision and anguish, she reined her mount to the right, and holding him to a walk, dropped down into the shallow ravine cut by Stony Brook on its descent to the bay. Splashing across the stream, they followed its gentle slope upward out of the mists that cloaked marsh and meadow, climbing toward Pierpoint Mill.

Shaking with exhaustion and the shock of her near capture, Elizabeth realized that her mount's owner had been right. Burdened with two riders, the horse would have floundered. She would never have eluded her pursuers.

He had sacrificed his life for hers, knowing full well what he did. And there was nothing she could do now to save him, no gain in going back. She would sacrifice herself also, and all that would accomplish would be to give Gage more fuel for propaganda against the rebels. Yet the thought that Patriot would die abandoned and alone was intolerable.

Nearing the top of the slope, she got a glimpse of clear sky studded with stars and now brightly illumined by the waning moon. To her left loomed the indistinct bulk of the mill, its great wheel turning with a muffled creak as the silver rill of water cascaded down the race and across its paddles.

She had to talk to her uncle and to Warren too, she concluded. Together they would figure out what to do.

Sick at heart, she whispered a prayer that somehow, in God's grace, Patriot had been able to elude the patrol. But even as the words formed on her lips, the certainty sank into her heart like a stone into a bottomless well that there was no hope of his escape.

She became aware of the slow tramp of feet and the rumble of wagons. Moving warily over the rise, she almost rode into a company of soldiers led by an officer swinging a shaded lantern. Rifles on their shoulders, they filed past where she had pulled up in the shadows beneath an overgrowth of pines.

As soon as they had moved out of sight down the dusty road toward Cambridge, she spurred her mount past the mill and over the bridge, then turned onto Tess's carriageway. The field behind the house was alive with urgent activity. Down the lane she could see soldiers moving in and out of torchlight, carrying barrels and boxes out of the barn and loading them onto waiting wagons.

Weaving her way through the rows of tents where the Lincoln regiment was already beginning to form up in columns, she made her way to the stable. Nowhere did she see Tess, Stern, or her cousins.

She hurried to lead the horse inside the dark building, found an empty box stall in the faint light from the open door. Making sure the animal had hay and that there was water in the bucket, she ran back outside and almost collided with Levi, who was striding down the path.

"Why aren't you with your company, soldier?" he demanded.

"I haven't been assigned to one yet," she answered, her tone tart.

Bending closer, he tipped up the brim of her hat and peered into her face. "I know that voice. What are you doing here, Cuz? Tess is in a state. She thinks you're still at Stony Hill, and Pa won't let anyone through the lines because we've been ordered to march."

"What's going on?"

"The Committee of Safety ordered Ward to fortify Bunker's Hill, and we're getting ready to move out. Looks like there's going to be a battle tomorrow."

"I'm going with you!"

He gave a short laugh. "You're a girl. You can't fight."

"Then what was I doing all the way back from Concord?"

He grinned. "What am I saying? You're the best shot we have." He gestured toward where his company was forming up. "We have a couple of men out on sick call, so nobody'll notice an extra body. Go get in line and I'll find you a musket.

"But stay out of Pa's sight—and Will's too, for that matter," he added as an afterthought. "Once we're on the hill it'll be too late for them to kick up a fuss."

She hesitated, torn between the imminence of the battle and the pressing need to find a way to rescue Patriot. At last, reluctantly admitting that for the time being at least there was nothing any of them could do to help her gallant savior, she gave a smart salute and ran to join the line.

Chapter Twenty-six

"IF THIS AIN'T A CASE O' PURE TREACHERY, I don't know whut it be! Them fools brung us up here 'thout the first danged notion o' what they wuz doin', and mark my words, they're sure as hellfire goin' to leave us all here to die!"

With a start Elizabeth came awake and sat up. Disoriented and groggy, she looked around her, dazed.

The cramped fortress was crawling with soldiers, some occupied in putting the finishing touches on the dirt embankment, others moving at a run on some urgent errand. Not more than two yards away a cluster of soldiers leaned against the wall, gesturing with angry intensity in the direction of the Mystic River.

Arriving on Charlestown peninsula shortly after one o'clock to find the work already well underway, the Lincoln regiment had joined in carving a fort out of the hillside with prodigious speed and as much stealth as could be managed in the darkness on unfamiliar terrain. But it was not, as ordered, on Bunker's Hill, which commanded the approach from the mainland, the entire peninsula, both rivers, and the bay. Instead, they were entrenching Breed's Hill, a lower prominence directly above Charlestown and well within range of British cannon.

Rumor had it that feisty General Israel Putnam was responsible for that decision, but for the moment he was nowhere in evidence. Commanding the force in the redoubt was Colonel William Prescott, one of the most respected officers in the rebel camp. Besides companies from his own regiment, the detachment included units from several others, including the Lincoln regiment and a detail from Putnam's brigade led by tall, handsome Captain Thomas Knowlton—more than a thousand men in all.

Stretching the stiffness out of her limbs, Elizabeth sprang to her feet. The air was still moist and fresh from the night, but with a sense of trepidation she noted a barely perceptible brightness in the sky to the east. As she followed the soldiers' angry gaze out across the embankment, she drew in her breath.

In the gradually strengthening light the raw umber walls of the small fort were cast in sharper definition against the waist-high grass that carpeted the peninsula's rolling pasturelands. The fortification they had constructed more by feel than by sight was roughly 130 feet square, with an arrow-shaped extension at its front that pointed toward the ghostly, deserted streets of Charlestown. Its walls by now were six feet high and a foot thick.

To their extreme right on the Charles River side of the peninsula and directly below Bunker's Hill, the mill dam blocked access to the narrow Neck from the water. Off to the left, however, open land sloped toward the Mystic River, broadening into a grassy valley of uneven terrain crisscrossed by numerous rail fences. At the farthest end of the peninsula lay a swampy area of clay pits and brick kilns, where she could make out the low, gentle slope of Morton's Hill. Except for their own position, the peninsula was deserted.

The scene on the water in front of her was a different story. Silently she counted off the armaments of the ships that lay anchored there: the sloop *Falcon* with sixteen guns; the transport *Symmetry* with eighteen; the *Lively*, twenty; and the *Glasgow*, twenty-four. To their extreme good fortune, just the previous day Admiral Graves had moved the sixty-eight gun *Somerset* from the Back Bay to a position he deemed safer, off Hancock's Wharf on the opposite side of Boston.

One didn't have to be trained in military tactics to realize that their position could be outflanked by a force circling to their right through the deserted streets of the abandoned town or moving along the narrow beach that rimmed the Mystic on their left, well out of range of their muskets and rifles.

The soldiers had begun to realize it too, and increasing numbers were casting anxious looks toward the higher hill behind them that blocked their view of the Neck as if wondering what was delaying the relief party everyone assumed must be on its way. But as she looked out over the brightening landscape, Elizabeth felt a sickening foreboding that there would be no relief party.

Levi and Isaiah joined her just as the church bells of Boston somberly tolled four o'clock, echoed by the melodious chime of the ships' bells in the harbor. A hoarse shout drew Elizabeth's eyes to the deck of the *Lively,* where a sailor pointed upward in the direction of the redoubt. His high-pitched outrage carried across the water as clear as the ring of metal against crystal, and a rush of scurrying movement and shouts followed. In seconds an officer ran to the railing to peer up at them through a spyglass.

The alarm spread like wildfire from ship to ship. Drums began to beat, then a boat slipped off from the *Lively's* side, the sailors tearing at the oars to drive the vessel posthaste in the direction of the nearest Boston dock.

It seemed to Elizabeth, watching transfixed, that time stood still while equally it unwound with furious speed. The *Lively* began to come around on her anchor rope, her bearing side revolving into view in the deadly dance of a serpent hypnotizing its paralyzed prey, until Elizabeth could see the intense activity on her gun deck.

They had no defense against this. All around Elizabeth the soldiers were staring, as she was, in mute, motionless, dismay, while along the shore of the town opposite the alarm washed outward as night's inexorable retreat exposed in the first, tentative light of dawn the gauntlet the rebels had carved into the dirt.

The *Lively* came to position, and instantly a jagged sheet of fire belched from one end of the frigate to the other. The ship shuddered, an ominous cloud of greasy smoke enveloping her from the gun deck upward and billowing outward across the water. The deafening explosion brought everyone in the redoubt to their knees, hands clapped to their ears.

Crouching against the forward wall, Elizabeth looked fearfully overhead as fiery arcs of solid shot traced across the brightening sky. Most of the balls tore into the hillside above or below them without causing any damage. But one plowed into the redoubt's rear wall, raising a geyser of loose dirt and small rocks that rained down on the fort's occupants.

Straightening with caution, they peered out over the top of the earthen wall just as the *Lively* unloosed another broadside, sending them once more to their knees. Prescott alone, Elizabeth noted, remained motionless, leaning against the parapet to watch the action with apparent unconcern, even when one of the balls furrowed the ditch outside the forward wall.

Already small details of men were busy patching the damage to the redoubt. Just as Elizabeth turned to throw a hasty look at the officers clustering around Prescott, her uncle swung around and glanced in their direction. His gaze found Levi's pale blond head, then dropped to his companions. Eyes narrowing, he excused himself and strode over to them.

"I should have known you'd find a way to get into the thick of things," he growled at Elizabeth before turning to his younger son. "And I suppose you're responsible for fitting her out." With a sharp jab he indicated the musket, powder horn, cartouche, and shovel Elizabeth had draped over her shoulders and hung from her belt in imitation of her comrades.

Before the two cousins had gotten out more than a few words of explanation and defense, shouting to be heard over the roar of the cannonade, Will joined them. He fixed Elizabeth in a reproachful look.

"I don't suppose you let Tess know you were coming with us."

"It's better she doesn't know I'm here." Elizabeth made an unsuccessful attempt to squelch a sharp pang of guilt.

"You don't think you're going to stay, do you? I want you off this hill—now! This is no place for a woman—" Stern broke off, throwing up his hands in a gesture of frustration as he unloosed a curse. "And how many times have I said that?"

"I won't leave you!" she cried, her voice choked with emotion. "Whatever your fate, it shall be mine as well."

Stern swung to look out over the wall, his face working as he struggled to maintain control. As he did so, signal flags ran up the halyard of one of the ships farther out in the harbor, and the barrage from the *Lively* ceased. By contrast, the sudden silence seemed so intense it echoed.

Indicating Prescott, who stood at a short distance, Will said, "I heard Prescott mention he needed a reliable messenger—one he could trust not to run off."

His father responded with a furious frown, then he grabbed Elizabeth by the arm and all but dragged her over to the colonel. He introduced her as James Freeman, and after a brief conversation, Prescott gratefully took her on as his messenger.

To block any British attempt to flank the redoubt, Prescott asked Stern to take a detachment and begin digging a breastwork down the hill in the direction of the Mystic. Stern strode off and in short order a substantial contingent, including Will, Levi, and Isaiah, filed out of the redoubt's single, constricted exit, shovels cocked over shoulders. Following Will's shouted orders, they spread out in a long line down the hill.

No sooner had the work begun on the breastwork than harsh orders rang across the decks of the *Glasgow, Spitfire,* and *Symmetry,* and all three began to come around, also bringing their bearing sides into line with the rebel redoubt while sailors swarmed to service their guns. This time all four ships opened the bombardment simultaneously. In moments the repeated volleys had become deafening, tearing at the nerves.

As before, most of the shots screamed past overhead or plowed into the hillside below them. But as Elizabeth dodged back up the hill to report to Prescott on the progress being made on the breastwork, a round hurtled over the earthen parapet, shearing off the head of the soldier standing in its path. All activity was suspended while the men stared at their gruesomely shattered comrade in wordless horror. At last a young officer edged over to Prescott and asked what they should do.

"Bury him," Prescott commanded grimly.

As if not believing his ears the officer mumbled something about a coffin, a minister, prayers. Prescott fixed him in a glare that could have melted steel and repeated the order through clenched teeth.

He was obeyed with reluctance, and the dead man was hastily buried, though not until prayers had been offered by a parson from one of the companies. But in the hours that followed a palpable unease settled over the fort. One or two at a time, men found urgent business back on Bunker's Hill, where they disappeared never to return. Elizabeth watched with concern as little by little Prescott's command began to trickle away.

Prescott noted it too, though he said nothing. In apparent unconcern, he substituted the tan linen duster he had brought with him for his uniform coat. The same color as the raw earth they had thrown up, it had the effect of making him less visible. Climbing up on the wall, he began to pace back and forth along the parapet as though taking a pleasant stroll on a particularly fine day. To all appearances oblivious of the hail of cannonballs, he called encouragement to the men cowering in the redoubt.

Steadying her emotions, Elizabeth took him as her example and carried out the errands he sent her on in grim determination that no one would see her fear. Others, she saw, began to do the same.

✱ ✱ ✱

FOR THE THOUSANDTH TIME Elizabeth resettled her hat so the wide brim would better shade her burning eyes from the sun. The wig was hot and made her scalp itch. She longed to pull it off, along with the stifling wrappings that flattened her bosom under her loose smock.

It was by now midmorning. The dust-laden heat inside the redoubt was smothering, and the roar of cannon had given her a violent headache. Long ago the soldiers had devoured the meager provisions they had carried with them. A stray round had shattered the two hogsheads of water, and there was no more to be had. She longed for a morsel of bread and a cool drink of water more than anything in the world, except for a hot bath and a soft bed.

A short time earlier an artillery detail had with considerable effort hauled four cannon through the narrow entrance of the redoubt, only to discover that there were no gun platforms or embrasures. Their solution was to blast openings for the cannon through the walls, adding to the already choking cloud that hung in the air.

Over the next few minutes the detail fired several ineffective shots at the ships in the harbor, which were answered when the Copp's Hill battery came unexpectedly to life. And before long the officers commanding the detail also discovered urgent business back on Bunker's Hill.

The muscles working in his jaw, Prescott sent Elizabeth to call his officers together. After Stern had reported that the breastwork now extended almost all the way to the swamp and was rapidly nearing completion, Prescott asked for an accounting of casualties. To everyone's amazement, besides the man who had been decapitated, only one soldier had suffered a slight injury.

"I expect the British will land at Morton's Point." Prescott indicated the silent cannon with a jab of his hand. "Gridley sent me guns, but his men seemed to find the air in here a trifle hot. Do we have anyone who can handle artillery?"

The answer was negative, and Stern insisted that Prescott send to Cambridge for a detachment to relieve the exhausted men. Prescott stared out over the peninsula, his face set in stubborn lines.

"The men who have raised these works are the best able to defend them."

Under pressure from the rest of the officers, however, he at last directed Major Brooks to ride to Cambridge to see if he could talk Ward into providing additional reinforcements and supplies. As they dispersed, Prescott gestured toward the top of Bunker's Hill, where large groups of men were visible milling around its fringes.

"Find out where Putnam is and why those men aren't down here," he growled to Elizabeth.

Relieved to get out of the redoubt's breathlessly hot, dust-choked confines, she plodded up the hill, dodging the unceasing hail of solid shot. At the top she found an even more chaotic scene than the one she had left below. Most of the units stood idle, fearfully watching the unfolding action, while others wandered about in helpless confusion with no clear idea of what they were supposed to do or where they were supposed to go.

The thunder of the cannonade made it almost impossible to think. Adding to the din, the floating batteries that had for some time been struggling up the Charles to the edge of the mill pond now began to lay a hot fire across the Neck, stranding substantial relief parties on the mainland.

She found Putnam just returned from his second trip to Cambridge that morning and in a foul temper. In an extreme state of frustration he accompanied her back down the hill to inform Prescott that early that morning he had managed, after considerable cajoling, to persuade Ward to order two hundred men from Stark's regiment to join the fight.

Prescott brightened at the news. A wiry, ramrod-straight Indian fighter from the New Hampshire wilderness, Stark was renowned for his toughness and the tight discipline of his men.

More good news was on the way. Shortly before noon Major Brooks returned to report that the Committee of Safety had ordered Reed's regiment to march, along with the rest of Stark's command. All they could do now was to wait for the British to show their hand and hope reinforcements would reach them in time.

AT ODD MOMENTS DURING THE DAY the haunting image of that meeting on the marsh the previous night flooded into Elizabeth's thoughts. Always she saw the dark figure in that instant after he had sent her off on his own mount, just as he turned to face the oncoming patrol, pistol leveled, facing down overwhelming odds with only one shot and nowhere to run.

Each time, a sliver of agony pulsed through her at the thought that it was all her fault, that she was responsible, ultimately, for his being there. Responsible for his death.

For he must be dead by now. The British would not delay hanging a spy in time of war. And looking out across the fearful scene below her, she was struck by the certainty that all roads back to the world they had once known were forever swept away. All she could do now was to push the searing self-condemnation out of her consciousness and force herself, however painfully, to do what had to be done in the hours that lay ahead.

THE SUN STOOD DIRECTLY OVERHEAD when the long lines of redcoats formed up in the square in front of North Battery wharf. Staring through Will's spyglass, Elizabeth made out companies of grenadiers and light infantry, the Forty-third and Fifty-second regiments, and six fieldpieces.

It was not until half past one that the loaded barges shoved off. In the redoubt taciturn soldiers jostled for position at the parapet. Wiping the stinging sweat out of their eyes, grinding their teeth on the grit that coated their parched mouths, they squinted against the sun's glare to make out the long oars that swept through the water in precise rhythm.

A fiery sheen glinted from the bayonets of shouldered muskets, rank on rank, intensified the blood red of massed uniforms, reflected each repeated image in the shimmering bay. When it seemed that every soldier in the garrison must be coming to oppose them, additional barges swept into view around the jutting piers of the North End, carrying still more grenadiers, light infantry, the Fifth and Thirty-eighth regiments.

To Elizabeth's relief the distinctive helmets of the Seventeenth Light Dragoons were nowhere in evidence. She tried to swallow, found her mouth too dry. Feeling nauseated, she raised her eyes from the barges to stare across the water at the town of Boston. By now every visible window and housetop harbored its share of spectators. The streets along the waterfront and the docks were jammed, with more onlookers filling up every height and vantage point all around the bay.

To cover the landing, the cannonade now became more intense. With the transports nearing Morton's Point, Prescott ordered the few remaining members of the artillery to haul two fieldpieces below to a position in the valley where they could more effectively slow the British attack. As an afterthought, he directed Captain Knowlton to take his company along as support.

The barges had reached the shallows off the peninsula, and the first troops sprang out onto the narrow beach. Hefting bulky haversacks onto their backs, they formed up in orderly rows while the barges returned to the docks to reload, this time bringing the Royal Regiment of Artillery and the officers who would command the assault force.

Elizabeth adjusted the spyglass, focusing on the clutch of officers standing in the bow of the leading barge. Prescott squatted down on the wall above her.

"Howe is in command," she told him. "With him are Pigot, Clark, and Abercromby."

"It looks like we're in for some action," a quiet but forceful voice said behind her.

Prescott straightened as Elizabeth spun around to face Warren. The doctor wore a cocked hat and was clothed in an elegant coat and breeches that matched the clear, light blue of his eyes, with a white embroidered, fringed silk waistcoat over spotless white linen. Powder horn and sword were slung over his shoulders, incongruous details, as was the fusil he leaned on like a walking stick, his long, slender fingers curving around the steel barrel with the same casual sureness with which she had seen them wield a scalpel.

"Don't you know it's dangerous out here?"

He gave her a lazy smile, his eyes lighting with excitement. "Ah, but that's precisely why I've come. It's too quiet at headquarters."

Prescott jumped down from the wall and touched his fingers to the brim of his hat in salute. "Sir, I await your orders."

Warren dismissed his words with a graceful wave of his hand. "I haven't received my commission yet and have no command here. I've come to volunteer." As Prescott began to object, he added firmly, "I consider it a great privilege, sir, to fight under an officer of your quality."

BY THE TIME THE BRITISH completed their landing, it was obvious that the rebels had used the long delay to their advantage. The few gaps that still remained in the rebel lines were being closed with desperate speed.

So it was to the astonishment of the rebel force watching from redoubt and breastwork, from behind rail fences and the alleys of Charlestown, that the British spread out across the top of Morton's Hill and sat down to eat their lunch in apparent unconcern while one of the transports skimmed back across the water. When one of the officers in the redoubt made a contemptuous remark, Warren and Prescott exchanged glances.

"Our men would welcome a taste of that hardtack," Prescott noted.

"I doubt Howe means to supply us with refreshments," Warren put in dryly. "More likely he's calling for his reserve."

Like the eddies left by a stone dropped into a pond, his words spread among those standing around him with varying effect, from dread to a bitter pride at this show of Howe's respect. But as she looked around her, Elizabeth realized that there could not be three hundred men left in the redoubt. There were perhaps an equal number in the breastwork below, in addition to Knowlton's troops, who had disappeared into the valley farther down. Even if all the promised reinforcements showed up within the next few minutes, Prescott might have at most fifteen hundred men left to face Howe's force, which already decisively outnumbered them.

It occurred to her that God had ordered Gideon to thin the ranks of his army until the only ones left were those fit for the fight. Bombardment, hunger, thirst, exhaustion had pruned the rebel army. Those remained whose resolve to defend their homes and country outweighed their fear and exhaustion.

She surveyed the tense faces around her. "We've stood up to them before and beaten them. With God's help we'll beat them again."

Her words also eddied outward, and in one face after another apprehension gave way to clenched teeth and the hard glint of an eye. Glancing over at her, Warren smiled.

WHILE HOWE WAITED for the reserve force to reach him, Prescott's concern mounted. The British ships had begun to fire red-hot balls into Charlestown to drive out the snipers posted there, and the Copp's Hill battery was shooting carcasses—hollow cannonballs containing combustibles—into the town. With each hit a lazy curl of dark smoke rose from a shattered roof or wall, followed by a thin tongue of flame. In minutes many of the buildings had kindled.

There was still no sign of the reinforcements the Committee of Safety had ordered out. From the redoubt it was impossible to see beyond the far end of the breastwork, where Knowlton and the artillery had disappeared in the direction of the swamps. At last Prescott sent Elizabeth to find the captain, then report back to him on the double.

Running to the bottom of the slope, she dodged through the small grove of trees shading the breastwork's lower end. Reaching the narrow, dusty road that stretched from the direction of the brick kilns on back toward the top of Bunker's Hill, she threw an anxious glance around her.

She was within direct sight of Morton's Hill, where Howe had just begun to form up his lines. Unconsciously holding her breath, she surveyed the British position.

It was nearing three o'clock, and by now the general's reserve had reached him, additional grenadier and light infantry companies, the First Marines, and the Forty-seventh regiment. As she watched, transfixed, the main body began to spread out to her right, moving in majestic deliberation all the way across the peninsula to curl around the base of Breed's Hill. Below the redoubt, Charlestown was a mass of roaring flames over which the wooden church steeples rose in towering pyramids of smoke and fire.

Wrenching around, she saw in dismay that a double battle line was already in position facing the breastwork and the area where she stood. What disturbed her most was the sight of a long line of light infantry and Fusiliers sorting itself into column four abreast along the narrow beach to her left, poised to sweep around the end of the rebel line.

Panting, her heart hammering, she looked behind her. A short distance back up the road a fence stretched from the road to the bank of the Mystic. Behind it bristled a sizable force, and recognizing Knowlton's lean form, she raced toward them.

As she slid behind the fence she saw that the position was much stronger than it appeared from the front. A stone wall topped with rails, behind which ran a ditch, it had been bolstered with a second set of rails to form a double wall. This had been stuffed with the drying hay that lay in windrows all around, broken chunks of bricks, rocks, sticks, any debris

384 ❋ J. M. HOCHSTETLER

that had come to hand. From Knowlton she learned that, moments before her arrival, an artillery officer had shown up with two fieldpieces, which he had placed in an advantageous position behind them.

At the fence's far end she made out Stark's tall, gaunt form, and then Reed, along with their tough New Hampshiremen. She ran over to Stark.

"Sir, the light infantry is lining up on the beach below us."

Stark gave her a keen look, then paced over to the edge of the bank, his leathery mouth drawing into a hard line as he looked down. Motioning some of his men over, he led them down onto the beach below the high bank.

On impulse, Elizabeth jumped down with them. Wasting no time, the soldiers dragged forward every rock they could lay hands on, and with a speed and skill that astounded her, piled them into a sturdy wall that stretched from the bank into the water. Behind this fortification Stark ranged his men three deep and gave the order to load their weapons.

Noticing Elizabeth standing idle, he motioned her peremptorily into the second row. Loading her musket with shaking hands, she squeezed among oak-hard thighs and torsos.

In front of her the first line crouched behind the stone wall, their muskets out of sight at Stark's command. On the other side of the wall, several hundred yards of smooth, wet sand strewn with dark patches of decaying seaweed stretched between them and the first ranks of the light infantry.

What are they waiting for? Elizabeth wondered as she rubbed her eyes and squinted at the terrible splendor of the enemy seemingly suspended in the taut, breathless hush. But she knew that all of them would wait until Howe, satisfied that his battle line was arrayed in tidy rows, chose to give the order that would wreak destruction upon them all.

Chapter Twenty-seven

FROM SOMEWHERE IN FRONT and above came a shouted order. At the same instant the column of light infantry, the Welch Fusiliers in the lead, began stepping toward them in a majestic, slow rhythm, accompanied by the deep, regular boom of the fieldpieces on Morton's Point and the louder, sustained roar of the ships' broadsides. Nervously fingering their weapons, Stark's men squinted through the shimmering heat waves rising from sand and water at the wavering image of the approaching scarlet line.

Behind them Stark strode back and forth, taut as a whipcord. "Don't fire till I give the order. Shoot low and aim for the crossing of their belts. Officers are in the brightest red—pick them off first."

The light infantry drew steadily nearer, shining bayonets advanced, and suddenly an unnatural silence settled over the peninsula as the ships stopped firing to avoid hitting their own men. In the hush Elizabeth could hear the squish of footsteps in the sand, punctuated by the occasional barked orders of an officer.

The redcoats were one hundred feet away, and she could make out the features of the men in the front rank. Not pausing, they closed to within seventy-five feet, seventy, sixty.

His voice quiet, Stark said, "Ready!"

All along the wall muskets were brought to level, steel barrels scraping against stacked stones, hammers clicking metallically to cock. The

Fusiliers and light infantry came on without pause.

Fifty-five feet.

"Aim!"

Sighting down the length of cold steel barrel, each man on the front line concentrated on his chosen mark, his finger tightening over the trigger. Elizabeth blinked the stinging sweat out of her eyes. She felt lightheaded. The beat of her pulse deafened her.

Fifty feet.

"Fire!"

A sheet of flame belched along the wall, and the acrid smoke of gunpowder momentarily blinded them, clogging their throats. The first line was up, rushing to the rear to reload, and Elizabeth stumbled forward to the wall.

Not waiting for the smoke to clear, Stark snapped, "Ready! Aim!"

Sighting down her musket barrel through the drifting smoke, she saw that the oncoming column had staggered backward. The first two ranks writhed on the ground as though cut down by a giant scythe, the third and fourth had lost half their men, and those coming up from behind wavered for an instant before stepping over their fallen comrades.

She had less than a second to sight her weapon before the order to fire was repeated. She pulled the trigger, jerking back with her weapon's kick, then scrambled to the rear, ears ringing with the muskets' multiplied report.

For an indeterminate period the wall's defenders blazed away at the advancing line, and still the redcoats came on. In turn, each new rank was cut down until flesh and blood could endure no more.

There was an instant when the scarlet line shuddered with an irresistible shock, then soldiers turned to push their way back through the jam of human bodies in frantic haste, and the ordered line disintegrated.

Elizabeth had just come up to the wall, but neither she nor her companions thought to fire. Open-mouthed, they watched as the might of the British army shoved and fought in terror all the way back to the barges that had brought them. Had it not been for the officers who blocked their way with drawn swords, the panicked troops would have thrown themselves aboard.

Glancing fearfully up at the sun, Elizabeth calculated in astonishment that the entire engagement could not have taken a quarter of an hour. With a shock she became aware that the roar of gunfire continued on the bank above them, but at that moment the firing ceased.

There was a brief, suspended silence, then they could hear a whoop of triumph from the direction of the rail fence. The sound broke the spell, and all around her, disbelief gave way to a jubilation of dancing, cheering, and shouting.

From what Elizabeth could see, the rebel force had suffered only a few minor injuries. On the stretch of narrow beach in front of the stone wall, however, the outgoing tide lapped against the piled bodies strewn across the sand, turning the water red. In spite of her comrades' elation, she could find little joy in the sight of the dead or the cries and pleas of the wounded.

Stark also remained sober, his calculating stare weighing the movements of the enemy down at the point. Quickly he began to settle his men down with a pat on a back or the squeeze of a shoulder.

"Good work, men, but the day ain't over yet."

Feeling lightheaded with heat and tension, Elizabeth clawed her way to the top of the bank, remembering guiltily that Prescott had sent her to bring back a report. The scene above reflected the one she had just left, with Knowlton's and Reed's men giving vent to an extreme of celebration in the belief that they had won the day. Here also the officers were working to calm their gleeful men, warning them to prepare for another assault.

As far as she could see down the width of the peninsula the British line had been driven back, retreating in disorder almost to the water. To within thirty feet in front of the rail fence, all along the breastwork, and in front of the redoubt the waist-high grass was trampled and mashed down, strewn with British casualties. Here and there broken men screamed for help or struggled to drag themselves to safety. In the distance black smoke rolled upward from the charred ruins of Charlestown, where beneath the dark cloud cherry tongues of flame still licked along a wall or engulfed a collapsed roof.

Glancing around, she saw that the British front was reforming with speed. As it began to snake back out across the peninsula, Knowlton shouted a warning to Reed and raced to pull his men together.

Desperate to get back to Prescott, Elizabeth took off at a run, her musket clenched in her hand. Crossing the road, she dodged through the trees and along the back of the breastwork. She was still yards from the redoubt when she realized that the long scarlet line had once more begun the inexorable march uphill.

"Where have you been?" a familiar voice barked. "Never mind— you'd better get down here on the double!"

Glancing around, she saw Will in the trench a short distance from where she stood, with Levi and Isaiah nearby. She dropped down beside them, and Will shoved her into the line.

"Ready!"

His shout was echoed by other officers down the length of the breastwork. Two hundred muskets swung into place across the top of the earthen wall as Elizabeth fumbled to reload.

She had to stand on a rock to sight down the musket barrel. Once more the double battle line paced toward them with maddening deliberation, companies pausing to shake out their tangled ranks each time they clambered over a stone wall or rail fence. Again the defenders of redoubt and breastwork and fence held their fire until the British closed to within fifty feet.

"Fire!" Will screamed.

Time seemed to stand still while they fired as quickly as they could reload. It seemed to Elizabeth she had become a machine, devoid of any sensation of fear or exhaustion or thirst. Rocked by the unremitting stream of fire from the rebel lines, the British still came on with furious determination, bayonets advanced, some stopping to fire while others struggled to within feet of the breastwork before being cut down.

For the better part of half an hour the redcoats clawed forward inch by inch, but it was at last too much. Once more the shattered line splintered and gave way. There was no order to the retreat. Many companies left half or three quarters of their men behind in the blood-drenched grass. As far as Elizabeth could see to either side, the rails of the fences were riddled with bullet holes.

Staring along her musket barrel, with a shock she recognized Howe standing a hundred yards from her, all alone, dead and wounded men tangled at his feet. His white gaiters and breeches were so splattered with gore they appeared red, and his face was fixed in an expression of horror that burned deep into her memory.

To both sides down the length of the breastwork, she heard again the fierce victory yell. But triumph tasted like ashes in her mouth.

Will accompanied her back up to the redoubt, detouring through the scene of joyful disorder to find his father while she reported to Prescott. When she went to find Stern a short time later, she found him conferring with Warren and Will. All three appeared visibly agitated, but as she came toward them they broke off their conversation.

Giving Elizabeth a look that sent a chill through her, Will stalked off to rejoin his company. Warren also broke away and returned to his position without speaking to her, and although it was clear that Stern was deeply disturbed, he could not be induced to tell her what they had been talking about.

More pressing concerns soon drove the incident from her consciousness. From the vantage point of the hilltop, she could make out through the drifting smoke small groups of defenders still moving among Charlestown's blackened ruins. On their right another detachment had found refuge in a small barn just down the slope from the redoubt, while others crouched behind the stone walls, trees, and rocky outcroppings from which they had driven back General Pigot's attempt to flank the redoubt.

It was by now nearing four o'clock. For the next hour the rebel soldiers watched as the British carried as many of their dead and wounded off the peninsula as they could safely reach. But just when they had begun to believe that there would be no further assault, barges loaded with reinforcements began to cross the narrow strip of water from Boston.

Their faces sober, officers and men began to take stock of the little ammunition they had left, then to share out their reserves of powder and ball. Artillery shells that had been left behind were broken open, the powder distributed to those who had none.

This time Howe ordered his men to shed their heavy packs and sent them forward in long columns. At the same time the artillery began to rake the rebel positions with grapeshot, and once more chaos engulfed the peninsula.

Firing on the oncoming column with frenzied rapidity, the rebel troops soon realized that this narrower, faster-moving target was more difficult to hit. Even so, each redcoat who stepped forward was dropped in his tracks, and the column crawled forward with excruciating slowness.

Yet as the minutes ticked by, while the mass of redcoats scrambled up the last few yards of the hill, more and more of the redoubt's defenders reached the end of their ration of powder and musket ball and scrabbled in the dirt for scraps of metal or nails that could be fired or a rock to fling. Stationed along the western side of the redoubt, Elizabeth stared out at the line of marines advancing in front of her.

In the lead, Pitcairn waved them on. "They've abandoned her, lads! One more push, and we'll be over!"

"We ain't all gone!" cried out a young boy near her. As if on cue, Salem Prince, one of the black soldiers, raised his musket and fired, sending Pitcairn reeling backward.

At once the attackers poured into the trench outside the walls. Repeatedly one or another of the redoubt's defenders, near crazed with exhaustion, heat, and thirst, leaned out over the embankment to fire down into the trench, only to be shot or bayoneted.

"Push on! Push on!"

Without warning, uttering a wild roar of rage, the British clawed onto the top of the wall *en masse*, bayonets stabbing through smoke and dust. In the melee, rebel soldiers fired their last shots and sprang to tear the muskets out of their enemies' hands and turn them on their owners.

For one tenuous moment the British force swayed backward. Then an overwhelming scarlet tide toppled over the embankment. Cursing, screaming, stabbing wildly with bayonets, clubbing their enemy with useless muskets, sticks, and rocks, men fought hand to hand as though bereft of reason.

At last, realizing that further resistance was futile, Prescott ordered his men to withdraw. Under irresistible pressure from the incoming British, coughing and choking in the dense cloud that covered the redoubt, confused, disoriented rebel troops began to grope their way toward the single, constricted passage through the fortress's rear wall.

Elizabeth jumped as a rough hand grasped her by the arm, then Stern dragged her toward the exit. Behind them Warren and Prescott strode along, swords upraised to ward off British bayonets as casually as though they swatted at an annoying swarm of insects.

They had to force their way through the jam-up at the exit. Once outside, the path of retreat ran between two wings of British troops who continued to pour a hot fire into the boiling tide of men. Clasping their muskets by the barrel, she and Stern beat back their attackers, their hands, coated with muddy sweat, slipping on the bare steel.

Amid the confusion, Will, Levi, and Isaiah materialized to surround them. As she turned to look back, she saw Warren coming wearily up, his fine clothing torn and fouled. As his clear blue eyes met hers, he gave a conspiratorial smile.

Without warning, her feet slipped out from under her on the trampled upward slope, and she fell hard onto the path. She was too exhausted to struggle to her feet, and Warren sprang to help her. As she watched with suspended horror, a British officer stepped out of the line that sagged in on them, musket upraised, then she heard the deafening explosion at point-blank range.

Warren jerked convulsively, his eyes widening. Blood trickling down his cheek, he fell to his knees, then crumpled to the ground at her side.

Will stepped between them to jerk her to her feet. She heard someone screaming, "No! No!" not recognizing her own voice as, shoving through the crush of men around them, a husky grenadier drove his bayonet deep into Will's chest.

He staggered and sank, blood foaming on his lips with each gasped breath.

Before any of them could move, Isaiah fired his last shot through the soldier's head. Grabbing Will's limp form up in his arms, the black man hefted him across his shoulder as though he were weightless and, motioning to Levi to carry Elizabeth, led the way up the slope.

How they reached the hilltop Elizabeth did not afterward remember. Nor did she have any conscious awareness of crossing the narrow Neck raked with cannon fire through the tangled chaos of a thousand men, some frantic to reach the safety of the mainland, others stubbornly holding their ground to cover the retreat.

In a state of complete collapse, she had only a vague consciousness of Levi's arms cradling her, bearing her along. Before her eyes swam Warren's smile, and then the image of him falling, replaced by the sight of Will's lifeless form slumped across Isaiah's shoulder as he led the way, and of her uncle groping blindly along behind him as though the heart in him had also died.

Reaching the other side of the Neck, the huge knot of men splintered into small clusters and single individuals, scattering inland across Charlestown Common toward the setting sun. Behind them the firing died gradually down. And as they turned onto the road to Cambridge, a somber quiet spread out across the land with the gathering night.

Chapter Twenty-eight

SEATED IN A WAGON by the side of the road, Tess was waiting for them when they turned onto the road to Cambridge just beyond Charlestown Common. At sight of Isaiah's limp burden, her face crumpled into lines of silent anguish.

Too exhausted and distraught for any display of emotion, they laid Will's body in the wagon bed and dragged themselves up beside it. Isaiah took the reins, and they began the sad journey back to Roxbury.

For Elizabeth, the hours that followed passed in a merciful blur. Because of the summer heat there could be no delay in burying the dead, and it was decided that Will would be laid to rest the next day in the Stern family cemetery in Brooklyne. Stern and Levi left for Lincoln to bring back Will's mother and his young widow and children as early in the morning as possible.

Huddled motionless in a chair beside the cold hearth, Elizabeth was grateful that the others seemed to have forgotten her, that no one mentioned it had been because of her that Warren and Will were dead. If she could only lay her aching body down and sleep, then perhaps when she woke up this horrible day would have been only a dream. But she felt too heavy and stiff to move.

She was dimly aware that Isaiah gathered her into his arms and bore her up the stairs, laid her across a bed, and wrapped her in a blanket. Summoning the last of her strength, she squeezed his hand in wordless gratitude before slumber claimed her.

All that night repeated alarms shattered the stillness with the deep boom of cannon as skittish gunners facing each other across Boston Neck fired at any sign of movement along the opposing line. But Elizabeth heard none of it. She slept as one drugged.

Just after daybreak Sarah shook her awake. She had brought hot water and soap. While Elizabeth soaked away sandy grit and oily gunsmoke, moving with caution to ease the soreness out of her muscles, Sarah laid out the mourning gown Elizabeth had worn two years before to her grandfather's funeral. Now it hung loose on her. Staring into the mirror, she noted with indifference the dark circles under her eyes and the hollows in her cheeks.

She could choke down none of the breakfast Sarah urged her to eat. Finally, with leaden steps, she crept downstairs.

The house was silent, the shutters still closed from the night. Tess sat all alone in the drawing room, red-eyed, her normally sure, quick fingers fumbling to sew a last bit of ruffle onto a coffin pillow. When Elizabeth came in, she gave her a look of sorrow and reproach.

Kneeling to bury her face in her aunt's lap, Elizabeth sobbed, "Oh, Aunt Tess, I'm so sorry. I know you were worried about me. I should have told you where I was going. Can you ever forgive me?"

Tess sighed and stroked her bowed head. "I know you don't mean to hurt anyone, Elizabeth, but you must learn to consider the effect your actions have on those who love you before you go so far the damage can't be mended."

Remembering a similar conversation with her father a few weeks earlier, Elizabeth gave way to bitter tears. "It's my fault Will and Warren are dead. If I hadn't been there, they would have made it out alive. But they were trying to save me."

"We can't know they would have survived. Joshua told me the

fighting at the end was so vicious it's a miracle anyone came through alive."

"I'll never act so thoughtlessly again, I promise." Raising her head, she hesitated, finally asked, "Will?"

Her movements stiff with weariness, Tess helped her to her feet and led her into the room where Will's body lay. All the marks of battle had been cleansed away, and a quiet peacefulness had settled over his features.

Brushing away her tears Elizabeth thought of how he had carried her and Levi on his shoulders when they were small, how he had teased them, played with them, scolded them, taught them so many things by making it all seem a wonderful game. How dearly she would miss this strong, patient, loving cousin.

After several minutes Isaiah came to lay Will in the coffin he and his sons had built, then he, Pete and Sammy bore it into the parlor. Within the hour the Sterns arrived from Lincoln with their pastor.

Each face was glazed with grief and anguish. Her throat constricted, Elizabeth noted that her aunt and uncle had aged in that night. With hesitating steps, each supporting the other, they groped into the room where their elder son lay.

Elizabeth embraced both of them, then turned to enfold Rebekah with her sleeping babe at her breast, mingling her tears with the young widow's. The worst was when she knelt to sweep up the little ones who clung wide-eyed to their mother's petticoat, struggling to comprehend why everyone was so unhappy and that their father would never hold them again.

In sorrow they gathered around the coffin as Rebekah bent, weeping, to kiss her husband farewell. In turn, she lifted up each of her older children to say good-bye to their father while Elizabeth cradled the baby, her cheek pressed against his downy hair.

His face contorted with misery, Levi said in a choked voice, "Why did it have to be Will? It should have been me. Will had so much to give, and I have nothing."

Stern's head came up, and he looked hard at his younger son. "Do you think your ma and I would feel better if it had been you? Do you think we would grieve less over you than we do over Will?"

Levi fought to blink back the tears, but couldn't. "I know you loved him more than me," he said raggedly. "He was the best. Compared to him—"

His mother gathered her lanky son into her arms while Stern fumbled for Levi's hand, clasped it. "We've never compared you to anyone, son. You're different from him, and that's all right. All I expect from you is that you be the man God made you to be."

Levi broke down and threw his arms around his father. Holding him, Stern whispered, "We love you, son. Don't ever forget that. If we had to lose Will, it's a comfort that we still have you."

When they had regained their composure, the Sterns' pastor read the Twenty-third Psalm, his deep voice hushed with emotion, then led them in prayer. At last a detail of soldiers carried the coffin out of the room, and together they left for the cemetery, joined by the members of Will's company.

Standing at the edge of the grave with her arm around Rebekah's waist and the young widow's head drooping onto her shoulder, Elizabeth let her handful of earth sift through her fingers to fall onto the coffin lid. She whispered a prayer for Will and for his little family so alone now, for Warren, too, who still lay where he had fallen on that battle-scarred hill.

The noonday meal back at Tess's house was a subdued one. All of them found it difficult to eat, and when the dishes were cleared away, Mrs. Stern, with Rebekah and the children, retreated upstairs to lie down. Elizabeth intercepted Isaiah at the front door as he headed outside.

"Please saddle Night Mare for me. There's an errand I have to take care of."

He gave her a searching look, then clamped his hat on his head and went out. Feeling as though the last familiar boundaries of her life had been erased during the past two days, she went into the drawing room, where Tess and Stern sat alone. Her aunt's head was bent over her Bible, but Elizabeth could tell that her mind was not on the words on the open page.

Across the room Stern sat uncharacteristically idle, staring out the open window with blank eyes. Elizabeth's heart ached to see him so.

Tess reached out to draw Elizabeth to her side. "At least this dangerous charade you've been playing is over at last."

Elizabeth hesitated, fumbling for the right words. "I'm afraid it isn't finished quite yet. I have to go back to Boston."

Tess stiffened. "You can't be serious! It's far too dangerous—besides, there's nothing more you can do."

"There is one thing I have to do." In halting words she described her meeting with Hutchins and her subsequent encounter with Patriot on the marsh the night before the battle. "I begged him to come with me, but he refused. As it was, I almost didn't get away. There's no way he could have."

Stern appeared visibly shaken, his face gone pasty grey. "You're sure they captured him?"

"It would have been impossible to escape on foot. So I have to go back. I'm responsible for Will's and Joseph's deaths. I can't let Patriot die too. I have to find a way to save him if they haven't hanged him yet."

"Elizabeth, sit down!"

She was already halfway to the door. Before she could reach it, Isaiah stepped inside, blocking her path.

"Why be Major Carleton's horse in the stable?"

She stared at him, taken aback. "You must be mistaken. I rode Patriot's horse up here the night before the battle. That should be the only one there other than our own."

"If that ain't Devil, then I gone blind."

She swung around to look at Stern, icy fingers tightening over her heart. What she read in his face sent her out the door, heedless of his urgent call for her to wait.

With Tess and Stern following in alarm, she flew down the path. Stumbling on her petticoats, she regained her feet and raced on, her breath coming in short, harsh pants.

The stable door stood open, and she bolted inside straight to the box stall where she had left her mount the night of that fatal meeting on the marsh a lifetime ago. Before her eyes could adjust to the dim light, she had the stall door open.

The stallion shied back at her sudden entrance. And coming to an abrupt halt, Elizabeth stared, stricken, at the gleaming bay stallion with black mane and tail and four black stockings who swung to face her, ears pricked as he whickered in recognition.

"Devil?" she whispered through stiff lips, and then, "Jonathan? *Oh, no!*" Slumping against the stall door, her hand pressed to her mouth, she repeated dully, "No. No."

In a rush the past two months shifted into vivid focus. Every seemingly innocent detail passed before her eyes, but now with devastating clarity.

Those probing questions. The cryptic comments that took on an agonizingly different meaning now. The sense that he had so often hesitated on the verge of saying . . . something . . . only to pull back.

Her own deceptions and outright lies. And his.

Everything had drawn her to him. But with all her strength she had fought the longing to trust him, the feeling she could not shake that he wanted as dearly to trust her.

There had been such good reason for caution, of course. But now the accusing memory of how often both of them had come achingly close to bridging that chasm of suspicion and mistrust pierced her heart like a dagger.

Too late she saw that all along God had called them to submit in faith to his perfect will. But they had both trusted in their own imperfect understanding.

Her knees gave way. Stern caught her, and sagging in his arms, she let him lead her to a worn bench against the stable wall outside while Tess hovered over them.

"If I'd known sooner, I'd have told you at once. But Warren didn't level with me and Will until yesterday in the redoubt, and then I couldn't . . . " Stern's voice trailed off.

She gazed up at him in despairing comprehension. Everything made sense now. She saw how at each crossroads she had chosen to race ahead without reckoning the consequences.

And this time her willfulness had led to disaster. If only she had sought God's guidance before rushing off to rescue Patriot in spite of her suspicions of Hutchins' motives, then she would have been directed to a wiser course, and Carleton would still be safe.

At last the dam of emotion broke. Burying her head against her uncle's shoulder, she gave way to a storm of bitter tears.

"Why did he do it?" she mourned when she was again able to speak. "If Jonathan was on our side, why didn't he simply join the militia?"

"Jon is a colonel in the Virginia militia."

Her mouth dropped open. All she could do was to stare at Stern in disbelief.

He went on to explain that when Carleton had returned to England ten years previously, he had held the rank of captain in the militia, a commission that, unknown to his superiors in the Light Dragoons, he had never resigned. Neither had he ever revealed his or his uncle's longstanding sympathies with the patriots.

Matters had come to a head the previous summer. False charges of smuggling had been leveled against Sir Harry by unscrupulous friends of Virginia Governor Dunmore, who had authorized the seizure of a warehouse full of goods on the pretext that British taxes had never been paid. Sir Harry had been there alone when soldiers from the British garrison in Williamsburg had arrived. When he had protested the seizure, they had beaten him cruelly, causing a concussion and severe internal injuries. He had died the following day.

It had not been until Carleton had returned to the colonies to settle his uncle's estate that he had learned the truth. In grief and outrage, determined to resign his commission in the Light Dragoons, he had accepted a commission as colonel in the militia to raise a regiment of rangers—irregular light cavalry—in case war broke out.

When he had received Gage's summons to Boston, however, Patrick Henry and Colonel Washington had forcefully argued that, instead of resigning his commission, he take advantage of the possibilities the orders presented. Although the role of spy was one Carleton despised, in the end the urgency of the situation had persuaded him to undertake his perilous role.

Elizabeth groaned. "Joseph told me that Patriot insisted he swear never to reveal his identity to anyone or Oriole's to him, so that if either of us was ever captured we couldn't be forced to betray the other. But Jonathan was obviously in grave danger these past two weeks. Why wouldn't Joseph let me try to help him?"

"You have to admit that your actions have often been so rash that you endangered not only yourself, but others as well," Stern reminded her. "Joseph feared you might be captured at any time, and if you knew Patriot's identity you could be forced to reveal it."

"Never!"

"Even if Abby or your parents or Tess were threatened?"

She wilted, knowing he was right.

"All of us admire your courage, Elizabeth," he said kindly, "but courage must be tempered by prudence."

Troubled, she said in a muffled voice, "I know Jonathan suspected

me of some involvement. He must have raised the question."

"He did the last time they met, but Joseph delayed telling him because of the danger you were both in. And then he never saw Jon again."

Tess put her arm around Elizabeth's shoulders. "You mustn't blame yourself, dear. There's nothing you could have done. If you've been exposed and you go back now, you will be arrested."

"Hutchins must have suspected you and meant to trap you as well," Stern agreed. "If he shared his suspicions with Gage, you'd be putting your head into a noose."

Elizabeth's stomach clenched into a knot. There was no way to pretend that anything other than her pride had led her to this disaster. Even now every pulsebeat urged her to rush to Carleton's rescue without stopping to weigh the possible consequences of her actions. But as she earnestly searched the faces of her aunt and uncle, she knew she couldn't do it.

How often she had closed her ears to the quiet, insistent voice calling her to submit her ways to God's leading. This time she had to get serious. She had gone as far as human strength, determination, and resourcefulness could take her. If it was not already too late and Carleton was indeed to be saved, it was not in her power to do it.

So there beside the stable as she knelt before the bench in the hot summer sunshine, enfolded by the loving arms of her aunt and uncle, she surrendered. "Lord, I want your will and your purpose for my life," she whispered humbly. "More than I want my own desires, I want you. Even if that means that you take Jonathan from me, I know your will is perfect, and I submit myself and him to your mercy."

As they prayed together, she was by degrees flooded with a sense of God's protection. It was as though an unearthly voice whispered a verse from Joshua 1: *Have I not commanded thee? Be strong and of a good courage; be not afraid, neither be thou dismayed, for the Lord thy God is with thee whithersoever thou goest.*

Suddenly she knew what she must do. She didn't have to persuade Tess or Stern, for both of them quoted the same verse to her before she could speak. And walking back to the house in awe and wonder, they worked out the details of a plan.

TESS ACCOMPANIED HER in the phaeton, with young Pete driving. Weaving their way around the outposts of sharpshooters stationed behind trees felled across the streets in case of British attack, they descended the road to the Neck in some trepidation. The opposing sides were still exchanging occasional scattered volleys, but although the British followed the phaeton with their guns, they made no attempt to stop them until they reached the town gates.

Pleased to find Captain Browne in charge, Elizabeth explained that they had been detained by the rebels, but had managed to persuade the guards to pass them through the lines. Indicating the medical case on the seat beside her, she added that they hoped to assist the surgeons, if help was needed.

His expression sober, the young officer admitted that it was. They had taken more than a thousand casualties in the battle, he told them, and over two hundred had already died, many of them officers. Doctors had been tending the wounded without respite, and burial details were still at work on Charlestown peninsula. Both Tess and Elizabeth were stricken to hear that Pitcairn was among the dead.

As Elizabeth tried to think of some way of learning Carleton's fate without asking directly, the captain's spiteful comment spared her the necessity. "At least they caught the traitor who's been selling us out to the rebels. It's your friend Major Carleton."

Pretending astonishment, Elizabeth elicited the information that Carleton had been arrested the night before the battle on suspicion of spying, for helping Oriole to escape, for attempted desertion, and for murder. At mention of the last charge, she and Tess exchanged puzzled glances.

Browne could give them no additional details other than rumors that were clearly preposterous and the information that a court-martial had been set for seven o'clock that evening. Relieved to learn that at least Carleton was still alive, they hurried to the Howards' town house.

Passing the Common, they stared in horror at the scaffold being erected on the grassy meadow, then hurried on by. It was past four o'clock when they reached the house, but to their consternation Andrews was nowhere to be found. From Mrs. Dalton they learned that he also had been arrested the night of Carleton's capture, and the housekeeper had not seen him since.

The house was still in considerable disorder from the thorough search Lord Percy and a detail of soldiers had made early that morning. Drawers had been pulled out and closets emptied, the contents scattered. Beds and chairs had been overturned, and mattresses, baseboards, and floorboards had been probed for any hidden evidence. They had found nothing, Mrs. Dalton told them, to Lord Percy's fury.

As they were speaking, Andrews came in. He was haggard and unshaven, his uniform rumpled and sweat-stained. With a sigh of relief, he embraced the two women.

"Thank God you've come. You know they've arrested Jon?"

While Tess went to see about tea, Elizabeth drew Andrews into the library and sat beside him on the loveseat. At her insistence he outlined the intense interrogation he had endured during the past two days.

"At first I was in a state of shock, then it all made sense. I should have guessed it long ago, of course. All those long, private meetings Jon had with Mr. Henry, and he was at almost all the social functions we attended. Colonel Washington showed up a number of times too, and the three of them along with several others always disappeared for extended periods."

He ran his fingers through his hair with suppressed frustration. "But Jon was on the most cordial terms with Governor Dunmore and all the leading Loyalists as well, so I didn't think anything of it at the time. He has a way of getting on smashingly with everyone. And there was always plenty of wine and any number of lovely young ladies to claim my attention.

"For months now I've had this sense there were things Jon was keeping from me. Thank God he did. They finally let me go because there was nothing I could tell them."

"Jonathan?" she whispered, fearing what he would say.

He gave a bitter shrug. "Smith led him through the streets behind his horse all the way to the gaol like a trophy of war. It was like they'd all become beasts—shouting, cursing, spitting on him, but Jon made no effort to resist. That night was bad enough, but today—"

He broke off, made a quick, distressed gesture. "This couldn't have come at a worse time, what with yesterday's disaster. We took horrendous losses, and feelings are running very high. I caught just a glimpse of Jon last night when they brought him back to his cell. It looked as if they'd beaten him rather badly. I was afraid they were going to hang him right then without waiting for a court-martial."

They were interrupted by Tess, who brought in the loaded tea cart. Gratefully Andrews accepted a cup of steaming tea and a large slice of cold roast beef on bread, mumbling through a full mouth that he had had nothing to eat since his arrest. Elizabeth watched him without speaking, feeling ill at the thought of what Carleton must have undergone.

Tess refilled his teacup. "Do they have any actual proof he's been spying for the rebels?"

Andrews shook his head. "They haven't found a thing, so they're charging him with attempted desertion. He was out of uniform and had gone some distance from his detachment in the direction of the rebel lines. They also know he intercepted Oriole and sent him off to safety on his own horse, so they can charge him with assisting a rebel agent. He could be hanged for either of those charges."

"Captain Browne said he's also being charged with murder,"

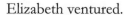

Elizabeth ventured.

Andrews's face hardened. "In the scuffle Jon shot one of Gage's spies who was with Smith. I think they said his name was Hutchins."

Elizabeth gasped. "David? He's dead?"

Seeing that Elizabeth was overcome at the news, Tess asked, "Have they been able to learn Oriole's identity?"

"Apparently not. They spent a good deal of time questioning me on that score, and I gathered they tried to beat it out of Jon. But if he knows, he isn't telling."

Elizabeth threw Tess a relieved glance. "There's a court-martial this evening?"

"It's just a formality. They're going to hang him in the morning." He laughed bitterly. "That scaffold they're building is for Jon. Lord Percy's regiment will carry out the execution, and I'm to personally escort him to the gallows. But they'll have to hang me too. The truth is I've been thinking about deserting for weeks now, but I didn't feel right about leaving Jon. So when he dies, I'll stand with him."

"Perhaps we can come up with a plan to avoid that."

It took several seconds for Elizabeth's words to register with Andrews. "What do you mean?"

"Escape, Charles. We've got to get him out of there—and you too, of course. I refuse to stand by and let either of you hang."

He dismissed her words with a short laugh. "Don't you think I've considered every possibility? The gaol is swarming with guards inside and out. Believe me, if I could have found a way to break us out, I would have. So what could a woman do?"

"In this case, perhaps more than a man. It may prove difficult, but it's certainly not impossible. Not, at least, for Oriole."

"Oriole!" he scoffed. "Jon's so heavily guarded even Oriole would need an army to break him out of there."

"I just may be able to arrange that."

He stared at her, nonplussed, his eyes widening. "Do you mean to say you're actually in contact with Oriole?"

"Charles, think a bit," she said kindly. "Who has had the trust and confidence of all the British officers, including General and Mrs. Gage? Who has been able to enter and leave Boston at will without hindrance or suspicion?"

At a loss for words, he looked from her to Tess, who returned a prim smile over the rim of her teacup, then back to Elizabeth. Starting to his feet, the color draining out of his face, he gasped, "You? You're *Oriole?*"

She conceded a faint smile. "While there's always a first time for everything, Charles, including failure, I have no intention of allowing this to be it. If I can smuggle guns, powder, and intelligence out of this town for nigh on a year, with God's help surely I can smuggle out a human being or two."

Chapter Twenty-nine

ELIZABETH KEPT HER GAZE fastened to the door on her left, through which the sergeant serving as bailiff had disappeared. While the majority of those present were officers, a sufficient number of rank and file had managed to find place inside to make her presence unremarkable, and squeezed among the restless crowd at the back of the packed room, she barely had space enough to breathe.

The presiding officer of the court, Burgoyne had been the last of the three generals to arrive, joining Pigot and Clinton, who were already seated at the table in the front and to Elizabeth's right. Taking advantage of the confusion, she had managed to slip into the courtroom in the wake of Burgoyne's entourage. She was dressed in the uniform of a private from Lord Percy's regiment, her disguise so perfect, from her powdered wig to the thick-soled shoes with raised heels that made her appear taller, that even at close quarters no one had given her a second look.

After what seemed an eternity, the door at last swung open. The bailiff entered first, then Carleton behind him, surrounded by guards.

Even though they were separated by the length of the packed courtroom so that she had to stand on tiptoe to see him between the shoulders of the soldiers in front of her, that first glimpse sent a thrill through her. Clad in the rough buckskins of a frontiersman, he appeared now vastly different from the ruthless British officer she had thought she knew.

His entrance was greeted with resentful looks and a swelling murmur from the crowd. Burgoyne was forced to demand silence several times before they stilled.

One of the guards gave Carleton a rough shove, causing him to stumble. As he straightened he turned his head, and for the first time Elizabeth saw his face clearly. She drew in her breath.

A raw scrape, bruised and puffy around the edges, crusted with dried blood and already discolored, ran across his cheekbone. A cut on his lower lip oozed blood. He was unshaven and unwashed, his fringed buckskin tunic streaked with sweat and blood, his blond hair tangled, hanging loose to his shoulders. Appearing to be near the point of collapse, he moved as though weak and in considerable pain.

Tears filmed her eyes as she watched him. She had to bite her lip hard to hold them back and keep from crying out in protest.

Without ceremony the guards prodded him into the dock to her left, opposite the tribunal. Leaning forward, she saw that his hands were cruelly bound. It was only with difficulty that he could clench his fingers over the railing in front of him to keep from sagging to the floor. But though it clearly cost him great effort, he threw back his head and directed toward the three generals a look that smoldered with defiance.

Burgoyne gestured to the bailiff. "Read the charges against the prisoner."

The bailiff stood forward and in a clipped voice began to read from the paper he held. "The prisoner, Jonathan Stuart Carleton, is charged with attempted desertion—"

Before he could continue, the rear door burst open, and Lord Percy strode inside. His narrow face pale and taut, he went to the bailiff, and after handing him one of the papers he carried, turned to confer with the three generals. As she watched them intently, Elizabeth felt a chill clutch her heart at the smile of satisfaction that came over Burgoyne's face.

Percy swung to face the packed courtroom. "This court-martial is dissolved on order of His Excellency, General Gage." With upraised hand, he stilled the commotion that followed his words. "The charges brought against the prisoner have been verified in all particulars by His Excellency. All that remains is to read the verdict and the sentence for these crimes."

As Percy turned a stern gaze on Carleton, his expression changed. "Have you been given food or water since your arrest, sir?"

Carleton returned his stare with a steady one, a sardonic smile contorting his cracked lips. His answer was an indifferent shake of his head.

Percy rounded on Carleton's guards. "We're not barbarians. Bring the prisoner water."

His orders were obeyed at once. His shaking hands still bound, Carleton clumsily accepted the cup offered to him, gulped its contents, then held the cup out in mute appeal. At the soldier's questioning glance, Percy motioned him to refill it.

Draining it the second time, Carleton returned the cup to the soldier with a hoarse "Thank you."

"See to it that the prisoner is fed as soon as this hearing adjourns," Percy snapped. He looked down at the paper he held. "This letter was received by General Gage half an hour ago. It was obtained from a courier on his way from Philadelphia to Boston who was intercepted by agents of Governor Tryon in New York. They immediately forwarded it to His Excellency. It is dated 16 June and is addressed to Jonathan Carleton, Colonel, First Virginia Rangers, stationed in Boston."

Stunned silence greeted his words. Elizabeth glanced in dismay at Carleton, but his only outward sign of emotion was a faint smile.

"The letter reads as follows: 'My dear friend, I have just received news from Mr. Henry of your faithful service to the cause of liberty and of the wound you sustained as a result. I know how abhorrent your present role is to you, but the value of your efforts on behalf of our brethren in Massachusetts is deserving of far greater reward than my poor thanks.

That must suffice, however, until I can offer a more fitting tribute.

" 'Yesterday I was elected commander of the newly constituted Continental Army, an honor I confess I do not think myself equal to. For the discharge of this momentous duty, I shall rely upon that Providence which heretofore has preserved and been bountiful to me.

" 'By the time this letter reaches you, I should be on my way to Boston to take command of the army there. When I arrive I hope to convey my gratitude in person and add my earnest appeal that you consent to become a member of my staff. The appointment carries the rank of brigadier with a commission to raise and command a brigade of light cavalry. I can think of no one more qualified to undertake this important charge at such a critical time.

" 'Until we meet again, my friend, the hand of God keep you safe. Your most obedient servant.' "

Looking up, Percy concluded, his tone heavy with malice, "It is signed, 'G. Washington.' "

The room was in an uproar now. Officers and their subordinates sprang to their feet of one accord, shaking their fists at Carleton.

"Hang the traitor!"

"It's his fault we lost so many good men yesterday!"

"Murderer!"

Carleton, to all appearances oblivious of the furor around him, was laughing exultantly. Above the shouts of outrage he cried, "Our cause could not be in better hands! He will fight you to the gates of hell!"

His face settling into hard lines, Lord Percy quieted the disorder to allow the bailiff to read the verdict. "Jonathan Stuart Carleton is found guilty of high treason. While sworn to uphold the laws of England as an officer of His Majesty's army, he did willfully and secretly take a commission in the militia of the Commonwealth of Virginia without the knowledge of his superiors and for the purpose of aiding and abetting the illegally constituted armies presently in a state of rebellion against His Majesty King George the Third. He did further act as a spy in providing military intelligence to said rebel army. He did attempt to desert. And lastly, he did murder one David Hutchins, an agent of His Excellency General Thomas Gage."

In a level voice, Carleton said, "A man cannot be held guilty of betraying a king and country to which he owes no allegiance."

Cries of fury drowned out his words. With a convulsive movement, the occupants of the crowded room surged like a red tide toward the place where Carleton stood, head thrown back, smiling with grim satisfaction at the effect of his words. Unmoved, he stared them down, undisguised contempt in his cool glance. Had not the guards around him fought the enraged mob back, they would have torn him to pieces.

Terrified that they would succeed, at the same time exulting at his courage, Elizabeth turned her attention to Percy. In contrast to the hate and fury that contorted the faces around him, the earl was staring sadly at Carleton.

"You've gone mad," he said, as though the two of them were alone in the room. "This is not the man I've known."

"You never knew me, Hugh," Carleton answered in a hard voice. "You pretend to be my friend, yet you invade my country to oppress and murder my people. You despoil the land in the name of loyalty to a tyrant not worthy to be called king. Your hands are stained with the blood of my brothers and sisters—and yours!

"By your own choice you have made yourself my enemy, and if I die fighting to drive you and your armies out of my country, I'll count my life well spent."

Visibly shaken, Percy said through clenched teeth, "You've heard his confession. The prisoner will hang at dawn tomorrow."

Carleton heard the sentence with an outward icy calm. As the guard nearest him reached to drag him out of the dock, he turned on him a stare so steely that the soldier's hand arrested in midair. Brushing past him, Carleton strode to the door without a backward glance, as though the tumult his words had caused was a matter of no concern to him, as though he shook the dust of that place from his feet.

Each pulsebeat of her heart and the throb of every nerve urged Elizabeth to push her way through the swearing, shouting men and run after him, if only in the hope that she might for one second touch him. But clenching her hands over the back of the bench in front of her until her fingernails bit deep into the wood, she forced herself to watch him walk out of her sight.

THE CEILING OF THE CELL was barely high enough for him to stand upright. His cramped surroundings were dank and filthy, the earthen floor so damp it was slippery with a film of foul-smelling mud. Pushed against the rough-hewn, chinked log wall, only a rickety bench just wide enough for him to sit or lie on furnished the constricted space.

Just below the ceiling was a narrow window, which, though it was too small for even a child to crawl through, was further obstructed by the addition of iron bars. It was just above ground level, but through it he could see the back corner of the gaol compound and, by craning his neck, a small strip of sky.

Guards were on constant patrol at every corner. No possibility of escape, even if he could by some miracle find a way through the cell's walls. These, though poorly constructed, were stout enough to eliminate that possibility.

For a long time he stood at the window with his face to the slight breeze, as though the hint of cool sea air could cleanse from his body the grime of his prison. He stared at the darkening sky until the last faint streaks of sunset faded and the stars began to blink one by one into the charcoal heavens. He wanted to engrave every detail, each faint star, each changing nuance of color on his memory in the hope that it might be so vivid to him when he came to the scaffold that it would blot out the terror of those final moments and give him strength that seemed woefully wanting now.

How bravely he had spoken at the trial. He felt now completely and hopelessly alone. He tried to pray, but again, as in his worst times, he could discern no response at all. It was like dropping a stone into a deep black hole and waiting for a distant splash of water that never came.

In England his troop had been forced to watch a soldier hang for stealing. The sight of a human being writhing in helpless agony at the end of a rope as he choked to death was not an experience Carleton had ever wanted to repeat. The thought of suffering such an end filled him with a horror beyond the power of words to describe. To face that fate alone was unendurable.

He had hoped against hope that Andrews would come to see him, but perhaps he wasn't allowed to. Or perhaps his friend was so disillusioned and disgusted by his duplicity that he wanted nothing more to do with him. That thought brought the most intense pain.

Of course, he had received a prime example of the dangers of revealing his hand when Gage, despite his promise to keep Carleton's role secret, had so carelessly exposed him. No one, no matter how noble the intent, could be depended on never to crack, either due to simple thoughtlessness or under intense pressure. Everyone possessed a weakness that could be twisted to the advantage of an enemy who discovered the point of vulnerability.

Yet he saw now with the blinding clarity of hindsight that he should have followed the nagging instinct that had urged him to open his heart to Elizabeth, an instinct that, too late, he realized had been the Lord's prompting. How often he had sensed that she also had been very near to confiding in him, only to shrink away. But the reasons for her refusal were also painfully obvious. Neither of them had had enough faith in God or in each other to break down the barriers of suspicion and doubt.

Was he being punished for that lack of faith now? Perhaps that was why he was left to die all alone. But if his discovery had prevented hers, then he would do the same again a thousand times over.

That he had no way of knowing whether Elizabeth was safe tortured him. The roar of cannon fire and the echoing volleys of gunshots the previous day had told him what must be happening, but not whether she was in the thick of it. All he had been able to learn of the battle had been snatches of conversation overheard from those who passed by his cell.

His only recourse had been to pray, pleading with God to preserve his brethren in the fight for their liberty and to keep safe the one who owned his heart. Even now he could only guess, from the savage retaliation he had been subjected to and the reaction of the mob at the trial, that the British had gotten the worst of the fight.

Absently he rubbed his wrists, chafed raw by the rough ropes that had bound him. His body ached from the beatings he had received. His head throbbed, and his shoulder was stiff, painful with each movement, much of the progress his wound had made toward healing undone.

His stomach burned with hunger, and he was desperately thirsty, for despite Percy's orders he had been given nothing to eat or drink. But the physical discomfort was nothing compared to the mental suffering that tortured him.

On leaden feet, yet far too rapidly, the night waned toward dawn. Too keyed up to sleep, equally too exhausted to stand up any longer, he stretched out on the bench.

THE SOUND OF A KEY RATTLING in the lock of his cell brought him upright with a jerk. He must have slept for some time after all. The small square of sky outside his window was just perceptibly lighter.

The door opened to admit five stern-faced guards who filed into the cell. So it was time. With reluctance he got to his feet.

He felt dirty, sweaty, chilled through, faint with hunger and thirst all at the same time. The ache in his shoulder left his arm so stiff it felt almost paralyzed.

He wished, irrelevantly, that he could bathe and change into clean

clothing, hating that the last sensations he would feel on this earth would
be his distasteful physical condition. At the thought he grimaced in dark
humor that such trivialities should concern him now.

The only light in the cell came from the faint rectangle of the window, and as the guards ranged themselves along the walls on either side
of the door, facing him, they seemed like little more than ghostly shadows. Uncertain what to expect, he waited for some sign as to what he
was to do.

Before he could move, the door opened again and a sergeant strode
inside, an older man with grizzled hair. He carried a pewter cup brimming with wine and a plate on which was a portion of fresh bread and
yellow cheese and a small piece of meat. This he placed on the bench
along with a knife and fork and indicated that Carleton was to eat and
drink.

He complied without hesitation, amazed at how acute hunger could
drive every other consideration from one's mind. The food and wine
strengthened him at once, and with the relief of a measure of physical
urgency, he began to think that there ought to be a better use he could
put the knife to.

The odds were decisively against him, of course, and the knife was
far too blunt to be useful, especially as the sergeant stood nearby, watching his every move with intense interest. As soon as Carleton had finished eating, the sergeant removed plate, cup, and utensils, then returned
carrying a tray on which were a basin of steaming water, a razor and
soap, a hairbrush and ribbon, and a towel. These items he placed on the
bench beside Carleton.

Surprised, Carleton hesitated before getting to his knees stiffly in
front of the bench. He hadn't expected any consideration for his comfort, and for a moment these simple graces were harder to accept than
the previous cruelty had been.

The water was gratifyingly hot. He buried his hands in it, brought it
to his face, relishing the feel of it on his sweaty skin and even its sting

against his raw cheek. As best he could in the darkness and without a mirror, he washed and shaved.

Again the sergeant watched him intently during the process, remaining just out of arm's reach. Carleton reckoned that with the sharp razor he could eliminate at least a couple of the guards, perhaps three if he acted quickly enough. But as before, he was certain there was no way he could take all six of them down.

The other alternative was to cheat the hangman. Finished shaving, for a moment he paused, staring at the gleaming razor in his hand.

He couldn't take a chance on the wrist, he thought with detachment. It would be too easy for the guards to staunch the flow of blood and summon a doctor. One swift cut across the jugular, however, and there would be nothing anyone could do to save him.

He swallowed hard and with a shudder set the razor down beside the basin, rubbed his hand across his face. As much as he dreaded the ordeal that faced him, he knew he was incapable of taking his own life.

With shaking hands he brushed as much of the tangles and dirt out of his hair as he could, fumbled to pull it back and tie it with the narrow strip of cloth that had been provided, no doubt to keep his hair from tangling in the noose. As he clambered to his feet, the sergeant picked up the tray and left the cell.

After several moments he returned with a different soldier, a young private hardly more than a youth. Dismissing the rest of the guards, the sergeant shut the door behind them.

As soon as they had gone, the private approached. Carleton saw that in his arms he carried a scarlet uniform coat, white breeches and stockings, shoes and gaiters, and a white wig and cocked hat.

Thrusting the articles into Carleton's arms, he commanded gruffly, "Put these on."

Puzzled, Carleton stared at the articles. A condemned soldier did not to go to his death in uniform, but this was not even the uniform of the Seventeenth Light Dragoons. The coat bore the same facings as those of his guards, the gosling green of Lord Percy's regiment, the Fifth Foot.

As he looked up questioningly, he saw that the young soldier was watching him with tears in his eyes.

"Hurry, Jonathan. We don't have much time."

Astonished, Carleton bent to get a closer look, squinting in the indistinct light, then drew in his breath sharply. "Beth!"

She smiled at him through her tears. "Could you think I'd let you hang when you saved my life?"

Stunned, he looked up as the sergeant, laughing now, came to pound him on the back. To his astonishment he recognized Stern. Just then the cell door was thrown open and Andrews strode inside.

Carleton looked from him to Elizabeth. "This is insane! We'll never make it out of Boston alive."

"Have you so little faith in me, and in God? You made me an offer, Jonathan, and if it still stands, I mean to accept it."

Tears came to his eyes then, and he pulled her to him. For a moment they clung to each other, neither able to speak. At last Carleton found his voice.

"I was afraid you'd try this. All I could do was pray you wouldn't see Devil by daylight until it was too late for any of your schemes."

"You almost had your wish," she murmured brokenly.

"How the deuce did you smuggle all these men into Boston?"

Stern grinned. "One of the burial details lingered a little too late on Charlestown peninsula last night and wandered closer to the Neck than they ought to have. We made a substantial substitution."

Andrews interrupted them. "I've been commanded to escort you to the scaffold, and you're due there within the half hour. We'd better get moving."

Giving a muffled laugh, Carleton saluted. "I'm at your command."

The guards stationed in the gaol had been trussed and locked up in the storeroom, their uniforms commandeered and their posts manned by members of Oriole's band, who would vanish back into the anonymity of Boston's alleyways as soon as Carleton and his "guard" had made their escape from the gaol. This proved startlingly easy.

Marching out a rear door, they mounted the horses waiting for them under Stowe's watchful eye and rode boldly off toward the town gates. Past the point of further astonishment, Carleton returned his servant's conspiratorial grin with a wondering shake of his head.

The light was strengthening in the eastern sky as they approached the gates. Well ahead of them they could see a phaeton that looked suspiciously like Elizabeth's moving off up the road a short distance beyond the outer British line. It was closing on Stony Hill and the highlands of Roxbury that lay beyond. With Andrews in the lead and Carleton riding in the middle behind Elizabeth and Stern, they drew up at the bars of the gate.

"Let us pass, soldier!" Andrews barked to the sergeant who blocked their way.

"No one's bein' allowed through 'thout a special pass, sir," the sergeant returned, his tone and expression sullen.

"What about that carriage?" Andrews indicated the diminishing equipage.

"That's the two Miz Howards with a cousin o' theirs. He's bad sick with the pox, and they're takin' him home to—"

"You fool!" Andrews snarled. "That's Major Carleton. Oriole broke him out not twenty minutes ago. Let us through before he gets away!"

"But . . . I saw his sores meself, and they showed a pass signed by General Gage," the soldier protested.

"Of course they had a pass, you blockhead! It's a forgery!" Andrews gestured toward the phaeton, which was already halfway up the hill. "If the major escapes, I'll personally make sure you take his place on the scaffold!"

Digging his spurs into his mount's flanks, he forced his way past the bars that blocked the gate. The others took their cue, and in a tight phalanx they streamed on through as the soldiers sprang out of their path.

By now the altercation had drawn a number of sentries down from the fortress walls onto the road, where they threatened to cut them off. In high theatrical style Andrews tore out his sabre and brandished it above his head.

"Stop that carriage! It's Major Carleton—don't let him get away!"

His words had instant effect. A group of soldiers raced for the vantage point of the fortress's walls, where they could take better aim, while others sprang to load and sight the fieldpieces on either side of the road.

As they swept past the outer line, Carleton brought his mount forward in a rush, Elizabeth hard on his heels. They pounded up the rising stretch of road, leaving behind them a cloud of dust and sand.

Carleton was laughing in spite of himself. "You've done it now! How good are you at dodging solid shot on horseback?"

Andrews guffawed. "Better than they are at aiming it, I'll wager!"

Twisting in the saddle, Elizabeth glanced back. A large detachment had just pulled up at the gate, and the officer in command was screaming something at the guards. In seconds the detachment came stampeding after them.

"I think we're about to get some company," she shouted to Carleton and Andrews, her voice almost drowned out by the deafening explosion of cannon fire.

Several balls arced through the air and plowed into the hillside a hundred yards ahead of them, still well short of the carriage. Applying their spurs, they charged up the road at a tearing gallop, increasing the distance between them and their pursuers.

The next volley scattered solid shot all around them, but this time the full-throated roar of rebel cannon answered it. A short distance ahead, the phaeton had made it to safety. Not looking back, they closed on it.

All along the rebel lines the sentries were shouting, waving their hats in the air as the riders swept past. When they were able to pull their lathered mounts to a halt, they all turned to look behind them.

Opposite Stony Hill the pursuing detachment had also come to a halt, glaring after their quarry in impotent rage. On either side the gunners exchanged a last round of fire, then a tense silence fell over the Neck.

Chapter Thirty

S URROUNDING ELIZABETH'S PHAETON, they rode back to Tess's house in a buoyant mood, trading good-natured insults with Tess and Levi, who had played the part of the pox-stricken cousin. He was bundled to the ears, with every inch of exposed flesh made up to simulate the ugly sores of the dreaded smallpox. Accompanying them was Andrews's servant, Briggs, clad in the gown Elizabeth had worn into Boston, with generous padding in the appropriate places, and demurely concealed behind the veil that hung from the brim of "her" hat.

Each time Elizabeth glanced toward Carleton, the message she read in his eyes brought a warm blush to her cheeks. As they turned onto Cambridge Road, he brought his horse next to hers, reached out his hand. Without hesitation, she placed her hand in his.

"Liberty has never tasted so sweet. I owe you my life, a debt I shall delight in repaying."

Her heart was too full for any reply. She contented herself with clinging to his hand.

As soon as they pulled up in front of Tess's house, Stowe and Briggs pried open the phaeton's capacious hidden compartments to reveal many of Carleton's personal effects. As the servants lifted out his violin, Carleton looked down at Elizabeth.

"Is there anything you haven't thought of?"

She considered the question with a smug smile. "I don't believe there is. I can't abide loose ends. So untidy."

His hearty laugh was sweeter than music to her. Once they were safely in the house and out of sight of any prying eyes, he pulled off his uniform coat and wig, then proceeded to divest Elizabeth of hers, tumbling her bright curls playfully in his hands as he set them free. She could tell he wanted to kiss her, but Stern took them by the arms and ushered them into the drawing room before he could make a move to do so.

Carleton clasped the older man's hand. "I hope I'll have opportunity to repay some small part of all I owe you." Turning to Levi, he said, "You played a most dangerous role, my friend. One wrong move and they would have arrested you on the spot."

Levi gave a broad grin as he indicated the spots of "pox" that covered his arms and face. "It wasn't too likely anyone was going to lay a hand on me."

Chuckling, Carleton conceded the point, then sobered. "I'll need to meet with Warren as soon as possible. But I'm most anxious to talk to Will. Where can I find him?"

Met by an awkward silence, he at last asked tentatively, "What is it?"

Elizabeth had known the subject could not be avoided indefinitely, but it was obvious no one had any more idea what to say than she did. In the suspended silence, a closed, hard look came over Carleton's face.

Blinking back tears, Elizabeth explained what had happened, adding raggedly, "We buried Will yesterday. We couldn't bring Joseph off. His body is still out there somewhere."

He stared at her as though he did not comprehend her words. "Warren—dead?" His voice broke. "Not Will too?"

He swung away, stood motionless for some moments. At last he reached out his hand to her, pulled her into his arms, and buried his face in her hair. His chest gave a convulsive heave.

"So many of our best men gone, and we've only begun the fight. How are we to bear such losses?"

She pulled back to look up into his eyes, hers full of pain and deter-

mination. "We have to find the strength to go on and to win—for them, for those of us who are left. We must never give up."

Learning that Will's widow and children were temporarily staying with Tess, Carleton asked to speak to Rebekah alone. Elizabeth had some idea of what their conversation might involve, and her guess was a good one. When Rebekah emerged from the library some time later, she came to Elizabeth's arms.

"Colonel Carleton insists on providing for me and the children, and he won't be dissuaded."

"Nor should he be," Elizabeth said with a nod of approval.

Smiling and weeping at the same time, Rebekah said wonderingly, "He's promised to provide a living for me for the rest of my life and for the children until they're of age, then they'll have a substantial inheritance. He even insists on seeing to their schooling.

"Oh, Elizabeth, I've been so worried. With Will gone, I had no idea how I could care for three little ones all alone. I've been praying, and—" She stopped, unable to continue.

"Then your prayers have been answered." Elizabeth gave her a tender hug.

As she cradled Rebekah in her arms, she looked up to see Carleton standing in the doorway. He dismissed her look of gratitude with an embarrassed gesture and crossed the room to talk to Stern and Andrews.

Rebekah went to find her children, and after a brief conference with the others, Carleton joined Elizabeth. "I must go to Cambridge this afternoon to see General Ward, then tomorrow morning Charles and I will leave to join General Washington. If he's already on his way to Boston, we should be able to meet him in New York."

"Don't forget, it was Governor Tryon's agents who intercepted the general's letter," she reminded him.

"I doubt they'll be looking for a couple of simple frontiersmen fr Kaintuck. Besides, I know some roads between here and there tha governor's agents are unlikely to be familiar with."

"Just remember, Charles, you'll always have a place here any time you want it," Stern broke in. "We need all the good men we can get, and you've more than proven your worth."

"If General Washington doesn't need me, I'll do so gladly." Shyly Andrews added, "I finally feel I have a home—that at last I'm where I'm meant to be."

Tess excused herself to see to provisions for a hearty breakfast, and one by one the others also discovered urgent business elsewhere. At last Elizabeth and Carleton found themselves alone.

He held out his hand for hers. She took it confidently, and he drew her with him out into the garden behind the house.

He had been wanting to kiss her for a very long time, and this time she responded without reservation. When he finally released her, she took his arm. Together they paced up and down between planting beds overrun by a profusion of colorful flowers and fragrant herbs.

Just beyond the head-high, neatly clipped hedge that bordered the large square of ground where they walked, they could hear soldiers hurrying back and forth between the Lincoln regiments' ordered rows of tents. But for all Elizabeth cared, they could have been a universe away.

There was not time enough to put into words everything that overflowed her heart, but at length she said, "Thank you for caring for Rebekah and the children. Not everyone would have been so generous."

"Will was a good friend. It's the least I could do for him. I couldn't see his family in want when I have so much more than I could ever need."

Hearing the familiar, lilting song of the oriole, both of them looked up, smiling. They had stopped below the spreading branches of the great oak tree at the lower corner of the garden. On a limb high above their heads swayed a pouch-like nest. As they watched, the male oriole came to perch near it, and four tiny yellow beaks poked out of the round hole, the imploring cries of the baby birds increasing in volume.

The male had no sooner stuffed the caterpillar he carried into the

mouth of the nearest fledgling than the female appeared with an insect in her beak to satisfy another gaping mouth. Not stopping to rest, the two birds flew off again on their ceaseless task of nourishing their brood.

The cycle of life never ended, Elizabeth reflected, and the thought comforted her. As surely as spring followed winter, new life followed death, fighting for its place on the earth. Let man do his worst, yet still the tentative shoots of faith and hope sprouted from the ruins of shattered lives and broken dreams. Resurrection was real, after all.

God's abiding love is like the oriole's nest, she thought with wonder. *Always he surrounds his people with walls of protection against the storms of life, nourishing them, keeping them safe, putting their lives back together again when they've been broken.*

It had been God's miraculous leading that had brought her and Carleton together. He had designed them to bless each other with joy long before they had had any inkling of his purpose. And in spite of their failures and weaknesses, in spite of their headstrong insistence that they knew what was best for themselves, God had patiently, steadily, inevitably brought them to a place of surrender to his perfect will.

Now his mighty hand would guide them in their country's valiant struggle for freedom. It was a journey she could not fear. For no matter what unseen dangers lay in their pathway, no matter where his leading took them, God's love would always bind them together, giving them the strength to meet with courage the challenges that would come.

Turning to Carleton, she read in his eyes that he was thinking the same thing. He took both her hands in his.

"That night I met you on the marsh—you knew then, didn't you?" she said.

His fingers tightened over hers. "I didn't figure it out until just a few hours earlier. I suspected you of considerable involvement, but it never occurred to me that you and Oriole were one and the same. You played your part far too well."

"I could say the same of you. But now my part is ended and yours only beginning." She could not conceal the wistfulness in her tone.

"Our struggle will be a long and arduous one, Beth," he reminded her. "Your talents, your resourcefulness and passion are too valuable to go to waste. Until our liberty is secured there will be a role for you and, I hope, for the two of us together."

She looked off into the distance, grateful that he had sensed what was troubling her. "Why didn't you tell me it was you that night?" When he didn't answer, she guessed, "You knew that only one of us could make it away and that if I knew it was you, I'd never leave you."

"One thought tormented me the day of the battle. That you were out there, that you might be killed. If I was going to die, then I wanted you to live on to fight for us."

Tears welled into her eyes. "When I saw Devil in the stable yesterday afternoon, I was certain they must already have hanged you. It felt as though my heart had been torn right out of my breast. I knew if I could never tell you how very dearly I love you, I couldn't go on."

He smiled down at her. "I've waited all my life to hear you say you love me."

"Oh, Jonathan, I think I've loved you from that first moment when you held me in your arms and wouldn't let me go. You asked me not so long ago to be your wife. Does that offer still stand?"

He drew her again into his arms. "You know it does—but on condition that there be no more secrets between us, my love. No more disguises. I must know all your heart, as you shall know all of mine."

Her only answer was to lift her face for his kiss, and for some moments they clung to each other. At length Elizabeth drew back to smile up at him.

And standing there in the garden, her hands clasped in his, she gazed with wonder into his eyes as though finding heaven reflected there.

If you've enjoyed this story or would like to offer feedback, we invite you to email the editor, Joan Shoup, at jmshoup@gmail.com. We'd love to receive your comments.

We always appreciate positive reviews posted on the book's detail page on Amazon, Barnes and Noble, Christianbook.com, and other online sites. Thank you for your help in telling other readers about this series!

Appendix

COMMON NAMES AND TERMS OF THE REVOLUTIONARY PERIOD

cartouche box: the case in which soldiers carried a supply of cartridges.

canister: cylindrical cases full of pistol balls shot from a cannon at close range to kill people.

gaol: jail.

grapeshot: iron balls the size of a tennis ball, bound together in a canvas bag to be shot from a cannon.

man of war: 18th century warship.

Discussion Guide

1. In Chapter 1, what concerned Colonel Stern the most about Elizabeth's behavior? When we face important or difficult decisions or crises, what should be our response as Christians? What underlying principles are we to follow?

2. Do you relate to Elizabeth's impulsiveness? When you face a crisis or an important decision, do you seek God's guidance and will before reacting? What steps do you take to determine God's will for you? How can you be sure that the choices you make are truly God's will?

3. Was Carleton a believer when he fell into sin? When we sin, what is the major consequence in our relationship with God and others? Are there any sins standing between you and God now? You and others? If so, what do you need to do to find restoration and healing for those relationships?

4. What were the obstacles that kept Carleton from receiving God's forgiveness? What was the deepest barrier? Have you ever felt that way? What is the only way to overcome it?

5. God used Elizabeth to call Carleton back to Himself even though she was not fully submitted to Him. Has God ever used you to minister to one of his prodigals or to a person who was lost, even though you weren't where you should have been in your relationship with Him?

6. Elizabeth succeeded in her impetuous actions for a long time, but they finally led to disaster for both her and Carleton. Have you ever

been afraid that if you totally submitted to God, He might deny you some things you really want or call you to do some things you don't want to do? Have your choices ever led to a less than desirable result or even to disaster that could have been avoided if you had sought God's guidance first?

7. Both Elizabeth and Carleton frequently had to lie in their roles as spies, and both wrestled with their consciences because of it. Do you believe there are circumstances under which it is acceptable in God's eyes to lie?

8. What was the consequence of Elizabeth and Carleton's refusal to trust God's leading in their relationship? Have you ever experienced the brokenness of a relationship because of your refusal or inability at that point to trust God's leading? What could or should you have done differently?

9. When Elizabeth came face-to-face with the consequences of her willful actions, she surrendered her will to God's. What was the outcome? What did God then call her to do after all?

10. When you withhold your trust and obedience to God's will for your life, how does that block the blessings He has in store for you?

11. Have you ever betrayed the confidence of someone close to you, or has your confidence been betrayed in such a way? How did you or the other person respond and what was the result? Do you need to ask forgiveness of that person or to extend forgiveness to him or her?

12. In *Daughter of Liberty,* what does the oriole symbolize? Do you think it is an effective image?